Secrets of Urthis

The Metalist's Journey - Book 1

KD Lumsden

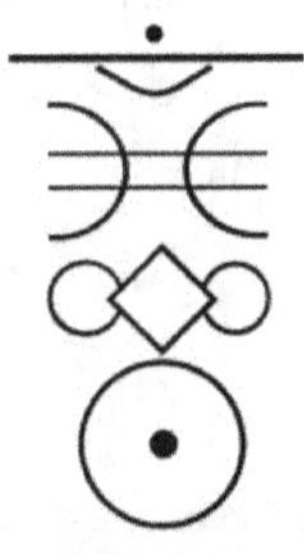

KD Lumsden

Dedicated to my loving husband, and son.
Thank you for always believing in me.

A special thanks to my editor & writing coach, Camille Cole.

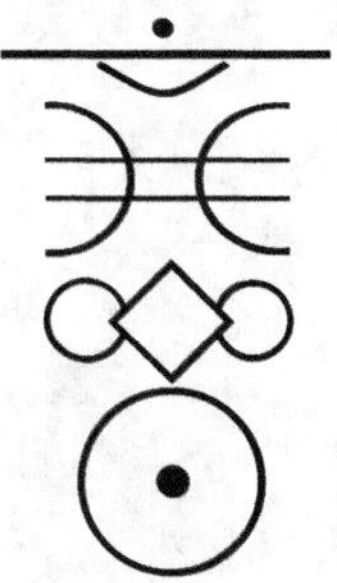

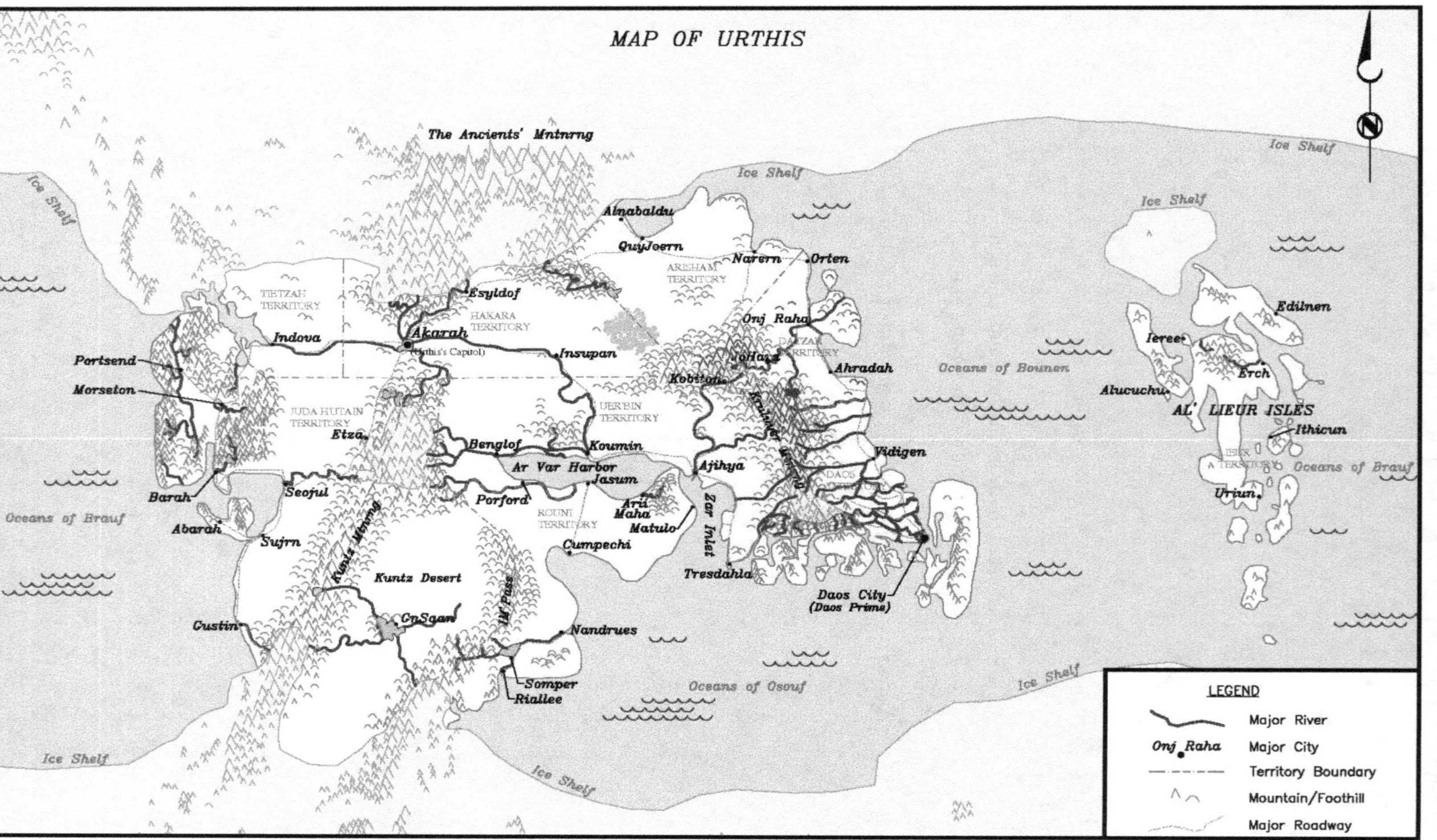

MAP OF URTHIS
N
LEGEND
Major River
Onj Raha — Major City
Territory Boundary
Mountain/Foothill
Major Roadway
The Ancients' Mntnrng
Ice Shelf
Alnabaldu
QuyJoern
Narern
Orten
ARISHAM TERRITORY
Onj Raha
DAEZAK TERRITORY
Ahradah
Oceans of Bounen
Edilnen
Iereet
Erch
Alucuchu
AL' LIEUR ISLES
Ithicun
Esyldof
TIETZAH TERRITORY
HAKARA TERRITORY
Indova
Akarah
(Urthis's Capitol)
Insupan
JoHaz
Kobsrou
Kreuiner Mtnrng
UER'BIN TERRITORY
Vidigen
DAOS
Oceans of Brauf
Uriun
JUDA HUTAIN TERRITORY
Etza
Benglof
Koumin
Ajihya
Portsend
Morseton
Ar Var Harbor
Jasum
Porford
Arü Maha
Matulo
Zar Inlet
Barah
Seoful
ROUNE TERRITORY
Cumpechi
Tresdahla
Abarah
Sujrn
Kuntz Mtnrng
Kuntz Desert
Daos City
(Daos Prime)
Custin
CpSgani
M Pass
Nandrues
Somper
Riallee
Oceans of Osouf
Ice Shelf
Oceans of Brauf
Ice Shelf
Ice Shelf
Ice Shelf
Ice Shelf

THE METALIST'S JOURNEY
Book 1 ~ Secrets of Urthis
Book 2 ~ Elements of Power

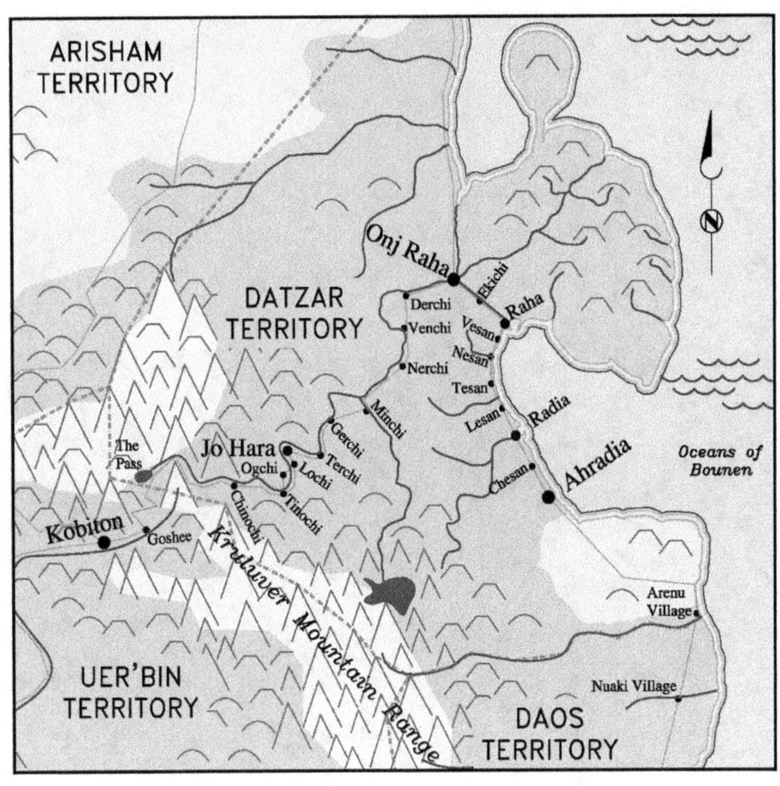

Contents

1

<u>Iron Irwin</u>

Metal.

Had Irwin any remaining within his flesh, like silver or iron, he would have recovered by now, but his father had stolen it all. His injuries would heal, and he would survive, but it would take time—time he might not have.

It was the rain on his ashen face that woke him. His wet cold clothing clinging to his skin. Then it came to him—the whole horrible night.

The light was gray deep in the woods where he lay by the road in the mud and his blood. Crows called back and forth in the fir tree canopy above. Bloodied and bruised, tears rolled down the side of his face and into his ear. He waited for Death to take him.

A crack of thunder shook more chilly rain from the trees. Irwin tried to move, winced in pain. His cracked ribs throbbed; his right arm was swollen, felt fractured; the right side of his face ached, likely a broken cheekbone; his right eye was swollen shut. Muscles in his left shoulder throbbed. He had defended himself from kicks to his head. Shifting his body again, struggling to push himself up, his arm gave way.

More thunder crashed, drowning his cries of agony and pain. Now the rain pummeled him, washing clean the dried blood. His clothing was torn and soaked with crusts of blood and forest debris, gray hair slick with mud. All the same, the copious wounds left by his father's boot were fading, fading because Irwin was what was known on Urthis as a Metalist—he held powers of instantaneous regeneration, and Ferro kinesiology (the ability to manipulate any type of metal).

His healing abilities had always been bewildering. The swollen eye began to open a crack. He needed metal within him to heal quickly, completely; the cracked ribs, his fractured arm, torn muscles, and the inflamed eye would take longer to heal without any metal. When he held metal in his body, the healing process was almost instantaneous. His father, also a Metalist, had stolen all of Irwin's metal before leaving him for dead.

I knew this would happen. I have never been the person Father wanted me to be, never will.

A splash of rainwater landed in his eye.

Where are my donkeys? I need to get up. I cannot remain here.

Struggling to get to his feet, first on one knee, and then the next, Irwin pushed himself all the way up. He peered up and down the roadway, half expecting to see his father, Albert. The muddy road looked heavily traveled—hoof prints in both directions, but now, nothing more than a dirty stream of slick muddy puddles. "Jenn Jenn! Nee Nee!" He cried, but there was no sign of his female donkeys. The hoof-printed mud bore little clue as to which direction they had gone.

He slumped.

I hope he did not take them. I hope he did not kill them. Where are my Jennies?

He called out for them again.

All those years of torment and hatred. Why has Father hated me all my life? What did I do to him? Nothing except for being born. He should have killed me when I was born if he hated me so.

He grunted.

He could not do it, not then and not now, so he left me for Death to find. What an asshole. I am glad he left me.

The years of abuse, mental and physical, had been more than Irwin could bear, but he had not understood it completely until right now. Right now, as he teetered in the middle of a lonely cold and muddy road in the middle of a forest. As a child, he believed he had earned every beating.

I never lived up to his or Grandpa Jebadia's expectations.

He might have flourished into the person he was meant to be if his Great Grandfather Edwin had not died when Irwin was only a child. The kindly old man had been the only person who ever loved him and accepted him for who he was. And when he sat with Saryh last night on her bed, she reminded him with her soft voice of those heartwarming times—of the kindness and care he deserved.

Each beating from his father Albert and grandfather Jebadia had kindled his resolve to hide his true self, but just the same, to not quit trying to taste everything that brought him joy.

They hated me being happy. They hated laughter.

He remembered how he had wrapped his soul in a shell, created a wall. As a child, he forced himself to persevere through the mire of his life. At times, he had contemplated his own death. Now he was older, wiser. And it came to him there in the mucky woodland that he wanted to live, wanted to recover what he had forgotten about himself—his love for the mountain's wildflowers, the mountain goats, and the soft white clouds drifting above.

Last night came into focus—the kindly Saryh; the woman to whom he had been taken to for his first time—the woman who understood why he couldn't and held no judgement.

I am glad to have met someone as caring and accepting as Great Grandfather Edwin was before he died. She opened my mind and my heart to possibilities I have forgotten.

Standing still and straight like a stone carving while his body and his mind began to heal, Irwin gazed up the sloping roadway. He now knew how much he wanted to live in peace and to be who he was without fear.

He shivered. His heart ached as he wrapped his arms around himself and felt the warmth of his own hug. "I am better than Father. I will never be like him, ever."

He winced and groaned and took one wobbly step up the muddy road. His bare feet were numb from the cold mud. Inch by inch, his body heat waned. He trembled, drew one leg forward and then the other. His shaking brought on sharp pains in his side. Gasping for air, he tried to think of warm thoughts—of fires and sizzling summer days—he needed to get warm.

Movement is the only way. I must keep going, just keep going, things will get better. Huh, how many times have I said that to myself?

On and on up the slippery forest road, one agonizing step after the other—Irwin made his way toward the trailhead that led to his home in the cave—the only home he had ever known.

The rain let up.

His feet found a good rhythm, and his body began to warm. There, at the intersection of the animal trail that led to the cave, a trickling stream meandered down the well-worn path. It would take almost two days to climb up the slope that had taken only one day to descend. The mountainside started out gently, but it would increase in steepness and effort. It was always a hard climb.

On a good day, he often dreaded the walk back home.

Where else could he go? Not back to the small city of Kobiton where his father had killed the whore and several PCP soldiers. There was a trading post village two days further north where Albert once traded for the young Jenny donkeys that became Irwin's pack animals. That was eight years ago. As far as he remembered, that village was full of tents where local miners spent the night. It was where they went for supplies, refreshments, and women. He and his father had then only stayed long enough to do the business at hand.

No longer cold, his clothes were still damp, his sandy-silver hair dry, and the color had come back to his pale skin.

I do not want to see my father again. He will never be sorry for what he did last night.

All this because I would not follow his one request to be with that woman—because I will never be comfortable doing what he wanted, but especially with a woman. He does not care what I want ... never has. He wants a son who will obey.

"All I want is to get my clothing and hunting supplies." Irwin called in vain to the crows flying overhead. They screamed back into the wind as if to agree with his decision to leave home, to escape.

What if Father is there?

If he is in the cave, then I will take my belongings and go.

What if he does not allow me to?

I will leave anyway. He cannot control me any longer. I can make new hunting gear, buy new clothing. I am resourceful. He cannot keep me prisoner in that cave. I will leave. I will find my place. I will find my way.

"I need to retrieve the rest of my metal," he muttered again into the wind.

Up the worn animal trail, he heard the trees rustle. Fearing the worst, he hid behind a giant fir, watching the trailhead.

Please do not be Father. Please do not be Father.

The shivering began again. He could not stop it.

Jenn Jenn stepped out of the forest—foliage protruding from the pack bags and bindings on the donkey's back. The pannier packs rocked toward her shoulder as she ambled toward him. It looked like she had tried to scratch them off. He laughed, shaking off his fears. "You silly!"

She brayed in what must have been great relief. He stepped away from the tree and stuck his hand out for Jenn Jenn to nuzzle. He laughed harder when he saw Nee Nee slide down a muddy section of hill on her butt, right into Jenn Jenn—her packs still upright and intact.

"I am glad to see you too!" He smiled and gave them scratches on their long ears. "I missed my Jennies."

After the loving, he stripped down and pulled a blanket from one of the packs and wrapped it around himself. His only change of clothes was wet and dirty. He found a tunic in another pack that was old, filled with holes and soot riddled.

No bother if it is dry.

He rummaged further through his packs, found dried goat meat in a small satchel, and ate a good portion. He guzzled one of his three flasks of water. Refreshed and somewhat dry, he considered the trail again.

A light mist filled the air, cooling what felt like a fever.

He put his arm around Nee Nee's neck. "I do not think father came this way."

Not wanting to be cold and wet again, Irwin found the wolf hide he had packed away. Wrapping it around himself, he fastened the packs and took up the donkeys' lead lines. Irwin and his Jennies inched up the slippery slope.

He was remembering the first time he traipsed down this trail with his father. They were heading to Kobiton after a late spring snowstorm. This was shortly after Grandfather Jebadia's death, and Albert had insisted Irwin come along. Since then, each visit to the hillside city of Kobiton was the highlight of every full moon. He recounted those memories as he trudged along, trying to keep his spirits up, trying to remember the times when he had learned something new about the world beyond the mines.

He thought about the woman, Saryh. They had talked a lot during their time in her room. He learned about her life and the quaint city of Kobiton.

Her daughter will grow up alone—an orphan now. She will have the life she has. There is nothing I can do.

I wonder what people do when they are without a family?

Irwin's Jennies are his family.

They do for themselves, I suppose, just like I am.

He did not need his father's help anymore. He could survive on his own. He could hunt for food. He could mine for ore. He could make a living off coal—if he chose. He could find love the way he chose, and maybe someday a loving family.

What else is out there for me? Mining is in my blood!

These thoughts disturbed him, but kept him going. By nightfall, he was still a half day away from the usual stopping point, and it was raining again. The sky had grown dark long before all the day's light was suckled away. Deep in the forest, he traipsed up an even steeper slope. By now, he should have found a flat spot for the night's camp and had a fire blazing. No matter, he was tired and needed to stop. There were only a few places between the trees where the ground was flat enough for a camp.

He inspected his packs and as he did he remembered packing Albert's Jacks while shopping at the markets the day before. His father had insisted that he wanted their newly purchased supplies and rations organized, that the important items were to go in *his* packs. Items carried by Irwin's Jennies now amounted to his personal camping supplies, wooden bowls, several flasks of water, a small satchel of dried goat's meat, and a bag of rolled oats for the Jennies.

That shitty asshole! All of this was planned.

But even with the metal cooking utensils gone, he could keep himself and his animals fed. He did not have enough food to make it to the cave—unless he went hungry tomorrow. He could hunt, but most of his hunting supplies were in the cave.

He remembered Saryh's words: "You might think you are a disappointment to your father, but in my eyes you are not." He remembered how she had looked at him. He remembered her smile, her bouncy brown hair, and how she had flirted with him.

I must stop thinking about her.

She was the one person who knew he was not attracted to women, yet she accepted and loved him anyway. His father's brutality to her and to him was fresh in his mind; he could not control his weeping.

It was only one night ago that Albert had marched back down the hillside toward him. "You are no son of mine! Go, you privileged asshole! May you have bad luck, you damn sniveling, pitiful, ungrateful child."

He had heard these words before, but not with such venom.

"You are a disgrace to our family name. I paid that whore to teach you something, and you conned her into thinking she did not have to teach you anything!

All you did was chit chat with a mouse of a whore!" Albert had been in his face, and with the force of his rage, knocked him about, flinging him onto the road like a dying chicken.

Albert kept on and on like the madman he was. "You are not a worthy Miner. You will never amount to anything more than a disgrace. You are no son of mine." He spat on Irwin, turned, and left.

The man raged on as he stomped back up the road. Before passing out, Irwin had struggled to find his center—knowing the metal in his bags would help. He could use his Metalist powers to absorb all the nearby metal. A Metalist's body can hold up to eight pounds total of multiple kinds of metals, and his cast-iron pot was three pounds. He pulled all he could from his pack and the metal turned to liquid—poured through the canvas fabric and into him without a tear. He was adept at extracting metal from the tightest of spaces.

But Albert had stopped, turned, and summoned the metal Irwin had begun to absorb.

It felt as if the metal was tearing through every muscle, organ, and bone in Irwin's body.

A Metalist's body was made to absorb and expel metal. Samuel Irwin Miner could manipulate the molecules of whatever metal he was absorbing, making it pliable. His skin could filter out impurities. He could separate ores used to make steel—iron and nickel. He could distribute metal throughout his body unless it was needed in one specific area. Pulling metal into his body was easy, but it burned and throbbed when it was unwillingly extracted.

He had screamed in pain. Weakened by the fight; he pleaded for mercy.

"I cast you aside!" Albert roared like an angry bear.

He had rolled away from his father's foot that was again looming above him. Albert's eyes were glowing gold. "Why Father? Why do this? Why? I have done everything you ever asked. I have always complied. I have—"

"You were daydreaming with that whore I paid for." Albert kicked at his only child.

Irwin knew he would not win this fight. He grabbed his head and tucked it toward his chest while his father beat him one more time.

"Goat Herder ... stupid, ignorant fool!" Albert kept on kicking Irwin in the gut, backside, shoulders, face, arms, and pushed him into the muddy roadside. "Stupid ... pathetic ... pitiful .... I cast you away ... you are no longer my son."

2

GOLDEN BOUNTY

I rwin chewed his meager supper.

I hope I never lay eyes on father again. I know things will not go well if he is in the cave when I arrive. He will probably try to kill me again.

He ate all but two strips of meat, saving them for the morning. He refilled his flasks with ice-cold mountain water from a nearby creek. He pulled out his other wolf hide and thick wool bedroll.

Then he prepared his resting spot at the foot of a giant fir tree. The Jennies bellowed. They had caught the smell before Irwin saw a wolf staring at them from the other side of the small creek. The large canine stood stone still, watching. Irwin stared back at the amber-eyed, dark-gray wolf. The animal growled, but then turned and jogged off. The Jennies trained their ears on the wolf's descent. He knew they would alarm him if that wolf, or any others, approached again during the night.

Exhaustion seeped into the core of his being. He found slumber while the creek babbled, and Jennies stomped. Nothing disturbed Irwin that night but dreams.

He awoke in the dark and fought hard to go back to sleep. But he could not. Every time deep sleep set in, so did the nightmares.

He got up from where he lay next to the tree as the black sky gave way to the shifting gray of far-off morning light. As he readied the Jennies for the rest of the trek, his feet already ached. He tried to ignore the discomforts.

I just want to be home.

He was ready for whatever outcome he would encounter in that cave.

He drank a good portion of water and started off again. He saved the last two strips of dried meat until he had to eat them—not wanting to hunt until he could leave his Jennies in the cave. There were plenty of mountain lions and wolves in this harsh wilderness terrain. Over the years, they had taken many donkeys—such a cruel way to die.

Late in the day, they broke past the timberline and took a brief break. Beyond the trees, food was a scarce find, but water would be prolific. Glacier-fed pools were full of clear icy water. He was now going at a faster-than-normal pace up the rocky mountainside. The Jennies balked at times, but Irwin pulled them along. He did not stop when darkness came. They were more than halfway between the timberline and the cave's entrance. The landscape was rocky, but Irwin knew this section of the trail. Home was close.

By midnight, they made it to the barren cave. They were soaked and starving. Irwin fed his Jennies and took a nap on his own bed of dead grass, fir-tree branches, and donkey hides. He woke at dawn and left his cave to hunt for food.

He sought out squirrels—wanting to bring back enough meat to dry, to have a cache. When the afternoon light began to form long shadows, Irwin took his bundle of dead squirrels and went back to the cave. His hunting excursion had taken him a long way along the forest's edge. He watched golden eagles soar overhead and brilliantly white goats grazed in precarious sunlit cliffs—made a mental note of where the mountain goats were located. The idea of hunting them was tempting, but his stomach told him to go home and eat. Without the Jennies in tow, he effortlessly scurried up steep mountain walls much like those mountain goats. This cold and blustery place was his homeland as much as it was theirs.

Finally, back in his cave, he made a warming fire and cooked his meal. That night, he ate well and readied a stash of dried meat. He made an inventory of what he had by way of rations and camping items. There were a few things left behind in the cave, but Albert had stolen all his personal belongings.

He was planning to leave me. I should have seen it coming.

During his hunt, Irwin made a final decision that he would not stay. There were too many terrible memories lurking in those caverns. He would pack only items of value and travel back downslope. He could not go back to Kobiton after what had happened, after the slaughter of Saryh and the killing of the guards, even if he wanted to. He would go to the trading post.

I hope I do not meet father there. I fear that man's wrath.

The next morning, he visited the family trove room and found it barren of silver; he decided to explore the caverns one last time. Albert had scraped the walls bare—a man who never shared his shiny loot. He brought Nee Nee, along with her packs, hoping to find a smidgen of metal. Along the way, he retrieved pieces of coal for fire-making later. Inside the caverns, he thought he heard a song—a quiet hum at first, and then he recognized the golden melody and followed the resonance. He found a narrow passageway; he had never been down this forbidden side-cavern. This was Albert's retreat.

Irwin also had his own personal spot outside the cave and up slope where he would go for peace of mind and meditation. His space was a small niche in the mountainside with a grand view—not an actual cave, but a place to get away. Up in his hiding spot, he kept a stash of gold, iron, copper, and silvery ore. He already packed up his small fortune—amounting to not much more than a few ounces—not enough even to buy the supplies he needed.

The golden melody humming throughout his body grew louder as he approached this new place. He squeezed through a small opening. Albert's secret place was coated in gold.

Why did he leave such a deposit behind? Probably so confident about leaving me that he forgot. Damn him. He is arrogant. But would he forget? Maybe ....

Irwin decided to take his father's gold!

What if he comes back?

I do not care. I will not be here.

He put his hands on the walls of the small enclosure. The gold was smooth, and it sang to him. It wanted to meld with him. He held back the desire to absorb it all. A study of the area had to be taken. Using his Metalist skills, he carefully withdrew the metal from the ceiling and the walls—about forty pounds of gold. He felt something else too. He peered up and realized that beyond the smooth golden-arched surface, the stones and rocks were ready to move. He paused in hopes of not causing the cave-in that surely was about to happen.

"Of course!"

Albert has always been at least one step ahead—plotting twisted setups. This is one more trick to eliminate me from existence.

"He would never have left this much gold behind, not unintentionally." Irwin spoke aloud to the ghosts in the cave and squeezed through the narrow passageway to get out.

I should have known! This was all pre-planned, every moment. How long has he been plotting this? How long has he wanted me dead?

Once on the other side of the short passage, Irwin put his hand forward to summon the gold, his father's gold—careful about pulling the precious metal from the collapsible chamber. The passageway rumbled around him. Above and below the cavern groaned. Nee Nee pressed against his side. Irwin pulled the golden bounty into one hand, pushed it through his body, and expelled it all out through the other hand, creating several five-pound rocks, making sure to distribute the heavy metal evenly into the packs on his donkey.

The cavern boomed louder. Nee Nee brayed and swayed from side to side. Irwin had retrieved almost all the gold. Tiny pieces of rock fell from the ceiling. The lesser chamber where he found the gold had already collapsed. And that cave-in loosened the section where Irwin and Nee Nee now stood.

Grabbing Nee Nee's lead line, he ran toward the entrance.

He heard the echoes of more cave-ins behind him. Dust clouds pushed them through the cavernous corridors. Rocks and pebbles rattled loose. Walls, ceilings, and even the ground rumbled. They ran faster. All the caves made by Albert and Jebadia were now imploding. The rumbling of death chased them as they fled.

This was a calculated tactic implemented over many years of planning and mine building. He could see the orneriness of Albert and Jebadia concocting their devious plan to bring down the mountain on some unknowing fool—a worst-case-scenario plan.

Larger rocks crashed down, and Nee Nee was pulling him away from the destruction. They rounded the last cavern corner—raced down the main passage toward the only exit.

Jenn Jenn bellowed at the cave's entrance. They raced toward her. "Get out of the way, Jenn Jenn!"

Dust and chunks of rock enveloped Irwin and Nee Nee before they reached the end of the tunnel. There was nothing they could do but run faster—the thunder of destruction rumbled around them. They were pummeled by the rocks, but neither stopped.

Irwin ran into the wailing Jenn Jenn and fell. He scrambled to his feet. Dust and debris swirled, nearly enveloping them all. He could not see through the dust cloud, but instinctively knew which way to go. Behind him, the key passage collapsed, sending more rocks, coal, and dust flying in their wake. He did not stop to watch the obliteration. He and the Jennies bolted down the rocky mountainside in the midst of the dust cloud. They would not be safe until they were far away from the rolling chaos.

Just in time, they reached the timberline.

His heart still raced, and the Jennies were still bawling as he located their camping spot for the night. He would be safe from Albert and any remaining tumbling rocks here.

All he could do for a long time was sit on the edge of a downed tree and stare off, occasionally looking up the mountain. Even the Jennies stood frozen in place.

It was nearly dark when he decided to make camp. He removed the packs from his donkeys and gave them water. He choked down a meal of dried squirrel. He made a fire with a small piece of coal. Curling up inside his hides and blankets, Irwin was warm for the rest of the night. He felt almost safe snuggled inside the soft, furry pelts.

Sometime during the night, he awoke to a soft rain. He had been dreaming about what had happened in Kobiton, about the soft caring woman who seemed to understand him, who died so horribly at his father's hands—her throat slit in one gory movement of his knife.

After a night of torment, he was glad when morning's light woke him one final time. It was early. He ate more dried squirrel once the Jennies were packed. They stomped their feet, ready to go. He glanced up the mountain toward his destroyed homestead. There were many memories he was happy to leave behind, but he would never forget his Great Grandfather, Edwin. He would carry him in his heart wherever he might go.

He and Edwin had toured the mountaintop meadows, hiked along precarious ledges in search of mountain goats, sat in the sun while his great grandfather rambled off all the precious ores he knew; shared lessons about life and how to live in the harsh conditions of the mountain. He had much insight and patience for Irwin.

"I will miss you, Papa Edwin." He muttered; a tear slipped down his cheek.

Since the age of six, after Edwin died, Irwin had labored in the mines beneath the fists of his father and grandfather. It was challenging work for a young boy, but he always obeyed orders, kept focused on the miserable work.

He would always remember that brief time of happiness before Edwin dropped dead one afternoon when they were out exploring the mountainside.

His great grandfather had brought Irwin into a new mineshaft to show him the construction his grandfather and father had crafted using giant timbers. Edwin told him to stay put, that he had forgotten something at the mine's entrance. But for reasons Irwin could not now remember, instead of obeying, he was drawn further into the mine—an internal pull he could not overcome. When Edwin found Irwin, he was plastered against the wall of the mineshaft, crying. His hands enveloped up to his wrists in liquid silver. He was magnetized and could not let go. Edwin was breathing hard when he pulled Irwin from the wall. He asked no questions of him nor scolded him.

Later that day, Edwin keeled over in the mountain grass and never recovered. From that day on, Irwin's childhood was over. He remembered the hot sun on his back as he leaned over Edwin lying on the ground, tears burning his eyes and his throat; he remembered Albert finding them there and yanking him away from the body.

After Edwin was gone, Irwin led Grandfather Jebadia and Albert to the lode of silver he had found the day Edwin died. The two beat him until his nose bled and warned him to never ever reveal to anyone what happened in that mine—what he had found and what that find did to him.

Young Irwin was then forced to work in the mines—where instead of playing and discovery with Edwin, his life was defined by cave-ins, stubborn donkeys, and his grandfather's and father's heavy hands.

3

<u>GOSHEE</u>

Sometime before midday he found the road that led to the trading post, and Irwin and his Jennies began another trek up an incline.

For two nights he slept under a canopy of thick fir trees. Each night, he built himself a fir branch bed that kept him off the wet ground. After dusk the first night, the rain was unrelenting. His cloak was not long enough to keep himself, or the makeshift bed, from getting wet. His nightmares and his cold, wet feet were almost more than he could bear. But he continued onward toward the trading post village. His list of camping and personal supplies grew longer each day. He had more than enough gold to purchase everything he wanted.

It was midmorning when Irwin neared civilization. He felt the metal in the village as they grew closer, some stationary, some moving around. Then came the smell of burned hooves; another indicator civilization was nearby. But it was the twang of metal against metal that called to him.

He ascended from the forest into a great valley. A flowery meadow once grew here, parting the woodlands, but now canvas and wooden structures cluttered the basin floor. He had found the trading post. He remembered from his youth when there were tents dotting the gorge here, but now there were structures—many more wood and stone buildings than before. In the center of the village, there was one lone three-story building. Whitewashed letters across weathered wood read 'Goshee Trading Post & Emporium'. The Trading Post had been modified—added onto over the years, reminding him how small this place had once been.

Entering the edge of Goshee, the Blacksmith Shop came into view—one long stone structure with several open bays, hot inglenooks, and smoking chimneys. The twang of metal resonated—a bittersweet song. Numerous types of equines were tied to a highline around the shop. From the looks of it, it was going to be a long day of hoof-trimming and shoeing for the smiths.

Outside the shop's doors, six large donkeys stood idle, tethered to a short hitching post. Two were being worked on by well-built blacksmiths—muscular men who wore nothing more than heavy leather pants and matching vests. They all looked alike: dark skin, thick black hair, and bushy eyebrows. Though their arms and chests were bare, each had a thick layer of body hair. Dust, ash, and horsehair coated the sweat-covered smiths too.

Hardened amber-brown eyes studied Irwin as he passed through the village. He averted his own curious stare under their watchful glare. He kept his focus on the muddy road, kept on toward the open doors of the trading post emporium. Outside that building, multiple donkey and horse lines were tied to hitching posts. Over two dozen horses and donkeys stood on either side of the road, waiting for their owners to emerge from the trading post. A few Jacks bellowed at Irwin's Jennies as they approached—none were his father's.

He kept his animals separated from the others. Tying them to the hitching post farthest away from the warehouse, Irwin examined his nearly empty packs. He untied each one and packed all the empty bags into one large bag. He would stuff them all with provisions before leaving Goshee. There would be no scrimping on necessities. Absorbing several pounds of gold into his flesh, he did not intend to walk around with forty pounds of gold left behind in his baggage.

Inside, every item necessary to live in the elements lined the shelves and the racks. Barrels and boxes filled with food supplies, some fresh and some dried, lined the walls of the main room. Adjoining rooms were marked with signs: clothing, camping gear, cleaning, and personal items; tack, mountaineering stuff, leather pieces. Had he just found that room he had sometimes explored in his dreams? He walked up and down the aisles selecting what he needed, what he wanted—things Albert would never have allowed.

A good part of the day was spent loading up his packs. Then he noticed he could buy more packs. He picked up the last large pre-oiled hemp canvas tent and a bedroll lining of the same thick material. There were oiled hemp jackets and pants for mine working—the type of cloth his best working pants were made of. Everything was waterproofed and ready for Irwin to start his new life. He picked out pants, shirts, socks, and a few items he admitted to himself he didn't need.

The best find was a smooth shirt made of a soft, thin material. The color of the luxurious shirt was red, and its sleeves were long. He imagined himself in it, sleeves rolled up for a cooler feel. He tried it on and decided it looked great.

He found two pairs of boots that fit perfectly; he selected six pairs of wool stockings. He chose a warm, wool-lined leather vest that complimented the red blouse. He laughed aloud as he stuffed his bags with the sort of items he never knew he wanted until now. By the time he returned to the front of the store, a giant grin stretched across his face.

He walked around the emporium several times, helped by an attendant who managed his expanding packs by the front doors. The attendant waited patiently for him to finish his shopping.

Irwin hefted a sack over his shoulder and strode over to the assistant. "I think I found everything I need."

By this time, it was late in the afternoon. The man was about ten years older than Irwin—and typically scruffy like others he had seen in Goshee. His light brown hair was oily and pulled back into a ponytail; he smelled as if he hadn't bathed in many moons. The greasy attendant said, "Ya said ya'd like a flint stone too?"

"Oh yes, please."

"Well, since ya be buyin' so much, I can give ya the flint free."

"Thank you. That is very thoughtful. I appreciate your helpfulness."

"Ya gonna go tavern after dis?"

"Yes. I was thinking about it ... for the whiskey, that is."

"Da beef stew is umm-humm."

"Good to hear. I might try some."

"And da women, and da drinks. Umm-humm." The attendant pointed at the pile of purchases. "I-ya have ta write dis all up."

Irwin watched as the man went slowly and deliberately about his business. "Might I help you?"

"Na, just takes time, that's all." He pulled items out of the first large bag. "How be you payin' for all dis?"

Irwin held tight to his personal pack containing all his worldly belongings: squirrel meat, dusty clothing, blankets, hides, coal, and his father's gold. He reached into the bag and looked at the attendant while he fashioned his gold rocks into smaller, more obscurely shaped chunks. Withdrawing numerous golden rocks, he placed them on the countertop. "I am hoping this will suffice. I am thinking this is about ten pounds, or so, of gold." He knew exactly how much sacred ore he was handing over. His smile never faltered. How exhilarating and liberating to trade his father's golden bounty for a new lifestyle!

The attendant chuckled as if in a drunken stupor. His eyes gleamed, staring at all that gold. He looked at his comrades who had also noticed the golden rocks. Giddy, the man began to itemize everything, pulling out the supplies one pack at a time.

No one else in the store was buying as much as Irwin. Once the other shoppers were finished with their business, all the workers stood around and watched as their coworker went sluggishly about his work. This man was not very fast nor very bright. Irwin had hoped that so much gold would have excited the dull-witted man to go faster. The guy grunted each time he wrote down a purchase. He inspected every piece of clothing—every bag of rolled oats, potatoes, turnips, beets, onions, and carrots were weighed twice. He checked the labeling on the sacks of nuts and dried pieces of fruit, opening each bag to verify the contents and the weight. Every satchel, no matter how big or small, was examined. He wrote down each item—broke his coal writing stick several times, and each time, he dawdled while looking for a replacement.

Irwin waited. He knew the man would be done, eventually. He felt the eyes of the other emporium attendants on him. He smiled. They were grimacing. None smiled in return, but conversed in low voices amongst themselves, occasionally looking over at him.

It was dark by the time Irwin made his way out of there. His head spun. The village was now a hub of rowdiness—well-lit for the impending darkness with torches and firepits burned low between makeshift tents and pathway intersections. Men shouted, and women screamed. The noise came from no direction in particular. His Jennies bellowed when they saw him coming. He went to them and untied them.

His newly purchased belongings were being piled up by his attendant outside the warehouse. He watched the man move in and out of the emporium door. He appeared livelier than he had all day. Then he was gone. Irwin brought the Jennies to the trading post door and stood there assessing how to situate all this onto his two donkeys.

The front door to Goshee's Trading Post & Emporium slammed shut. He heard it lock from the inside. Irwin ignored the clanking of the metal lock humming near his ear, and he focused on packing.

Goshee seemed somehow larger at night than during the day. Many of the local miners had returned from their long day toiling underground. Grizzly-looking men walked around, some drunk, some plain belligerent—goading and badgering one another. A few walked alone, glaring off into the night.

He felt many sets of eyes watching him. Every man who walked past had some type of metal on their person, and now there was an undeniable chorus of metals in his ears. The village of Goshee was not at all like the tranquil city of Kobiton. The sound of women screaming, moaning, and yelling came from somewhere. Some of those calls sounded distressed, and yet he had not seen any females on the roadway. Back in Kobiton, women and children were everywhere.

He tried to keep his focus on his belongings. He paid just enough attention to what was going on around him to be aware of those who passed by. The energy they exuded reminded him of Albert—unpredictable. He would never return to this place.

One lone PCP soldier rode down the well-traveled road through town. The indigo uniform was easy to spot, as were the dark-skinned man's features. This man had a scar up his face, gripped his sheathed knife with a dark-skinned hand. He was heading straight toward Irwin who could hear the ringing of the horse's new metal shoes as its feet moved across the muddy and rocky roadway. The metal bit inside its mouth was dripping with saliva. There were metal tie downs on the saddle and metal spurs on the rider who carried several knives and wore a golden ring. Irwin felt the PCP soldier's fingers gripped tightly around the ring and reins. He watched the shrouded guard riding toward him.

He remembered Albert standing before those massive wooden gates as they were fleeing from Kobiton. He was shouting at a guard atop a guard tower to let him pass through the closed exit. Irwin had slowed his donkeys but heard the rhythmic beat of the hooves of PCP soldiers' steads in pursuit. He had not been able to muster the nerve to look back.

A red-headed soldier had shouted at Albert from the tower. "I'm afraid I can't allow you passage at this time of night." The soldier's comrades thundered toward the scene at the gates.

Large black beastly horses had slid to a halt right behind Irwin. He glanced up at the menacing riders. They all looked similar in their indigo uniforms, neat and clean, three were brown-skinned, and two sets of eyes were reflective, like an animal on the hunt.

One of the mounted soldiers shouted to the others, "I'm guessin' we've got ourselves a couple Talented miscreants 'ere."

Irwin had put up his hands. "My father is the miscreant."

Albert was clearly ready to bring about an all-out brawl. He threw down his lead line, and all his donkeys halted, waiting obediently. Irwin watched Albert look around, calculating. His voice boomed. "Miscreants are creatures that morph into predators who then feast upon their prey." He then stepped around Irwin and the Jennies, heading toward the PCP riders.

Staring down a soldier, Albert said, "Miscreants are people who take advantage of unknowing souls. They convince them to believe lies—sell them snake oil that cannot cure what ails them." The seasoned Metalist flooded metallic daggers at the horses, magnetically manipulating the blades to pass through their jugular veins. "Miscreants plot up diabolical ways to harm their prey." All four horses fell dead, crushing their riders, breaking their legs, and trapping them under the weight of the giant steeds. "They have no regard for the safety or livelihood of anyone other than themselves. They are amused by others' distress." Albert had wiped his lips in satisfaction.

The horses did not have time to scream out in pain, but their riders wailed in agony. Irwin watched his father use his metal to silence the first three riders. He had showed no mercy.

"Miscreants are PCP hiding under the shroud of a false Hakra. He cannot save you. And yet, without him, your kind would not exist. This is not a world for people like you." He moved toward the last soldier who screamed in agony, his dead horse crushing his leg. Albert summoned the soldier's squat sword from its hilt, inserting the blade into the belly of the screaming man.

A flame burst from the tower. The gate below had been drawn open. Another flame exploded and a soldier from above shouted, "Go from Kobiton; never return!"

Albert spun on his toe and stomped toward the tower's entrance. "You cannot tell me what to do!" A fire appeared in the soldier's hand, and the red-headed man threw fireballs at Albert. "Do you think you can kill me with your paltry fireballs? You cannot!"

His father stepped into range of the raining fire and cackled as it flew into his outstretched arms and hands. All that fire snuffed out the moment it made contact with his skin. Irwin then felt Albert's energy magnify. His father retaliated; with outstretched hands, small daggers flew with precision and were thrust into the soldier above who cried out as his life ended. His body slumped forward and toppled over the side of the rampart. Landing face down, his head had cracked like an egg as it hit the cobbled road, blood splattering all around.

This wretched memory would haunt Irwin for the rest of his life.

4

<u>THIEVES</u>

I fear not the Hakra. His words may sting, but they cannot kill me. But those PCP ... even though Albert has shown me they can be defeated ... are unlike anything I have ever imagined. There may be other beings out there with powers comparable to mine.

He was ready to leave Goshee, but the emporium did not sell alcohol. He would have to go to the only tavern in town to purchase hard spirits. He had purchased an empty jug and was given instructions on how to acquire whiskey.

I would like some alcohol. It helps me sleep. Oh, who am I fooling? It will help me forget.

The tavern was located around the backside of the emporium. It was full of commotion, so easy to find. He followed the sounds of drunken jubilance. All the windows were open, as were the two main doorways. Long tables with benches were lined up throughout the establishment, and the place was packed with male patrons. The bar was in the far corner of the room, the kitchen just beyond.

Men sang songs and carried on, gripping glasses of ale. Various types of card games were being played at some of the tables where miners bragged loudly with stories of grandeur, and others groped females who walked past carrying trays of provisions. The ratio of miner to tavern wench was about fifteen to one. The women had to shuffle around greedy hands and slobbery faces. These men, like Albert, showed the hard-working women no respect. They grabbed and kissed, hooted and hollered, all while the serving wenches went about their arduous work. This unnamed tavern was the wiliest place he had ever seen—sheer pandemonium with stinky miners carousing and drinking. Trying to be nonchalant about using his metal magic, he hobbled his Jennies so that they could not be moved—a tactic used by Albert on many occasions. Irwin clutched his jug.

A group of four angry-looking, soot-covered miners stepped around Irwin's donkeys. They glared at him. He followed them inside where resonating voices were drowned out by the singing metal throughout the room—the metal that now surrounded him, rattled his very being. Everybody sitting, standing, or moving, possessed some type of metal, and he heard and felt all of it—all different types of ores—iron, lead, bronze, silver, and gold called to him. Coins, blades, jewelry, teeth. It all rang out. Each piece of metal had its own sound. It was as if a bout of vertigo had hit him with great force.

Keep focused. Find the bar. Breathe. Breathe.

A large woman with dark reddish-brown hair stepped up to him. "Ah. What can I do ya for Hun? You look a bit lost in here."

A handful of coins protruded between her large breasts. He could feel the knife secured outside her left leg. "Yes, please. I would like this filled with some whiskey."

"Ah, you be cute!" She said and took his empty jug.

A platter of stew bowls passed by. He asked, "May I get a jug of the stew also?"

"Yup, uh huh, we got jugs. But ya pay for dat jug! I bet ya want some of dat bread too, huh!"

"Yes, please."

"Ah, ya mama raised you up too sweet, Hun." She pinched Irwin's cheek. "Will be back wit some whiskey, soup, an' some bread. How ya be payin' for dis?"

The men sitting closest to Irwin hushed their conversation and looked over in his direction. He shoved his hand in his pocket.

He had learned at an early age how to stamp metal with emblems. It had been with Albert's insistence and influence that he learned to replicate coins. He pulled out six gold pieces. "This is all I have. I assume it will be more than enough for the whiskey, jug of soup, and bread?"

The woman smiled at him. She put the gold pieces between her breasts and said, "I'll be back, Hun. Wait here."

Irwin went back to the door and looked out at his Jennies. They were what kept him grounded. He was trying to ignore the singing of metal. He felt several more miners approach the tavern. They came inside and grimaced at him as they passed. He watched them move toward a table across the room. He heard their banter. Then two more scruffy looking men passed. Both carried satchels of silver, daggers, and blades. Everyone was apparently fully armed.

I have never been in any place so full of people.

Miners came and went. Irwin waited. At one point, he saw his serving wench. She passed him by and went on to help other patrons. When she came past again, he reached out for her arm. She was quick to deflect his contact. But he did not let go. "My jug of whiskey?"

"It be comin', along wit ya stew jug an' bread."

He released his grasp. "Thank you."

Now she had many more coins between her breasts. He waited and watched her come and go a few more times. She was swift to move between her other female workers and out of the way of groping hands.

After a long wait, she returned to him, carrying two jugs and a bundle wrapped in cheesecloth. He could smell the freshly baked bread inside the cloth. "'Ere ya go, an' tanks."

A sigh of relief came over him as he stepped outside the tavern. He peeled back the cloth and bit off a chunk of the hot bread—delicious! The bread had just come out of the oven; that was why he had to wait so long. Now the wait was worth all the glares, stares, and murmurs. He tied up the jug of stew and took a pull off the jug of whiskey. As he took a long hard swig, he felt several men coming out of the tavern, straight toward him.

One of them spoke to his comrades. "I don't see a blade!"

"Me neither. Measly mate ain't got no metal to speak of."

Irwin felt their daggers, knives, and coin satchels. Two men held their weapons ready to fight; the others stepped forward. Irwin just listened to their banter.

The first man spoke again. "How come you're so clean cut?"

"Speakin' like mama's boy back 'her."

"Go back home, you Kobiton freak."

"I say we take his stuff."

Irwin held his ground and shoved the cork back into the jug of whiskey. "You did not see this blade?" He smiled and made a sword appear between his hands. The blade was impressively large, and most likely intimidating. "It is good for taking heads off. It slices through bone easily."

Grunting and mumbling among themselves, the men walked, and then ran, away from him. The young Metalist summoned their daggers into his skin, further disarming them.

Okay, I am ready to leave and never return to this place.

He removed the hobbles and checked the donkeys once again. Everything he had packed was still in place; nothing had been removed. He took up the lead lines and set out. Using firelight, he steered them along the main road. Metal weaponry gave away men lurking in the shadows alongside the road. He was being followed.

He stopped at the northern side of town to light his new lantern, securing it to a hook on the tip of his new walking stick, and continued along into the forest and followed the road away from the trading village of Goshee. As he sauntered with the sounds of nightlife close by, Irwin felt men prowling in the shadows beyond his light.

The would-be thieves lessened in numbers the farther away from the village he strode, ever mindful and aware of what was going on around him. But when he finally stopped for the night, there were still three men stalking him in the forest nearby. The bandits were surveying him, his camp, and his belongings. Of that, he was sure.

He went about his business, knowing they were out there. He hobbled his Jennies and used a chunk of coal to make a warming fire. All the while, the men and their armor moved around, closed in, just beyond his camp's light.

Trying to use the Jennies as shelter from Irwin's eyes, a man darted into camp. He had crawled around the animals and a few large rocks. He was headed toward Irwin's backside.

Irwin felt the long thin dagger held tight in the man's hands moving toward him. He turned, absorbing the metal right before the thief tackled him. He used the momentum to toss his foe to the ground, hard. Then he kicked the fiery piece of coal at a second invader who was approaching his flank. The coal bounced up the man's body, burning his clothing and even his facial hairs.

That grizzly man screamed like a scared child, batting off the charred piece of coal. Irwin did not hesitate to disarm this man too. Now Irwin—who was honing his Metalistic powers—was quick to use these powers, though he did not want to cause actual harm to these men. He had no reason. Not yet.

The first thief jumped to his feet and raced into the forest. He had been neutralized by the loss of his weapon and the hard throw to the ground. Irwin heard his footfalls circling around toward yet another thief while the burned man also managed to find the shadows. That man was loud enough to follow by ear. They lingered close by, waiting for the third man to confront Irwin.

The third man stepped out from the shadows, soot-covered and sweaty. He moved toward the lantern, ready to challenge Irwin. A knife clutched in either hand. This man was ready to kill.

"I do not want to hurt you." Irwin said, staring at his opponent.

"You ain't no Talent. And there ain't no PCP 'ere to save ya either!" The man's eyes glistened in the light as he approached.

"Stay back," he said as the thief encroached. With his hands out, Irwin did what he knew to do to keep himself alive. He pulled for the blades, and they disappeared from the man's grasp—who did not yet appear startled, still grasping the wooden hilts. Maybe he was ready to beat Irwin for his fortune.

Irwin did not want to be like his father. He needed an intimidation tactic. "Do you think that since your blades are gone, it is still wise to fight me?"

The thief did not look at his hands, holding only pieces of wood. Instead, he frothed with anger and continued to step forward and backward, trying to intimidate Irwin with his fighting dance.

Irwin was bewildered by the audacity of this man. He had feared many things, mostly his father's wrath, but not this thief. Anything that this mere Mortal would attempt to dish out would be nothing like the punishments Irwin had endured throughout his life. The bandit kept on dancing and grunting, spitting at him like a vicious dog.

Frustrated by this Goshee native, Irwin tried the only intimidating act he could think of that did not involve cutting this would-be thief into pieces. Flushing his gold forth, Irwin coated his whole body, including his clothing. He could still move, even with his body encased in metal. The metal was fluid and would not drip, unless he specifically made that happen. His power held the metal on the surface of his skin and clothing, creating his own golden armor.

That was enough to scare away this last thieving miner.

Not wanting to lose sight of them, Irwin shot out pieces of metal that adhered to the man's clothing and another's boots. Only one thief had a few coins on him, making tracking that crook easier. He felt all three startled burglars racing away, heading back down the road toward Goshee—nearly two kilometers away.

Irwin sighed and reabsorbed the metal into his flesh. He was not one who wanted confrontation. Nor did he want others to know that he had this power. But he had to defend himself and his Jennies from thieves and assassins.

I need to learn a better, more tactical way of intimidation. One that does not reveal my power ... something that does not end in brutality. That leaves only my words, I guess.

He held vigilant in the center of his makeshift camp. He sensed the men feeling the metal adhered to them—watching and listening as they traveled farther away.

Hope I do not see them again.

He pulled out the jug of stew and the loaf of warm bread. With a woolen blanket as his seat, Irwin enjoyed the warmth of his coal fire and his fresh meal.

5
<u>Captured by Emotions</u>

He felt somehow victorious after scaring off the thieves. He made camp—set up his tent and laid out his purchases. No expense had been spared to create this new life. He layered his bed with his new woolen blankets and thick animal hides. He set aside all the produce, rummaging through each bag, nibbling on some of the items. He bought twice his weight in supplies, and that would keep him warm, dry, and well fed for some time. He slept in comfort under his new warm covers that night, listening to night birds in the forest as he drifted off. His new tent was roomy—large enough to stand up inside—and it would house all the packs and still allow ample space to spread out for sleep. If necessary, his Jennies could also be in there, standing up or laying down. The bad dreams had left him.

That next morning, there was a chill in the air as Irwin packed up camp. He continued up the road, heading north into yet a higher elevation. The chilly wind picked up. He was glad to have his new wool vest snug under his cloak.

At last, I am well-dressed for any occasion.

The roadway twisted and turned back and forth up the mountain slope. Trees that once were thick amongst the underbrush began to thin, allowing the stiff wind to howl down the hillside and occasionally up his sleeve. Irwin and his Jennies were pushed and pulled by Mother Nature all day long. But they did not stop.

By late afternoon, the clouds grew dark. Irwin had been deep in his thoughts and did not notice the change. But the Jennies had and bellowed. Then he saw it: a sheet of sleet in the distance. A low rumble pushed ahead of the storm front. An onslaught of fierce weather moved down the mountain toward Irwin and his animals.

Irwin watched the darkness descend and hurried to set up the tent. The Jennies stood in the middle of the road watching him secure the shelter between two sapling-like pine trees. He hoped the small fir trees would offer some protection from the shifting winds.

The drone of sleet grew louder and swept straight toward them along the roadway. He had just enough time to stake down the sides of the tent as the hard-hitting icy chips sliced through the air. The Jennies clustered close to the side of a tree, their packs on—their heads and necks exposed to the bitter cold moisture.

He opened the large doorway into the tent and hollered at his Jennies. Pointing inside the tent, he said, "Go to bed!" The packs scraped along the sides of the opening as both donkeys obediently filed inside. Irwin's head was soaked and slightly frozen as he, too, entered the dryness inside the tent.

He tied up the front door and then peeled off his partially frozen cloak. The sides of the tent breathed with the wind and sleet. The trifling trees creaked and brushed on both sides of the tent. Every foreboding sound worried him. He did not want to be impaled by a tree, but knew this place was safer than the center of the exposed roadway. The Jennies stood patiently while he removed their bags and packed panniers.

Irwin wrapped himself up in a blanket and pulled out his meal from the night before. There was no place for a fire. All he had now was the lantern, lit and hanging from its stick. That light source, his blankets, and the warmth emanating from the donkeys would have to do. He ate his meal, enjoying the cold stew and bread.

This is better than dried squirrel.

He ate well and then enjoyed some of his whiskey.

That will help me keep warm.

He wrapped himself in a few more blankets and leaned against Jenn Jenn who had already lain down. Once the lantern was snuffed out, the hum of the wind and sleet droned on and on and put them all to sleep.

At morning's first light, they all needed to get out, but the sleet had frozen shut the front flap. Peering through a crack in the tent door, he could see that snow had dusted the surrounding landscape. He had to use his Metalistic powers to escape. Slicing through the ice was easy. Once freed from the tent, they all stepped out into the frozen terrain. The trees that had protected them from the wind and sleet wore a layer of ice and snow on their northern sides. Firs were encased in ice that shimmered in the morning's light. The roadway was frosted underneath the snow, blown here and there by gusty winds driving the snowy flecks and icy chips along the road. Irwin watched the wintery whirl carry fluffy clouds across the sky. The donkeys rolled around in the cool winter delight. He looked upslope, assessing their options. Steep drop-offs lay ahead, burnished by severe winds. Though the sun was on them now, Irwin was not sure for how long. Clouds moved overhead like racing birds in early winter, but the wind on the ground remained mild. Pieces of loose snow and ice pelted his bare face and hands. He knew that in time this would chafe him and his animals.

I hope this is the last snow of the year.

If he went on, the trek would be tough. But if he stayed ....

Why would I stay? I am not stopping here.

The mountain was omnipotent, with its wild, wintery conditions swooping toward them. The trail could disappear, especially if the conditions worsened. He might accidentally go off-route—end up frozen to death along with his Jennies.

That's positive thinking!

He shuddered at his thoughts and from the cold—tried not to worry about what could happen. He was well-prepared. Besides, he had been a mountain dweller all his life, had lived through far worse conditions and had traveled across worse trails with horrific cascading drop-offs. What was before him was easier than what he had already endured.

This is supposed to be an adventure!

Being on his own gave Irwin a new sense of pride and accomplishment. He had never imagined in all his life being truly alone like this. He had wanted a change in his life for so long; it was nice to feel free. Now he could envision many ways of being liberated from the curse of his family. It was his time to shine—to be a responsible adult.

Irwin was diligent about feeding and watering his Jennies before feeding himself. The food and drink were cold, but that gave him vigor. He surveyed the wintery landscape. He knew the snow and ice would make it a difficult hike, but he would not shy away from the climb. He had bought the clothing and the tools he would need and was prepared to set out on this adventure.

After double checking his packing, he ate one more time. He would need the strength and the energy. While he ate, he wondered if there was anyone else out there like him, wondered if there were other men who felt like he did.

The Jennies complied with his decision to continue, but they moved at their own pace. Nearing the timberline, he knew the weather would be more extreme the further upslope they traversed. But he was not going to turn around.

Albert could be out there!

Irwin's mind never ceased with a litany of worries and predictions. He imagined his father watching him—maybe from a higher elevation, or lower, lurking in the woods, waiting to pounce again. He was aware that this trail was not in his best interest, but there was no way he would turn back. Goshee was not hospitable, nor was the surrounding landscape.

I would have liked to live in Kobiton. The people were always nice. My father is a madman. I am nothing like him. I will never be like him.

Since he had not seen any trace of his father along the roadway, Irwin decided that he probably would not.

If I stay on the road, I can see what is out there. This is the only way for me to remain free from Albert's tyranny. I will get past him. He will not bother me ever again. And I will find a way to live as I am with people—a special person—who will love me.

Since an early age, he had been constantly reminded of his inadequacies. Grandfather Jebadia, Albert's father, had complained to Albert on many occasions; said that Irwin was an abomination. He would shout and Irwin could hear from his bed, "The boy is too skinny and malnourished! His legs are too weak, and his arms are too thin. His eyes lack confidence, and even his teeth lack strength. His feet are flat; his back is not strong enough to pull his own weight. And there is something *odd* about that runt, I tell you. You should never have coupled with that light-haired woman." The man had been blunt about cutting Irwin down to a scrap of donkey scat every chance he got. His father was no different. Without his great grandfather Edwin's hand there for him as a child, Irwin would probably not be alive.

The hike that day was perilous. The wind pushed him this way and that. Ice shards whipped at the exposed fleshy areas on his body and his face. The donkeys' heads were down, their noses just above the snow. They followed their master, stepping in his tracks and using him as a windbreak. Jenn Jenn's head was his back brace against the fierce winds. Her lead line was secured around his waist.

The road was many years old—had been built for all types of weather and vehicles. It was something to be marveled at. But as the snow piled up, the road was barely wide enough for two donkeys abreast. He could make out ruts in the road. It was apparent that wagons could—and recently had—traveled this narrow and winding way.

Wagons dared traverse this treacherous mountain pass during this winter storm?! I could have opted to go a different route through the forest, at a lower altitude, but I would have seen father if I had done so. No, this was a good choice.

The hard wind never died. He could see no more than ten feet ahead. The wind whipped the snow around his feet, yet on he trudged.

Without warning, Jenn Jenn put her head down between her legs, pulling at Irwin to a halt. But there was no place to pause, even in the middle of the road. It was too narrow and too windy. The landscape above him rumbled, hinting at an avalanche. Up ahead, there were large piles of snow blocking the roadway from previous avalanches. And there were drifts where the wind had blown the freshly fallen snow. He had to get them moving again.

We cannot stop. Not here. Not now. We must push on.

He tried to coerce them with treats, but the donkey's orneriness was stronger.

"Come on, walk ... walk up. Walk up! Please Jenn Jenn! WALK UP!" He hated using his powers on them. But they were not in a safe place to stop. So, he used the nails secured within each hoof and summoned the donkeys to walk, just as his father would have. It was for their own good.

Late in the afternoon he had to light his lantern. The wind was as stubborn as his donkeys. The lantern swung around on the end of the pole until he made sure, with some Metalistic ingenuity, it would not fly off.

It was past dark by the time he found a valley where they could camp. The area appeared to have been created for camping—a small bowl-shaped valley carved into the hillside, a place where people with wagons could stop for a reprieve.

How did they calculate where to put these camp spots? To build such an engaging passage would mean there was a need for respite. Those hard workers needed slumber, time off their feet, and to eat and resupply along the way. But why build a route through such difficult terrain? Saryh had mentioned something about pilgrimages. This must be one of the routes taken to see Hakra.

Along the back of a ravine-like valley, a frozen waterfall met with a pool below. He hoped he would be able to break the ice and refill his water flasks and canisters.

Large seat-like rocks were fashioned around a circle of tightly knit, medium-sized rocks. This was the place where people came together for rest and food. The firepit was well used. The circle of rocks was deeply charred, but as frozen as the landscape they sat upon. To the side of the firepit, a large stone slab had been placed on top of four large rocks to create a table; the creek separated sleeping areas from a congregating area.

He tossed several pieces of coal into the firepit, poured oil across them, and used the fire from his lantern to ignite it. For a while, the entire valley glowed with light. He moved in close to get warm, and so did the Jennies. After a while, he led them to the creek to break open the ice water with their hooves. Chilly water raced along below the frozen surface.

Soon Irwin removed the Jenny's packs and set up his tent. The girls were now free to move around. The wind stopped. Now the world was as quiet as the innards of a cave.

He warmed up the last of the stew by setting the jug at the edge of the fire. Along with the boiled meat and vegetables, he enjoyed the last of the bread. After they ate their bags of oats, the Jennies got more carrots. Then he ate a few pieces of dried fruits and savored several pulls off his whiskey jug.

Treats for everyone!

The alcohol warmed his insides; it would also make sleep come faster. The Jennies would spend the night outside near the firepit.

Irwin slept snugly in his tent, wrapped in his packs and blankets. At some point during the night, after the fire had died, the donkeys pushed into the tent and laid down to sleep.

It snowed again that night—a light dusting. When he woke the world was still. He was preparing for the day's journey when the snow began to fall again. After a warm breakfast, he refilled his water containers. The Jennies appeared happy about their time off; Irwin also felt a sense of calm.

Their reprieve was short-lived. After an easy start, the winter tempest was soon more arduous than the day before. Avalanches had washed across the flattened surface and trekking across the uneven ground took up precious daylight. Irwin and his donkeys arrived at the next camping spot well after dark. They had drunk most of the water. Usually, that much water would have lasted two days. They were all working too hard. They had barely made it. Estimating tomorrow's travel time, he felt wary about making it to the next camping spot. They were all tired and sore from pushing up the hard slopes. The wind and icy weather were relentless. Nevertheless, the next morning, they started out on an unknown trek once again.

That night they were stuck in the middle of the road in a half-pitched tent huddled together for warmth. He let the donkeys stay inside while he built a fire outside in the cold to melt snow, to make water for the next day's journey. As the sun set, he looked at the sparkling crystals of snow glowing on the powdery puffs on the tops of the fir trees down below. He sighed. Had he made a mistake? Was there no place in the world of Urthis for him to be happy and free? Then the sun sank completely, and it was dark.

Huddled over the fire, he worried more about his uncertain future.

I made the wrong decision. I was wrong. I should not have followed this road. I know better. I should have cut through the timberline. It is not plausible that I would have met father below. He did not want me around. He wanted me dead. Besides, there are so many valleys and ridges out there. I made the wrong decision. Wrong decision.

"What was I thinking?" He hollered into the dark chilly night. He thought he heard an echo.

I have more forethought than this. I wish I had I not been captured by my emotions ... I cannot stop seeing Saryh slaughtered by my father's hand. I hope I never see that man again.

6

<u>NIGHTMARES OF SARYH</u>

S aryh stared at Irwin. Her deep brown eyes pleading for him to do something as his father dragged her toward him.

"Now if you do not want the whore to have your child," Albert pulled Saryh up by her hair, and Irwin saw the metal ball Albert had wedged in her mouth, gleaming from the reflection of candlelight. "... produce your dagger." He placed his other hand across Saryh's mouth. "... and slice her throat." Albert summoned the metal from her mouth, morphing the silver ball into a sharp dagger, bringing the blade across her neck.

Irwin had never imagined they would use their secret power to kill. "No!" Bright red blood splattered across Saryh's white bedspread.

He had never seen this look in his old man's eyes, and now it was too late to help Saryh.

"That is how it is done, boy. What is wrong with you anyway?" Albert tossed her head down, stepped back from the bloody mess, and pulled up his pants. "Where are your clothes?"

Saryh lay face down, lifeless. Blood oozed from her neck, soaking her bedcover. "No! No ... She did nothing wrong!" Irwin touched her hand; it was already turning cold.

"Get off that bed, you foul-mouthed child." Albert reached for, but missed, Irwin's hair.

Irwin reached around Saryh's body and pulled her across the bed, blood spilling everywhere on his arms and his chest. "Why!?"

Irwin called out again. "I am an idiot! I should kill myself."

Good luck, you have tried and failed many times ... idiot.

"What do I want?" His words echoed through the valley.

Not this ... anything but this wintery bleakness.

Though he was resourceful when it came to living off the land, boiling snow into water took too much time and energy, and this was not what Irwin wanted for his life.

This shit is shit!

"Goat herder." He recalled wanting to change vocation, wanting to herd goats, but not any longer.

They are mountain creatures. They love this type of environment. I hate this place.

He looked into the infinite blackness and felt the bitter cold envelop him. He truly hated this place.

He was at odds with the mountain and his thoughts. He did not want this choice to be his downfall. He did not want to die on this frozen slope. He tried not to imagine the worst-case scenario.

Anywhere else but here. I wish I could be anywhere else right now. There are better places than this.

Saryh's room had smelled like her. Sheer drapes billowed in the night breeze coming through the open windows. Long and narrow, her room held a massive bed in the middle covered in what looked like clouds and soft, fluffy animals. Candles flickered in the far corner, their soft light radiating into the room. Irwin looked around; his gaze rested on two paintings of places that he thought must be far beyond Kruluver Mountains.

"Take a seat on the bed," she said, and began to undress.

He lay back, enjoying the comfortable covers and soft mattress. He did not watch her. She approached the bed with only a feathery stole draped across her bare shoulders. "This is so comfortable." He brushed his arms across the bedspread.

Saryh spread his legs apart and positioned herself between them. He kept his eyes closed. So many emotions raced through him—fear above all else.

"Irwin. Look at me."

I cannot bear to think about her anymore.

Tears froze as they dribbled down his face. He took a long drink of whiskey.

There must be places warmer than here. Anywhere but here would be nicer. I want to see the world. I want to see truly flat land. What would that look like? Flatter than this, and probably warmer!

His mind kept on churning. Then he called out again, "An endless meadow!"

A calmness swept across his tired body. He had found a resolution sitting on the frozen land.

I want to find some place warmer and flatter. I want to find another man to love. There. I have said it. I must learn to own it.

Down on the flats he could make an honest living being a smith or a tinker. People did not have to know about his certain abilities. He could work a reclusive lifestyle, as he always had. He could still be interactive with the locals—get to know the world around him. He envisioned living in a town and mingling with others. These thoughts warmed him, along with a cup of hot, steaming water. After refilling all the flasks, he served warmed oatmeal to his Jennies and himself. Then he found sleep, and more nightmares.

Once again, morning came too soon. He felt like he barely slept. His body was still cold, still tired. Yet he summoned his inner strength and pushed through another day of trudging in knee-deep snow. The slope lessened at the break of two merging peaks. He had reached the pass.

Finally!

As they traversed through the summit's passage, the wind came at them from the other side. For a while, he had been warmed by the sun. Now he pulled the cloak across his shoulders. He took up the lead lines and mustered the Jennies along. Frozen snow whipped around their faces again, obscuring the roadway. He could barely see, but as he looked up, he saw the pass widen. A few fir trees speckled the white landscape, congregating along the base of the mountainous slopes. He had tramped through a narrow passage and out into a meadow.

Though he could have, Irwin did not stop. He felt a large amount of metal in the distance. Some of it moved, but most of it stood idle. They passed two trees and emerged onto a snow-covered, iced-over lake. A thick layer of snow obscured the solid surface below. The Metalist followed the resonating melodies.

As he walked across the frozen lake, his tired eyes made out two large, mostly dark wooden structures. One building was a lofty two-story log cabin, the other a long, narrow barn. Snow drifts pushed up under the eaves of both buildings. The cabin was enwrapped by a wide porch; the barn was closed tight. There were a few smaller out-buildings. Attached to a hitch post, just outside the barn, close to a dozen donkeys stood huddled together for warmth. Their packs looked empty. Only a few had stuffed packing panniers. He tied up his Jennies to a hitch post alongside the cabin.

The log lodge was made from massive timbers. Lights shone in every room, and the large wrap-around porch held back snow drifts. Two stone chimneys towered at either end of the building. Smoke billowed, and the smell of cooking food lingered in the chilly air.

He took the steps up to the front porch one at a time, and now he could hear music just beyond a large front doorway.

Ah, good! Sounds as inviting as it looks. I hope I do not regret this.

He reached for the wooden doorknob.

A very hairy man stumbled out of the doorway, laughing. His cheeks and forehead were beet red. Thick white hair curled around his face. "Better get in there, young man!" He stumbled down the steps and headed toward the long string of tethered donkeys. He had come outside to relieve himself and began pulling at his trousers.

Irwin gave the man his privacy. He turned away and entered the lodge. The warmth inside blasted away his partial frostbite. He peeled himself out of two of the three layers of clothing. Then he ventured toward an enormous dining table in that front room.

A middle-aged man with sandy blondish-white hair was tuning a lute. He sat at the end of the long table, long enough to seat fifteen people. It had been made from one huge timber, several benches and a few chairs were pushed snug against the monstrous slab. The diminutive musician, perched furthest away from the door on a grand head-of-table chair, began strumming his lute and singing a storytelling song. Two older women clapped their hands to the rhythm. None seemed to notice Irwin enter. But the bard smiled and hit his lute, creating a new sound and a unique beat. Irwin took a chair at the other end of the table and sat down to enjoy a reprieve. He stared off for a long time, listening to the peculiar song.

A cup of hot water was placed in front of him. "You look like you need this," said a young red-headed woman. She could be his age, but he wasn't sure. He was intrigued by her tightly curled red hair—had never seen a redhead up close before.

Nor had he ever envisioned anyone having such curly hair. "Can I get ya anything else? Meal? Bath? Bed?" Her words were thick with a strange accent.

"Yes, please, to all of that! And I have two Jennies that need to be put up for the night, if that is possible."

"Of course; what's your barter?"

"I have a few gold coins?"

"We prefer food barters, or personal houseware items such as linens, or cloth, or soap, lye, or hard brushes. But for one night's meal, a bath, and bed to rest in, for both you and your two Jennies .... I say twelve silver pieces."

He stuffed his hand into his pocket and thrust out two golden Hakra-stamped coins. Irwin was glad for the one Talent his father had taught him. He handed off the coins, and she looked them over before stuffing them into her apron pocket.

A twinkle in her eye, a smile upon her lips, and a lift in her step, she walked away—her red hair bouncing. When she returned, she said, "I'm Fay, by the way. Go speak to Yuri. He's in the stables." She pointed out the small window behind them. "He'll take care of your Jennies. I can bring you a bite to eat now, or you can wait and have supper with everyone later." She smiled and waited. "We usually serve meals in the evening and in the morning. But we have a few things ready for consumption now if you prefer. And you're allowed one hot bath, or two cold, whichever you prefer. Just let me know when you want any of it."

Irwin liked the idea of a hot bath after enduring the endless, bitter weather.

He noticed the Bard was trying to catch his attention with his clamoring and singing. Irwin ignored him. "Nothing right now, thank you. I will eat and bathe later—after I get my donkeys settled in."

"Very good then." She tilted her head.

She reminded him of Saryh, in a way, but he shook off that thought.

He enjoyed his hot cup of water, listened to the music. He watched Fay pick up a dance with the older women. She appeared to be related to them, but was much younger. They all had red hair of different lengths, shades, and curliness. But when they giggled, they all sounded the same.

Like a gaggle of turkeys.

The women fell into a heap, giggling and singing. Their enthusiasm was nearly out of control. Then the old man who had encouraged Irwin to come inside thrust open the door. A frigid wind blasted the warm room.

The Bard cried, "Harold! You've returned." Placing the lute on the tabletop, he moved toward the bear of a man.

With a gleaming smile, Harold chuckled and shook the Bard's hand. He slipped the Bard a few silver coins. "Yeah, I must be leavin' ya'll. It takes me about a half a day to return home from here."

"Well, thanks Harold for walking this way with me." The Bard said, taking the monetary gift.

"Cheryl, Fay, Eliza, as always, thanks for the hospitalities. It's my pleasure to bring you necessities, and of course, the coal." Harold hugged each woman, "See ya'll when the snow parts."

"Hopefully, that's soon." Fay said as they embraced. "I'm done with all this whiteness for the season."

Harold said, "So are my donkeys. They'll be angry I took my time leaving today."

Cheryl, the oldest of the three women, kissed the furry-faced man. "We'll take just as much coal next time. Thank you, my friend."

Eliza winked and leaned in for a kiss on her cheek. "See you soon, you old miser!"

"I always set aside one donkey for your coal."

Cheryl said, "Have a safe journey, Harold."

"Much thanks to all you ladies, as always." Harold turned to open the door.

Feeling the pull of his Jennies for leaving them out in the cold, Irwin trailed after Harold. The man turned to him. "You better not be leavin'."

"No. My Jennies dislike being idle in the snow. Just like your team, they will heckle me if I do not get them a meal and blanketed."

"Ah!" Harold said as he moved along his donkey line, checking every pannier, making sure everything was secured and ready. "You be a miner?"

"Yes, I was born and raised in a mine."

"I've been one only half my life," Harold chuckled. "It's demanding, though, ya know. And the elements constantly weather us."

"Oh, yes, I know." Irwin untied his Jennies. "You live around here?"

"'Bout half a day away," Harold pointed, "Up that slope. And yourself?"

"I come from Kobiton."

"Ah, that is a lovely place. Magnificent sunsets, friendlier people than Gosheens."

Irwin stared at the frosted barn doors. "Indeed."

"It's too cold out here. Better deal with your donkeys and get back in there and enjoy those ladies." He spoke to his animals. "Hurry up. Get going," Harold then waved at Irwin and began his trek along the road, heading back the way Irwin had just come.

He called to Harold, "Be safe!"

"You too." Harold took a few more steps and then stopped. "Hey, you know, if you are looking for a new place to trade, there is always Chinochi. They take coal barters any time of the year. The pay is a little less, and the distance is about the same as Goshee is from up here, but the people are nicer."

"Thank you for the advice."

"My pleasure."

7

MEETING NEW PEOPLE

I rwin knocked on the barn door several times. Yuri peered through a small viewing portal. Grayish-black hair coated the man's head and face; only his nose and greenish-brown eyes could be seen beneath his thick mop of hair.

Irwin smiled, feeling at once timid.

Yuri sniffed him, gave him another core-chilling stare.

"Fay sent me," Irwin said. "She ... she said you are Yuri? And that I can stable my donkeys here for the night."

The stable hand closed the small viewing window and opened the barn door. "Come in."

Once the Jennies moved inside, the barn door was closed. Yuri held one lantern. He was dressed for the weather in hairy animal hides. The aisle way was bare dirt, but each stall was piled deep with musty-smelling pine needles, woody pieces, and dusty straw.

Irwin said, "They can sleep in the same stall. They are used to close quarters."

"Packs go on wall," Yuri pointed to a spot along the front of the appointed stall where there were pegs and hooks for hanging tack and packs.

Yuri left the lantern on a peg outside the stall and stepped out of sight.

Irwin managed to remove the packs and panniers in record time, if only because he wanted to be back inside the warm cabin. Even though the barn was warmer than outside, it was still cold compared to the toasty household he had just left. He made a small pile of the baggage he would take inside and left everything else behind. Then he handed a small portion of oats to each of his donkeys.

Yuri was standing near the door, perhaps waiting for Irwin to leave.

He hustled and handed Yuri the lantern on his way out of the barn.

The sounds of music and laughter had subsided in the cozy cabin, and the table was empty. He removed his cloak and hung it on a wooden coat rack next to the front door, still gripping his baggage. He heard voices in the kitchen.

He walked over and opened the kitchen door, just slightly. "Come on in," Fay said when she saw his face in the doorway. Behind her, a back door swung closed. Someone had just left the house.

"I never did catch your name?"

"I am Samuel Irwin Miner. But you may call me Irwin."

"Come in, Irwin. Sit down. Tell me of your adventures."

He took a seat on a high stool near a central kitchen table. His gaze picked apart the cluttered kitchen. It was an enormous room with a large fireplace and a stone oven. He spotted a massive cast iron stovetop beside the stone hearth. Dirtied pots had been piled onto the idle stove. There was a lot of counter space and cabinet spaces below the counters. Piles of dirty dishes were strewn across the counter, waiting to be washed. Clean dishes were stacked and drying on wooden racks. Fay stood at the far wall washing dishes in a large mason sink. He noticed a drain that went through the flooring, probably to the cellar—probably into a water collector. He guessed the dish water would be reused for cleaning clothing.

"Adventures?" His life did not seem adventuresome.

"Your journey here—how was it? Which direction did you come from? Where are you heading?"

"Cold." There was a long pause. "The walk was tough."

"Oh."

A basket on the table held potatoes that needed to be washed and peeled. They smelled freshly picked and were riddled with spots of soil. He studied the fresh produce while Fay carried on.

"Well, tonight you are in for a nice treat. We're going to have stew that Cheryl started two days ago. It's full of the last of our venison, the last of our carrots, and some potatoes. Bread will be baked later. Harold brought us a generous supply of potatoes and beets, rhubarb, and flour. I would have thought he'd stay another day. Bernard probably wore him out with all his song and dance. He wore us out, holy Hakra!

"That Bard has such energy, and his stories are so wild. It's been a long time since we've been entertained. Do you know he's fifty-seven, and still traveling? Fifty-seven! My mother was dead long before she turned fifty-seven. All she ever saw was the city of Ajihya. She never toured the canal or went up the road to the eastern villages. But Bernard says he's toured across all the land at least twice around. Twice around! I wonder how long that has taken him. I should ask him later." She glanced over her shoulder at Irwin. "Oh, sorry, I tend to babble. What is your story, Irwin? You don't dress like a typical traveler. Are you a miner? Where are you from?"

He picked up a potato, smelled it, and put it back into the basket. "I come from Kobiton."

"Kobiton, really? I love Kobiton ... such a beautiful place. I've been there about a dozen times. We visited there last summer. Oh, it was so much fun. We just happened to arrive when the Celebration of Summer was going on. My sisters and I got there on the first day. They had just finished putting up all the decorations.

"Oh, my ... the dancing ... the crowds, everything was so inviting! We planned to stay one night to shop, but ended up staying three nights to enjoy all the festivities. Goat races and chicken catches. The bake-offs and all the other contests. So many children enjoying the sweets! Oh, you must have been there. No one would want to miss that. It was so much fun. What do you like best about Kobiton?"

"I ...." Irwin had never heard of that celebration, and now it was hard for him to think of Kobiton. He blinked away a tear and said, "I lived outside town. I only went there when asked."

"You seem to have deep feelings for something."

"My father died. And I left. I just started walking and did not look back."

I do not want to have this conversation.

"Oh!" Fay wiped her hands dry with a cloth in her apron. Then she came and sat down opposite him. "I'm so sorry for your loss, Irwin. My mother died when I was very young. It's so hard to lose a parent, no matter how old we are."

He tried not to be angered by the conversation, but he was. "Can I have another mug of hot water, please?"

"Sure." She smiled and got up from her seat. "This time I can drop a mint leaf in it for you."

"Yes, please; that would be nice. And thank you."

They shared a quiet moment while she retrieved the tea and placed a hot mug, a mint leaf floating on top, between Irwin's hands. She took a seat again. "Why did you leave the Kobiton area? If your father died, you could have moved into the city. It's such a lovely place with so much color and nice people everywhere. Are you really a miner? What do you mine?"

"Mostly coal—sometimes gold and silver."

"Gold?"

"Yes. Well, my father was the one who found the gold, and that was many years ago. Silver is more prolific around here than gold."

"You've found silver too? Wow, that's impressive. Most miners only find coal, but dream of finding precious ore." She returned to the pile of unwashed dishes. "Gold is something only Hakra or Governors have."

"Well, someone must find it for them."

"True. I guess there are some people better-suited, more so than others … like my family. We live in this summit cabin to greet all those who make it over the passes, and we like it here. We are made from men and women with fiery bellies who thrive in the cold and snow. We enjoy being gate keepers for those traveling from Datzar Territory to Uer' Bin. It's a good place for us. From here, either way it is at least five days' walk to any trading town—and it's all downslope.

"Sometimes we're swamped with visitors, and sometimes it's quiet for a whole moon. But when people do arrive, we always enjoy the company. I can tell you that the visiting men are kept honest by Yuri. He can be a bit intimidating at times. But he is very trustworthy and can be pleasant if he applies himself."

"Is Yuri your brother?"

"No, Yuri is the stable master. He prefers to be the recluse. It suits him to sleep with the animals. So, if you come from Kobiton, that means you must be heading east?"

Irwin nodded.

"I would have to say there seems to be more people heading west than east these days. Of course, families have been heading into Uer' Bin Territory for years now.

"From what I understand, Datzar Territory is not very friendly to newcomers. The north side is alright, I guess. But the south … well, they are close to Daos, and that place is inhospitable. That's what I hear. I have never been in Datzar territory farther than Chinochi. And Daos. Well, I've only heard one story, so …. You seem so quiet, Irwin. Do you have any siblings? Or friends your age?"

"No. My friends are my Jennies. They are good companions." Making small talk was not a simple task for him. "That barn of yours looks strong. It must be to have that much snow on top of it. Does it ever not snow up here?"

"We do have incredible summers … not a bit of snow on the ground, only on the peaks. But yes, this time of the year, the snow does pile up. Tending the snowy roofs and steep banks is one of Yuri's jobs. He's supposed to keep all roofs clear of snow … not an easy job if time is taken with it. Yuri can be a bit lazy if you ask me. You don't look like you are lazy at all."

"I have worked hard for as long as I can remember. I was about six when I began to mine." He glanced up at the wagon wheel chandelier holding a dozen candles all lit up. "Did your family build this place?"

"No. It was built long before we arrived. Yuri was already here. He has lived here at the summit his whole life, or so he says. He doesn't talk much about his life before we arrived." She paused to take a drink of water. "We moved here after our mother's death. Before here, we lived in Ajihya. I was born there ... then my sisters, and I, we went on a pilgrimage that brought us here.

"I had never hiked up a steep slope, or seen fir trees, or mountain tops until we came here. But now ...." She looked around at the timber-walls. "It would be hard to get me to leave. We've been here for years."

"You do not appear much older than me."

"How old are you, Irwin?"

"I have seen nineteen winters now. How many years ago did you move up here?"

"Oh, I don't know. I was much younger. Much smaller. I have not counted the winters, but at least a dozen have passed, I would imagine. Probably more. I might be your age, but I might be older. Growing up here has been incredible. My sisters brought me here to enjoy all the opportunities living with nature can offer." She paused from her work, wiped her hands clean and gazed through the window at the gray day. "I will admit, this is better than serving Hakra and doing his work. We like it here. It works well for us. Living in the snow is not for everyone, but we manage."

"How long have you known Harold?"

"Oh, he's been wandering past our door since I can remember. He's told us a few stories about the men who inhabited this place before us. They were a rowdy bunch, apparently. But Harold has lived in these mountains since he was young. His family split up when he was a child, leaving him with an uncle. He was raised outside Chinochi, and he lived and then worked there for several years. He didn't like it much. My favorite stories of his are about the women he courted and how none were suitable. Funny thing, now he's too old to tolerate anyone but himself. He's a picky old man.

"It just so happened that one day he decided to learn how to mine coal and never looked back. Some people die after just a few years at that work, but Harold ... he just keeps on going." She walked away from her stack of dishes. "This winter was hard for him. He usually never travels during the winter—not until after the last snow. Hopefully, this is the last storm of the season. I want to plant my garden as soon as the spring flowers pop up. I'm hoping to still have a few potatoes to do it with." She took a seat and picked up one from the basket between them and brushed some dirt off it.

"I imagine, from all this snow, we'll have a full lake this year. When the lake is full, the fish are plentiful. We catch and smoke as many trout as we can, and when it gets cold, we freeze the rest. Sometimes we trade the trout for other meats; trout is only good to eat every other night." She giggled to herself.

The smell of the ripe stew was thick, and she sniffed at the aroma. "But tonight is venison stew. It's been cooking for two days. Two days!" She pointed to the cast-iron pot. "You're in for a real treat, Irwin. Hopefully, you'll like the bread too. I'm using our mother's sourdough start! Getting hungry just thinking about it."

"Actually, I would like a bath, please."

"Alright then." Fay took his hand and led him out of the kitchen.

It wasn't that long ago that the kind Saryh had made the same gesture. "Follow me," she had said and took his hand. She led him around the saloon kitchen in Kobiton. They went through a narrow passageway that connected to a back door and a stairwell that led to the upper floors. "First, we are goin' to the basement. Have you ever been in a basement?"

"What is a basement?"

"It's a below-ground floor, like a cellar, but much larger. We have a cellar too—where the whiskey is made. Basically, it's a hole in the ground, down below the basement."

It smelled musty down there. Three lanterns hung from thick crossbeams. He had ducked his head several times as he moved with caution through the large space.

"We store food down here, and after the whiskey is brewed, the casks are brought over here to cure. It usually takes three years to make a good batch—the kind your father buys. We do most of our laundry here, too. Though, on hot days, we take advantage of the sun." Saryh pointed into a room where an old woman was piling folded sheets, dresses, and clothing onto a wooden shelf.

"This is massive." Irwin took it all in.

"Over here is the bathing room." Saryh had motioned for Irwin to pass through two sheets she had pulled open. "Sit on that bench and disrobe. There're hooks to put your clothing on over there." She pulled the sheets closed and moved toward him. "Any clothing you want washed; we can do that too."

He did not take the seat; he had never been naked in front of a woman and didn't think he could start now. "Do you do this for all the men?"

"No, I don't. Though sometimes I wish I could bathe them! Come on, let me help you take off your clothes."

"No, I can do it. Thank you." He tried to fill the silence. "My father usually watches me undress. He ridicules my body."

"Your father doesn't respect you, Irwin."

He took off his shirt and put his hands on the button of his pants. He knew he had a man's body, well chiseled by years of demanding work. Saryh was staring at him.

"I respect you," she said. "I don't want your first time with a woman to be jaded."

"Thank you. Thank you for respecting me, Saryh." Irwin stopped mid-motion with his pants still straddling his hips. "I hope doing this will finally earn father's respect."

"I don't see that happening. I don't believe Albert respects anyone other than himself. If he hasn't shown ya love and respect until now, I don't think he ever will. What interactions I've had with your father .... He is a very disturbed man."

Now was the first time since Saryh that Irwin had physical contact with another person. Fay's hand felt warm and smooth—a kindly grasp. He did not want to appear callous, but separated his hand from hers.

She opened the door to a narrow stairwell that led to a cellar and lit a wall-mounted lantern with a flick of her fingers. He had never seen this kind of magic. She motioned for him to follow.

The stairwell was a tight fit, but wide enough for one person to descend. He ducked his head to avoid hitting the underside of the stairs heading to the second floor, and he kept both hands on the walls that turned from wood to stone as they went. They stepped into an even warmer room filled with hanging clothes. Clothing hung in rows from a myriad of ropes drawn from one end of the room to the other. Fay walked through the middle of the long drying room, leading the way. He noted the thick stone walls and arched doorways supporting the massive building above. The next area of the cellar felt cooler.

Fay led him through the basement into a secluded bathing area in the far corner, where the floor sloped toward a tub. Again, hanging lanterns came to life. Had something supernatural transpired? Too startled to say anything, he pretended to not be alarmed, if only because Fay acted so nonchalant.

She pointed to a changing area—an ornately carved wooden partition, tall enough to cover the body but not the head. "You can remove and leave your clothing behind that screen. Use the pegs or the basket for your clothes."

The bathtub was made of iron. Irwin had felt it and the heavy cast iron oven all the way across the snowy tundra—his markers toward this small piece of civilization. Even while standing in the kitchen, the iron stove and tub had called to him. Now as he stood aside the tub, he felt the iron molecules expand, heard the tub groan, and could hear the metal changing its tune as warm water poured into it.

Boiling water poured from a tin pipe that appeared to come from the kitchen above while ice cold water trickled from another tap. Fay showed him how to operate the ice water faucet. "Turn this to the left and the cold water comes on. Turn to the right, and it's off." She demonstrated as she explained. She then pointed to a hanging lever over the center of the tub. "Only pull this when you're done. It's a cold wash and will release the water stopper down there in the tub."

Everything she had explained about how the bathing system worked, he understood. Still, Irwin was amazed by the technology, the metal pipes, and the iron tubs.

Fay left as he fiddled with the cold-water faucet, leaving him to contemplate this turn his life had taken, to be here in such a remote and spectacular circumstance. Seeing these new applications for metal usage was broadening his knowledge of how to manipulate his Metalistic powers. Levers, faucets, and piping filled his mind with wonder. He played with the cold water, tested the spigot valve—cold water flowed until the bathing water was tolerable to his flesh. At first, the hot bath made his feet tingle as if pierced by needles. And as Irwin lay back, a rush of heat prickled his spine. His vertebra and ribs popped and cracked. His body wanted to connect with the metal tub. The song and the urge to allow the metal to be as fluid as the water were strong.

Remain calm, ignore the calls.

He had to keep that pull at bay. He fought with his muscles to relax, starting with his legs and knees. His body tensed as his mind tried to rest. Then, without warning, all his muscles jerked before going limp. His head sunk below the water's surface. He relished the depth of the tub—to be completely surrounded by heat, especially after all those days of chilling cold. He would have liked to do the same for his Jennies, but he did not think these people would allow him to bathe the donkeys in their tub.

Once the water cooled, he took the icy wash and watched the cold shower flow between his legs and down the drain. He stepped out of the tub and toweled off.

His dirty clothing had been removed from the changing area, and he would find it cleaned and almost dry in the laundry room, but his bags were still there. He did not remember anyone entering the room while he bathed, but he might have fallen asleep.

He pulled out his silken red blouse, looked it over contemplatively, and stuffed his new fancy shirt to the bottom of his bag. Taking his time, Irwin dressed and then went to find his clothes hanging to dry and then emerged from the basement. It was now mid-afternoon. He found the kitchen doorway and stood at the threshold. The kitchen was clean—all the dishes in drying racks or already put away.

The woman he thought they called Eliza sat at the kitchen table sipping on a mug of tea. She smiled warmly at Irwin. "Is there something I can do for you, young man? Irwin, was it?" She looked almost too old to be Fay's sister, but their resemblance was apparent.

"Yes, and you are?"

"Eliza."

"I do not know where my bed is, Miss Eliza."

"After a good hot bath, a nap always feels good," she said. "Please, follow me." She led him into the main room and up a flight of stairs he had not noticed before. She climbed the stairs to an open loft. The entire second floor was one large, shared bedroom. Chimneys at either side end of the long room, there were small windows here and there. This would make for a cozy place to sleep. Wooden bunk beds lined the walls, but the middle section was open. Slumped in a chair near the living and dining room chimney, the Bard snored loudly.

Irwin looked around and selected a bunkbed, the farthest away from Bernard the Bard. He took refuge on the lower bed.

Eliza left the room, and he placed his bags underneath the bed and pulled out a woolen blanket from his pack. Fully dressed, he wrapped himself in its familiar warmth. He closed his eyes and fell into a much-needed afternoon nap.

8

<u>KOLOTO THE GIANT</u>

He awoke to the sound of Bernard tuning his lute and people chattering downstairs. Muffled conversations echoed up the stairwell and into the vaulted sleeping space for visitors. He could hear them from where he lay still, resting on his bed. He was slow to get moving. The warmth of the house and the bed made it difficult to even want to move.

Once downstairs, he found an older couple who must have arrived while he slept. They were sharing home-brewed beer—raving about their brew as they poured mugs all around. The staff moved in and out of the kitchen as people took up seats around the table for the ale, conversations, and in anticipation of an evening meal.

Once his lute was tuned, the Bard began to play a ditty.

"Here come ye Maidens three, stuck in duality." He strummed the chords and sang. "It's cold outside, but warm in here. I sit with new friends, and a good pint of beer." He leaned forward and took a sip of his mug of homebrew while his fingers continued to strum. "Yuri waits with the animals in the barn, to keep them safe an' free from harm." He picked at individual strings while humming. The Bard looked to be in deep thought. His dark blue eyes stared at the front door while producing the next progression of the tune.

"From somewhere outside a noise echoes, loud ..." What sounded like a tree branch falling against the porch caused the entire house to rumble. "... whilst the women in the kitchen are bein' proud. But suddenly the noise grows louder ..." There was another hard thud outside. "And louder ..." Again, the front of the house rumbled. "... And louder." The Bard's voice faded, and his eyes grew wide. Was he afraid?

Irwin ventured all the way down the stairs, unintentionally matching his foot falls with the loud noises. All sets of eyes downstairs were on the door.

The Bard strummed another chord as Irwin entered the room and made his presence known. "And the boy over there is crapin' his trousers." Bernard held the note, and another loud crash was followed by the door bursting open.

Irwin jumped back and out of the way.

A large, grizzly man with brown eyes framed by icicles and knots of snow stepped through the entrance. He slammed the door shut behind him and heaved a hot breath of air. Encased in snow, he peeled off his jacket. Everyone fell silent at the sight of this massive man-bear.

Irwin took another step back, trying to escape the man's intense glare. He stumbled around the man and took a seat near the Bard.

Tossing the iced-over jacket of hides and furs aside, the gargantuan man kept his stance near the door—his deep brown eyes a contrast to his reddish-brown skin. "Eliza? Fay? Cheryl? Where are my women?!"

The women screamed from the kitchen, and they all spilled into the main room and raced into his copious arms. "Koloto!"

After the excitement died down, Fay introduced him. "Everyone, this is Koloto—one of our newer neighbors."

He took in all the women but held onto Fay longest. "You should see what I killed today!" He urged them to follow him outside.

Two massive black furry horses stood with heads low to the freezing wind. They looked too strong to be held by such small ropes that had been tied to the tiny wooden hitch post. But there they stood, patiently waiting for their master. Beyond the stout horses lay his fresh kill—a large moose tied to a wooden stretcher.

Only the women of the house followed Koloto down to the moose's side to inspect the dead beast; everyone else stayed on the porch. They commented amongst themselves as Koloto's horse drug the moose's body to a smoke house around the corner of the cabin. Fay led the way with nothing more than her long-sleeved dress on, but she did not appear fazed by the cold.

The freezing wind tugged at Irwin's lungs. Everyone went back inside. The dark horse snorted at him. He thought the giant beast resembled the warhorses he had seen in Kobiton—the ones his father had killed—but this animal was even larger.

Both his donkeys could easily stand underneath either of those giant horses and still have room to move.

I would hate to be kicked by one of those beasts.

He shivered and left the porch for the warm cabin.

The couple with the homebrewed beer sat across from one another. Bernard sat at the head of the table between them. The Bard once again was tuning his lute, while others conversed. Cheryl had taken a seat with a mug of beer. There were several jugs of beer and many empty mugs to choose from. "Come sit down. Don't be shy. You'll like it." She shoved her mug toward Irwin, insisting he try. "They can brew a mean beer. And there are two to choose from—apple ale and berry ale. That's the one I like the best." Out of politeness, he took a small sip.

Usually, just the smell of any type of ale made his stomach turn. But after getting past the hoppy flavor, Irwin could taste boysenberry undertones. "This is pretty good," he said, letting the beer run around his mouth before swallowing.

"This is not as good as what we usually produce," the man said, his white hair askew. He and his wife looked well-fed. They wore matching dark clothing, had kind eyes and genuine smiles—a perfect match.

The wife also had white hair and well-aged wrinkles. Her dark green eyes shone as bright as the fire. "Yes, this last year was definitely not our best."

The husband started, "There was not enough sun in the spring ..."

"... And the fall was long and dry," the wife finished.

"I am Samuel Irwin Miner—call me Irwin."

"I'm Maeve."

"And I am Chet ... She's a better talker than I."

"Watch out for Chet. He can be quite a handful." The wife goaded the husband.

Irwin sat in silence, enjoying a small mug of berry beer Maeve had poured for him. He nodded and listened politely to Maeve and Cheryl chatter. The older woman was ready to share all the samples they had brought with them. Cheryl was working out a trade for some of the moose meat.

After a while, Fay came out from the kitchen and marched out the front door. Koloto followed, but took one of the benches. He asked for a taste of the homebrew, and without hesitation, consumed half a mug. He had sharp features under his frock of black hair. His eyes were almost as dark, between a deep charcoal gray and brown, but they glistened with specks of other colors.

Those eyes were trained on Irwin. Koloto looked deadly, but soon those eyes transformed from disapproving to genuine kindness.

"You a miner?"

Irwin nodded.

Koloto sniffed and said, "Figured. You look like a miner."

And you, Koloto, look like a PCP soldier, but deadlier.

Koloto grunted at Irwin and took another gulp of the beer. "There are many miners around here." He watched Fay as she came in the door and hustled into the kitchen. "Many come here trying to look for a good time with these ladies. Sometimes to lay claim to a fortune that is not theirs. Some look for quick way to make money or make a con." He sniffed at Irwin again. "What brings you to the summit lodge?"

"My father died, and I realized I am not cut out for mining. So, I just started walking."

"Not every man is meant to do his father's work."

Lifting a mug of his brew, Chet said, "That's right! Some fathers are neglectful work horses and show emotion only through aggressive acts and behaviors."

Maeve said, as if finishing his thought, "And some of them just aren't there."

"Some men never know they are fathers," said Fay, stepping between Chet and Bernard and placing bowls of stew in front of them.

"Bastards are bastards." Koloto said, slamming his mug on the table and then grinning at Fay.

"Koloto is our resident trapper. Chet and Maeve have met him once before." Fay seemed anxious to inform Irwin about the gathering of people.

Maeve looked kindly at Koloto. "Such a nice young man, you are."

Chet added, "So strong and able-bodied."

"And helpful!" Maeve finished.

"I am here to keep you safe," Koloto said, though his eyes hinted at something different.

Fay winked and smiled at Koloto. "You do keep us safe. You bring us big game, and we put up with you for a night, or three."

Koloto took a long drink and looked at Irwin. "I live a reclusive lifestyle. Or at least I did until I found these women. I come out of my den for them."

"I'm glad you arrived tonight." Fay said, and her eyes locked with his. "We were just arguing about ice-fishing for our next meal."

Koloto spread his lips in another lustful smile. "I will always bring you a meal, Fay. Besides, I'm better suited to hunt than any of you."

"You are definitely better at it than Yuri. All he ever brings home are old elk, already injured, or infected, or just too stringy even for stew." Fay said and then returned to the kitchen.

"But you made stew out of the last deer I brought ya!" He shouted at her as she disappeared. "Ah, women. They are hard to please sometimes. But if we please them, they tend to be kind in return."

Cheryl said, "Hey! We had to use what little venison we had left last. As it was, it would be fish soup had I not found this last flank steak. Thank me for going through the food cellar one last time."

"Ah, that's why I love you, Cheryl." Koloto threw her a kiss from across the table. "Always triple checking everything." He turned his focus back to Irwin. "What did you mine? Was it coal or dazzling ores?"

"Coal, mostly."

"A hellish job—stuck in a dark place, laboring for hours in hopes of finding enough to feed yourself. Trapping in the winter is just as hard as mining, I imagine, but so is living upon this Hakra forsaken planet."

"Agreed!" Kane saluted Koloto.

Irwin gazed into his mug of beer—embarrassed to talk about his life. He did not want anyone to know about him or his past. He would never see these people again, but he did not see a reason to inform them about himself. He continued to just listen.

Maeve's greenish eyes stared at him from over the rim of her mug. He could tell that she, too, was curious about him. "Fay said you were from Kobiton—such a lovely city ... a good place to live. I imagine there must be many jobs a young man like yourself could obtain there. And lots of pretty ladies to woo! Why would you have left, regardless of your father's death?"

Irwin kept on staring into his nearly empty mug. He felt the alcohol begin to spin his mind. "I do not know what to do." Then he confessed his true thoughts. "I do not want to go back to mining. But that is all I know." He drained the last bit of liquid and swallowed. "I am not used to being alone and on my own, unsupervised. Living in a city ... being in a city longer than half a day ... I have never done that. I am not used to being around a lot of people. I get overwhelmed in a tavern if there are more than a dozen faces. I know that sounds silly." At once he felt embarrassed. He bit his tongue before any more words could spill from his lips.

Cheryl said, "Life is not easy."

Chet had been listening. "I agree! People can be mean and judgmental—outright hostile sometimes. I say do what you are good at, boy. It makes life easier. That's what Maeve and I did. We know a lot about growing plants—about growing hops, and how to cure it into ale. We grow and harvest a variety of fruits and vegetables. But hops is what we like best to grow." He sounded drunk. "Even this high into the mountains, our crops are always prolific with all the rainfall. We cultivate our own fertilizer and maintain our gardens methodically. The landscape provides what we need, and we use that bounty as often as we can."

Maeve added, "But even this late into the season, we don't have all the resources to keep us going. Five days ago, the snow was melting, flowers emerging. We thought it was time to replant, but Mother Nature fooled us!" She laughed with the energy of a young woman.

"Flowers? Already?" Koloto harrumphed.

"Yes, but then Mother Nature can do whatever she wants, and we just have to live with it." Maeve shrugged, nodded at her own thoughts.

Chet said, "What I was trying to say is that we often use what is around us to cultivate our needs. And maybe that is what you need to do, my boy."

Cheryl pointed at Irwin. "Sometimes going for a walk helps—a change of scenery. Sometimes it's necessary. Sometimes it's what brings us back to ourselves and our true mission in life." She, too, sounded slightly drunk.

Eliza came in, following Fay with plates of sliced fresh-baked bread and the rest of the stew bowls. She placed the bread platters down and then sat next to Bernard.

Everyone chimed in with compliments. Fay passed Irwin and Koloto their bowls and returned to the kitchen. She soon returned with spoons, forks, and knives, and placed each by every bowl.

These fancy silver utensils were something Irwin had never seen. His family used wood, and he marveled at the size and length of each utensil. Even at the Hairy Yak Saloon, they used wooden accouterments in the dining room.

Ideas abound!

"We hope you all enjoy this meal," Fay said. "Is there anything else I can get anyone before I enjoy this food too?"

"Na, sit down, woman." Cheryl grabbed her sister. "Eat some stew."

Fay took a seat between Irwin and Cheryl. She took a few bites of bread-soaked stew, and then she stared across the table at Koloto.

Irwin tried to ignore the young woman's eyes flirting with a man who was too large to be just a man. He tried to keep his focus on the meal. The succulent bites of deer in the thick stew fell apart in his mouth and the hot bread.

Everyone said yes to Fay's offering of second helpings. Cheryl went to retrieve another loaf of bread. Everyone watched as Koloto took a third. Only a few said yes to dessert. Eliza had made a mixed apple and berry cobbler from the fruits Maeve brought for trade. She retrieved it from the oven. And as it cooled, the aroma of cobbler wafted around the warm and cozy homestead, nearly everyone wanted to try a bite.

Bernard the Bard began again with his lute, strumming chords without singing.

A few went outside to cool down from the hot atmosphere, while others stood before the great windows overlooking the roadway and the frozen lake beyond. The cloudless night sky was bright enough to make out the distant landscape.

Bernard kept his seat and his instrument in tune to whatever he felt like playing. He strummed another song, humming along for a while, until it turned into a singing melody.

"Once before, when I was young, I lived alone as always. A time or two, I traveled the shores of oceans and of lakes. What I've seen and heard would quiet lips and shatter your ears. People move and people stay, but in the end, we all go away. When we go, what do we see beyond this land of luscious green?"

He paused and looked around the room. The clanking of dishes being cleaned in the kitchen and the murmurs of Maeve and Chet near the front door provided a chorus for Bernard's song. "No one believes what they know of the future, or of long ago. We go along in this crazy dream without a shout or a scream. We don't forget what we have seen in this long and lonely dream. Do you believe what you see in this long and lonely dream?" Bernard's strumming cut out, and he added, still singing, "Don't believe what you see in this long and lonely dream. You won't believe what you see in this long and lonely dream." His dark blue eyes shifted around the room, and Irwin had an uneasy feeling the man was trying to gain his attention.

Irwin said, "I don't get it. Why would I not always believe what I see?"

Bernard looked for a long time into Irwin's eyes, his dark blue eyes probing him. "Which way are you heading?"

Irwin pointed to the door. "East."

"Good choice." Bernard smiled and nodded. "There is more to see in the east. I had been thinking about heading back to Kobiton. 'Tis a wonderful city with many patrons who always like a pleasant song, but my talents would be wasted in such a stagnant place. I, too, think east is a much better option than west."

"Anywhere is better than Kobiton."

Bernard leaned in and raised an eyebrow. "You thought Goshee was better than Kobiton? Why didn't you stay?"

"Goshee was worse than Kobiton."

"And yet Kobiton is bad too? Huh."

Irwin said nothing.

The Bard studied him, then sat back in his chair and took a draw off his ale. "Something else beyond your father's death made you leave. What was it?"

Irwin said nothing.

"I mean, don't get me wrong, Kobiton seems to have everything a young man like yourself would want—like Maeve said ... work, women, and a most hospitable environment! And they do not overly preach Hakra's rules—unlike so many other towns and cities I've visited. That in itself makes it an appealing place to live."

"I am a miner. I live a solitary life. I have no need for cities or women." Did he sound like his father? He did not want to say anything more on the matter.

With a roll of his eyes, Bernard tuned his lute to another melody and picked a few chords.

Fay came back without her apron and sat down with a mug of beer. "This has been a fun night. It's been half a moon's time, if not longer, since we've had anyone stop by. And then, boom! Half a dozen patrons come through our door in two days' time. I'm exhausted." She drew the mug up to her lips and took a long drink. She burped. "Dang, that's excellent beer."

Bernard said, "You've good neighbors."

"What few neighbors we have, they seem to always stop by around the same time every moon cycle. Last time, it was just Chet and Maeve." She surveyed the room. "... and it gets boring sometimes because they talk about the same things all the time. Growing crops and making ale is all they know. I'm not complaining, mind you, they give us produce and liquor." Her eyes settled on Bernard. "What is the scariest person you have ever encountered, Bernard?"

Bernard the Bard strummed his lute with vigor. "The scariest? Or the most intriguing?"

"Um, intriguing I guess."

Bernard commenced with a simple chord progression. "I came upon him on a working day, when many a folk were not out to play. Work, work, work was in the air, and no one seemed to notice or care, but he was frantic for flight, because soon they would notice and want to fight. Yet he was unlike any other and came to me. He stuttered. Shield my path, keep me low, and allow me the space to exit, to go. They are in pursuit and will not quit until I am executed. So, with my embolden right, I shielded him, and halted a fight. I was honored to meet him and upon his departure he called to say that I was the most noble man he had met in ten-thousand days. He was unlike any other, and he had a studder, if you see him again, tell him 'hi I am your friend'." He held the final note for a long time and then broke back into his song once more.

"He wore drab clothing, with an earnest smile, tall—gangly thin—and azure eyes. His skin is translucent, but don't be afraid. He's unlike anything that has been made." Bernard was gazing at Fay. "He seemed to disappear before me, yet he spoke, truly honored by my yoke. He never showed rage or anger, especially when the henchmen attempted to take, but we gave them the fake.

"I was glad to have met him, for he was a most intriguing person!" His song ended and Maeve and Chet moved toward Bernard with wide smiles and arms entwined.

"That sounded so good, Bernard," Maeve said.

Chet said, "You have a way with the music and the words."

"We're glad to have stopped here on this night."

Fay smiled and nodded. "Bernard's been fun to have around. Did you know he arrived with Harold?"

"Harold was here?"

"Yup, you missed him by a hair."

"He didn't stay for supper?"

"He said he needed to get going before the weather turns again."

"Oh, too bad. We haven't seen that old buzzard since autumn!"

"Yeah, as a matter of fact, I was impressed he didn't stay for dinner," Fay said. "Oh, that reminds me! If any of you would like, we're going to barter some of the moose meat." She looked at Maeve. "I know that Cheryl already guaranteed some for you two and thank you for the ale. We've already stripped much of the meat and put the hindquarters out in the smoker's house. The shoulder and flank strips should be ready by midday tomorrow. We might be able to cure some a little sooner for those of you who plan to leave earlier." Then she looked at Bernard and Irwin. "I just need to know what your barter is. We have more than enough meat to trade. Most likely, Koloto will go hunting again and bring us another moose, or elk, or deer—so don't feel you are putting us out."

Irwin knew that when fresh food was practically being given away, he should take whatever was offered. He made another five golden coins in his pocket and passed them to Fay. "I have nothing to offer but a few gold coins. I will take whatever this gets me."

"Thank you, Irwin, but this is too much." She passed back three coins. "I'll have several pounds cured and wrapped for you whenever you are ready to leave."

Instantly Bernard the Bard flew into a song.

"A thousand years of red rain and Urthis is reborn. Everyone to blame, but no one is scorned." His voice churned from high to low, and he held each final note. "Through conflict and non-resolution, the people were execution'd. Now we follow the empowered Hakra, for he shall bring us further-rah—living between thick and thin, no one loses, and no one wins. All people die, but we must march on, for so soon the light guides us to dawn. If we follow Hakra do we know who is right? Do we know who is wrong? When the truth shall be told—we'll face up to the bold. So, we march in the night, shouting 'Hakra you are ours'. We know, yes we do, the owners of powers. When we find what is right, and see what is wrong, we shall all stand tight and fight on and on." His voice trailed off.

Eliza came back to the table and sat next to Irwin. Bernard's song ended, and she said, "I've heard that song before—it depresses me. I wish people weren't forced to believe the Hakra and his teaching."

Bernard said, "That song highlights the mass incarceration of Volatile people who have stood against Hakra and his indoctrinated beliefs, and that we ... I mean, they will continue to do it."

"Every day," Eliza muttered, and took a sip from her ale. "He's the reason we live here and nowhere else."

Koloto pondered, "I've often wondered what life was like before it rained red for a thousand years. Were people even here?"

Bernard looked around the room again and returned to his lute—this time, he sang a more cheerful song—a melody everyone picked up and sang along. "The sun came up to play today, the sun came up to play, the sun came up to play today, the sun came up to play ...." It repeated, over and over, and everyone caught on, except Irwin.

He watched Bernard play, and he thought he saw the Bard conning everyone. His words, his melodies, all of Bernard's songs were interlaced, and seemed to make people change—their moods, their demeanor, every aspect of these people who gathered around the table. Bernard sang, staring at Irwin, waiting, it seemed, for him to change his mood, his attitude—but the spell was not working on him. Everyone else clapped and sang along, as they probably had been before Irwin's arrival. Bernard looked as if he might be confused, almost concerned. His attention then returned to the rest of the group.

Irwin studied the Bard, trying to figure his trick. The musician went from tuning to playing, back and forth, all the while luring everyone into a sense of ease. Fay never asked Bernard again about his barter for the moose meat. Irwin watched but was cautious. Although these people and their ways were foreign to him, his soul longed for this kind of cheerfulness.

After a while, he grew weary. He was worn out from all of it, from Bernard the Bard's theater. He longed to uncover the mystery of this singing man and his magical melodies. He wanted to know why everyone was so drawn to the annoying man and why he was repelled. Even though his body was exhausted, he was hesitant to leave the Bard here with these oblivious folks. He did not trust the man or his magic.

Soon Irwin excused himself, and everyone wished him a good night's sleep when he retired from the table. He dragged himself up the stairs in search of his bed. He felt drunk from what little beer he had consumed. Sleep found him within minutes of putting his head to the pillow—his dreams filled with snowstorms and magicians, with hot baths and frightening strangers. He had met more unfamiliar people in the last few days than throughout his entire life.

9

<u>Never trust a Bard</u>

He woke before first light to the sound of mining machines, but it turned out to be Koloto snoring. The corpulent creature of a man slept across the room. The stench of alcohol was thick on the man's breath.

Irwin sat up, nearly hitting his head on the bed above, remembering it was there before grazing his skull. He leaned forward and grabbed his bags, pulling them out from underneath the bed. He rummaged through each. He was still tired and peered out the small window next to his bed. It was still dark, and a few clouds obstructed the moon's light. He could make out dark shadows of blustering tree limbs outside. He laid back down and returned to sleep.

By the time his eyelids lifted again, the light was streaming through the window and burning his eyes. He rose from the bed and looked around the quiet room. Koloto was gone from the sleeping loft. Bernard was sitting on his bed. The strange man was staring at his lute until he noticed Irwin. The Bard stood, grabbed his belongings, and went downstairs, winking at Irwin before stepping out of sight.

Irwin looked down at his bags again. They looked to be pulled out farther from his bed than they had been when he woke in the dark of the early morning. His new red silken blouse separated from its paper wrapping.

I thought this shirt was at the bottom. Well, I did wake up and .... That was odd too because I rarely wake up that early unless I must piss. Snoring Koloto is what it was.

He rearranged his clothing and then tied his bags shut.

The aroma of apple-berry cobbler wafted from out of the kitchen as he descended the stairs, bags in tow. His stomach grumbled. He put his bags at the front door and rushed to use the outhouse.

Returning to the warmth as fast as he could, he found a place at the table, far away from Bernard. The Bard smiled at him and then returned his gaze to Cheryl and Maeve who were recounting a story.

Ignoring the story, Irwin stared off into nowhere, gathering his thoughts about the day, assessing how much he wanted to walk, and how much he would have to wear to keep as warm as he was right now.

Fay appeared at his side. "Would you like some cobbler, along with a meaty breakfast?"

He was famished, and probably because of last night's consumption of ale. "Yes please, that sounds great. And a mug of hot water, thank you."

"No mint leaf?"

"No, thank you." He was ambivalent, lost in thought.

Fay returned to the kitchen and the front door swung open before the kitchen doorway shut. Chet entered and tossed his coat onto the large rack, packed already with other people's outerwear.

"It's not too cold out there today." He called to Fay, who shut the kitchen door behind her. Chet walked over to Irwin. "A perfect day to leave the summit—return to our abodes. If you leave soon for Chinochi, you should make it past the boulder field and into the forest by nightfall. You don't want to be caught out on that boulder field after the light descends. Winds are wicked along that passage."

Chet moved closer to his wife who was still chatting softly with Cheryl.

Bernard excused himself. Irwin watched the Bard exit the building and return in a trice.

Fay returned with Irwin's meal and mug of water. "Is there anything else I can get you, Irwin?"

"No. Thank you, though." He ate the large piece of pie first, then the slice of moose meat and skillet-fried potatoes. The hearty meal was accompanied by a mug of hot water. This would keep him going all day. He was grateful and happy to have come across this welcoming log cabin and its charming hosts, to have had a warm place to spend the night.

"Wait, Fay." He put his hand into his pocket, summoned another gold coin, and handed it to her. "Thank you for being so generous."

"Irwin, you don't have to." Holding the coin tight in her hand, she said, "You're always welcome here, and you can stay for more than one night. When you're here, you're safe. Oh, that reminds me. You need that moose meat! I'll be right back with it."

Bernard had his lute in his hands again, and instead of tuning it endlessly, he began at once to play. Irwin had a feeling this Bard was trying to encourage him to eat faster with the lively music. Feeling lucky he had realized what was happening, he slowed his chewing and glared at Bernard. He wanted to enjoy, to savor, each bite in the warm cabin. The Bard had already eaten the same breakfast and was watching Irwin intently.

Bernard was impatient to leave, and it came to Irwin that this Bard did not want to travel alone.

He took his empty plate and mug into the kitchen, where Eliza and Cheryl were gabbing with Koloto next to the enormous fireplace. "I wanted to thank you for giving me delicious food and friendly conversation. It was enjoyable to have met you all." He felt himself blush, intimidated by all the eyes upon him.

"Hope to see you again, Irwin." Cheryl said, as Koloto grabbed her and Eliza in an intimate embrace.

"Thank you," he said again, and headed for the door. Fay appeared just then and handed him the meat for which he had already paid. He bundled into his jackets and grabbed his baggage. Ready to move on, he opened the door, leaving the warm cabin behind.

It was slightly warmer outside than it had been the day before. The sun shone above the treetops, warming the alpine air. He strode toward the barn.

Bernard was already in the stables. Yuri stood in the shadows, watching as Bernard brought out his only donkey. The Bard finished securing his worldly possessions onto his donkey's back. His animal was taller than Irwin's Jennies. The Bard's dark blue eyes were trained on him the moment he entered the barn.

Bernard said, "Is there any town or village in particular you want to get to? Or is it just east that you are heading?"

"East."

"Ah!" The Bard replied with a sly smile. "I see! You have no real destination in mind?"

"Some place warmer than here." He hoped his deep sigh had not been too noticeable.

Yuri grunted from the dark corner. His brown eyes glowed with flecks of green as he watched the two patrons engaging one another, preparing to leave.

The Bard said, "Warmer weather is a promising idea, especially after all this snow. I'm sure glad to have someone to travel with. Traveling alone is just that; but with a friend, it becomes more pleasant." Bernard walked past the man in the shadow and out the barn door. "It's about what, Yuri, five … maybe six days to Chinochi from here?" Yuri grunted again, and Bernard made his way out into the bright day.

Irwin watched the Bard from the corner of his eyes, took his time to ready his Jennies. He brushed them down; fed them dried apple pieces. He reattached and secured the packing frames, panniers, and all his gear onto his animals. Then he retrieved and secured the meat package and the rest of the baggage he had left outside the stall.

He was apprehensive about traveling with Bernard the Bard and considered that he had talked to himself during these past cold nights. But for now, he did not really want to be alone. It might be pleasant to have a companion. Perhaps they could entertain one another. On the other hand, he was not so sure how much he wanted this so-called Bard as a traveling companion.

He led Jenn Jenn and Nee Nee out of their stall.

Yuri stepped into Irwin's path. "Nothing good will come if you follow that man." His words were rough. At first Irwin did not understand, but Yuri repeated himself and pointed in Bernard's direction, "Don't follow that man."

Irwin was not sure about heeding the grizzly stable hand's words.

I feel mostly safe. I know where his blades are, and I know I can defend myself if I really need to. I am not too worried about this situation.

He stepped out into the sunlight, studied the tracks leading east. He glanced back the way he had come when he felt Yuri's eyes on his back. A dusting of snow fell when the barn door closed. He hated making the wrong decision, but now he hated the cold even more. He stood there looking at the snow-covered roadway. He wanted to go back into the warm cabin and stay a while longer. And then he thought about going back to the one place he called home. Then he remembered it was all destroyed by his father. But he could not help to think of and worry about Albert. He had to remind himself that his father had left him, not the other way around. He missed the monotony of his old life.

I am enjoying this adventure. I know how to stay safe, keep warm, and provide for myself. What do I really have to worry about? Besides being next to a man I know little about. I knew little about Saryh and yet she let me into her world freely. She was a whore, and that was what she was supposed to do. That sounds like my father.

He did not want to regret any of his actions, but already did. Even though things turned out relatively well, so far, Irwin could not help but judge himself. It was as though he was still living with Albert—taunting him, making him second-guess himself. But he knew he could keep others from harming him. It was not in his nature to be violent, but there were many years of degradation stuffed deep inside that he could call from. Even so, he did not want to hurt or kill anyone. Moreover, he did not want to make a wrong decision that could lead down a path of death and destruction.

Saryh is not a whore. She is a woman. I hate my father.

Maybe I should heed Yuri's words. No. Fay was right; he is a sour old man who lives with his animals. I could tell he does not like me. He might have been trying to dissuade my thoughts. But why? What would he have to gain? Why lie? Maybe it is his thing. It was obvious that Yuri really did not like me.

He felt foolish for a moment for leaving his old life behind.

Do you want to die in a mine?

Images flashed in his mind's-eye of crushed bones and bodies of miners he had either discovered or seen over the years.

You want to be those bones, buried under layers of coal? I chide myself if I do and chide myself if I do not. Ugh! Just sit around and die already.

He must follow through with what he has set out to do. He was a man of his word. He turned to the east, regardless of Yuri's warning, and set out to catch up with Bernard. He had already agreed to the journey. Even though it would be nice to have someone else to help set up, maintain, and watch over camp, his skepticism about Bernard the Bard grew and shrank the more he thought about the man. There was something different about that nomadic Bard, but he did not know what. So, he decided to follow along. He wanted to understand how Bernard the Bard lured people in.

Maybe there is something about the music. But what could it be? How could he use the music to enchant someone without them knowing what was happening?

Still, deep down, he wanted nothing to do with the eccentric old man. It was the fear of the unknown, and the want to understand his fear, which made him continue onward.

He remembered Edwin saying, 'how do we learn? By doing, by watching, and by reading the situation. Doing that, you learn in mind, body, and spirit'. He recalled many other insightful things his elder had taught him, but this one rang true right now.

Bernard the Bard was half a kilometer ahead, and that distance grew throughout the day. Irwin's Jennies lagged. The day was warm—mostly sunny and very bright. Only a few clouds blocked the deep blue sky; the winds were calm.

Although there was fresh snow on the ground, the trail was easy to manage. He followed Bernard's donkey's hoofprints. After a while of walking in the open, the trees grew in thick and hid the sun in some places. The wagon trail followed a gentle sloping landscape until a long wide ravine began to stretch the downward side of the slope.

The road left the soft summit valley. Now the landscape was rough, mostly frozen, tundra. It wound through patches of trees, followed the hardened terrain, and slowly descended the mountainous peaks. Then it took a turn through a large boulder-riddled field. In all directions, brutal gravel, rocks, and enormous boulders rippled along the land, blocking views upslope and down.

Irwin had lost sight of the Bard. The treeless boulder field stretched on for many kilometers in all directions. From behind, he felt the sun leave the valley. Hues of orange, pink, and purple glistened across the snowy landscape, but it had begun to turn dark. The sight was beautiful, but perhaps deadly.

Once the sun was gone, the temperature dropped, and the winds picked up. Nee Nee stopped, a hard icy breeze goosed her backside. Jenn Jenn stopped too. Irwin pulled as hard as he could to get his girls moving again. The sky was turning a deep crimson; soon it would be night. There was no time to waste.

He could hardly make out the tree line along the other side of the field—over a kilometer away, it was a long distance to motivate donkeys through. He hated using the nails his father had sunk in their hooves, as he had done reluctantly already so many times. But he understood the necessity.

It was times like this when Irwin appreciated his Metalistic abilities. With apple pieces in one hand, he got them to the edge of the boulder field. The night sky sparkled with stars and planets. The air was crisp.

He saw a fire light along the tree line. As they approached, sheltered by the safety of the trees, Irwin saw Bernard tending to a small fire.

"Glad to see you made it!"

Irwin stepped up to the warmth of the campfire.

"One of us needed to set up camp before dark. I'm not one for traveling beyond light. This high in the mountains, one can freeze quickly." The old man's breath hung in the air in front of him, where he huddled near the flames. "I suspect it's going to be a chilly night.

"Why don't you go over there and tether them donkeys to the line I hung? I say leave their packs on. It keeps them warmer. I sure do like these makeshift camps—such nice amenities."

This was another one of those carved-out camping spots made for travelers. There were stacks of firewood between the trees. Irwin led his Jennies over to Bernard's taller Jack. He was eating from an oat bag and pinned back his ears when Irwin tied up the Jennies.

Bernard said, "I've already pulled out some of that dried moose meat Fay handed out. And I have a pot of water set to boil. Like I said, all you need to do is tie them and come get warm."

Irwin took his time. He wanted to remove all the bags from his Jennies before watering and feeding them. They each got a wool blanket across their backs. He put off his own needs until his hands were too stiff to move. He clutched his blanket rolls and headed to the fire.

"That is some road," he said and tossed a blanket across his shoulders. He folded one of his animal hides up on the ground and set another blanket down for more warmth. "How they cleared the roadway of those large boulders is beyond me. They probably used Koloto's horses."

The Bard laughed, and said, "Clearing boulders is an easy task for some men—that is, compared to carving roadways across vertically dropping mountain slopes. However, I believe the road coming from Goshee is worse than this one." Bernard was cool, almost aloof. "But, of course, I am not one for steep drop-offs. I have a bit of fear of falling from a high ledge." He drew himself closer to the fire.

10

<u>Shifty Travelers</u>

"Where exactly are you heading, Bernard?" Irwin broke a long silence.

The Bard sighed. "I have no final destination except to meet death at some point. I trust that will be many years from now ... I hope. I've traveled for many years. I've seen many places–entertained many people.

"You see," Bernard said, "I come from a family of travelers. I've toured across this mainland several times—followed any road anywhere. My feet might tire, but I don't care. As long as I can wander, my mind and feet will get me there."

Irwin studied Bernard and decided he was trying to use his rhythm and rhyme to lure him closer.

I made a wrong decision in traveling with this man.

But he was still curious. The Bard's hair was not quite white, gray, or blonde; it was a mixture. His wrinkles flattened when he was not smiling. His hands were calloused from years of playing his lute.

"How old are you, Bernard?"

"Oh, I don't really know. I tell people fifty-seven. It's a good age, I think. At fifty-seven, you are old, but not as ancient as mold. People appreciate that you've seen much, but realize you are still young enough to go on. I'm fairly sure I'm old enough to be a great grandfather. I haven't celebrated my name-day since forever ago."

"Have you ever traveled this way before?"

"Yes. Last time I traveled across this pass, I was heading west. It takes about a moon's time to go from the last city in Datzar, called Jo Hara, to the first major city in Uer' Bin, Kobiton—as you must know.

"Last time I came through east to west, the would-be town of Chinochi was nothing more than a trading post the size of Goshee. The Goshee emporium was only one story tall, and there were only about a quarter as many tents. But I'll tell you, that tavern has not changed."

"Did these camping spots exist back then?"

"They've been here since the beginning of time," he said. "That's the one wonderful thing about this road. There are ample camping spots. As you might know, many people travel this road at all times of the year. It's the only passage from the Oceans of Bounen to the Ar Var Harbor, unless you take a ship. Now, from what I understand, that passage takes just as long, and you're on the open ocean. Merchants, families, and travelers do not shy away from this passage—though it's much nicer to travel during the warmer seasons.

"Did you know that this is the only mountain range in all Urthis that you'll ever cross to see an ocean? Do you know what an ocean is? Ever seen the ocean?"

Irwin said nothing.

"It's like an endless lake. And by the way, the warmth you crave is only a few days away."

"What about the cabin?"

"What cabin?"

"The log cabin at the summit where we just were. Did you stay there last time?"

"That summit cabin was not as hospitable last time I journeyed this way. Let's just say I was thankful for the new inhabitants. Those Erthin women guard that passage well. It was hard for me to say goodbye.

"Alas, a Bard must travel. I have encountered much along my journeys. The one thing I can tell you for sure is that everything is colder to the west—including people's attitudes. It's the same the more south you travel too. But all-in-all, people are much the same everywhere you go. Most are genuinely pleasant. But when you run into individuals with sore teeth, offer them a drink. And you'll always have a good story to tell if you don't over-stay your welcome."

Irwin still did not like Bernard's odd rhythm in the way he spoke.

Maybe that is how he does what he does, through his words. It is not the song at all.

"Why do you travel around? Why would you not want to live somewhere more ... permanent?"

"I am a Bard! It is my destiny to keep on moving, to come up with rhymes, to play music, to spout off stories. I am meant to entertain. It's what I am good at. If I were to stay in one place, I wouldn't have experiences to draw from.

"To tell you the truth, Irwin, I probably wouldn't be as much fun."

Irwin stood and wandered away from the fire to retrieve more kindling. He tossed the pieces onto the fire and the Bard pulled the boiling water pot from the fire's edge. Irwin took his seat and accepted a mug of hot water.

"Thank you, Sir," he had replied to the offer.

"Sir? I am no Sir." He chuckled. "You're a Commanding Officer's dream, Irwin—all the yesses, pleases, sirs and such."

"What's a Commanding Officer?"

"Just how sheltered are you, boy?"

"I am sheltered by the trees. And my blanket offers a good wind block."

"Too sheltered! Your father must have slapped you around one too many times."

Irwin kept his memories of those beatings to himself.

The Bard continued to pry. "And I bet your mother wanted you to be respectful—all those pleases and thank yous."

Irwin pulled the blanket tighter around his shoulders. "My mother died when I was born."

"I can tell you hadn't been coddled."

"My great grandfather raised me. He taught me to always be polite."

If I wanted, I could kill you right now, you old coot. Take a breath. Calm down. He is like Albert—trying to provoke. Remain calm.

The Bard was staring at him. "A polite miner—I have never met a polite miner. Most miners look and smell of sooty mines—reclusive, volatile, or have a mental deficiency of some sort ... or maybe a combination of it."

I am none of those.

He stared back at Bernard.

Yes, another unwise decision. I should know better than to travel with anyone. How do I get out of this? Do not freak out. Take a breath.

Yuri had warned him. Bernard the Bard was shifty with his words and his actions.

Bernard salvaged another handful of meat strips. He passed a piece of the moose jerky to Irwin. "Here you go. What really made you leave home? I don't believe you when you say your father died. You would be more shaken if that was the real situation. That is, unless you killed him?"

Those blue eyes kept trying to penetrate his soul, his life story. So, he stared back. Bernard looked like any other person, but there was something about him. "My father was not easy to live with."

"Whose father is? Consider yourself lucky to have grown up with a father. My mother raised me. I never knew my father. None of the men in my life were good to learn from. I think I was ten when I took my own road. I never looked back.

"Many of us wanderers don't feel that we blend well with normal society."

"Why not?"

"Not everyone is created equal on Urthis."

Irwin shivered. Was Bernard alluding to something more than what was obvious?

What is he hinting at? I know I am a recluse, struggling to come out of my cave and explore this planet. I know I am different. I am used to hiding my true self.

Albert had made a strict point for them to keep their Talents hidden.

Maybe I am supposed to roam like the Bard. And maybe Bernard has the power to manipulate people, altering mindsets perhaps. It sure seems like that is what he is trying to do. Did Saryh call those like him Telepaths?

Though Albert never said it outright, he had hinted to Irwin that their family were the only people with magnificent powers—one of the reasons they hid in the mountains. But Irwin was beginning to realize that there were others with powers.

Father lied about many things. I wonder how many people out there have powers comparable to my own. Beyond that one who could make and throw fire, what other types of powers are there? Telepaths and what else? Is everyone powerful? Father said everyone was Mortal. I am starting to believe he lied about many things. Do not panic, take a deep breath.

His heart banged against his ribs.

Breathe!

The old man moved away from his seat and opened his lute bag. He took out the lovely wooden instrument, plucked the strings, but several notes faltered, so he tuned the instrument again. "It's never good when my lute gets cold. The strings become brittle and might break."

"What are the strings made from?"

"Sometimes horsehair, or intestines, or tendons."

"Oh."

That is one way to reuse parts.

Irwin drank down the hot water and poured himself another. He ate all the jerky.

Bernard strummed his lute. A smile crept across his reddened face.

"A long, long time ago, before the wind, before the snow, there lived Telepaths, Erthins, and Clan-Duins. Oceans churned and tides changed, it was they who changed the planet's name.

"Distant creatures from a land long lost, they travel on at any cost. Some who were born here, and those who remain, are all somewhat the same. And those who are surrounded by walls, will never hear their spiritual calls.

"All those who travel are not all lost, but they'll keep on travelin' no matter the cost."

This melody was better than anything he had heard the Bard sing. He pondered the man with wonder as he repeated the song. Irwin did not listen to the words, just the hummable tune. And when the song was done, he clapped.

"How do you do ... what you do?" he asked.

"Strumming the lute? Making the notes? Or composing the music?"

"All of it."

"It's a fluid motion that gets easier the more you do it. There are notes." He plucked the strings. He strummed and hummed. "I can lure you in with a changing rhythm and by harmonizing." He sang while changing the chords. "When I compose a song, it comes from my soul, you see." He played and sang. "I use my words to bring out the best in people."

The wind blew across the fir trees, and it started to snow. The fire flickered and Bernard fed it another thick piece of wood. "I am not as good as other Bards, but we all have our own way." There was a spark in his eye—maybe reflecting the flames, or maybe something else Irwin could not understand.

"How many other Bards are there?"

"Traveling or stationary?"

Irwin shrugged.

"Thousands I suppose. I've only met about two hundred or so over the years. We have a way of not mingling. Some stay at one tavern, while others might service Inns. Some go to the city center and play, and some travel around all day. For every day I spend traveling from one place to another, I stay that many days in the next settlement. If it's a larger town, I'll travel around the different districts. Sometimes I work the streets; sometimes I work the Inns. I stay for a time, gathering up a few stories and money, and then I head back out into the world.

"You will find stationary Bards, but like I said, they lack experiences. Like what you witness at Saloons, there are people who put on shows, singing and dancing and such, but they live and work in much a different style than myself. They are considered Dancers, Ladies of the Night, or Exotic Entertainers, but not Bards."

He leaned toward the fire. "If I can give you some advice, and this is something a young man like yourself needs to hear, don't trust anyone who entertains. They usually want one thing—your money."

Irwin sat back. The Bard's words were rattling him. He looked over at his Jennies and his bags leaning against the far tree. "Did you go through my belongings this morning?"

The Bard nodded his head. "I had to know what type of man your age travels the wintery pass alone."

"Why would you go through my stuff?"

"We're traveling in the same direction. During wintry nights like these, you need to know who you can trust. I wanted to know if you had any weapons."

"Were you looking for weapons, or were you looking for money?"

"Both. But I found neither." Bernard pointed at Irwin's baggage. "Most men carry some sort of weapon. I have a short knife for killing ferocious animals during the night. But you carry nothing for protection unless you stow an ax in your pack bags. If that's the case, then you would have to sift it out before assailing some bear, or wolf, or mountain cat. How are you going to defend yourself against the wilds?"

"I have lived in these mountains all my life. I have never been approached by any ferocious animal." That was a lie, but none had ever come at him with the intent to kill. "All the animals I see usually turn and run. They stay away from us two-legged creatures—they do not like our smell." Irwin's grayish-silver eyes never left Bernard's beady blues. "Besides, as long as there is a fire, I guarantee the scary creatures will stay away."

"Is that what your father told you?" He pointed at the flames dancing in the night between them. "You think that fire will keep you safe? You do not know what lurks in the darkness that surrounds us. The PCP might be out there!" His eyes glistened.

Irwin knew what the Bard was trying to do—provoke him, physically and emotionally. They continued to stare down one another. Bernard was looking for information, but Irwin made sure he remained unreadable.

The old man strummed his lute. He struck up a song he had sung the night before.

The Bard was trying to use his musical magic to lure him in, but it was not going to work. Irwin was now certain he could not trust this man. The slang he used in his songs confused Irwin, and he decided this was part of the Bard's well-practiced lure.

He gathered his blankets even tighter around his shoulders—moved his hides lengthwise along the bottom blanket. He made a pillow with the smallest blanket and lay down; he wrapped up in the rest of his blankets. He would ignore the Bard for the rest of the night. He concentrated on the fire, the leaping flames, crackling wood, and the white smoke spiraling up toward the night sky. He was safe. He knew exactly where the Bard's short knife and hidden dagger were located. One was always secured to the Bard, serving as a beacon to his whereabouts in the camp. Irwin knew he could defend himself against this bold, theatrical man.

After a while, Bernard wrapped the lute in its sheepskin hide and tucked it atop his bag. He poured himself another mug of hot water, and then he pulled his blankets around his rotund body.

Sleep crept across the camp.

11

<u>Twisted Words</u>

It was first light, and Irwin was aware he had barely slept. He lay there listening to the Bard snore, and to hungry nocturnal creatures calling out. All the donkeys had lain down. Nee Nee and Jenn Jenn were back-to-back. He shifted his body several times, and then sleep came to him again before the sun was up. It was a brief but deep sleep. He was up before dawn and gathered his belongings and secured them onto the Jennies. He and his donkeys left camp before the Bard was up.

He had not bothered with breakfast, and soon his stomach wished he had. But he wanted to get far away from Bernard the Bard as possible. Pulling the donkeys along the snow-covered roadway was difficult. Though he believed he would out-pace Bernard, there he came, riding up behind them on his larger donkey.

"I see you're trying to get to the next camping spot before nightfall. Clever idea, my boy."

Irwin did not reply.

"I want to ask about that red blouse?"

Irwin's body stiffened. He said nothing.

"Is that what got you kicked out of your cave? Did your father find out that you are a reclusive female trapped inside a male's body? It happens. I'm not one to judge. I've met many people in my days."

Irwin wanted to keep the forward motion with his Jennies, but he stopped right there, growled, and spat, "You do not know me! You do not know my situation! All you know is what I have told you, so stop trying to read me."

"You can trust me, Irwin. I was honest with you about what I did, right? Besides, I cannot rob you at this point. If I did, you could track me down easily in this snow ... unless I stab you and leave you to die. But that is a most callous action for an old Bard. So why would I? I already know you have no way to defend yourself—and that in itself is rather odd." He swept his hand through the mountain air. "And you have nothing I want. I suppose I could take your food, but most travelers have more valuable possessions than donkeys, rations, and panniers. Something made of silver or bronze, or gold perhaps ... but you have nothing of real value! No extra coins. Well, maybe your cooking wares are worth something—"

Irwin stared at Bernard. "I cannot believe you went through *all* my things!"

"I didn't go through all your baggage. You came into the barn too quick. Besides, Bards say and do a lot of things. It's in our nature to be curious about others, as you should be too. Curiosity might save you ..." His voice dropped. "... or get you killed." Then his voice rose again. "What I'm trying to get across to you, Irwin, is for you to be curious about others. Learn what you can from those you surround yourself with. That's the best way to keep safe." He paused, pulling at his beard. "But remember to be cautious. Don't trust everything you see or hear. People will boast about this and that, and those who say you should believe in what they say or do are likely trying to convince you of something that is not real—not based in this reality. That's rule number one here on Urthis. Most people are not genuine—have ulterior motives."

Irwin stopped listening.

Keep calm. He is leading me along ... but for what reason? What are his motives?

This was a game to Bernard; a mental game that he did not want to play. "You say you are an itinerant wanderer, but all I see is a manipulating thief! You steal food and drinks, kindness, and who knows what else."

"I'm not a thief; I am a Bard. I've stolen nothing. If anything, I give pieces of myself to everyone I meet." His eyes narrowed. "It's obvious that you're very naïve in the ways of this world. I'm trying to help you, Irwin. You grew up in a mine and weren't exposed to new things, new experiences. You know nothing about the world or the people you'll meet in it. You need to be guided by someone who has."

Bernard sighed and shifted on his mount. "In retrospect, though, your family may probably had good reasons to keep you so far removed from society. There are many bad people out there who steal away naïve, able-bodied youngsters. They use these children until they are spent of life, and then leave them to die with no repercussions and no remorse.

"Maybe you are not ready for Urthis. Maybe you should go back to your father. Ask for forgiveness." The blue eyes turned to Irwin and held firm. "Or you could be stubborn and thoughtless."

Irwin held his tongue and his rage.

"Go back to that cave of yours and grow up a bit more before you come back out to explore the world and its inhabitants."

He is trying to provoke me. He is testing me. Breathe.

Had you met my father instead of me, you would be dead by now.

"You cannot tell me what to do."

Putting up his hands across his face, Bernard said, "Hey ... Hey. I am just trying to help!" He snorted, urged his donkey backward. "It's obvious you need guidance, you and your narrow mindset."

"Narrow mindset? You told me not to trust anyone; people are not genuine. Now you want me to believe that you are here to help. But I see what you are trying to do. You are the one who is not genuine. You are trying to manipulate to your advantage, trying to get something from me that I will not give. You are two-faced, Bernard the Bard. There is no way I will ever believe anything you say. And you will not convince me to do anything I do not want to do."

The old Bard laughed raucously.

It is unfortunate for me that we just happen to be traveling in the same direction.

Bernard's laughter grew more boisterous.

Irwin growled. He did see himself as naïve, at times uneducated, but surely not narrow-minded. His father and grandfather had been obstinate in their thoughts and attitudes. But Edwin taught him to be open, to change; allow for all pos-sibilities life would offer—to think differently than his other family members. He knew he was uneducated in the ways of the world, but he was educated in the nuances of verbal manipulation. He was not ready to back down, nor he was about to take unsolicited advice from some itinerant. "Yuri was right."

"What was that grizzly old Clan-Duin right about?"

"Yuri is a man, like you and me, not a-a 'Clan-Duin' as you refer to him. Calling people names is no way to make friends."

"You're an idiot, Irwin. Your father should have taught you better. He might have taught you how to mine ... how to find a buyer for your coal, but do you know how to interact with anyone else?"

Irwin knew the Bard was right.

"After our interactions last night ..." Bernard made a sound out of his nose. "... and from what else I've seen of you in the last few days, that's a no! And speaking names like Clan-Duin and Erthin, you might think that is slanderous, but that is what *They* are! And you'd know that if you knew anything about *Vols* or the PCP."

Irwin flinched.

"Oh, so you have met them. So, you know what Erthins and a Clan-Duins are?"

Irwin had no clue what the Bard was talking about.

"Your father and you, did you have an altercation with them?"

Irwin turned to escape from the conversation. The Bard was trying to read him about something or someone.

Bernard said, "Maybe somehow you two were separated? Did the PCP intervene in your squabble over the red shirt?"

You have no clue what you are talking about.

Irwin pulled his Jennies along, wishing he was kilometers from here, from this Bard.

"Well then, Irwin, you might as well stay here in the mountains. This is where you'll be safest from the PCP. If you go downslope, there are people far worse than me who will take you. They will own you; corrupt you into something not yourself ... mentally and physically."

Irwin drew his Jennies to a halt. "You do not know me or my situation. And your words do not scare me. I have met people who corrupt, who manipulate, who beat and berate worse than you ever could. You do not scare me. So, whatever you believe you are trying to do to me, I will not fall for it.

"And as a common traveler of the roads, I find it sad that I cannot trust you or your words, Bernard the Bard. I figured that you, someone who has seen the sights, might have empathy toward others and their ways—a false assumption—poor judgement on my part."

"I cannot trust you either, Irwin the Miner! I've never met anyone who walks around with no blade. No axe in your baggage. No sword at your side ... no dagger to speak of. And your words are just as misleading as my own. It's obvious you are withholding as much as I, if not more. We are stalemated. As I see it, you need me just as I need you."

"We do not need each other." Irwin pulled on the lead lines again.

"Yes, we do. We are here to keep each other company on the trail. You do have a unique story, Irwin the Miner; and I have much knowledge about the world. We'll both benefit from this journey together."

Irwin's lips tightened. "I know we are each other's entertainment. But are you going to make a song about me?"

"Maybe," Bernard kicked his donkey onward. "Better get going. See ya at camp!"

Irwin watched the Bard's donkey wade through the snow. His Jennies looked tired, and he kissed Jenn Jenn and Nee Nee and pulled them gently down the sloped road.

Wind whipped around them, chilling Irwin to the bone. It was skin biting cold when they passed through the shaded areas and the wind chill lowered. They pushed on.

After a few kilometers, when he came upon Bernard, he was stopped in the middle of the sunlit roadway. The sun had hit its apex and started to descend into the timberline. The Bard stood next to his Jack eating jerky. He tried to pass off a canteen and stick of jerky to Irwin. "This is really good. They gave you some too, right?"

Irwin did not acknowledge him. He did not want to engage the Bard more than necessary.

No ratty old Bard will interfere with my goal of finding warmer weather.

The bitter cold and snow were as annoying as this weaseling man.

The Bard said, "I have a few ales we can share this evening to help keep us warm. It will help you sleep better."

"You would like that. It would allow you time to search my bags again."

"So, how long have you been separated from your father? After I left my mother, it took me some time to forget her—now I can't even recall her face. I remember feeling jaded ... slighted even, if only because of what she didn't teach me about people. It was a foolish mistake on her part to not inform me about those who do harm to others, and there are a lot of them out there."

Irwin's growling stomach urged him to stop several hundred feet out of earshot of Bernard. He fed and watered his animals first, as always, and then pulled out his meal of moose jerky. He did not want to share. He knew he owed Bernard for the night prior, and tonight Irwin would lay out provisions. For now, his contempt got in the way of his need to share. He did not dally. He was off again, as were his thoughts.

How can I rid myself of this man without killing him? Outpace him.

His imagination was running, and his feet set his speed along the road. He envisioned a time when he and his animals could be alone again. He wondered about the next town. Did he need to stop, or should he just continue walking—leave Bernard behind? No matter what he did, he was certain that his time with the Bard would soon come to an end.

By late afternoon, his pace slowed. Bernard and his donkey followed only a few strides behind. They barely made it to the next marked camping spot before dark set in.

While they made camp, Irwin felt Bernard's eyes. Not a word was exchanged as they removed tack and set their donkeys up with water and grain bags. Afterward, Irwin decided to set up his tent—hoping that erecting an enclosure would bring a reprieve from Bernard's prying eyes.

Bernard stopped setting up the firepit, and Irwin soon noticed the man's eyes held a mischievous sparkle that increased as the tent was completed.

"This is for my Jennies. I let them have this tent so that they will travel better. They are too cold, and that's why they are going so slow." He knew the Bard was aware of his false truths.

"Wow! A miner who loves his donkeys more than himself? I've never met anyone so selfless." Bernard's eyes narrowed. He said, "What's baffling is last night you didn't pull that tent out for them. And it was much colder upslope than it is here. I don't think it's the cold. I believe it's my presence that has created this unsettled air about you. And though I find it funny that you are hesitant around me, it is I who am afraid of you." Bernard approached Irwin.

"I offer no hostility," Irwin said. "Why would you be afraid of me?"

"Do I really need to give it to you again? You have no weapons—unless you have a leg blade I have not seen."

"Why is not having a blade a bad thing? There are many people who do not carry blades. I happen to be one of them."

"Everyone carries something to defend themselves." The Bard stepped closer, staring Irwin down as if he were prey. "I know! Should we line the inside of the tent with pine branches? No, those would poke your precious Jennies. Maybe we should find them exotic grasses downslope."

"You are not afraid of me. You mock and ridicule me. Why?"

"Oh, I'm afraid of you. I've never met anyone who would travel without a blade. And your satchel of coins at your side is empty. Did you spend all your cash at the cabin? Are you that unprepared?" The man was unrelenting. "Did your father not teach you about blades? Did he not want you to have a knife to defend? Was he afraid you would kill him? Or was he afraid you would kill yourself because you were miserable living under his scrutiny? Or maybe," He paused. "Or maybe you hold a power? Maybe you are more than you let on! What *is* your story, Irwin?"

Just like Albert. Do not buy into it. He is trying to provoke. Breathe!

"You do not care about me. It is all about manipulation for you. Trying to get what you want. I have nothing to say to you."

"You're acting like a madman! If you were more civilized, more educated—"

"I am not the person acting mad!" Irwin wanted to be away from this man, but he did not want to leave the warmth of the camp.

"No! No, you're not. You should be though! You should be mad! You should be mad at your father for withholding so much about Urthis. He denied you access to people, making it hard for you to have a good relationship with anyone other than an animal. When was the last time you had a conversation about yourself with another person? See ... even now you cannot speak. You cannot rebuke!"

Bernard's close proximity made Irwin withdraw further.

"Your father made you this way. Look at you. You cannot even function." Bernard changed his stance and his approach. "Luckily, you are still young enough that you can remake yourself in your own image."

Irwin wrapped his arms around his chest and took a step back. "I do not understand why you want me to believe that you care about me. As you said, you are a Bard, and you travel around and make up stories. I may be your amusement, but I am not amused. Besides, no one made me this way. This is who I am."

Bernard chuckled, pulling again on his beard near the firelight. "You know what? I do care! I care because I live on this plane of existence, and so do you. I need to know if you are one of the good guys. Are you going to hurt me or help me? From what I've seen, Irwin, you're a good person. But you are also a very simple young man. Your approach to life is straightforward, so thinking abstractly is difficult for you. And you don't trust easily, which is sad. Not everyone is out to get you. There are kind people, and I do meet them often. That is an issue we could work on.

"I can also tell that you're scared, wary of this life given to you."

He was fishing for more information.

"I'll tell you, Irwin, that you should embrace this world like a prickly bush … a prickly bush with sweet fruits. There are parts of this world that you want to eat up, to savor, and others that will poke you, maybe hurt you. It's hard to be prepared for any of it, especially with your meager background."

Irwin was stuck on this cold roadway with a man who appeared hungry for drama. He wanted to be done with this conversation and this miserable trip. But it was cold, and the thought of leaving camp was daunting. He wanted to be done with all of it, especially the conversation.

"I'm glad that you brought out your tent! We'll stay warm and sleep inside tonight. Excellent job, young man, excellent job!" The Bard went back to gathering firewood. This camp, like the last, was stocked with firewood, flat camping spots, and a watering hole.

Irwin watched the Bard walk over to the large stone-inlaid firepit with an armload of cut wood, branches, and twigs. That's when he noticed the camp had been recently used.

Bernard placed his armful down and cleared off the stone firepit. Fir branches were piled over many dead but dry coals.

I need to remember to set up the camp for the next travelers before I leave tomorrow, as someone did for us.

He wondered who.

Harold, maybe?

Then he remembered Harold had traveled with Bernard from Goshee.

I wonder how those two got along.

There was a sturdy structure of kindling ready to be ignited. While kneeling, the Bard pulled out a small metal tin and slid it open and removed a thin wooden stick. He rubbed the stick on the roughened back of the tin and a flame shot forth. He lit a small piece of oiled cloth, then put the fiery cloth into the stack of kindling and blew.

Irwin stood back and inspected this interesting phenomenon. He made his fires with his flint and stone. He used dried donkey manure, or moss, to ignite the fire. The sight of Bernard's tin now gave Irwin ideas of what he could craft with his powers.

Bernard handed him the device. "This is a match tin. I traded a song for it."

"You traded a song for this?"

"I've traded many songs for many things." Bernard went to his saddlebags and returned with a large pot. He filled it with snow and perched it between the rocks and the fire. He watched it melt and then added more snow.

Irwin took a seat on a rock near the fire. Although he did not like this man, he was curious. While Bernard melted the snow, it gave Irwin a chance to ask questions. "Did you trade songs for your night at the summit?"

"Of course. I stayed three nights. They fed me and Erp very well." He pointed at his donkey. "I got two hot baths out of the deal, and many meals. I think I sang two dozen songs, maybe more. I'm not sure I got enough out of them for my time. A dozen songs will sometimes take me at least six town visits to make. Multiply that by the days it takes me to get anywhere, and yup they got the better deal."

Bernard pulled out a few corked bottles of ale he had bartered for with Chet and Maeve. He opened both and passed one to Irwin. "In three days' time, we shall reach Chinochi." He toasted to Irwin, who stared at his bottle. "Take a drink, boy."

Irwin coughed at the smell of ale, but he took a tiny sip and put the bottle into the snow. Bernard drank up half of his bottle of ale before Irwin took another sip.

The snow inside the pot had condensed into a small amount of water. Bernard continued to add ice and snow until it was two-thirds full. Pulling at a steady pace on his ale, he dipped a rag into the simmering water. He rang it out, wiped his face, and hummed with satisfaction. He cleaned his hands. Pulling another rag from his bag of supplies, he dipped it in the hot water and passed it to Irwin.

Irwin just wanted to leave camp, but he was tired of walking, of the cold, and he knew his Jennies were tired too. He looked at the hot rag with distaste.

"Do what I just did. It'll feel good. It'll remind you of that hot bath we are both entitled to when we arrive in Chinochi." He smiled and dipped his rag again.

The hot cloth felt good. The warmth on his stiff fingers, ears, and on his nose was indeed soothing. He became lost in a daydream about the bath he took with Saryh. He dipped his rag again. "Why did we not do this last night?"

"Well, I was just about to when you showed up," Bernard said. "And then we got busy with formalities. I know it's true that we both have things we need to keep private, but it's okay to share things common among men."

"Alright," Irwin said, looking down at his bottle of ale. He picked it up and tried to choke down another swig, but the taste was too bitter. "Sorry, but I cannot drink this." He passed the ale to Bernard.

"What's the matter with it?"

"Too bitter."

Bernard sniffed at the bottle and took a taste.

"That was why I did not buy any ale from them."

"It's not so bad. Yours is a bit fresher than the one I'm drinking." The Bard leaned back, taking drinks off both bottles, one in either hand. "They would've done better if they left them in the cellar through this last phase of winter. It seemed to me that Chet and Maeve were trying to get food out of their trade. I imagine finding food during this time of year is a struggle, especially being so high up in the mountains. Good thing that Koloto man-beast came along. Damn, he was large."

Bernard drank down both ales and opened a third. He did not play any songs that night. And he did not eat. The Bard chose to get drunk instead of eating the moose meat Irwin had set out for him.

After a while, Bernard retired to the tent, taking with him his pile of wool blankets.

The quiet camp felt pleasant—an occasional snort from one of the donkeys. He was relaxed for the first time in two days. He ate all the moose meat he set out for both of them. He sipped from the jug of whiskey nestled between his packs and watched the fire dance in the dark.

A howl from a distant wolf pack and an occasional hoot from an owl lingered in the night atmosphere. The crisp air was not as cold as it had been the previous night. He decided to seal up the tent with tiny metal clips. The idea of keeping the Bard contained was far more appealing than sleeping in the same tent with the man. It took only a moment for Irwin to lock up the front flap of his tent. Now there was no way the Bard could violate his private space. Now he could get some real rest. He lay down upon the hide and woolen blanket, wrapped himself up in two more. There was a gentle snowfall before he drifted off; he knew it was covering the campsite with a soft white blanket.

12

<u>CHINOCHI</u>

The passage through Uer' Bin territory into the Datzar region zigzagged back and forth and around the steep mountain pass. The forest grew thick, blocking the pass from the hard winds—but not the snow. It was a grueling trek and very steep, along several sections through the heavy woods. But it was a long straight line down the thickly wooded mountain as it descended toward the foothills.

By dusk of the sixth night, they passed by two dimly lit cabins and then the lights of Chinochi came into view. The town was modest in size; a wood mill sat next to a small river, and several merchant buildings lined the streets. Only the Inn and a barnyard were upslope from the rest of the settlement, centered on the main thoroughfare. Freshly covered with a dusting of snow, he could see that the roadway had not worn any footprints in quite some time.

He sighed when he saw the lights and smelled the smoke. And since Bernard the Bard had miscalculated their arrival to Chinochi by a day, during the past four days of mild snow, he took respite in this small trading post town. The bitterly icy winds gnawed at his core. He craved the warmth he had envisioned during their tramp and trudge through the mountain. That, and his need to contain the Bard at night, wore his nerves thin.

Bernard insisted that a few days off their feet would be a good thing. But Irwin only wanted to stay one night. Though he wanted to be rid of Bernard the Bard, he had conceded mostly because of the cold. He realized this journey with a companion was not without merit. He was learning many things about traveling with others, and why he should not in the future. He loathed the thought of being around the Bard much longer. Yet he felt coaxed into agreeing with the Bard that they should not just yet part.

They approached a hospitable-looking Inn. It was three stories tall with a large covered front porch. It was warm inside and smelled of freshly baked bread and roasted mutton. The two travelers startled the family of ten who worked and resided there.

Both men were glad to have arrived at suppertime. Bernard stepped into the large dining room, beaming, and greeted everyone in his usual manner. He put down his baggage and his wrapped lute. With no hesitation, he struck up a conversation with the husband while the wife ordered one of her three sons to go open the stables and take in their animals. Irwin stood behind Bernard, trying not to stare at the enormous family. He was awestruck, as were the children, upon seeing him and his animated companion this late into the day. Were they wary of seeing people traveling during winter? The youngest gawked at Irwin, apparently forgetting his dinner.

The middle boy moved toward the door, and Irwin followed. "I will make sure my Jennies and Erp are well kept." He told Bernard before stepping out into the cold and closing the door behind him.

The large family scared Irwin. Although he had just spent six days with a stranger, Bernard was only one person. The more he was around lots of people, the more overwhelmed he felt. Taking in their features, reading their expressions, gauging their emotions—making sure he would not say or do the wrong thing—it was all extremely hard for him to take in.

Happy to be outside with his Jennies and Erp, Irwin suffered to think this was how his life would be from here on out, being overwhelmed by strangers, and by his loath to talk about himself and his past.

We just got here. I cannot let my fears get in the way of enjoying the warmth and hospitality of others. Keep calm. Take a breath.

The young boy, Travis, introduced himself as he escorted Irwin, Erp, and the Jennies into a long barn. He explained that they would have to pay the livery owner in the morning, but it would be alright to stable the animals for the night. Travis wasn't dressed for the outside and shivered as he hustled to bring buckets of water into the stalls. He helped Irwin bring straw for the donkeys to eat and bed upon.

Irwin thanked the child and told him to go back to the warmth of the Inn. He took his time removing the tack from Erp and his Jennies. He brushed the animals down, which allowed his anxieties to calm. His mind wandered to a conversation with Bernard:

"I don't understand why you put up with pulling those donkeys along." Bernard had cut through Irwin's quiet moment on the trail. His tone and his criticism reminded Irwin of Albert. "You need to make those animals work for you. You work too hard as it is, young man. The first thing I'd do is ride one of them. Halt all this walking through knee-deep snow.

"Yeah, so they're a little bumpy to ride without a saddle. And you'll need better control than a halter and rope. So, buying new tack will be in order. Just so you know, riding isn't a bad way to get around. Many travelers prefer to ride. You definitely go faster and have less of a load to bear."

Irwin had frowned at Bernard's insinuation. Yet the Bard had a point, even though Irwin did not want to hear it.

"Or you could look into selling one of them and use that money to purchase a few things to help you in your travels, like a saddle and leather bridle. Most of those panniers can hang off a saddle.

"My saddle has many types of rigging and such. It's easy to bundle all your belongings on those. Anything else you need, you can tie down on the back of the seat, as I have here. Most saddles are made to be well-used. Some people keep theirs even after their animal dies. So, finding one that isn't already worn in might be tricky. Those are the best to find. Of course, you could get something new. It takes a saddle maker at least two moons' time to make one, but they are well worth the investment, especially if you're going to keep that animal you're riding. You know, you could always have one specially made for all that baggage you carry around."

Irwin had grumbled to himself that he would never part with either Jenny. He loved them too much. They were his only family. "I could never sell them. And I could never ride them."

Bernard did not hear him and continued to talk over him. "Or you could always trade them in for a larger animal, like Erp, here. He can pack as much as your two put together. Besides, those Jennies are looking a bit old."

"They have been part of my family for seven years."

"Do you know how old they were when they came into your possession?"

Irwin shrugged. He had tried to ignore Bernard the best he could. "How many times were they bred?"

"They were bred twice by my father. They both produced twin offspring, and both sets were female. My old man sold, well traded, their babies for new Jacks. He wanted to sell all the Jennies, but I told him I would take care of these girls."

"Well, that's special, twin Jennies making twin babies. You might be able to use that as a selling point. You know, Jennies are of more value than Jacks, especially if they can reproduce in numbers."

"I am not selling them!"

"I suggest you think about it. One animal to feed and coerce instead of two! You might get somewhere before dark." He had kicked Erp on, around Irwin and his Jennies, through the knee-deep snow.

That conversation had unnerved Irwin to no end. He could not let go of it, even now, and it played over and over in his mind, always angering him. He longed to be apart from Bernard, but was exhausted from their long days of walking.

When he finished grooming the donkeys, he managed enough gumption to go back into the Inn. He closed the front of the barn and heard the lute, laughter, and happiness. A touch of cynicism crept into his soul as he tried to understand how Bernard worked his charm. He was perplexed by it all. The old man came off very forward and kindly. He did not appear scared to meet new people, nor were new people cautious of him. But Bernard had spoken of bad people lurking everywhere. How could he tell the difference? How could they not see he was a thief?

Irwin stepped up onto the porch, slipped past the door, and peeled off his outer layers of clothing.

This is the warmth I crave, but not the place I want to be.

The tables that had been pushed together in the middle of the room for supper were now separated. The large room was more open now, tables and benches were pushed snug against the walls. Bernard regarded Irwin with a smile, but kept his attention on the youngsters. The oldest of the daughters came over to take his oiled overcoat and his pack of belongings.

He was hesitant to give up anything, but the girl smiled kindly at him and leaned in to speak. "I'll hang this up near the window. Would you like to see your room?"

"Thank you, and yes, please." He followed the girl to his room.

The music trailed them up the stairs, and the girl hummed the melody as she brought Irwin to his bedroom door. "Is there anything else I can get you?"

"After I get settled, may I please have some supper?"

"Why yes. Of course! I'll make sure there's a plate waiting for you."

Her eagerness unsettled him, and he watched her head bob to the Bard's music as she walked away.

I should leave tomorrow—be done with that man and his peculiar ways.

His stomach grumbled.

I wish I could eat here in my room.

He placed his belongings down, glanced around the single-bed room, and then left, following his calling for food.

Irwin entered the large downstairs room and realized the music had stopped. Bernard was drinking a cup of ale—a plate of partially eaten food next to him. The children were all gathered around, hoping for a tale.

Bernard wiped his mouth with a cloth napkin and then began strumming a story song—one Irwin had heard before.

He did not bother to listen. He ate the meal, drank what was given, and returned to his room without enduring a conversation with anyone. The family was otherwise enthralled by Bernard the Bard.

He enjoyed the warmth and comfort of his bed almost too much, and slept in. Upon waking, Irwin contemplated what to do next. These kinds of thoughts made him weary. He wanted to be lazy, if only for a brief time. There was no set schedule for him to follow. He could be leisurely if he wanted.

After a while, contemplating the day ahead, Bernard came in and sat at the foot of the bed. He was waiting for Irwin to stir, though he was already awake.

It took a while before Bernard figured out that Irwin was faking his slumber. "I want you to offer your help in trade for their board. There are hundreds of things you can do for this family of mostly females. They could use some help. The father has a bad back and his young boys cannot lift much more than a box of apples. Nor are they as tall as you." He slapped the side of the bed and stood. "You're obviously not Talented like me. You need to learn to earn your way." The old man sat there a while longer, waiting for Irwin to stir. "You have to learn how to work for others."

He banged the door shut when leaving the room. Irwin pulled the blankets off his head and stared at the door. He threw out some gold and sealed the door closed.

What is Bernard expecting from me? I am not here for him or anyone else.

Beyond straining porous rock for precious ore, all Irwin knew how to do was to create and contain rock walls, make supports for caverns, and set explosives. There were more qualified people here in Chinochi who could help this family—those more trustworthy than a sly Bard or a wayward Miner. Besides, he was more than willing to pay for his room, meals, and for boarding his animals.

He was not the Bard's accomplice. They were just two travelers moving along at the same pace from the same place. He did not appreciate the Bard ordering him around. He wanted to rest and recuperate from his journey.

I did not come all this way to pretend to help fix a problem I know nothing about.

He sighed and pulled up the covers again. Being around Bernard was draining. He felt as if he had traded an enemy he had known for one he knew nothing about. Wrapped in his thoughts, Irwin emerged from his bedroom around midday. The younger children were cleaning the tables, chairs, and the floor. Bernard played his lute. He did not sing; it sounded as if he were trying to make up a new song, playing the same progression over and over, providing the children a rhythm to work to.

The youngest boy stepped away from his task and approached Irwin, asking if he was hungry.

"Yes, please!"

The boy ran off and came back with a few dinner rolls leftover from the night before. He then went back to scrubbing the floor.

Irwin took a seat at the edge of the already-cleaned table. He ate as many rolls as he could and packed the last one into his pocket and took it upstairs for later.

Back in his room, packing the dinner roll into a small satchel, there was a soft knock on his door. The same daughter, still bobbing her head to Bernard's rhythm, blushed when he opened the door.

"I've come to ask if there is anything you need?" Her bright brown eyes averted from his. And then they crept up to meet his gaze, waiting for a reply.

He was startled by her intensity. "Actually, yes! I know I need to pay for the stables."

"Oh, Bernard the Bard already did that," she said. Her smile grew, and her bobbing head slacked.

"Wow! That was …"

Amazing that Bernard would be so kind.

"… very nice of him. Uh, I was going to ask about getting my clothing laundered, and maybe a hot bath?"

"Chinochi has a bathhouse. They can tend to your needs. I can take you there if you like." She was younger than him, but only by a year or two.

"I did not catch your name last night."

"Lucile."

"That is a nice name. My donkey Jenn Jenn had a baby several years ago. I named her Lucy … the other baby I named Lucky."

"Only my friends call me Lucy." She blushed and glanced down at the two buckets she carried. One held clean sheets, the other a small amount of soapy water and a rag.

"What are those for?"

"Oh these? I'm just … I'm here to clean your room."

"Thank you. But you do not have to do that. I already made the bed. And I have kept the room as clean as I found it."

"Many thanks to you; that was thoughtful!" Biting her lip, Lucy set her buckets down.

He thought she looked to be caught off-guard.

"Well then, if you will follow me, please." She turned and Irwin followed. "Oh," she said, spinning around, bumping into his chest. She jumped back, and her eyes darted around the hallway. "Don't forget your dirty linens. We can take them with us and have them washed."

Nearly all his clothing was dirty and stinky. "Thank you, Lucy."

"You're welcome. It's the least I can do." Her brown eyes stared at him.

He followed her down the stairs, and they left through the back door. Lucy led him down the slope along the middle of the street toward the river. He could whiff it in the distance. They passed several storefronts with different types of merchandise, including a Tannery and Saddle Shop. An oiled saddle in one of the window fronts caught his eye, but he kept one step behind Lucy who strode up to the front door of the Bathing House.

The town of Chinochi was busy during the daytime and appeared larger than Goshee. It smelled better too. This place did not look like a trading post, as Bernard had insinuated—more like a quaint logging town.

Lucy opened the door for him. She then came up behind him and informed the front desk clerk what he wanted.

Irwin handed off a gold coin and was given five silver pieces back. He gave her his bag of sour smelling, dirt, and sweat-encrusted clothing. She handed him a wooden stick with several holes chiseled through it.

"Isabell will help you from here, Irwin. See you later." Lucy said and hustled back out the door.

"I'm Isabell. I can have the clothing you wear cleaned as well; just trade them for this robe." She too appeared to be around Irwin's age, and pregnant. Her clothing was tight throughout her midsection. She looked tired, and there were dark circles under her light-brown eyes. Her long brown hair, although pulled up, lay in a mess around her head.

Irwin decided that Isabell needed a bath and her clothes cleaned also, but she had to work instead.

"How long do I have to bathe?"

"You can take as long as you like. There is a sunning deck outside the bathing room. We also have sleeping areas, just find yourself a cot. Your clothing will be washed and dried by dusk." She handed off the robe and led him to a small changing room. "Swap your dirties in here, then bring your clothing to me." She left.

He changed into the robe and brought his clothing to Isabell. She took them from him and gathered it all into her arms. "Follow me, please. If you don't mind opening the door for me, thanks."

When he pulled opened the thick wooden door, hot air escaped, wafting past them. He had felt that type of steam up at the summit cabin. Isabell took the lead and brought him to a washer's platform, boots in hand. There were cubbies along the wall behind him for footwear.

Several red and white-haired women waited there for the clothing. They pulled out all his dirty clothes from the bag, shoving them in wads into a barrel of steaming water. He could smell the sourness of his own garments.

"These women will be the ones you speak to about your clothing when you are done bathing." Isabell then addressed the wash women. "He has number six." She turned to him again. "Bring them your number when you are done enjoying the bathing house, and hopefully they will have it all dry by then."

Irwin did not know what to say. Every time he had washed his clothing in the winter, it had taken days to fully dry. How clothing could be dried in such a brief time was curious indeed. But there was all this hot air ....

He followed Isabell past closed doorways, down a long corridor, and into an open room with a partially opened rooftop. Two fireplaces blazed on opposite sides of the room. One couple lounged together in one of the tubs. Irwin had his pick of a large pool, or one of several small private pools in alcoves.

The room was made from one type of stone—all uniform. He couldn't see any cut lines on this sandstone. It was peculiar to think that all this stone had been here since the beginning. But he knew the landscape—knew this was all imported from further upslope, had seen it along his desolate hike through the Kruluver Mountains. As he looked over the room, he could see that all these pools had been softly chiseled, almost to a polish. Most of the interior walls were highlighted by stone and shell mosaics of flowers and aquatic landscapes. There were random colored tiles strewn across the walls—some etched with text or handprints.

"There's an inside outhouse over in that corner. We call it the water closet." Isabell pointed to a secluded room that melded into the rest of the mosaic scenery. "The large pool is not as hot as the small ones, but feel free to sit in any of them. Our Mayor Earl Yurpton is over there with his wife, Marisa. They're very friendly," she said. "Enjoy your time here."

13

<u>WHO TO TRUST?</u>

Irwin approached the large pool and stuck in a toe. It was warm, but not as hot as the bath at the summit cabin—the kind of heat he now craved. He moved to the next pool, glancing at the mayor and his wife who were quietly enjoying themselves.

The next pool was too cold. He moved on.

The rotund mayor said, "This is the perfect pool, young man. It goes from coldest to hottest right along here." Like the rest of the people he had seen in Chinochi, the mayor had sandy-blonde hair, blue eyes, and pale skin. Now that he had traveled all the way across the mountains, he noticed slight changes in the people he encountered. Hair color, for example, transformed from brown, to red, to brownish blonde.

The mayor chortled. "Wild cat got your tongue?"

Irwin said, "No sir. Why would you let a wild cat get your tongue?"

The mayor jubilantly replied. "Why, it's a phrase we use. If one has no tongue, that would explain why they are silent."

"Oh."

The mayor's wife smiled at him. "I'm Marisa Yurpton, wife to the mayor here, Earl Yurpton. We love to meet new people. You're more than welcome to sit with us."

"I ... I do not think that would be appropriate."

Mayor Earl Yurpton gestured with his hand. "Come on in, young man. Even a passerby is welcome to sit with the Mayor of Chinochi."

"Thank you for the invitation, sir."

Marisa gleamed, "This is the best pool out of them all."

Irwin flushed, dropped his robe, and stepped into the nice, warm pool. They moved so he could have a good seat.

"This is the finest place Chinochi has to offer," she said. "We hope you like it."

Irwin dunked his whole body under water. He let the heat wrap around him, waiting for it to warm every inch of flesh. He came up for air and batted away his soppy wet hair.

"This feels good," he said, and found a seat against the edge of the pool.

"What's your name?" The mayor wanted to know.

"Are you the young man who came with Bernard the Bard?" Marisa asked.

"I am Samuel Irwin Miner. And yes, I traveled here with Bernard the Bard." How did they know of his traveling companion, and of him?

Marisa's smile widened. "It must be fun being an apprentice to the Bard?"

Irwin said, "I am just a miner. I am only following Bernard because he was heading downslope from the summit lodge. I am no apprentice."

The mayor said, "Most people don't travel this late into winter unless it's necessary. We understand why the Bard is here. But if you are a miner, do you have coal to trade? Or are you in the need of mining supplies?"

"Neither, Sir."

"Where are you from, Samuel? You have a little accent I cannot peg." Marisa smiled at him from the far side of the tub.

He did not know what to tell these people. The truth was the only thing he knew. "I come from the mountain tops, beyond the summit. My father died. So, I decided to leave my cave." His reply clearly stunned the mayor and his wife. "I have never traveled this far before. I grew up as a miner in the high mountain tops. That life is all I know."

"Oh! I am so sorry for your loss," Marisa said, after a long silence. "It sounds like it was a good thing you met the Bard. Have you two been traveling together long?"

"Six days."

"And you met him at the summit?"

"Yes."

"Tis a bitter time to be traveling," The Mayor said and cleared his throat.

"You know, Hakra brings people to us when we need them. It's probably good for you to be with Bernard the Bard. Are you going to stay with him? Be his understudy?" Marisa kept on, not waiting for a reply. "I hear he is really good with the lute and sings and dances too. We don't have anyone around here like that. It's been many years since we've been entertained. From what I understand, he is fun to watch, and I hear he has many exciting stories. Tuck and Travis were talking about Bernard the Bard earlier today."

Irwin tried to figure who it was she had talked to.

"They are the youngest of Tara and TJ's children. The family who owns the Inn. Those two boys were gloating about his stories when I saw them this morning."

"Bernard has a few good stories to tell. But I am no storyteller, not like him," Irwin said. "I have a hard enough time talking at all."

The Mayor said, "Did you come down from the mountain tops looking for work? Because if you did, and want to stay in Chinochi, we can always use a hard laborer. There is logging if you are up for climbing steep slopes. But you said you are a miner, so you'd probably prefer climbing down into dark shafts. There are mines about two days south that are being worked for coal. We've got a few crews that rotate the work in ten-day shifts. It's good to find men who know the trade. From what I understand, mining is not for the lighthearted."

"Indeed! Mining is a tough job. My family mined coal. Sometimes they found other ores of value. When I was younger, my father and grandfather found a sizeable chunk of gold—a deposit of significant size. It had to have been twenty pounds or more."

It was actually over a hundred.

"I remember them arguing about it a lot. Neither spent an ounce, that I know of. They kept it for themselves."

"Gold! Really?" Marisa's eyes grew wide. "Gold is such a rarity around here. There were silver mines east of Tenoci many years ago, but they dried up, and the miners went across the river." She turned to her husband. "Wasn't there an incident about a dozen years ago at the brothel, over gold?"

Mayor Earl Yurpton growled at his wife. "There was, yes. That was the reason it was shut down."

"Oh! I thought it was the fighting."

"It was because of a fight. Don't you remember? The place was destroyed."

"Oh, that's right. Wasn't there a fire and the fighting? I forgot about that. That's where the fabric store is now."

Her husband nodded.

Soon, voices echoed down the hallway leading into the bathhouse. A few young women, giggling and socializing, came into the steam-filled room. Two were pregnant, and another held a young baby, just old enough to enjoy the water. They all disrobed and slipped into the large pool. Their voices grew louder, dissolving the conversation between Irwin, the Mayor, and his wife. Their pool grew quiet. Irwin enjoyed the warmth a while longer and then got up out of the soothing water.

"You look tired." Marisa said as Irwin picked up his robe. "There are a few cots in a room just beyond," she pointed, "where you could catch a nap if you want. If you want a hotter bath, that pool over there is excellent for a quick dip. And there are cold showers for soaping and scrubbing yourself around the corner."

"Thank you very much, Lady Marisa, and you too, sir, Mayor Earl Yurpton."

"Do enjoy your stay, Samuel Irwin Miner," the mayor said. "And if you are looking for a job, let me know. We can always use another miner."

"Thank you for the offer, sir, but I am just traveling through." Irwin yanked at the sash on his robe and walked toward the water-closet. Then he found the dimly lit showering area. He used a lever-pull cold shower to cool down from the hot bath and scrubbed the remainder of dirt and smell from his body. Then he went to see if his clothing was clean and dried.

"Go back to your bath, take a nap, do something." The elderly laundry woman flicked her hand at him. "Come back just before sundown. It will all be ready by then."

Irwin was done being in this Bathing House, but his clothing was not. He decided to take a nap. The sleeping room was not hard to find. There were signs pointing the way. He lay down on a cot in the farthest corner and enjoyed the quiet reprieve.

He slept for a long time and woke to the sound of Bernard's laugh. He sat up and looked around the small sleeping area. The Bard was out there mingling, projecting his voice so that all could hear. Irwin picked up on a story he had not heard before, but he would not listen to it now either.

Collecting his mind and the robe, he emerged into the light of the main bathing room. There were many people gathered now, soaking off the day's tensions. Bernard was in the middle of one of the warm pools. His eyes lit up when Irwin emerged from the sleeping room.

"Come here Irwin, my boy! Here is my apprentice now! Irwin, my lad, fetch me some ale, would ya?"

Still somewhat lost in a sleepy haze, he stared at Bernard. He felt as though the people were laughing at him. There were at least fifty people in the Bathing House, all socializing loudly. He suffered a bout of vertigo. Everyone appeared fine with the way things were, but he was not. He had to breathe and keep his focus.

It was nearly dark outside. Excitement tickled his belly and Irwin turned and walked past more people streaming in for an evening dip in the warm water. He found the empty hallway and finally his center. He retrieved his still-warm clothing—changed out of the robe and into a warm pair of pants and a long-sleeved tunic. It was the warm stockings he enjoyed the most before sticking his feet into his boots.

Clothing bag across his shoulder, Irwin walked back to the Inn. He was not impressed by how quickly Bernard had acquainted himself with the whole town of Chinochi. And it disgusted him to hear how people were talking as if he and the Bard were longtime friends. On top of all that, he was irritated that the Bard had ordered him around—like Albert would have done. He packed up his belongings.

Had he made the worst mistake of his life—leaving the high mountains behind? Even though Albert had not cared about him, he still cared about his father. He wondered what the old man was up to. Then he remembered Albert had disowned him. There was nothing he could ever do to remedy this. He wanted to go back, but at the same time he wanted to go on. Either way, he did not want to be here.

I hate second guessing my actions.

This situation felt oddly familiar.

But where will I go? It is dark and cold outside.

I am being brash.

He did not want to make the wrong decision again. He made himself carefully consider all the possible outcomes. The thought of finding a mine played around in his head. The people of Chinochi needed coal. Harold had said he traded with them. He received less in payment, but they took coal in trade.

Yes, I could run back to the lifestyle I do not want to have. Or I could continue going forward.

Chinochi is not the place I want to be. I am still on a frozen slope.

He wanted warmer weather and flatter land. The decision to do anything else had to come from him, and not be influenced by outsiders. He would not be bullied or conned anymore.

There is nothing else to do but go forward.

He stood there staring at the door of his room, reminiscing. It had been nearly three-quarters of a moon's cycle since Albert had left him to die by the road. The memory of what had happened in Kobiton was, by now, fogged over. And the farther he walked, the further removed he was from those horrors.

There was a light knock on his door. It was Lucy. She poked her head inside the door. He stood but a foot beyond the door, staring back at her. The sudden change in her expression made Irwin drop his bags.

"You aren't leaving, are you?"

"No, I was just getting everything ready for an early departure tomorrow morning."

"Bernard didn't say you two were leaving!"

"I am leaving tomorrow. Bernard will most likely stay a few more days."

Lucy cocked her head. "Why wouldn't you? I thought you were his apprentice. He seems to really like you, Irwin. He sang songs about you and talked about you. He said you are his apprentice, and that you two are traveling together. Why would you leave him?"

Did she see something Irwin did not?

"Bernard the Bard is amazing. Don't leave him! He can show you the world."

"We were traveling together from the summit to Chinochi; that is all."

She stared at his baggage.

He pushed the bags toward the bed with his foot.

"Oh," she replied, averting her light brown eyes. There was a long pause, as if she wanted to say something else. "Well, I came to tell you that it's suppertime."

"Oh good, I am starving."

The twang of a lute string sent a shiver down Irwin's spine. It felt like the Bard was taunting him. Now he was more than ready to leave the old coot behind. Morning light would not come soon enough.

Many of Chinochi's people had flocked to the local Inn to watch the Bard and enjoy a meal.

"It's a packed house down there," Lucy said. "All the seats are taken. And people are willing to stand just to hear him. We have never been this busy, ever.

It would probably be best if you eat in the kitchen." She smiled at him. Was she flirting?

Lucy's blue and red plaid wool skirt coursed down the stairs, and she led him past the filled dining area. Everyone was clapping with the rhythm of the music. Bernard tried to signal Irwin, but he ignored the Bard and followed Lucy.

Inside the kitchen, the sound of the music was muffled. Tara, the mother, and Lucy's younger sisters were making meat pies. They were chattering about the business turnaround because of the Bard. He ignored that conversation and asked if there was anything he could do.

"You can cut these." Tuck, the youngest of the boys, said. He handed Irwin a bowl full of pealed potatoes. "Cut them into thumb-size pieces."

Irwin began to cut potatoes into edible sizes. After the first few slices, he noticed how dull the knife was. It had jagged edges, and a broken end point. He manipulated the metal, straightened out the edges, and restored the knife's tip.

He noticed the young boy watching him. "Do you even know how to use a knife?"

Irwin began slicing again. This time, the blade parted the potato effortlessly, and the chore was completed in no time. He most certainly knew how to handle a knife, and he knew how to slice potatoes. He waited for the boy to pass off another bowl of freshly cleaned spuds. Again, the blade slipped through the potatoes. The boy watched with apparent amazement.

"You sure did fake me out there."

"'Fake me out there', what does that mean?"

"You made me think you didn't know what you were doing."

The mother stepped up to the table and took two bowls of sliced potatoes. She smiled at Irwin but scowled at her son. "No small talk, Tuck. Get back to work."

Tuck dropped his eyes and head and went back to cleaning potatoes. After his mother was gone, he said, "I'm going to be a miner when I grow up."

"Mining is not all that much fun."

"Neither is cooking. But I won't have to cook if I'm a miner."

Irwin shook his head. "Someone must cook for the miners. How else will they get energy to work through the day? Not everyone is suited to cook."

"I can't cook, but my mother thinks I can. She makes me cut potatoes and beets and carrots. I hate it here." Tuck passed Irwin another bowl of cleaned potatoes. He appeared to be no older than six, but the child had dreams of grandeur.

"At least by being a cook, you will always be fed."

"Yes, but if I'm a miner, I can find gold! Then I can pay someone to cook for me."

They had fed almost all of Chinochi by the time they were done with the evening's festivities. Family members, and Irwin, were fed only after the dining hall was cleared. It was nearly midnight. Bernard, however, had been fed early. He was now done with playing and retired to his room. It was past midnight when the kitchen finally closed. The Inn's family had a fat purse and gifts of food in return for the many meals. The younger children were sent to bed, while the older girls helped clean up the kitchen and prepare it for the next day.

The mother boasted, "Never have we been that busy."

Everyone seemed pleased with the outcome the night had presented; though they had not prepared for such a flow of patrons who consumed all their winter rations. But if the Bard stayed in the Inn, they would have a packed house every night. While women boasted about business, Irwin slipped upstairs to his rented bedroom.

He was not sure if Lucy, her mother, or her younger sisters ever went to sleep that night. The smell of muffins wafted through the floorboards early the next morning. The scent coaxed Irwin out of bed and downstairs. He managed to eat several muffins before the tavern was bombarded by patrons again.

The tables began to fill, and the food orders piled high. Patrons asked about Bernard the Bard and then, like magic, the Bard stepped down the staircase and into the dining room. As he appeared in the main room, all conversations went silent. He seemed pleased to have everyone's undivided attention.

Irwin tried not to listen to the Bard engage these people. He slipped past Bernard and headed to his bedroom to gather his bags. He returned to say good-bye before the singing commenced. He stopped at the kitchen and left a small satchel of gold coins on the counter where he had sliced potatoes the night before. Then, just as quick, he departed from the Bard's path.

14

<u>A Silver Mine</u>

The further from the steep slopes of Kruluver Mountain Range Irwin ventured, the faster his pace. Descending out of the lowest reaches of snowfall, he found himself occupied with sporadic weather patterns and denser forestry. The roadway was well-used. Lined with small rocks like cement mixed with mud, his journey took him along a hard, well-traveled surface. He came across several heavy-duty wooden bridges spanning deep creeks and wide chasms—a remarkable sight. Had the Hakra instructed man to build those bridges?

This new world he journeyed through was vibrant in flora and fauna. And through random breaks in the trees, he could see how far he had already come. The high mountain tops, usually occluded by thick clouds, shone bright when the sun did hit them. Though most days the sky was a dull gray.

At least instead of snow it now rained. Albeit cold, he continued to pull the Jennies along at a moderate pace. He appreciated the sun breaks, although they were few and far between. Even though this weather was warmer than upslope, the rain was still wet and still uncomfortable. It soaked through his canvas jacket, but not his canvas tent. Every evening, when his tent was up and water boiling, he enjoyed the warmth and his solitude. This only made his resolve to seek warmer weather a top priority.

It was nearly a full five days of walking, obstinate donkeys in tow, before he reached the town of Tenoci. As in Chinochi, there was only one Inn along the main roadway. It towered above an intersection between roads that went from low to high ground. Irwin bought a room for the night, and two warm meals. He left early the next morning—no reason to stay. He still had rations, as did his Jennies. During his brief stay, his interactions with the townsfolk were minimal.

The further away from his comfort zone he traveled, the less he wanted to mingle with the people around him.

He knew he needed to change something about himself, but he was intimidated by people. The more he was around them, the more he wanted to turn away. He felt he must force himself to interact with others—a grueling task. He knew he had nothing to fear. Yet, his father's presence was still there with him, making him question everything he wanted to do.

He preferred the hospitality of the forest. The sights and sounds were a comfort. He knew that another town would come along and test his willingness again. And again he would force himself to have exchanges. He hated that he had a challenging time with *wanting* to talk to people he would probably never see again.

Jenn Jenn and Nee Nee were the best of companions. They did not need much from him other than a handful of oats, love in the form of scratches, and time for grazing. The further down the mountain they traveled, the tall grasses were greener and hung like luscious gardens he remembered from Kobiton. Irwin watched them mow down with precision small sections of grass. He made an extra effort to be kind to his Jennies and allow them time every day to graze. Usually this happened in the evenings as he was setting up camp and eating his meal.

With a river at his side, he could catch a fresh meal. For Irwin, fishing was a fun adventure. Sitting by the water's edge, sometimes he would find small nuggets of silver lodged between rocks under the chilly surface. He scanned the forested hills as he trudged along with line and hook, looking for a long-forgotten cave, hoping to find larger pieces of ore. While fishing, he would also let his mind wander while waiting to feel a fish snag the worm on his hook.

During his first day's trek heading east of Tenoci, he passed several off-shooting roads—overgrown, long forgotten, and leading to abandoned mining caves. Those rutted and grassed-over roads branched off from the main roadway he was on and wandered up the gentle slope. He had seen this before when traveling to Kobiton where there were ancient mines, long abandoned and totally forgotten. There were no fresh tracks coming to or from any of these roads he passed that day.

I wonder if there is still silver up there.

His curiosity grew.

That night, he made camp at the junction of one of those narrow roadways. A babbling brook flowed through a stone constructed culvert, beneath the main roadway, and spilled out into the river just beyond. He wandered along the off-shooting road that meandered along the edge of the brook and found several flecks of silver, iron, and nickel in a short time. He then stepped into the river, scaring off any of his fishing prospects, to claim a large piece of silver he had felt beneath the flowing water. He looked upstream and noticed the mouth of a mine farther upslope.

The metal in that cave sang to him; perhaps this was because he had some ore already in his flesh. He glanced at his donkeys eating along the stream's edge. They would not be bothered if he stepped away for a while. The evening hours were close, but his curiosity drew him on.

He left his fishing line, hoping it would catch something on its own, and hiked away from camp. It was still light as he followed the brook up the gently rising slope. Almost one hundred feet upslope, the coursing water ventured away from the cave's opening, and then turned into a trickling waterfall. While the stream was laced with silvery pieces and specks, Irwin sensed larger pieces of ore inside the cave's entrance.

There had been a cave-in not far inside the cave where large slabs of rock jetted down from the old ceiling. Remnants of a body lay in broken pieces not far away—arm and skull, smaller bone fragments scattered here and there, possibly mauled by an animal.

The sweet hum of silver ore buried beneath layers of rock pulled him forward, beyond the cave-in.

I should get one of the Jennies to help carry the bounty.

Unlike Mortals with no Talents, all Irwin had to do was place his hands on the cold, roughen surface and concentrate. By the time he was done extracting all that was hidden to the unknown eye, Irwin had nearly a hundred pounds of silvery ore lying before his feet in large eight-pound rocks.

Without much daylight left, he raced down the incline to retrieve Jenn Jenn.

After packing the cache of silvery rocks, Irwin was now intent on the hunt. He led Jenn Jenn toward the waterfall. Rolling up his pant legs and taking off his boots, he pulled her up the slippery rocks. When surveying the stream, flecks of metal beamed brightly against the darkening sky. The silvery ore glowed from yellow to pink as he approached. The closer he stepped, those specks and pieces of metal swam through the water and into his exposed feet and legs. Jenn Jenn followed him toward the waterfall where at the bottom of the pool, where the water fell, it was coated in pieces, large and small, of iron, nickel, and silver.

He congealed all the pieces to form another eight-pound rock. He kept the remnants within his skin. It was on the brink of night when he found his camp. He had forgotten to catch a meal, and ate dried fruit and meat pieces again, satisfied with the day, with his finds.

Irwin and his Jennies followed the river for three days after leaving Tenoci, where it merged with a much wider, yet shallower, river. After that, the road and the river played hide and seek with the dense forest foliage where the grass grew muzzle high—the perfect height for Irwin's donkeys. They swung their heads to and frow, trying to eat all they could as he pulled them along. They were more reluctant than usual to follow. He tried to goad the hungry animals forward with a stick, to no avail.

An indescribable clatter in the distance roused his attention. He could feel and hear metal on metal screeching, singing to him. He soon realized it was a wagon rattling along an old roadway upslope from him, squeaking loudly over every hard bump. The vibrations echoed through the forest and shifted upslope. He stared into the trees, waiting to see where the vehicle might be.

His reluctant donkeys were not distressed by the noise, unlike Irwin. He watched for and listened to the wagon clamor down the mountainside. He could tell that there was a heavy load on the back axle, causing the loud squeaking and creaking. The load shifted back and forth. He was still looking for the vehicle when it emerged several hundred feet ahead of him. He spotted the wagon briefly and then the roadway curved away from the river. There were three large deer bodies with heads and legs strewn across one another, hanging off the backside of the wagon.

Three people were perched up high on the wagon, two faced forward and one sat in the back, blankly staring off. That man seemed to wake up when seeing Irwin. They made fleeting eye contact. Then the wagon rolled out of sight again. He wondered if this was a clue as to how far away the next town might be. The thought of cooked venison was the only thing that pushed him forward toward the inevitable human contact.

He had not fished the last few nights, choosing to eat rations instead, and he was tired of dried meals. His tongue longed for a fresh meal of meat and gravy, potatoes, fresh bread, and perhaps some cheese. His morning meal of warm oatmeal never sustained him for a full day.

I did not eat a midday meal. No wonder I am so hungry!

The afternoon light slid behind the mountains. He growled and grumbled at Jenn Jenn and Nee Nee, trying to coerce them away from the grass. The only way to convince them forward was to use a stick. He hated being aggressive with his Jennies, but he wanted to be at the next camp and done with this day.

I want fish to cook, and fishing takes time.

The day's gray clouds shone colorful streaks of orange and pink as the day's light shifted. The river mirrored the radiance, although it hid behind thick fir trees, but the tree line finally broke, revealing a large meadow where the next camping spot was.

Finally!

Yet as he settled into the large space, he noticed what seemed like a hundred different animals grazing contentedly at the other end of the open grassland. There were horses, oxen, donkeys, milk cows and calves, goats with their small kids, and chickens—all intermingling. Beyond the motley group of animals, he observed a large caravan of carved and painted carts, carriages, and wagons. He now suspected that this was a local camping spot. He sized up the brilliant scene of art and animals.

Between the caravan carts and carriages, tapestries were strung up for privacy and fluttered in the evening breeze. He heard laughter coming from within the enclosed camp, murmurs of conversations.

The road moved like a bow's string and curved around the edge of the forest. From within the dark shadows came a deep, foreboding growl. His Jennies sidestepped away from the trees, taking off immediately with Irwin in tow. He had a good grip on their lead lines and would not let go. They began trotting eastward, following the cleared pathway. His feet hit the ground every other stride as the donkeys flew forward. They skirted across the edge of the meadow at an increasing pace. Irwin tried to gain control, shouting at them to slow, but neither Jenny listened. He barely kept up.

From his periphery, Irwin saw a black-furred wild cat standing in the middle of the roadway, looking after him and his fleeing donkeys.

A wild cat so close to those animals!

Yet none of the domesticated animals were racing away, unlike his Jennies. Only a few of the grazing animals popped their heads up from the luscious grass to watch Irwin struggle against his Jennies, pulling him away from the meadow.

Why are none of those animals spooked by the sight of a vicious cat?

He kept up, his feet leaping with their pace.

When they wanted to, Jenn Jenn and Nee Nee could and would use their force together. This time, they pulled Irwin beyond the meadow and back into the dense forest. The startled animals stayed on the roadway, knowing they could see what was ahead and behind them. They fought against Irwin's powerful arms as he attempted to slow them. He battled with his donkeys, shouting at them to halt, but they were willful.

Nearly a kilometer passed before Irwin managed to slow his donkeys. They all puffed hard with breath. The Jennies were still agitated and pulled on their leads to go faster, but it was clear they too were winded by the scare. They soon calmed down enough to walk at a decent pace. Before long, Jenn Jenn and Nee Nee stopped all together to catch their breaths.

Mouth dry and breath heaving, Irwin needed a drink of water. He cursed at his animals while hydrating himself. Then, finally, he convinced them to walk at his pace.

Though the evening light had almost completely faded, he decided to continue along the roadway where it parted the forest to reveal the river again. He stopped to let the donkeys drink from the water's edge. A smaller meadow bloomed along the river just ahead.

Again, this appeared to be a good place to camp. Water babbled softly, and he relaxed. Then he spotted firelight nearby and heard it crackle and snap. Someone else had also decided this was a good place to camp. He stiffened at the thought of sharing this small space of land.

A woman's laughter caught his attention. He studied the situation and concluded there were two people over by the fire. Both were staring in his direction. The male looked like a shadow at first, shrouded in dark clothing.

The female waved at him. Their fire highlighted her young features. She was as pale as snow. Her long platinum hair cascaded down her dark-colored cloak. She appeared to be a two-toned other-worldly type, perhaps not from Urthis. She moved toward the rocky and muddy roadway and waved again, signaling Irwin to come forward. He was slow to approach her, but he did.

"Good evening." She said, smiling. "I am Yace. Yace Yellsen. And that is my friend Kipp Hauler."

"Good evening. I am Samuel Irwin Miner. These are my Jennies, Nee Nee and Jenn Jenn."

"You are welcome to share our campfire tonight. That caravan of Gypsies took over the local campsite upstream. This is the only good spot for quite a ways."

"Thank you for your offer, but I am nervous for the donkeys. There was a ferocious wild cat stalking a herd of grazing animals back by the Gypsy camp. I saw no shepherd or anyone caring for the herd. By now, it probably does not matter. They are most likely all dead."

The woman did not appear concerned. She simply muttered, "Hm."

She must not have understood what I said.

"What was really odd, though, was that the grazing animals did not appear scared, or to even notice the beast. I do not think that wild cat followed me. But it could have. You must know they like to chase things that run."

"Oh, I would not worry about any wild cat." The young woman dismissed his fear. "They are fickle creatures. It was most likely surprised by you and your donkeys. You probably startled it. It was probably heading for a drink at the river."

"Going for a drink? I do not think you understand. There are chickens, goats and baby kids, and cows. Those are all decent meals for a hungry wild cat. I think it was going for a meal, not a drink. Do you not care that those people may need our help?"

"I don't see you turning around to go help." She said, hands on her hips. "Besides, I am confident those Gypsies can take care of themselves, especially against a wild mountain cat. Come, relax by our fire."

Irwin hesitated. Her lack of care for the people of the caravan put him off. At the same time, she had made a good point—he was not returning to aid them either. Maybe this Yace knew she could not help. He studied her watching him. She appeared pleasant, and spoke honestly, but there was something different about her. She smiled at him, encouraging him to come with her to her camp. Cautiously, he did so, and so did the Jennies.

There was enough space in the shallow meadow next to the river for a small camp. But not enough for one more tent. "You can put your belongings there. And if you are comfortable with your Jennies being loose, they can graze down whatever they can find along the road." She pointed here and there. "I really wouldn't worry about any wild cat stalking us."

Every time he looked into her light blue eyes, he felt startled. She continued to stare at him. Those eyes complimented her pale skin and hair. Yet the sight of such paleness disturbed him. She studied him exactly like Bernard the Bard had. The man she called Kipp was glaring at him. His deep brown eyes glistened in the shadow of light and shimmered like a carnivorous animal on the hunt.

Kipp's voice was deep and smug. "What did the wild cat look like?" He was trying to penetrate Irwin's eyes, just like Yace.

Irwin studied the dark-haired, dark-skinned young man by the fire. He reminded Irwin of Yuri, or Koloto; he was roughly grizzled and appeared somewhat jaded. He felt drawn in by the stark difference in skin color and attitude between two people who appeared to be good friends.

He responded to the man's question, "What was that? You mean, what did that cat look like?"

"Kipp, not now. Ignore him. He can be torpid sometimes."

"Torpid?"

"A bit slow and dimwitted."

Kipp grumbled. "I heard that."

Maybe this is not the best place to camp.

He didn't appreciate how this woman was speaking about her counterpart. "You know ..." He began to pull his Jennies along, circling around the tent. "... I believe I will find another place to camp." He stepped over branches and underbrush and made his way toward the roadway.

Yace said, "There isn't one."

Irwin did not stop.

"We already walked up and down this section of road trying to find a spot big enough for the two of us to camp and not strangle each other."

He continued to walk away with his Jennies.

"Kipp and I don't always get along, but he's the one I choose to be with. I know we are not a typical couple, where the man dominates the woman. But that's how we like it! The only other place to make camp is back with the Gypsy caravan unless-unless you camp on the roadway. You could ask the Gypsies if you can camp there, but most likely they will scare you away. They're definitely scary people." She looked over at Kipp, watching their exchange while sitting fireside.

15

<u>YACE THE TELEPATH</u>

I rwin stopped. It was dark, and he was tired of walking. He wanted to make camp and get some sleep, having walked all day in hopes of finding an Inn. "People do not scare me." He grumbled, knowing he was lying. "What about the next town? It should be close to here, right?" He already knew the answer. He could go back through the meadow and the Gypsy camp, across the river, then upstream to the small village he had seen on the other side, or he could stay here.

"You mean the city of Jo Hara?"

"I guess." He never knew the names of the upcoming towns or cities until he saw the welcome sign. He wondered how she knew the name of the next town.

"I think that city is about two, maybe three, days away." She peered at Kipp again who remained quiet at the fire's edge. "You wouldn't get there tonight, if that's what you are thinking. Nope, this is the only place for you to stay, Samuel Irwin Miner."

Irwin turned to Kipp. "Why do you ask what the wild cat looked like?"

"I was just wondering if it was a roan feline, or a black feline that chased you and your donkeys off." Kipp said.

"It was black."

"Olei!" Kipp seemed excited about this.

Yace growled at her friend. "Kipp! Not now." She glanced back at Irwin. "Are you still leaving? Or will you stay and share our fire?"

He could leave. He could go off and camp in the middle of the roadway. He had done it the night before. But his body hurt worse than it had the day prior. He did not want to sleep in the middle of the rocky and muddy road again. It was hard to ignore his want to be done with this day. Nor did his feet want to take any more steps. Right here and now was a camp with acceptable accommodations. Besides, there were things about these two that intrigued him. Yace sort of scared him. But it was Kipp who drew Irwin back toward the campfire.

Irwin did not really want to be alone tonight. He had hoped to have found an Inn; something to get him away from the monotony of his daily routine. The Jennies were not as entertaining as they once were. And he knew he could deal with these two easier than a whole family at an Inn. He hated responding to massive questioning, and it seemed that all Inns' residents were always curious about where he was from. Where was he going? What was he going to do with his life? "Were you two chased off by more than one feline?"

"Kipp saw a black one earlier." Yace glared at her counterpart. She wanted him to keep quiet, that was clear. There was something she was trying to hide. "And then I saw a roan-colored one. Wild cats are present here, that's for sure." She continued to smile and be pleasantly engaging, but there was something devious behind those bright blue eyes. "We were deciding how many fish to catch for supper. Will you be staying?"

Perhaps these two are more prepared for the world than I am.

He might have something to gain by spending a night with them. Their stories might be more entertaining than Bernard the Bard's. He saw nothing wrong with talking to them, though he would remain cautious. He knew Yace held a small dagger against her thigh, and two other knives were close to the fire. Kipp had a small carving knife under the cloak.

What unnerved Irwin was the way Yace commanded Kipp. It reminded him of Albert. He missed his father, and at the same time he was glad to be so far removed from Albert and his wrath. What dealings he might have with these two would keep him going until the next time he yearned for interactions with others.

He shrugged. "Sure." He pulled his Jennies back toward the camp, but then decided to leave on their baggage. He would be ready to leave with haste if necessary.

Kipp's hard brown eyes never left Irwin—assessing this new person. "So, your last name is Miner. Does that make you a miner, or is that just your family name?"

Their eyes locked. Indeed, there was something uniquely different about this young man. He assessed that Kipp was probably about his age. And Irwin was curious to learn about this brown-skinned man.

"Um, yes, I am a miner. And yes, it is a family name." He filled the Jennies' grain bags and slipped them across their faces.

Kipp sniffed loudly as Irwin stepped toward the fire. "That explains a lot." His lip upturned in disgust.

"Kipp," Yace growled. "Be nice."

"He smells! He smells like something we should not be associating with."

"That isn't a nice thing to say to our guest, Kipp. Have you smelled yourself lately? You stink!"

"I know I smell! I'm supposed to smell! I'm supposed to smell like a wet dog." His eyes shimmered like a wolf's in the dark. "I've never met someone who smells like ... like Death."

Irwin raised his arm up to smell his odor.

Yace said, "Can you be kind tonight, Kipp, please? Ignore him, Samuel Irwin Miner."

"I'm hoping he's just a guest. I'm hoping he's not the person Dana spoke of."

"Kipp!"

The expression of anger washed off Kipp's face at the sound of Yace. His demeanor turned soft, and his eyes looked off into the night—looked vacant.

"You can be bothersome sometimes." Yace scolded Kipp. Then she turned her attention to Irwin. "And other times ... well, he practices being silent."

He had witnessed something similar happening with Bernard the Bard. Bernard hypnotized people with his song and dance. Yace did something more drastic. "What just happened? What did you do to him? What did you do to your friend, Kipp?"

"Whatever do you mean?" She stammered and stared at Irwin with those pale eyes and an intense energy. She moved toward him, but he jumped away.

He wanted to keep his distance from this spooky woman with the white hair. There was something quite different about her. She came off as nice, but then turned evil like the onslaught of an unexpected storm. "You changed him!" He was witnessing something he could not understand. The darker-skinned young man appeared statuesque.

"I did nothing wrong. Kipp is alright ... probably hearing something off in the distance and concentrating on it." Her eyes turned bluer, watched him as he moved around the fire toward Kipp. "He gets that look when he hears something."

Irwin went to place his hand upon Kipp's shoulder, but Yace reached for him. He grazed Kipp, making physical contact, and melted away a spell Irwin knew nothing about. When she reached for him, an intense burst of energy repelled Yace and Irwin away from one another. And because of Kipp's proximity, he fell to the ground, rolling with that burst of energy next to the firepit, barely missing the flames.

The dark-haired man jumped up to his feet. "You did it again, didn't you? You bitch!"

"What just happened here?" Irwin struggled to his feet also.

"You've got to stop messing with me," Kipp shouted at Yace.

She pointed at Irwin. "He's the one Kipp! You don't see it, but you need to."

"Why must you take my mind? I wasn't doing anything wrong." He strode toward her, his fists clenched. "How many times have I asked you not to do that?"

Yace stepped back, her hands up.

Had Kipp grown larger?

Irwin's head hurt. He watched Kipp take a swing at Yace who was quick to dodge the flying fist.

"Kipp, I am sorry, but I had to! You were going to make fools of us. And now he's going to leave, and it's going to be your fault!"

"My fault?" He lunged at her again.

This escalating of words and physical threats had to stop. There were many ways he could use his own power to halt the quarrel. They both had metal on them. But he did not want to worsen the situation or expose himself. Instead, he tackled Kipp.

The dark-haired man screamed like a scared child, "Get off me! Get off me!" Kipp kicked and threw a few wild punches. "He's trying to kill me, Yace!"

Yace stood back from the brawl, laughing at Kipp's outburst.

Irwin jumped off Kipp. He had only meant to stop Kipp, not scare him. From now on, he would keep his distance from both of them.

"I hope he's not the one. I don't want to travel with Death," Kipp said.

"Are neither of you concerned about what just happened here?" Irwin was confused about the powerful charge of energy that had sparked between them. "When I touched you, Kipp, you physically changed. And I want to know what you did to him, and to me, Yace."

"You are powerful, Samuel Irwin Miner." Her eyes locked onto his and he stepped back. He felt she was much more powerful than he was.

"What happened there just confirms it," said Yace.

"We shouldn't be associating with him. He's Death, I tell you!"

"You think he was going to kill you, Kipp? I don't think this man is Death." She looked at Irwin, her eyes probing his. "There is something amazing about you, Samuel Irwin Miner ... something very grounding. You changed Kipp back to himself. Only another Telepath could do that, or someone more powerful like a Coterie." Her eyes twinkled at Irwin and then shifted to her friend. "And would you stop being so stupid? This man isn't Death. Death would look darker and deadlier! Kind of like you Kipp."

Irwin did not like this exchange. "I have no power. You think I'm powerful? What about yourself?" He hated to think that she somehow knew about his abilities. Her eyes were trained on his. "That was all you back there, Yace. You obviously have a power I have never experienced." He had not shown her anything of himself, nor would he.

"That was not all me. Oh, you have power, Samuel Irwin Miner. You might not know it yet, but you are powerful indeed! That spark we felt says it all. You melted my spell from Kipp's mind. That was all you. I'm far from powerful, and that's why I'm going to see my father."

"I don't look like Death." Kipp kicked at the dirt next to the fire.

"I do not understand why you think I am Death. It is obvious that Yace is the one who acts devious." Irwin said. "From what I witnessed, Kipp, I saved you from her. She is the one who put a spell on your mind, not me. She is the one who has laughed at you, made fun of you, called you names in front of me, a perfect stranger."

Kipp seemed to disregard what he said and winced. "I know what Yace is. I know she can be evil. But she does not turn my stomach like you. You're an unknown evil. You smell like Death," Kipp said. "You taste like Death. And I don't like you ... you must be Death."

"You not liking him does not make him Death. Besides, if he were Death, don't you think Olei or Alio would have stopped him?"

"No! They would have shooed him on toward us! Maybe that's what they did. Maybe Samuel Irwin Miner is a test they have sent. Were you paid to come here and rile us all up?"

"Oh, now you are just being silly, Kipp." Yace said, rolling those eyes.

"I am the one who has been the most genuine here." Irwin looked at them both. "I am not evil. I have done nothing wrong. Yet I witness you two badgering one another, fighting each other, placing some sort of magical spells, and trying to lure me into your madness. If anything, it is you two who are Death." He was tired from his day. But watching these two was slightly entertaining, nonetheless. They were an odd couple, indeed. "Trust me, if I really wanted to, I could slaughter the both of you in a moment. And neither would see it coming."

"See! I told you he's Death."

Yace took a long look at Irwin. "I don't think Death would come into our camp the way Samuel Irwin Miner came to us. He is one of the good ones."

"How do you know? You were the one who invited him to come and share our camp. How could he say no? I could see Death coming to visit you, Yace. And you'd deserve it after all you've done!"

"What's that supposed to mean?" She snorted and glared at her friend. "You think Death would admit that he could kill us, and then not?" She spoke. "No, he would just spill our blood and enjoy our camp and all our amenities."

This reminded him of how Albert and Jebadia tangled, but kinder.

I do not have to be a part of this. I can leave at any moment.

Irwin moved toward his Jennies.

"No, you are not leaving! And no, he is not Death! Let's try this over again." She said and faced Irwin. "Hi, I am Yace Yellsen, and this is Kipp Hauler."

"I am out of here," He muttered and kept on toward his Jennies.

"You cannot leave!"

He turned and stared at Yace.

Why is she trying to command me?

He could not help but chuckle at the absurdity of it all. "Your mental tricks do not work on me. I am not a doll." The Jennies' feed bags came off, and he slung them across his left shoulder and took up their lead lines.

"Wait!" she screamed. "No, you cannot leave!"

"Yeah, go!" said Kipp.

Is he jealous that I can walk away freely?

"You cannot leave!" Now she was dancing around, trying to work her magic on him. "Kipp, help me make him stay."

"I say leave! Good riddance!"

"Kipp! He's supposed to help you! He's supposed to help me. He's supposed to escort me to my father's residence. Dana says he will keep me safe in Onj Raha. This is not how it's supposed to go. Dana told me he is here to help us! Do you want to deal with me by yourself?"

Now her pitch was higher. "Dana saw you, Samuel Irwin Miner. She saw you! She said she saw you in Kobiton. You were horribly hurt by an older family member. She thought it was your father.

"And then she saw you again at the trading post ... Goshee was it? By then you were healed, in mind and body. And then ... then you met the Erthin women at the summit lodge. There was music ... a large moose or deer in front of you. And that was when Dana said you were followed by a dark specter. Does this make sense, Samuel Irwin Miner? Was there a dark presence with you until a handful of days ago?" She took another step forward. "Were you followed by a stranger pretending to be a friend? Someone who made you feel more uncomfortable than I am right now ...?"

Irwin stopped.

How would she know what I have gone through? Shit, I need a drink of whiskey.

"Who is Dana?"

"She is my mother. Not my birth mother. That woman is long dead," said Yace. "Dana took me in as her daughter long ago. She is a dreaming Telepath. She sees visions of people and places and things going on. Her visions are usually in her dreams. Sometimes she has visions when she is awake. Her visions can be of future events or past. Sometimes she has ones that are just moments into the future. Some dreaming Telepaths can make the visions happen. They can summon them at will, but that takes years and years of training." She continued to take small steps toward him.

"Dana had several dreams with you in them. She said she saw you hurt, then healed, and then followed by a Telepath. She saw that you are a novice to this world. This world is cruel to novices, especially Talented ones. She told me that our time together is twofold. I get to teach you about Urthis! And you will keep me safe." She stopped just beyond arm's reach of him.

"How am I supposed to keep you safe? I carry no weapons."

"Kipp carries no weapons, but he is a deadly assassin."

"Does this mean he's staying?" Kipp said.

"You can leave tonight Samuel Irwin Miner and continue on with your doldrums life. Or you can stay the night and decide tomorrow's fate tomorrow."

"Why did your mother dream of me?" He stared at her, trying to figure out why she was trying to lure him in and scare him off at the same time.

She is so much like the Bard.

There was something he could not deny about Yace's words.

But how could Dana see me? Dreaming Telepath? I have heard of Telepaths before. But how could she know about me? Dream about me? What else about me does she know?

He wanted to run away, but more of him wanted to stay and get answers. He wanted to find out why he felt drawn into and repelled by this new situation.

"Because she did, Samuel Irwin Miner. It could be coincidence or ominous fate. But Dana cannot deny what she saw. We are here for each other."

Every time Yace said his full name, it made him flinch. "Please address me as Irwin."

16

KIPP THE CLAN-DUIN

"Are you gonna stay the night?" asked Kipp.

Irwin was not so sure. "What is a Telepath? And why would Dana dream of me?"

Yace did not answer both of his questions. "It's more like you came to her in her dreams. She saw what you were doing, maybe even when it was going on with you. The first set of dreams happened a while ago. I remember we were a few days west of Chinochi, camping along the road—that was about a moon ago.

"When you came to her, Dana told me that you were in Kobiton on the main road at the edge of town. Something bad happened to you and your father. She did not go into detail but was saddened by that dream. I'm guessing someone died. Someone you know, perhaps? Or maybe that was when you were hurt?"

Yace was trying to read him, he could tell.

"She also saw flashes of you being in Goshee. Your mind was in a better place, and you were without your father. You appeared happy then.

"And maybe a dozen days ago, she dreamed of you again. You were having a struggle of some sort with a dark specter. I'm guessing it was a Telepath. Dark specters usually are. She also said you are very kind and thoughtful, and that you tend to take the peaceful route ... thorough in your approach to problem solving, almost to a fault." She paused, as if being directed what to say. "Oh, and though you hesitate with your instinct, you are a good judge of character. She said you are a grounding type of person."

"She saw all that in dreams?"

Yace stepped backwards, toward the fire. "You know, we don't have to stand here in the darkness. We were just about ready to get supper started. I'm not sure about you, but I'm hungry." Even though Irwin could feel she was slightly deceptive, Yace spoke mostly with honesty.

"You look tired and hungry. You've probably been walking all day. Let's talk by the fire." She turned to Kipp. "Go fetch us a large fish, Kipp. Please."

Perhaps Yace will be more forthcoming than Bernard the Bard, even if she goes off on tangents.

Irwin decided. "I will stay for the fresh meal. Thank you." He would try to get more answers. He brought the Jennies back and secured them near the tent. Again, he placed the grain bags upon their faces, and kept the panniers on in case he felt it necessary to leave in a hurry.

Kipp glared at Yace with an upturned lip. He pulled his cloak and shirt off, revealing muscular arms and torso.

Then he shape-shifted his body. The black hair on his skin grew across every inch of exposed flesh. Even his arms and legs contorted and grew longer. Multiple joints popped as he went down onto all four limbs, now looking like a long-legged, sleek-bodied wolf.

Irwin felt hypnotized by the well-built young man. He stopped breathing in order to take in this spectacle, realizing why Kipp's facial features looked the way they did. Kipp's nose was broad and long, his large eyes set slightly closer together, his dark hair thick across his head, and his eyebrows now blended into a mask of brown and black across his face. He had canine features, and Irwin had not completely realized that until now.

I never would have fathomed anyone could actually turn into a four-legged creature. That means Koloto and Yuri might have been wolves as well.

The shapeshifter darted along the river's edge, then dove in. Irwin watched and tried to speak, "How the ...."

"Kipp is Clan-Duin, Irwin." Yace spoke softly, reminding him of Saryh as she began to explain things he had never known before. "A Clan-Duin is a being that can shapeshift into an animal form. They usually have one specific totem they can transform into, like a wolf, or wildcat, or bird, or even an air-breathing water creature. Kipp comes from canine lineage. He can transform into all different sizes of dog. Big ones and small. I don't know how he does it exactly. It's a fluid movement for him. He thinks 'wolf' and becomes one. Sometimes I wish I could do what he does."

"Clan-Duin," Irwin whispered. He now understood why Bernard the Bard had labeled Yuri. "I have met a few like him."

"There are hundreds of thousands of Clan-Duins across this planet. The Clan-Duin species is unique in that they are the only creatures that can change from a human into animal. It truly is remarkable to watch them."

He listened and watched Kipp splashing through the river. "That is something special."

"Oh, he's special alright ..." She paused to watch Kipp dash through the water. "... but I am more talented than he will ever be.

"What I mean is .... Well, I'm told I'm a Coterie, considered a 'Children of the Universe', something special, right? I mean, lore says the Coterie are bastard children of Guru. They mixed with mortal blood somewhere along the way, long, long ago. Now the Gurus are direct descendants of the Ancient Dwellers. And Ancient Dwellers are all-powerful beings. I mean, who wouldn't want to be the kin of Ancient Dweller? They get to make things at a breathtaking level of complexity." She spread her arms wide. "They are what the Hakra wishes he were!

"But Hakra will never be an Ancient Dweller. The Ancients ... they just create and go. Hakra says he creates, then delineates how life is supposed to be. He doesn't like the idea of free will.

"Instead, Hakra has given the people a false ideology to follow. Yeah, he's given people things they need to succeed, but it's only for his gain. He is using them. In the grand scheme of things, he's using all of us." Pausing, she then added, "If we could all be accepted as we are, powerful or not. The Ancient Dwellers want us to enjoy the bounty of the universe. Not follow false deities.

"I don't understand how people can be so torpid about believing only one entity created everything we see when there were many. We all created this, really." She watched her wolf disappear downstream. "What it is, well, it's under educated people. Those who live on plantations mostly. They don't get taught much. And what little they are taught is practically force fed." She made a gagging sound when saying, "Tomes. Yuck! They only know what is told and cannot help but believe the hype.

"If only people could see that the Ancient Dwellers made all of this." She spread her arms wide again. "There are no attachments, just eternal gratitude. And that's better than having to work your whole life at a job you hate, and not being rewarded for it. This place, everything we see, is the reward, yet some don't get that! Who would want to work their whole life and get no rewards for it? Everyday life rewards you if you pay attention, if you believe in yourself.

"But some people need reassurance." She then turned overly dramatic. "Why does my life suck? Why can I not do this or that? Why must things be cruel? Why are people so hopeless? Why, oh why?" Thankfully, she stopped tossing her eyes, arms, and head around.

"Yet since the Ancient Dwellers do not exist on this plane of existence, the Hakra has taken that ethereal position to delineate how life is. He tries to answer the Whys, but .... Then there are self-appointed deities who try to control everyone. Of course, some people can't think independently. They actually need to be told what to do. And that's how it comes back full circle.

"What do you think the Ancient Ones would say if you asked them why? Why all this? Why life? Why whatever? They would probably say, why not?" She waved her hands through the air again. "But if you ask Hakra, he'd tell you because of this and this and this, now get back to work for me—instead of just go and enjoy it!

"Thankfully, there are people smart enough to not buy into any of it. I surely don't. Nor do the Gypsy. Nor do most people with Talents. We see through shit like that. Most people though ... well, Mortals really, and some with Talents, are conned into believing the hype Hakra spouts." She drifted off.

Irwin remained silent, taking it all in.

"What I really find silly is that the Hakra has said he will smite all that do not grovel and pay homage. He finds Telepaths and other PCP to help promote and enforce his propaganda. It's all about fear, fear, fear. But for the Hakra it works. As sick and twisted as it is, he figured out how to unite an entire planet.

"I understand it though, why he does it. I mean, I was raised to fear Hakra's wrath. If I did not work, if I did not believe in his words, I would be beaten. So, I understand the hype. But now I know better." She took a seat by the fire. "It's about controlling the masses ... about fear mongering."

Irwin remained standing, mesmerized by this woman's long-winded diatribe, but his foot was going to sleep.

"You know you don't have to stand."

He had been listening to her, but some of his concentration was upon Kipp. He looked for the Clan-Duin. "Yes, I know." He listened to Yace rant, curious about all of it, but still he waited for signs of Kipp.

Yace shrugged. "As Gypsy, we've met rogue soldiers along the way who worked for Hakra. The things they saw while working for him ... even though their minds were messed with by Telepaths, some memories are hard to permanently erase.

They saw firsthand what the Hakra really was ... and that was why they were relocated out of Akarah."

He felt her eyes on him.

"Many soldiers who work for Hakra resent all he stands for, because, well, he is fraudulent. They see it, but a good portion of the people who live on Urthis believe he is an actual God. We Gypsies know the truth; Hakra is a false deity laying claim upon people who don't really need him. What they need it to learn to believe in themselves."

She grabbed a flask, drank in gulps, and said, "I'm not full Coterie. So I am only partly connected to the creators, the Ancient Dwellers. Not that I wouldn't want to be full Coterie. Nonbry says I'm lucky to be part Coterie. I guess no one is of pure Coterie descent anymore because of generations of crossbreeding with other species and Mortals. That dulls the lines, whether it's Clan-Duin, or Erthin, or Telepath, or any of the other Talented species which still reside upon Urthis."

Irwin had lost sight of Kipp. He kept his stance, though his legs begged him to sit. Clearly, this woman enjoyed talking. His legs wavered, and she egged him closer to the fire. "Come on, take a seat. What about your family? Did they always mine? Is it a generational thing? Or is it bred in? I mean, to want to mine probably is rare, right? It takes a certain breed of people who want to live inside caves, away from everyone else ... risk their lives." She paused, but so briefly, Irwin had not a second to speak. "It's weird that some men don't need contact with others. Did you always live in a mine, Irwin? Did you ever live in town? I imagine there are only so many resources to mine other than coal."

It was quiet, and Irwin realized he must respond. "I have always lived in a mine, but in mining you find other things, like jewels, or ores like ..." He counted on his fingers. "... silver, gold, lead, copper, bronze, nickel, quartz ... and there is always a demand for slate, marble, graphite, sandstone ...."

"Wow, did you mine all of that?"

"No. Only coal."

"Well, everyone needs coal. It's more compact than wood and burns hotter, though it probably comes at a price. I can't imagine how many miners' lives are lost due to cave collapse. That's probably why whole families get into mining. I mean, they must support one another, right? If one member dies, there must be another waiting to take their place. Did that ever happen in your family?"

Irwin stared at her, sitting there in the glow of the firelight.

She does not stop.

"No. Not that I know of."

I wish I had listened to more of Bernard's stories and songs.

"Was that black feline that scared me and my Jennies a Clan-Duin? Did I use that term correctly?"

"Yes, Clan-Duin, and yes, that's why the grazing animals did not react the way you thought they should. That Clan-Duin was their Sheppard."

"That makes sense. Are there a lot of dreaming Telepaths?"

"There are many types of Telepaths. Dana just happens to be a dreaming one."

Not sure that Saryh had defined telepathy very well, Irwin wanted clarification. "What exactly is a Telepath then?"

"A Telepath is someone who can read minds, or speak without using their mouth, not like we're communicating right now." She twisted the edge of her hair around her finger. "They can see visions, whether awake or asleep. They can also hear random thoughts from people standing around them; and they can manipulate pliable minds."

"Pliable minds?"

"Unlike yours."

What does she mean?

"Some minds are gullible or easily tricked by words. Telepaths can probably do other things, but I'm not versed in all telepathic abilities."

"So, Dana is a Telepath? ... but only a dreaming one?"

"Well, she can converse with me telepathically. But yeah, her primary telepathic trait is dreaming."

"And you say you are a Coterie?"

"Yeah."

"But you did telepathy on Kipp."

"Yeah."

"Then you are a Telepath too?"

"Yes. Being part Coterie means I can do it all!" She stretched out her legs in front of her, closer to the fire. "Well, at least I can do some of it. See, the plan is for me to go meet my father in Onj Raha. He is Coterie too. He's supposed to help me unlock my true potential. That's what Nonbry says. But I cannot travel there alone. I must have an escort. You can probably understand why women don't travel alone."

"No, I do not. I travel alone. I do not understand the issue."

Her expression flattened. "Traveling alone is not a good thing for most people, especially if you have certain skin colors. But you, you are different. First off, you're a man. Second, you have pale skin. Third, you are kind of skinny and don't look like you've had much work experience. Fourth, you don't appear an easy target. You appear highly suspicious, which is good, I suppose. And finally, you could be overlooked because you are so quiet."

"Why is that?"

"There are terrible people out there, usually Telepaths, who prey upon unsuspecting minds and bodies. If you appear to be an easy target, then you are taken advantage of. Telepaths look for specific traits in their captives. Mortal minds are the easiest to control, Clan-Duins second. Erthins can be more of a challenge, but they can be controlled too. Now Telepaths controlling other Telepaths, now that can get a little tricky. Telepaths are powerful creatures who don't like to be controlled. Of course, there are some species we've met along the way who have Talents to keep themselves warded, so to speak, from Telepaths."

Bernard hinted at something like this, but I did not think it was so complicated.

"No one likes to be controlled."

"But that's the way of things on Urthis. Free will happens, but it's not a common occurrence. Telepaths have had a hand in controlling people on this planet for centuries."

Huh. How much of this should I believe?

17

MAKING FRIENDS

"**W**hy do you not live with your father?"

"The long and short of it is that he impregnated my mother many years ago, not knowing. I'm guessing she was a pretty whore. And he did what men do. It's obvious to me that my mother was young and not very thoughtful about things. After I was born, she sold me to a family." She pointed westward. "In lands far across the great plains of Urthis."

This Yace enjoyed leading the conversation. But he had more questions. "I still do not understand why Dana dreamed of me. Why me?"

There came a thrashing of water, but he still saw nothing near the bushes or in the water.

"You are heading east, correct?"

Just like Bernard, hoping to follow along.

His silver eyes rested on her brilliant blue eyes. "Yes, but that is not an answer to my question. Why did she dream of me?"

"Like I said, you came to her in her dreams. She told me you are supposed to be here for me as I am supposed to be here for you. You and me, Irwin, our lives are linked for whatever reason."

"Sounds like mere coincidence." They kept on staring at each other. Were there ulterior meanings behind her words? "Wait a minute, you and Kipp, you two came from that caravan upstream? You are Gypsy, correct?"

"Yeah. Yes, we are. We departed from them for three days to make sure we could tolerate each other before going on the long journey together. Like I said, Kipp and I are traveling together. We have a mission. We are heading to Onj Raha to meet my father."

"You were not up front about your journey to see your father when we first met." Irwin swayed from foot to foot before taking a seat on a large stone. "It was only when I started to leave you threw a fit and confessed your true motives.

Before that, you just came off as travelers, slightly angry that a band of people you labeled as Gypsy had taken over the local camping ground."

Yace made a noise out of her nose and shrugged.

"But now I see you were sent here to wait for me. It is presumptuous to assume I would help you. I do not know you. And from what I have seen, I am not so sure I want to be around you. Besides, you do not know what type of person I am. But beyond that fact, you have Kipp as an escort. Why would you need me?" He stared at her. "How do you even know you can trust me? What if Kipp is right? What if I am Death?"

"I think I know enough about you, Samuel Irwin Miner. What Dana saw about you and told me about you is true. She knows people and their motives. You cannot lie to her in a dream, and they are always very revealing, even if she is not."

What is she up to?

"She said you are someone who can keep me grounded. She said I could trust you with my life ... and it's not that Kipp can't keep me safe. He can. But he can't keep me grounded. We already saw that you ground out my powers. Besides, we're heading in the same direction. Why not walk together for a while? You know, get to know each other better."

The boldness of this woman.

"Just because we are heading in the same direction does not mean we must travel together."

"Why not?"

"Are all Telepaths alike?"

"Like what?"

"Manipulative?"

"Not all."

His head hurt.

It is obvious that Telepaths have a way of talking and do not know when to be quiet. Of course, it does explain a lot about Bernard the Bard and why he could not allow a quiet moment.

Irwin put his hands up to his face and closed his eyes, wiping them. He was weary of this woman who used her words to run his mind around. He glanced around again for Kipp.

I hope that Clan-Duin fellow returns soon with a meal!

He did not want to make eye contact with Yace any longer.

"I understand why you are cautious, Irwin. I would be too. There are many evils out there far beyond our imaginations. Bad things happen to good people all the time. But you survived the dark specter that followed you, so that means you are strong enough to endure time with me."

Yace had to fill any void with her words that was clear.

"Sometimes in the midst of the river of chaos, it's good to find a branch to lean on."

I can leave at any time. I can leave at any time. I am not bound to stay here.

Suddenly Kipp dashed through the camp, a large trout between his teeth. He brought it to Yace and held it in his jaws for her to take. The fish was alive and tried to flop out of her hands.

"Ugh, Kipp!" Grasping the fish's tail, she raised the flopping trout above her head and thrust it upon the rocks—a quick kill.

"I hate it when the fish is still alive, Kipp, you know that."

He panted a happy dog smile and went off to the side to shake off the water. Then he mutated and retrieved his clothing.

Irwin watched the spectacle and could not help but stare at Kipp's body, wondering how his skin changed so fluidly. The young man's body hair was not as thick or as coarse as the wolf's hair. It appeared that hair had slipped back into his dark flesh. He pulled his pants on, tying them with a cord. Then he slipped on a well-worn indigo-colored tunic, wrapping his cloak back across his shoulders, and became a shadowy man once more. The Clan-Duin sat down next to Irwin, staring with his canine eyes.

Irwin tried to ignore the insistent gaze, but he could not bring to an end to his own curious stares.

Yace snarled, "Kipp, what did I say earlier?"

Kipp threw his hands up at her. "What!" He looked back at Irwin. "Am I intimidating you?" He pointed toward his old seat. "I didn't chase you off my rock. I'm sitting below you, behaving. What more do you want me to do? I'm in the beta position! Should I grovel? Should I show my belly?"

"Just be nice to our guest."

He sat back further into his dark cloak and became a broody shadow.

An uncomfortable air shifted between the two of them. Irwin took that as a cue to move around.

"You are not going anywhere, are you?"

"I need to tend to my donkeys." He walked over to his Jennies he had left tied up.

I should leave. But there is fresh food, think about it! I do not have to cook tonight.

He stood there for a long time; he took several deep breaths, hoping to calm his anxieties about joining these strangers at their fire.

Maybe these are the people the Bard warned me about.

They appeared to be like people in the songs Bernard had sung.

Magical and transforming. Hm.

He had been warned about those who wanted to do harm to innocents. But he did not see these two as bad, or evil. In fact, Yace had been more honest than Bernard. The Bard had run Irwin's mind around and around. Now he realized what Bernard the Bard really was, a wayward Telepath hungry to use people for his own gains.

Yace and Kipp are different. They have a mission, a reason to be traveling.

On the other hand, she is trying to manipulate me, just like Bernard. They all want to travel with me. Why me? Why are all these people drawn to me? At least Yace has been more forthcoming. She did answer my questions. Well, most of them.

His belly fluttered.

I have more questions. What is an Erthin? And what types of creatures throw fire?

He was genuinely excited to have learned something about the people around him, but scared at the same time. His family had never mentioned others with power. But now, he did not feel alone amidst the confusion and wonder about other people, and himself. Although he could not allow this new information to deter him from his primary goal, these new facts invigorated his interest. I want to know more.

I think it is a good idea to stay for the meal, at least. All I must do is ignore her insistence that I must travel with them. And ignore Kipp's distaste for my smell.

He then smelled his own odor.

Kipp is right! Tomorrow morning, I will bathe.

He pulled out his bedroll, two water flasks, and a tin cup. He set those articles aside and then removed the packs from his weary donkeys. Leaning his panniers against the nearest tree, he allowed his Jennies the freedom to graze. Then he brought those few items over to the fire and made his own seat, interrupting a quiet conversation between Yace and Kipp. She had started to fillet the fish but was not paying much attention to what she was doing.

"I was just telling Kipp we are leaving tomorrow morning."

Kipp said, "You didn't say that. Besides, we can't leave tomorrow!"

"We must leave tomorrow," she said. "Now that Irwin is here, we must leave. He's ready to go."

Her eyes flashed, turning from blue to white and then back. It was a quick change, but Irwin saw it. Her voice softened. "Just days ago, you were ready to journey east. You even denounced your family because of the lie your mother kept from you and Flinn. What's your reasoning now? Why don't you want to leave? I know you know Flinn cannot come with us. She's not old enough."

It was obvious to Irwin that Kipp was hesitant to say too much in front of him. The Clan-Duin glanced at the Metalist, his lips as flat as his tone. "I am still mad about everything."

Yace waved the fish knife around. "You see, Irwin, our friend Kipp here, his mother died only two moons ago."

Irwin spoke softly. "I am sorry for your loss, Kipp. It is hard to lose a loved one."

"Not as sorry as I am." Kipp said, "Or Flinn, my younger sister is. You see, our mother didn't share everything with us about why we left our father. And since I was young when it happened, I did not know what exactly happened or why. All I knew was that Dinill was hurt, and mama had Flinn."

Kipp grumbled and shifted on his perch by the fire. "But what I'm still mad about is that Hauss knew the whole time that Flinn was not truly our sister. Yet he said nothing to me about it."

"Kipp, it shouldn't matter that Flinn is not your full sister, made from your mother and father. So, what if she's your half-sister, and half-niece—"

This woman has no filter when it comes to speaking about intimate family affairs. She does not seem to care if she shares personal secrets in front of a man neither of them know.

"—She is still your sister, regardless of breeding. Her relationship to you will not change unless you want it to." Yace looked at Irwin, gauging his reaction. But he was more concerned with what Yace was doing with her knife. She was not paying any attention when cutting the fish.

"Besides," she said, "it wasn't your mother's fault your father was raping your sister. She didn't even know what was happening … too busy working and keeping children … until Dinill was pregnant with Flinn." Her knife ricocheted off a throat bone and sliced her thumb. "Damn it." She threw the knife to the ground. "That's the last time I'll hold that blade again. I hate it. It hasn't worked properly for moons now." She suckled her injury.

Irwin did not feel drawn into their family drama. Instead leaned over and picked up the knife. It had a rusty, dull edge. "Do you wipe this clean after every fish you cut?" He knew the answer by the obvious lack of care on the blade.

Kipp shook his head. "It's her knife, not mine."

Yace said, "Not every time, no. Why?"

"I figured the answer was no, not ever." Irwin snorted, running his fingers down the blade, working his Metalist magic. The imperfections drew flat, and the rust fell off; the blade gleamed in the firelight. He handed it back to Yace.

She examined the blade, then handed it to Kipp. "How did you do that?"

"I have a way with metal."

"Maybe that explains your smell," Kipp said, passing the refurbished knife back to Yace. "You surely don't smell like a miner. You smell more like a dead miner."

Yace took the knife. "No, really? How did you do that, Irwin?"

Irwin was not comfortable showing his powers the way these two had done. There was no way he could tell them what or who he really was. It was too hard to explain. He held his breath. They were waiting for a response.

The Clan-Duin came to his defense. "I thought you said you were hungry, Yace. Our guest was kind enough to fix that dang knife of yours. Why don't you finish what you started?"

For once, it seemed to Irwin, Yace was humbled. Her eyes penetrated his. They stood there like that. Then, after blinking away that moment, Yace brandished the knife, saying to Kipp. "So, are you coming with us tomorrow, or are you staying?"

Is she hinting that I have already agreed to their journey?

He shook his head, snickered under his breath.

"Kipp, I would like to know."

Irwin said, "I have agreed to nothing at this point," before Kipp could answer, before he was any deeper into this than he already was.

The Clan-Duin studied him, then said, "We can leave tomorrow. I don't have a problem with it. I'd just like to go say goodbye, that's all."

"It's not like we are leaving them forever."

Irwin could tell she was trying to calm Kipp.

"We're just going on ahead. They'll meet us in Onj Raha. I'm sure my father will put us up in his manor until they arrive."

Kipp didn't look convinced. "Are you sure? Or are you guessing?"

"I'm fairly sure he will. You might have to work off your food and board."

"Are you fooling me? I'd rather join the PCP if that's the case. I've heard that on this side of the mountains they are more lenient about Hakran rule."

"Don't fool yourself, Kipp, you'd rather clean dishes for my father than for the PCP!" Then Yace used the newly sharpened knife and began slicing again. "Wow, Irwin, you are amazing!" The fish opened right up, making it effortless to de-gut, and she went about cleaning the fish and putting it into a pan with a good amount of lard she scooped from a ceramic container.

18

<u>Sharing Secrets</u>

The fish started to simmer in the pan.

"How long have you two known each other?" Irwin wanted to change the subject.

They looked at one another, postulating answers. "It's been about eleven years since I joined the Gypsy." Yace nodded at Kipp to confirm. "Kipp and his family have been with the Gypsy for what, almost fourteen years now? He had been with them for about three years before I came along. I want to say Kipp was about ten when I met him." She spoke about him as if he were not there. And in that moment, he stared off into the distance, pretending not to be there. "We've been best friends ever since my first day." She glanced at Kipp and back at Irwin. "But we are not in a relationship or anything like that. I mean, our relationship is completely platonic."

Irwin believed what Yace was saying, but when he glanced at Kipp, he saw that the Clan-Duin did feel something for the pretty young woman. Kipp ogled Yace when she was not looking, much like the men Irwin had seen at the Hairy Yak Saloon, in Kobiton. He could see that Kipp had deep feelings for Yace, but held them behind his stoic facade.

He felt the tension rise. "So, you two are traveling ahead of your Gypsy family to see your father? Why? How far away from here is he?"

Yace smiled with an air of satisfaction. "Yeah, we are. That's the exciting and scary part of the journey. But once we reach my father ... once we reach my father ... my time with him is going to be twofold. He'll teach me about my powers, and I'll be taking care of him. He is old and ill and needs my help.

"From what I understand, he lives in Onj Raha and has for some time. That city is located close to the eastern coast." She drew a map in the air. "We are maybe three days away from Jo Hara, about here, in relationship to distance and time. From here to there, Onj Raha is approximately fifty days, give or take a day of rest." She stared at her invisible sky map. "We don't have to travel solid without a break, but we must make good time. My plan would be for us to hike quick enough to cover all this land." She pointed at her invisible map. "In say, forty days."

He was still skeptical about this new situation. "Will it be warmer there than here?"

"It's the east coast, I don't really know. I'm from the west coast, and they've got warm and cold weather, depending on the season, of course. But I'm guessing it will be warmer there than here. It's much lower in elevation than where we are now, so it should be warmer.

"I mean, it makes sense. From what I've heard, Onj Raha is a grand city. Lots of people probably flock there. It's hundreds of years old and home to hundreds of thousands of people. And it's one of the largest cities on this side of the mountains. I've seen the maps. I know it's close to the ocean; they have a massive port, but it's not by the ocean.

"I know this is the river—" She pointed at the stream they were alongside their campsite, then again to her map in the sky. "—which runs through Onj Raha. From there it's diverted north and south, and mostly used to transport goods from all these villages, towns, and ports of call beyond ... out into the oceans of Bounen."

Irwin was amazed by how much Yace seemed to know, and her excitement about all of it. He turned to Kipp. "Is she always like this?"

"Yeah. She's always in her own world. Always smart and very stubborn." They both looked at the beautiful young woman. "Yace knows enough about everything to make you feel like a fool when you learn something new."

"I do not."

"You tend to ruin things for everyone else, Yace."

Hands upon her hips, she said, "I only did that once. Well, maybe twice." She counted the instances on her left hand. "Okay, so it was more like four times."

"You act like you know the answers to everything, even before the questions have been asked."

"That's because I do."

"You never allow me or anyone else to find solutions to problems our elders might present."

"That's not true ... well maybe ...."

"You make hard tasks look easy using your powers, which you know is forbidden. And you act like you are above everyone else when you really aren't."

"None of you work hard enough. If you worked with more thoughtfulness, then you could be as good as me."

"You complain about how disappointed you are by everyone, and you can't help but look for something new to control." He tossed a sideways glance at Irwin. "I wish you would stop trying to control everyone and every situation. If you want us to escort you, you need to be nice."

"Hey! I am nice."

"You need to allow us to make our own decisions. You know we're just as smart as you."

"In your own way, yeah," she said.

"Ugh! You'll jeopardize us with your arrogance. You and I both know Dana would say the same thing if she were here."

Their attention turned to the fish, watching it sizzle in the pan. Yace said, "Well, look at that ... I don't know everything, but I do know enough to keep me alive."

"Get us in trouble is more like it." Kipp turned to Irwin. "I wouldn't follow us. I'd go some other path if I were you." He sat back and pointed at Yace. "You'd think we were siblings with how much we bicker."

The cheeks on her pale skin turned rosy. "Thank the Ancient Dwellers we aren't!"

They sat in silence, waiting for the fish to cook.

Kipp grumbled, "A, Yace, you're gonna burn the fish!"

She tried to move the fish around on what little grease she had put in the pan that had become too hot. The grease was already beginning to sear the fish against the cast iron pan.

"I thought you were a woman, Yace. There's that old saying 'all women can cook, and all men can hunt'." Kipp said.

She glared at him. "I can cook." She scraped the wooden spoon under the fish, trying to pry it up.

"No, all you can do is burn."

Irwin noticed Yace was having difficulty trying to pry the fish from the pan. He moved in to help. "Let me try." As his fingers touched the cloth-wrapped metal panhandle, he was able to manipulate the structure of the cast iron pan.

The metal was rough to the touch—a newer pan that had not been properly finished. He flattened the rough edges. Neither Kipp nor Yace had any clue what he was doing. All they saw was the fish flip up into the air. The half burned, half undercooked trout flipped twice, then landed in the pan, uncooked side down for a thorough cooking.

Irwin handed the hot pan back. "It's all in the wrist."

Now they both stared at him. Yace said, "How did you do that? It was good and stuck. Look at how burnt it is! How'd you do that? How'd you flip that fish?"

Kipp bemoaned, "Look at how burnt it is."

"Cooking fish is easy, though I usually do not have lard. Water usually does better in these kinds of pans—keeps the fish moist."

Kipp put his head in his hands. "Why do you always burn the food, Yace?"

"I am no Patrice, Kipp. Just let me be." She turned to Irwin. "I'll let you cook. You have a better handle on this. Besides, I think Kipp's done with my cooking."

"All two days of it, yeah! I'd rather eat food raw, like I'm supposed to."

Irwin said, "I don't mind cooking. I much prefer it to setting up camp. And I have well-worn pans, better than this one."

"What's wrong with my pan?" Yace's mouth turned downward.

"Well, it was not finished with an oily sealant, nor was it cast correctly," Irwin said. "It is slightly off balance in iron weight; and because of that, it is not flat enough on the inside. So, more often than not your food will burn." He realized both Kipp and Yace were intent upon his every word. "I suppose."

"You could see all those imperfections with just your eyes?" Yace was clearly prying.

He did not want to say anything more.

Yace leaned in close, too close. Her eyes were trying to penetrate him. But she could not. "Can I touch you? To see if I can see what you are?"

He was reserved about any more contact with this woman. And yet he was curious to see what she could reveal about him. He did not want to give himself away. Nor did he want to talk about himself. He was still too afraid to open up to these two, but at the same time it was they who had already displayed their powers. "Sure. I will allow it."

As she leaned forth, he sat back. Irwin watched Kipp from his periphery. The Clan-Duin sat quietly by the fire, statuesque, listening to something off in the distance again. Had Yace used her powers to make Kipp appear quiet, or had the Clan-Duin actually heard something? Her hand moved toward his. The moment she touched Irwin's flesh, her eyes dilated, turning even bluer there in the firelight.

"Whoa!" She pulled her hand off him and looked over at Kipp. Immediately, Yace put her hand back on Irwin's hand. Her eyes never left Kipp's as she touched and retracted her hand from his a few more times. He let her play touch with his hand, then he pulled away.

"What are you doing?"

"That was amazing! You are amazing. I have never known of any being like you." She put her hand on Irwin's again and closed her eyes.

I want to know more about you ... all of you!

He could hear her thoughts, loud and clear. "Okay, I think we are done here." He jumped up and moved away from the fire.

"No ... No. Irwin, I am so sorry. I did not mean to invade your mind, nor your space."

It was too late.

"It's just that when I touch you, I cannot hear Kipp's thoughts. Kipp doesn't think much, but when he does .... And for whatever reason, I believed you had no thoughts, but you have thoughts, lots of them. But somehow you can keep them to yourself."

The Clan-Duin's attention was still focused outside their camp, but he said, "I don't have much thought beyond the primal notions someone like me should have."

"But I can hear your thoughts, Kipp," Yace said. "I can't hear Irwin's unless I have contact with him. And when I touch him, I can't hear your thoughts at all. It's a pleasant change of pace. But I wonder why that is?" She placed her hand on Irwin's again. They peered at one other.

Irwin felt her looking into him, into his memories, into his recent images, thoughts, feelings, dreams—some he had been ruminating over. Yace took her hand away. She was soft as the expression on her face. "I'm sorry, Irwin."

The fish sizzled loudly.

Now Kipp's attention was on the food.

Irwin said, "It is alright, Yace, you did not hurt me." He did not know exactly what she had experienced, but he watched her demeanor change after their connection. He was hesitant to ask what she had seen and felt in his mind. But as he watched her withdraw, he figured it was the images of Saryh he could not be rid of.

He moved the pan out of the fire and placed it between the three of them on the flattened ground. He took the wooden spoon and cut the fish into pieces, making an offer to Kipp. "Which piece do you want?"

Kipp picked the largest slab of fish.

It was obvious to him that Yace had seen something he would never have shared with anyone, ever.

He could see that she was deeply troubled and wished he had not allowed her access into his mind. Her reaction confirmed his conviction to further isolate himself.

The Clan-Duin ate his meal with his hands. "It's not that burnt."

Yace left the fire to relieve herself, but she did not return. Irwin left the rest of the cooked fish in the pan and moved, leaving Kipp and the fire in search of her. He took a lit twig and grabbed his lantern off its pole. Lighting the oil-soaked wick, he ventured into the forest. He could hear Yace sobbing.

He could see her watching him approach. "I am so sorry, Irwin. My powers are so infantile that I don't know how to use them. Dana has told me to not go probing without permission.

"I know you said I could .... I just wanted to know what made you so grounding. I did not think ..." She sobbed lightly. "... I didn't think."

There was a long pause. "The funny thing is," she sniffled, "Dana warned me several times I might see something not meant to be seen. Obviously, I did not listen to her. I thought I could ... I wish I had some other power ... any other power but telepathy. I am sorry, Irwin. What happened to you in your past is yours. I did not mean to see it."

He felt her shame. He was not angered by her probing. "What did you witness?"

Yace stared at Irwin the way Saryh had looked at him. He felt her wanting to draw him into her chest and coddle him.

With a hint of watery eyes, Yace leaned into him. "Your father should be held accountable for all the things he has done to you, all the torment he has put you through."

Still not knowing the depth of what Yace saw, Irwin tried to put off her worries. "I have been through worse." He sighed. A large pang of regret filled his belly.

I wish I had not let her touch me.

"Though, Saryh's death still wakes me at night."

He wondered how much of the unexplainable brutalities done against him while under his father and grandfather's care she had seen. Irwin had known pain. He had known misery. He had wanted to end his existence. But now all of that had changed. Walking away from the lifestyle he had lived, he now felt lightened from those burdens.

Yace's eyes filled with water. "We share similar lives, Irwin, but I was the youngest of six and lived in town." She looked away, then back at Irwin. "I don't remember my biological mother. The family that adopted me told me my mother used me to pay a debt to them. That was why they took me in. In retrospect, I feel they adopted me so they could have another child to mistreat.

"My adopted family owned an Inn where the children did all the work. We had chores, but I was made to do them all." She shook her head as if to shake off the memories. "At a young age, I was doing chores that my older siblings were required to do, but they made me do them. I was forced to do things a young child is not ready for. And if I did not do as told, my siblings or my father would beat me. I would get whipped with a belt, or locked in a box, or suffocated in blankets. I was hit all the time and called names.

"While my siblings all had rooms above ground with windows and beds, I was forced to live in the cellar. My room was nothing more than a cot between a shelving unit full of preserves and the wall. I should have been happy to have a cot at all, but I wanted more. I wanted to be loved and accepted. There was no love in my family, but especially for me. Mother only loved me when I worked. It was a twisted existence.

"I wasn't allowed to have friends; In fact, I didn't have any friends while I lived at the Inn. And because my siblings were, well, who they were, I made up a friend named Nalabeth. She saved me from the torment and torture. What I went through was not as bad as what you've gone through, but my older brothers did light my hair on fire once. I remember them saying, 'It looks like hay; it should burn just like hay'. I remember my older sisters calling me a ghost. They threw mud on my face and told me that if I wore mud, I might make a friend, meaning that people could then find me.

"Thankfully, they weren't home all the time. They went to seminary. I was too young, or too pale. I don't remember the reason I never attended. But I'd steal their books and teach myself what they were learning. I've always loved reading books and learning new things." Her mouth curved into a smile. "I kept to myself, for the most part, and played with Nalabeth. She helped me discover my powers.

We would play with jacks and marbles. It was because of Nalabeth that I learned I could levitate marbles." She sniffled. "I tried to keep it secret. No one knew for a long time. But when I was caught levitating marbles, I was beaten and thrown out. I knew I could not stay in that town; I had to leave everything I knew behind.

"So I ran. For several days I went. I remember walking all day, stealing what I could, sleeping where I could. It's hard to fend for yourself when you are Talented. I had to deal with people running after me, stoning me, shooting me with arrows. I didn't know you're not supposed to show your powers. But Mortals are afraid of those with Talents. And the more obscure you appear, the more likely they are to believe you have some power, some ability, and that really scares Mortals." She sighed again. "You're lucky you look Mortal. Had Dana not told me about you, I would have overlooked you on the roadway tonight.

"I remember finding a plantation that allowed people like me ... like us, to stay. They brought me in and locked me up."

Irwin felt her pain as she recanted distant memories, still fresh in her mind.

"I was young and innocent, and naïve. And the people at the plantation relished young, naïve children like me." Her words faltered. "I think I was trapped in a windowless room for more than a moon's time, or longer, but it felt like years. A moon can seem like a lifetime when you're being violated in every way imaginable.

"I thought Nalabeth was the only one who could save me. But, at the same time, I knew she couldn't." She kept inhaling deeply, as if reliving it right there. "And as I cried out for her to save me, I cried out mentally, you know, telepathically ... loud enough for Dana, Nonbry, and Captain Hari to find me.

"Dana had dreamed of me before they found me. She always knows when Talented people are in distress." She peered up at Irwin. "She knew where I would be. I am so lucky to have Dana as my mother."

She chuckled, as if laughing at fate. "Though really, it was Nonbry and Captain Hari who came and rescued me. Captain Hari is not one to be reckoned with. He is a powerful Erthin. And Nonbry is a Telepath like Dana, but ... but stronger mentally, and older, and ornerier. I don't know how many people they killed while trying to rescue me, but they lit the whole plantation on fire."

Irwin kept his questions to himself, allowing Yace to compose herself before continuing with her story.

"Tamera, the Gypsy's healer. She's a remarkable Erthin. She can give life and take it away in an instant. You don't want to mess with her. Tamera healed me as best she could. I was beaten, broken. I don't know how long I was unconscious, but the Gypsy drove through the town where I had lived my whole life without any incident.

"I remember waking up at the local watering hole where the children went after seminary. I could hear my adopted siblings playing and shouting. All the while, Dana was at my side. She said I would always be her daughter. And ever since, she has been loving and caring. I'm grateful to have had Dana as a representation of what a good mother should be. She made up for all the terrible years with my former family, that's for sure." Yace paused for a long time.

"Irwin, you deserve all the happiness the universe can provide. I am sorry I saw so deep into your mind."

She moved forward, perhaps wanting to embrace, but Irwin felt awkward as usual. He did not need to hear her life story. And he still did not know exactly how much of his past life she had viewed.

19
<u>Telling Stories</u>

"**I** promise I will never probe your mind ever again."

She leaned into him, and he put an arm around her shoulder.

"Apology accepted. What all did you see?"

"I saw abuse by your elders, especially by Jebadia. But your father was just as bad, if not worse." She smiled warmly at him. "We should get back before Kipp eats all the fish."

"He would not do that. Would he?"

She shrugged as she took Irwin's hand to pull him along. He allowed it, and the lantern swung in his hand. They stepped over decaying downed trees. Yace's long locks touched Irwin's arm, tickling him as they headed back to the fire. He let go of her hand, encouraging her to take the lead.

"I happen to know that Kipp is really hungry. He was pretty mad at me for burning the fish again. I am no cook, no matter what Kipp says women should be able to do."

She steered them toward the light of the camp.

Irwin said, "I do not mind cooking. It gives me time at the end of my day to do something soothing, to take away the stresses of the day."

"Well, good because I don't trust Kipp to cook anything all the way through. He prefers his food raw."

Both Jennies were eating grass along the edge of the trees. Only Nee Nee perked up to see him.

Yace turned to face Irwin. "Before I make more of a fool of myself, do you mind telling me what your power is?"

So, she had seen into his memories, but she had not seen what he really was. She had seen his experiences, physical and mental, but had not beheld his power. All those Metalistic actions he performed were innate; they came without thought. What Yace had seen were his burdens and secrets.

"I am a miner. I mine ores."

She stopped in her tracks. Her eyebrows furrowed. "Mine ores, what does that mean exactly?"

"I can find ore like lead or copper, silver, gold, zinc, you name it. I mine it. That is what miners do." He stepped away from Yace and went to the fire.

He noticed her stand next to the Jennies, petting them and watching him walk away. He sat down next to Kipp who had eaten his fair share of fish and was about to eat more.

Irwin pulled out a chunk of fish from the pan and placed it on a rock. "Is this how you two eat? Because I have wooden plates."

"Yace didn't do the dishes."

Yace shouted as she entered the camp. "I don't do dishes."

Kipp snarled back at her. "Wait! You'll do them for Patrice, but not for us?"

"Of course, I'll do the dishes for Patrice's cooking. You do them too!" She came up to the fire and took her seat, her eyes on Irwin the whole time. "You'd do the dishes for the entire Gypsy too, Irwin! You'd do anything for Patrice's food. Trust me. Even though she feeds two dozen people, and the dish buckets are always full ... her food is amazing! Well worth an evening's time spent at a creek washing dishes."

Kipp pointed at their small dish bucket in the shadows near the river's edge. "But you can't clean our dishes, which amounts to two bowls, three spoons, and the other pot?"

"What makes you so incapable of doing our dishes, Kipp?"

"I fetched the meal. What more do you want?"

"I want a million gold coins, a chariot lined with a dozen white horses ... and ...."

"Sorry, but I can't deliver on that until next life."

"What about some more fish?"

"More fish? That's all the fish you're gonna eat. I know you; you only like things freshly cooked and still hot and always in small amounts."

She sneered at him and took a bite of the cold fish in her dainty fingers. "I don't overeat unlike you."

"I eat today because I don't know what tomorrow will bring."

"Well, unlike you, I eat fruits and vegetables!"

"I eat apples and pears. You don't like squashes, or figs, or—"

"I do too like squashes!"

"Only when Patrice cooks them."

"The figs are a textural thing. They feel slimy on my tongue. And the taste is not something I like either."

Irwin shook his head. He could tell that they were poking fun at each other. And though it was reminiscent of Albert and Jebadia, this was more pleasant. These two were not badmouthing anything he had done. He quietly ate his fish.

Kipp asked of Yace, "Are you gonna eat all that?"

She nodded and continued to eat the fish.

"Maybe I steal something sweet from home."

"Nope. You can't leave, remember?" She picked up another bite with her fingers. "We made the agreement with our elders." She placed the bite into her mouth. "We would not go home." She chewed and swallowed. "We would learn to live off the land, as we already know how, but by ourselves. We must be here, live together, and tolerate each other until they come to visit. Don't worry, they'll bring us more of Patrice's cooking." She turned to Irwin. "And then, after that, we'll be leaving."

Kipp's question sounded like a sour note. "When will this happen?"

"Tomorrow morning. Dana already knows Irwin is here."

Irwin puffed up his chest. "You are still assuming that I am willing to travel with you?"

"You told me that you liked to cook better than making up camp. Well, you have until tomorrow morning to decide."

"So, you're not coming with us?" Kipp looked at Irwin.

"Like I said, I have not agreed to anything."

The Clan-Duin studied Yace. "But you acted like he was coming."

"Details, details."

Kipp's nose flared; he stood.

Yace mimicked him.

"You can be so annoying," he said, staring at the barren frying pan. His attention then turned to the west. "Maybe I go steal us some bread rolls. I'm still hungry."

"What did I just say, Kipp? No! If anyone gets to steal anything, it will be Irwin."

Irwin raised his hands. "I am not a thief."

"Good answer, Irwin." Kipp smiled at him. "They'd smell you coming. Most likely, Olei is already trained on you. So, Irwin can't leave. It has to be me."

"None of us are leaving," Yace said. "Our elders stressed that we learn to be resourceful."

"I'm resourceful, unlike you," Kipp said. "Besides, I thought you were supposed to be working on lessening your control over others."

"I have been! I've been working on it."

"How so?"

"Well," she said, "By letting either of you go and get something sweet to eat from camp."

"What!" Kipp scoffed, "You just said I couldn't."

Irwin said, "I have some dried apple pieces. Not a lot, but I do not mind sharing." He hoped to quiet the bickerers.

"Thank you, Irwin," Yace blushed and smiled a flirty smile.

Once more, Kipp's eyes and ears were trained westward.

Yace watched him as he continued to look toward the forest, toward the Gypsy Camp.

"What is going on?" Irwin was even more curious.

"I feel Dinill angered … and Flinn too. They're probably fighting again." Kipp sighed and gazed back into the fire.

"You can feel them?" Irwin studied the Clan-Duin called Kipp.

Yace said, "The farther away from home we get, the less you will feel them. Remember? That's what Tamera said."

"Good! Because I am done with feeling them."

"Good to hear." Yace turned to Irwin. "It's kind of hard to explain the type of bond a Clan-Duin has with others. But yes, he can feel his family members' emotional states. He knows approximately where they are, but only if they're close by. And anyone he bonds with sexually; he has a special attachment to them too. He can feel them like a family member. Sometimes it's a stronger bond than with family. It's a good thing for animals to have that connection. It's what keeps them loyal."

"Oh." Irwin fell silent now, as did Yace and Kipp.

He enjoyed the quiet moments. Yace stood and carried the slightly burned pan and wooden spoon toward the soaking bucket near the river's edge.

Irwin heard her humming and clanking of dirty dishes.

He stirred the embers of the smoldering fire, stoking it back to life by adding a log and a few pieces of kindling. "Is this how every night is with you two?"

"Ever since we were sent away from the Gypsy, yeah. She does what she does, and I'm the sentry. My job is to keep us safe, to keep Yace safe."

"Is that what you want to do?"

"It's better than being with my family right now," Kipp said. "Frankly, I can't wait to be done with this."

"You have not even left yet, and you want to be done?"

"Oh, I want to leave, don't get me wrong. I just want to be done with the journey."

"Why is that?"

"When I'm done, I don't have to come back to the Gypsy. I can just go off and do whatever I want. Onj Raha might be the perfect place for someone like me. I have never enjoyed all the moving around; we have never been stationary. Seeing fresh sights is fun, but there are things that go wrong … all the time." Kipp paused. "But in Onj Raha … I could work for some rich person, or work on a fishing boat, or become a barterer in the markets, or join the PCP—not that I would join the PCP. There comes a time in every man's life when he must go off and prove something to himself."

Irwin nodded.

Sometimes we are proving ourselves worthy of this life.

The farther from the high mountain tops he traveled, the lighter he felt. He was beginning to appreciate himself and the world around him.

"What did Yace tell you over there in the forest?"

"She apologized for prying into my mind. Apparently, she knows she is not supposed to, but she did it anyway."

"She does a lot of stupid things for being as smart as she says she is. So, what made you leave the mining lifestyle, if I may ask?"

What should I tell him? The truth.

"My father deserted me."

"So, you didn't really leave. It's more like you were abandoned."

"Something like that."

"Why would your father desert you?"

I think I can trust him. More so than Yace. She already knows all of this anyway, I suppose.

"He said I was not his son." This was hard for Irwin to admit, to hear himself say it aloud. "I try not to be like my father. In fact, I do the opposite of him as much as possible." He shook as if the cold and snow had returned. Thinking about his father made him angry. "But there is no denying it. I am his son. I mean, I look and sound just like him. And sometimes anger is quick to find me. He uses his anger for evil purposes. I try to do the opposite."

"Did you do something to piss him off?"

"I have done a lot of things that irritated him. But refusing to mate with a Brothel Lady was the last straw. He said it would make me a man if I did. But I already think of myself as a man."

"Really, he did that? Over you not coupling with a woman? Was she ugly or something?"

"Saryh was far from ugly. I am just not ready."

Too much has happened to me that I need to heal before I can move on.

He did not want to reveal any more.

"What an asshole!"

"Yes, he is definitely an asshole."

"Couldn't you have continued mining?"

"I have been a miner my whole life, and I am only nineteen years old."

"So, you decided to do something else?"

Irwin nodded.

"Good for you."

"My goal is to find warmer weather and flatter ground." Irwin felt safe alone here with Kipp. "I have lived in the tops of mountains my whole life. It is a rough existence. I want something completely different now."

"I've always wondered what it would be like to live a stationary life. To have a house, not a wagon, and a big garden—a family. I'd go hunting with my boys every day." Kipp was gazing into the darkness again.

Irwin listened to his new friend daydream out loud.

"I want children, lots of them." He glanced at Irwin. "What's it like to do the opposite of what you're used to doing?"

"I like it. After being inside the same old dark mines, doing the same grimy chores day and night. Nothing ever changes, except the weather outside the mine."

"Where did you mine?"

"We lived upslope of Kobiton, about a day's trek. Two days west of Goshee."

"Dang! You went through those mountains all by yourself?"

Irwin pointed toward his donkeys, "I have Jenn Jenn and Nee Nee. They help me every day."

"They're donkeys! What good can they be?"

"Well, they keep the tent warm enough for all of us to survive the cold. They've packed hundreds of pounds of rations and gear through days of cold and snowy trail between towns. And they keep me company. Luckily so far, in every village there has been a warm hearth and a warm livery for my Jennies."

"Dang me! Takes a lot of coin to live that way."

"I am a miner."

"You have money? Don't tell Yace."

She had finished cleaning their dishes and was returning to the fire. "Don't tell me what?" Her eyes darted between the two men. "Oh, you have money! How much?"

Irwin shook his head in dismay at how these two worked together, and yet fought to be apart. "Enough to get by." Yace probably already knew some of it since she had tapped into his psyche.

She put the clean dishes down along the fireside. "See, there, I can clean dishes. And if Irwin decides to be our cook, I'll clean the dishes every night."

"We'll see about that." Kipp stood, stretched, and yawned. "Well, I guess this is good night."

"What? Wait? Really? Now you want to go to bed? The night is young, Kipp!"

He rolled his eyes at Yace. "And you want to get up how early and walk how far?"

The fair-haired woman in the shimmering lavender cape said nothing.

"That's what I thought. If you want me, I'll be asleep." Kipp pointed to his worn patch of ground where he must have slept the previous nights.

Irwin yawned and stretched too. It was time for bed and only Yace wanted to stay awake. He felt her eyes on him as he laid out his bedroll. He lay down and pulled a layer of woolen blankets over himself, then turned his back to the fire.

20

THE GYPSY

Irwin woke early. He emerged from his blanket roll and watched Kipp rise from his dusty bed. Sometime during the night, Kipp had apparently transformed into his wolf form, probably to keep warm. Shaking his body clean of clothing, a plume of dust wafted off Kipp's fur. As if in slow motion, the Clan-Duin shifted once more into his naked two-legged form and walked toward the firepit, still smoldering from the night before.

Kipp stoked the fire alive by tossing on a bundle of kindling. He then pushed the log they had been burning back across the rock-encircled firepit.

Not fully awake, Irwin retrieved a tin kettle from his packs. He filled it with water from the river and placed it at the fire's edge. At some point, the water would be warm enough to enjoy after his morning bath.

He rummaged among small pouches and large sacks, looking for a clean change of clothing. He found cleaning soaps, scrub brushes, and a soft drying cloth. He walked over to the river and watched the swiftly moving water float past. It was shallow right there, but a few steps out into the river and the ground became difficult to mark out.

Kipp, only a few steps behind, must have had the same plan. They stood together at the river's edge and the Clan-Duin said, "It's chilly, but once you get in it becomes tolerable."

Irwin glanced back at Yace's tent.

Kipp said, "Don't worry, she'll sleep until the sun is on her tent."

Irwin kept staring at the water. "You are washing up too?"

"I've got to! Yace said I stink."

"And you said I smelled like Death."

"At least I can wash off the wet dog smell. Changing that deathly smell to something more pleasant might take a lot of soap."

Irwin took out a small square bar of soap and placed it on the ground next to his scrub brush.

"You have any extra soap?"

"You do not have your own?"

Irwin would later discover that Kipp owned nothing more than the clothing he wore, a pair of boots, and the dark and thick wool cloak.

"Yace has all the smelly soaps, oils, and such. Most of it smells of lavender. I'd rather smell like nothing."

Irwin pulled out another square and gave it to Kipp. "That is yours. Keep it."

Kipp took the chunk of soap and jumped into the water. Although the river looked deep, it only came up to his knees near the bank. The water was frigid. Kipp meandered into the deeper, swifter water.

Irwin removed his clothing once piece at a time, not looking forward to the inevitable chill of the water. He pulled off and folded each piece neatly and put his dirty clothing into a bag. He picked up his bar of soap and scrub brush, but then stopped where the water met the bank.

The ore in me will freeze me.

There were several rocks, all different shapes and sizes, along the riverbank. Irwin leaned against one and after a bit, he figured out what to do. With his left hand on the rock, he shoved out all the metallic ore from inside his flesh and encapsulated that boulder with nearly eight pounds of mostly silver, with some gold, iron, copper, zinc, and a little cadmium. The giant rock shimmered in the rising morning sun.

Kipp asked, "What is that?" He took a step toward it.

Irwin stepped into the ice-cold rushing water and his flesh stung like a thousand bee stings. He groaned and gazed back at the shiny metal rock he had left behind. "That is my fortune."

The Clan-Duin moved closer to the glistening delight. "How did you do that?"

"I am a miner." He, too, was amazed by his own abilities at times.

"I get that you are a miner, Irwin, I just … I can't see how …? Dang me! You have an amazing Talent, Irwin … one of the rarities." Kipp stared at the sparkly rock. Then humbly, and Irwin felt loyally, Kipp said, "As long as you stay with us, I vow to keep you safe." His eyes sparkled like a golden nugget in the summer sun.

Abashed to hear such earnest words from a man he had only known one night, Irwin said, "Thank you, Kipp. But I do not need protection." He felt embarrassed for showing off. But, at the same time, he realized he would no longer be judged by this man.

They bathed together, scrubbing each other's backs with Irwin's stiff brush. Kipp no longer pressed for conversation, for information.

After their cold bath, back at the fire, Irwin's tin kettle was full of hot water. He poured them each a cup of hot water to drink, to warm them from the inside. Irwin then pulled out a clean hand cloth and dunked most of it in the nearly boiling water. He waited and then used it on his face, limbs, and torso.

Kipp followed suit, pressing the hot rag against his arms and legs. "I will remember this trick!"

"It is a wonderful thing to do on cold nights in the mountains. A bard showed me."

Kipp said, "You've gotta watch out for bards."

"Yes, I figured that out early on." Irwin retrieved clean clothing from his other bag. "Bernard the Bard was quite deceptive."

"Bernard the Bard, I feel like I've heard that name a few times. It is highly used, as well as Villard. That's funny. His name is probably Kevinn." Kipp crawled into Yace's tent and pulled out his own bag.

Irwin said, as if to himself, "He was definitely a dark specter."

Kipp and Irwin were cleaned, dressed, and fed by the time Yace emerged into the bright morning light. Yawning and stretching, scratching her braided hair, she stumbled toward the fire. "Why are you two up so early?"

"To bathe and eat," Kipp said.

"You're always hungry—" In the middle of her sentence she saw the shiny metallic rock at the river's edge. "What is that?"

Irwin followed her over to the rock, nervous he had left the metal-encased boulder. "My fortune."

She touched the coated stone—her hand glided across the metal. "How is this possible?"

It was confession time. He felt anxious to do so, but relieved at the same time. Irwin showed her how he did it.

He felt Kipp stepping closer to get a better view. Pointing his finger at the rock, Irwin did not have to make contact in order to extract the metal. All the burnished ore was then sucked into his flesh, floating through the tip of his finger, leaving the rough and weathered boulder behind.

Kipp and Yace stared at the rock, then at Irwin, then at each other.

The Clan-Duin and the Telepath stared at the Metalist.

He saw Kipp's attention shift toward the roadway, toward multiple people approaching, exiting the forest. They walked straight for the little meadow. He heard the Gypsies' voices as they entered their campsite.

Yace whispered, "Say nothing to no one about this, Kipp."

"Duh!"

The Gypsy had brought a saddled horse with ration-filled bags. A young girl broke free from the pack of four adults, shouting Kipp's name, running down the road toward them.

Kipp was the first to move away from the rock. He strode swiftly toward the road and his younger sister.

Yace called to Kipp, "Be careful with Flinn. She's emotionally weak right now."

Kipp raced to meet his sister, and there was a loving embrace. The young girl of perhaps twelve years looked much like Kipp. She had the same lovely bronze-brown skin, deep dark-brown eyes, and shadow-black hair. Kipp twirled Flinn around in the middle of the roadway, both giggling.

Yace took Irwin's hand. "Come on, let's go meet my mother." She pulled him away from the river and over to the roadway.

Three men of different generations of Gypsies strode alongside an older woman. Their look was as ornate as their vehicles—whimsical clothing in wild patterns and bright colors, tattoos, and body piercings. Yace leaned into Irwin's side, perhaps to comfort him. He tensed when he saw the two large and powerful Clan-Duins scrutinizing him with their dark eyes.

She introduced Irwin to each one. "This is Nonbry. That is Alio, and Hauss." The two Clan-Duins did not look alike. Irwin recognized the younger of the two as Kipp's older brother. Hauss looked identical to Kipp, except for his constantly furrowed brow and pursed lips.

Alio, the middle-aged Clan-Duin, walked beside an enormous, dark warhorse carrying ration bags stuffed full of provisions. The older Clan-Duin showed more confidence and was clearly less intimidated by Irwin than Hauss. His skin and eyes matched both flaxen. Alio's older and scrupulous eyes surveyed the camp and what Irwin had brought to it. He stopped short of the elders, Nonbry and Dana, as did Hauss. Alio studied Irwin. He appeared cautious of the miner, but more engaged than Hauss. The older Clan-Duin whiffed his scent.

"And this is my mother," Yace introduced, "Dana."

The older woman stepped up to Irwin. Her teeth shone brightly, as did her violet eyes. Her wrinkled hands revealed years of hard work—veins bulging and liver spots covering the creases. She wore a dark-green woolen shawl that was draped across her shoulders and head. She pulled it down, revealing wiry white hair. Irwin could feel her loving heart shining through those violet eyes as she smiled at him. Dana was a kind soul.

It seemed like a long time that she looked at him and into him. He tried not to notice Nonbry who appeared soured by something. The old man was comparable to her in age and wrinkles, but he was fully bald. Dana's icy hands pulled at Irwin's.

She spoke with a raspy voice, "You are a strong young man, Samuel Irwin Miner, a grounding post for those around you. You bring fortune without wealth to all that you meet. Your caution will be needed along the road. Their needs are as great as your own. You will keep them safe, my son. I foresee it." She leaned in close to Irwin, and he bowed. Dana then placed a soft kiss on his forehead.

He thought he felt something happen when her hands were on his, when her lips met his flesh. But he could not assess what had transpired. Once her hands let up their grip, the feeling was gone, as was his thought about it. Dana's focus went to Nonbry who was talking to Yace.

Nonbry's blue eyes were stern. He said nothing to Irwin, though his eyes held Irwin's gaze for longer than was comfortable. Then Nonbry regarded Yace who was still at Irwin's side. He passed to Yace a hand-carved talisman attached to a string. "I give you this charm for your journey. With this, you will have the ability to contact me anytime, though I prefer nighttime when we are done moving." Then he added, "Be sure Irwin does not touch it. His powers will ruin the spell." His words seemed to be more for Irwin than for Yace.

Nonbry kept addressing Yace. "Your father and I spoke last night. He stresses that you get to him as quick as possible. That's why we are allowing you to have Blacky, enough rations for a moon's time, and an adequate healing kit. Keep Blacky with you at all costs. He is a rarity on this side of the mountains—swift and surefooted, he will take you faster than feet alone." The old man glanced back at Alio, signaling him to bring forth the black-furred horse. "Be safe."

"Thank you Nonbry, we will." Yace turned to hug her mother. They embraced for a long time and pulled away with moist eyes. She looked at the middle-aged Clan-Duin as he brought the hearty steed forward. "Thank you, Alio. I guess we will see you all soon." She glanced at Hauss where he remained still, watching Kipp and Flinn reconnect.

Alio's gruff voice spoke to Yace, "This is the one who will keep you two safe?"

"Yeah, I trust him."

The older Clan-Duin's flaxen eyes were intent upon Irwin. "How can you trust him? How can you trust he won't poison you, or kill you in your sleep?"

Dana put her hand on Alio's shoulder. "Please be kind and trusting. He is one of the good ones, Alio."

The older Clan-Duin was adamant. "He doesn't smell right to me. He smells like rotten metal."

Irwin said nothing.

Yace scowled at Alio. "Don't worry, Irwin, I think you smell great. Besides, Alio has too keen a nose. And he's not a good judge of character."

"I'm a better judge than you ever have been, young lady."

Nonbry appeared ready to intercede.

With a deep sigh, Kipp dropped Flinn. He looked at Hauss and said, "Although I am going for a long walk with Yace, we will all see each other soon." He moved to embrace his older brother. The hug was rigid and Hauss maintained a defensive posture, not reciprocating the embrace.

Nonbry was firm. "It's time for you to depart."

Dana smiled at her aged counterpart. "So must we." She took up Nonbry's hand. "Be smart, Yace, my child. Keep her safe, Irwin, my new son. Watch over them both, Kipp, you are their guardian."

"Yes, Mam."

"I love you mama."

"I love you too, my sweet."

Hauss grunted at Kipp, nothing more. Flinn was the only one who held him tight and kissed him upon the cheek. "I consider you my brother and nothing else. Dinill is not my mother. Our mother died two moons ago. I am an orphan, just like you, Kipp. And if you'll have me, I'd love to go with you and Yace."

Hauss grumbled at her. "You can't go with them, Flinn. You're too young."

"Shut up Hauss! You're not my uncle, nor my father, you're my brother! And as such, I expect to be treated like your sibling and not some pathetic child you must look after. I can keep myself safe. I don't need your help."

Kipp said, "Flinn, I'm sorry, but you cannot come with me. You need to stay here with them. I need you to stay and keep Hauss and Dinill from killing one another."

"Ha!" Flinn was a lively one. "I can't stop them. I don't want to be their toy." She glowered at her brothers, then at her elders. "I know everyone means well, but I want to be with Kipp. Since you've been gone, Kipp, everything at camp is so boring. There's nothing to do. Why can't I come with you?"

"No," was the immediate response from all the adults. Flinn bounced up and down. "This bites!" She roared directly at Irwin.

He understood she was jealous that this unknown person was allowed to join in, but not her.

Flinn sneered at Irwin again, but then she turned away. Her hair flew around her head as she stormed off with Hauss a few steps behind.

After Flinn was a good distance away, Yace said, "She's feeling spicy today."

Kipp glared at Yace. "Don't start."

It was obvious Kipp was emotional about leaving his family behind. But this is what Yace wanted.

Kipp grumbled under his breath, just loud enough to be heard, "The sooner we go, the sooner we get back."

Irwin stood there, in the middle of the roadway, unsure how he had been convinced to go with these two. As far as he knew, he still had a choice. But the moment he thought about separating from Kipp and Yace, his thoughts shifted to breaking camp, readying himself for the journey. He did not know why, but he had to leave with them. And he did not know why he didn't come out and ask why Dana had referred to him as her new son.

21

<u>WHAT IS AN ERTHIN?</u>

I am doing alright by myself. I do not need help from others. Besides, why would they want me in their family? They do not even know me.

While he tried to make sense of what had transpired with Dana, again those thoughts disappeared with the wind. As if by rote, he went to his Jennies and began attaching the wooden frames and canvas panniers to their backs.

Yace stood back and watched Kipp tie up their cleaned dish bucket, with dishes tucked inside, to the back of the saddle; watched him retrieve his satchel of meager belongings and fix it behind the saddle too. Irwin then saw her dash into her tent. After a long time, she emerged with four oversized bags tight in her arms.

By this time, he and Kipp were done and waiting to go—waiting for Yace. She whined and appeared anxious, so he and Kipp took down her tent and packed it up. While they were busy, he could hear Yace arguing with her baggage, trying to secure it onto Blacky's saddle. She was short, and the horse was enormous. At last, she conceded to strapping her bags across the saddle and securing them to the stirrups. After everything was tied up, Yace took Blacky's lead rope and started down the road at a good pace. Irwin and Kipp hurried to keep up.

They traveled only a brief time before the forest fell away to terraced fields of immaculately cultivated crops. Channels had been dug throughout, allowing river water to flow through partitioned areas. Before they left the protection of the trees, Kipp shifted out of his clothes and transformed into his canine form. This time he became a short-haired, brown dog. Kipp kept to Irwin's side as they followed Yace. She let up on her pace as they walked through the riverside plantation. It looked like a small farming village with all the outbuildings, but Yace informed Irwin it was not.

"This is one of those places where, if you go in for one night, you might never leave. They take people like us, those with Talents, and zap our minds. And then they tap into our physical potential until we are dead. Mortals are more likely to be allowed to leave than people like us." They passed by the main building, three stories tall and in the shape of a T.

Children were scurrying around the building, adults were out in the fields harvesting produce, planting more. Down by the river, a small paddle barge held crates of harvest.

"Why is that?"

"Mortals are seen as less-than, not worth the price of a Clan-Duin, or Erthin, or another Telepath. A powerful Telepath knows how to use their power to corrupt." She shrugged. "Not all plantations are like that, though. This might be one of the better ones. It's hard to know the good from bad until you're knees deep in melons."

They continued to pass people, buildings, and animals.

Irwin knew they were being watched.

Yace picked up her stride again after they had passed all the plantation people. She was in a hurry. And if Irwin's donkeys were more than willing, he could have kept to her side. As it was, by the time she stopped to water Blacky near midday, Irwin was at least a kilometer behind.

Kipp waited for Irwin in the shadows of the forest next to the creek crossing. Meanwhile, Yace resumed her grueling pace, probably guessing, or knowing, they would meet her at the next camping spot.

Tired and angered that his donkeys were behaving so stubbornly, Irwin found a place to sit and take a rest. Kipp approached and stared at both Jennies.

The Clan-Duin said nothing, but after a while of locked eyes, Kipp had both animals' attention, and had no problem getting the stubborn donkeys to follow. They walked through the shallow stream and out the other side. Kipp called for Irwin to keep up.

After that, the donkeys made a good pace; rivaling the stride Kipp had set to catch up with Yace's hard tempo. "She seems adamant about a forty days' walk," the Clan-Duin commented. "If she were to ride, Yace could probably get there in that amount of time. But that means you would ride too; and I'm not sure these girls are up for it."

"Thank you for sparking them to go faster." Irwin said, walking along with Kipp.

"If it's any consolation, they preferred the miner's life to this one. They told me they miss standing around all day ... that, and the companionship of the rest of their herd."

Secretly, Irwin did too. They all were used to a more sedate lifestyle—one of the reasons he felt the need to keep moving. "I could tell they were depressed about the Jacks' absence." He did not like thinking about his past or talking about it. They walked along for a few more feet, and Irwin felt the nerve to pry. "After all the conversations with you two yesterday, I have a few questions."

"Like what?"

"What is an Erthin?"

"You don't know?"

"I did not know what a Clan-Duin was until last night."

"Okay. Well, there are five powers Erthins can have, but usually you'll only meet one with one power, or two. They can use fire, or water, or both."

"What do you mean use?" Irwin asked, "Like shoot fire balls from their hands?"

"Yeah; exactly."

"Okay, I have met one of them. How can they use water?"

"Harness water, like the river. They could make it smash you, suck you into the water, drown you. Or if you're swallowing a drink, they can make it flush into your lungs, drowning you. Or they can make it rain torrents upon you, causing a flash flood, killing you. Or if you're in a—"

"Alright, I think I get it. Those who harness water are the ones to fear."

"The ones who harness fire are the ones to fear. They can ignite you, externally or internally."

Irwin stared at Kipp, startled by this new revelation.

"Then there are ones who can harness air."

Shit. Where have I found myself?

"Let me guess, they can steal your breath."

"Or cause a windstorm. They can use air to knock you off your feet or overturn your wagon."

"Good to know. Any others?"

"Then there are the ones who harness the earth. They can make the ground eat you whole, or rocks roll across you, or trees smash you."

They walked on and after a while, Irwin asked, "Yace mentioned Tamera was an Erthin healer. That she could give life and—"

"She can take it away, yeah! Healers are not ones to mess with either."

"Any other types of Erthins I should know about?"

Kipp counted on his hand, "Fire, water, air, earth, spirit. Yup, that's all."

"They all sound deadly."

"Yeah! You don't want to mess with a redhead."

"Redhead?"

"All Erthins, well, the ones I've met, though some have darker, reddish-brown hair. And their skin can vary from an olive green-brown to pale, like yours. I guess there could be a blonde Erthin, but that would be a rare find."

The women at the summit were Erthins then. How interesting. It explains why the house was always so warm even though the fires were low.

They walked on a while longer before Irwin asked, "How is it that Yace even knows about her father?"

"Nonbry knew him."

Slightly confused by the knowledge that Nonbry knew of Yace's father, Irwin probed further, "So they telepathically communicated with one another, and he invited Yace to come and live with him?"

"Something like that, yeah."

They walked along in silence again.

Irwin appreciated how candid Kipp could be. "What would you do if you were free to do what you want?"

"You mean what am I good at?"

"Sure, I guess. Well, what I mean is, do you know how to make money? A trade like wood cutting, making ceramic wear, or rope making, or ...."

"I can pickpocket. I'm good at slighting hands and eyes. And I've been working on card games, getting better at deciphering people's ticks."

That is not really being a productive member of society.

"Sounds like you are a thief."

"Hey, for me, it's either canine fur or servant garb. I can work as cheap labor, doing gritty jobs, work for rich Telepaths who corrupt minds, or the PCP. Those are my options. Or be a canine. Either way, my people aren't easily accepted. Most see Clan-Duins as a threat, or a nuisance. That is, unless we're wearing the right clothing."

Interesting philosophy.

"So, you would rather be seen as a dog? Is that why you changed before we walked through the plantation?"

Kipp nodded. "Not every dog you see is a mutant. But every mutant is a dog, in one way or another." He chuckled. "Now I'm sounding like Yace. Dang me. I've spent too much time with her already."

"But what if you did not have to be like that? What if you could do what you really wanted? What would that be?"

"I don't know." Kipp took a few more steps. "I'm not really good at any type of work. I mean, I can be taught to work, but I don't know what I'm doing until I do it."

"Did your elders teach you anything of use? Any way to work and live with society?"

"I can hunt."

Another stretch of silence ensued. "At least you will be well fed." The forest was shaded from the sporadic sun. "Does this mean that every wolf I have ever seen was a Clan-Duin?"

"No. Not all."

"What is the difference then?"

"If I took on my animal form and not shed it, ever, I would become it. Whatever that form is, bird, dog, cat. Clan-Duins know not to keep their animal forms indefinitely." Kipp said, staring up at the blue sky. "It weakens the mind if we do. We become more animalistic with our impulses and forget our human selves."

They strode through the rich green forest. "Yace explained that there are other types of Clan-Duins. Wolfs, wild cats, birds, and air-breathing water animals ...."

Kipp shook his head. He used his fingers again to count the diverse types of Clan-Duin species. "Well, there's canine, which means anything dog-related, from small harbor dogs to wolves. Felines can be anything cat-related, and cats can be big and small, and all different colors. Raptors are anything that flies, and I mean anything. So that sparrow could be a Clan-Duin. Or that woodpecker." He pointed at the birds in the trees above. "And there are several others—bear and monkey, oh, and dolphins, which are the water-dwelling air breathers. Basically, anything that is considered a predator ... can be ... could be Clan-Duin."

"Then why did you say that every mutant is a dog?"

Kipp slapped the side of his face.

Was he frustrated at having to explain this?

"Some mutants are downright assholes, no matter what type they are, Erthin, Clan-Duin, Telepath .... I used the word dog as another word for asshole."

"So, you are an asshole?"

"Yace tells me I am some of the time. Other times she thinks I'm cute. I try not to take anything she says seriously."

They continued down the roadway until evening light diminished behind them. Yace had found the next camping spot and was trying to set up her tent, but she was struggling. It lay in a heap on the ground. The fire smoldered because she had tried to burn wet wood. Only a small section of one branch crackled and burned. Yace did not seem to care. She sat there happily eating rations from one of the bags when Irwin and Kipp entered the campground.

"Tomorrow we are tying them onto Blacky." Kipp summoned the donkeys and tethered them next to Blacky. He did not take off their packs or give them any food. Instead, he went to Yace who handed over a pouch of dried venison.

Irwin could not help but take care of his animals before tending to his own needs. He fed them grain before he joined Kipp and Yace.

She passed a flask, and a pouch of little sweet rolls Patrice had made.

"Tomorrow, we will go faster than we did today," she said.

Kipp chewed and spoke. "That's why we need to tie Irwin's donkeys onto Blacky." Food fell through his teeth and spit off his lips.

"That's so gross Kipp. Please finish your bites before talking," Yace sneered at him. "But yeah, you're correct. And when you're done eating, I need you to set up my tent."

Irwin thought she was talking to him. She had been looking right at him as she spoke to the Clan-Duin.

Kipp was not looking at Yace when he said, "You'll have to learn how to do it on your own sometime." He caught her startled eyes glaring at him. "Maybe now is the time."

"Kipp! Come on, you can't do that to me."

The Clan-Duin said nothing, but the smug look on his face said it all.

It was obvious to Irwin that Kipp was thinking, *I can and I will*. He watched as he took another piece of venison and stuffed it whole into his mouth, not about to budge from his seat or his meal.

"I do not mind helping you, Yace." Irwin said and immediately felt Kipp's eyes on him. He looked at the man at his side, then into the smoldering fire.

Yace said, "Thank you Irwin."

Here he was again, caught between Yace and Kipp. Only the meager fire separated them. Kipp was glaring at him. Yace had a smug grin. He imagined Flinn in a similar situation, pegged between older siblings. He smiled at them and then focused on his food.

Night was setting in and he listened to crickets and a chorus of frogs, hoping for a few minutes of peace while he ate.

Kipp had found more pouches and was pulling out dried fish and fruits. Patrice had sent along more than enough meals for everyone. Potatoes, carrots, beets, ginger roots, and who knew what else were organized and labeled in bags. There were nuts, all different types, dried and bagged, a multitude of spices, and butter! Kipp tried some dried fish and handed some to Irwin. They ate well from the rations stockpiled for hungry travelers.

"Let me help you with your tent, Yace," Irwin encouraged after the meal.

Kipp went about stoking the fire, and Irwin did the best he could to keep Yace focused on helping him with the tent. But after holding the posts for a brief time, she became 'tired'. She returned to the growing fire's edge and sat down, watching Kipp and Irwin work from her stone seat. Irwin kept on trying to engage her by explaining how to put the pieces together and pull the canvas over, but her attention had drifted elsewhere. Pulling items out of her bag, she proceeded to brush her long, white hair.

Kipp tended to the animals once the fire was roaring. He removed their tack and took them all to the river's edge for a drink. After that, it was free time for foraging. He took a stiff brush to groom their herd while they grazed.

Once done with Yace's tent, Irwin took a moment to rest by the fire. He watched Kipp going about his duties and smiled to himself. It was nice to see someone else caring for his Jennies in the same manner as he would.

Yace broke him from his reverie. "What about your tent, Irwin?"

Clouds had mottled the evening sky. Now that it was night, not one star could be seen.

"It's going to rain soon, Irwin."

Kipp sniffed the air as he brushed the donkeys and nodded in agreement. The Clan-Duin did not look up from grooming, until Yace added, "Of course, you can always sleep with me."

Irwin saw Kipp's head rotate like an owl's—those brown eyes looked to him for a reaction. "Thank you for your offer, Yace. There is more than enough room in your tent for all of us, and the Jennies too." Irwin felt Kipp staring at him.

Yace's smile widened. "The donkeys and horse sleep outside. And Kipp doesn't like to sleep inside tents. So, it would just be you and me."

Kipp sounded bitter. "I do like having cover from a storm. But if I remember correctly, you said that I'm a dog, and that dogs sleep outside."

"You're our guardian, Kipp. Guard us." She looked at Irwin who saw her angry glare change to a kind smile. "You are more than welcome to share my bed, Irwin."

Now he realized what Yace was insinuating. "I think I will sleep in my own tent," he said, and then felt the first drop of rain hit his head.

Her smile faded. "Fine." She retrieved her overstuffed belongings and tossed the bundles into her tent. Then she took a small lantern tethered to the saddle, stopping at the fire to light the lantern. Without another word, Yace went into her tent.

Irwin sensed Kipp's relief as he watched him dig his tent from the pannier baggage. He wanted to be quick about erecting it before the onslaught began, but it was already drizzling.

The Clan-Duin helped him finish pitching his large canvas tent. With a forlorn look, Kipp peered from inside the open doorway of Irwin's tent to the smoldering fire.

"You can sleep in my tent, Kipp." And without another word, the Clan-Duin began removing his clothing. Kipp placed his pants, tunic, and cloak in a pile next to the open door.

"Thanks, but no," Kipp said. "It's better for everyone if I'm out here listening to and watching the forest." He mutated into his canine form and stepped into the downpour.

22

Jo Hara

Darkness passed and morning light began to shine, but the rain never relented. Their cold morning meals were consumed in haste. They did not sit around hoping the rain would stop, and though it was coming in sideways, the two men followed Yace's lead. She seemed even more determined now.

The next two nights were much like the first, full of rain. At night, Yace did most of the talking, reminiscing, and complaining. Kipp sat next to the fire, tending to it and his sentry duty. There were small conversations between Irwin and Yace that did not amount to much. Yace encouraged him to speak, but like Kipp, only if he had something to say that mattered would he talk. The interactions were enjoyable for Irwin; this was what he had wanted in his journey—a bit more companionship than his donkeys offered. It was reminiscent of the summit lodge where everyone was kind and supportive and enjoying each other. Nothing was too uncomfortable for Irwin to handle.

Is this how most people live? These two, unlike Bernard the Bard, do not hide anything.

Yace and Kipp were open about their thoughts and feelings, and foolish to a point, making his time with them enjoyable.

On the fourth night, they came across several large plantations spanning long across the low-sloping, well-farmed land. By the looks of the landscape, they were closing in on the city of Jo Hara, but the lack of light forced them to stop. The unrelenting rain had slowed their pace and their timing for arrival at Jo Hara. That seemed to unnerve Yace to no end. She admitted that she knew they could not continue into the dark and stormy night. But she wanted to. It was raining hard. There were plantations and outbuildings everywhere. But Yace drove them on into the darkness before finding a good place to sleep.

They camped away from prying eyes in a large orchard. It offered shelter from the rain and wind. Plum, cherry, apple, and pear trees grew in the well-kept grove.

Leaves were sprouting, and most of the branches were bearing fruit buds. The smell was pleasing, and the sight was beautiful to wake up to.

When morning came, and they were amply fed, Yace set in motion her quick pace. "We will stay in Jo Hara tonight." She announced as they started out.

She told Irwin to walk by her side with the large war horse and donkeys in tow. Kipp stayed close by in his brown canine form, loping across the landscape, following the smells like the wild creature he was. At some point, she said to Irwin, "There are a few things we need to buy before going any further east. I want you to wear tailored clothing from now on. As for Kipp, he needs an updated PCP uniform."

"Tailored clothing? Why do I need tailored clothing?"

She slowed her pace. "For a miner, you dress better than most. But you don't look like a wealthy traveler, like I do. You look like a hermit, or a wannabe mountain PCP without the large warhorse. Well, we have the large warhorse, but ... anyway. Your dark clothes might draw undue attention."

"Why are you so worried about what I wear?"

"Have you ever met any PCP?"

Irwin nodded. "Yes, but what does that have to do with—"

"Do you know what PCP are?"

"Men who enforce Hakra's laws." They exchanged looks. "Enlighten me."

"PCP are Population Control Patrol."

"I thought they were called Planetary Constable Patrol," he said, "peacekeepers of all."

"That is true, but their primary responsibility is to keep people, Mortals really, *safe*. They're here to make sure everyone in every land on Urthis is following the rules ordained by Hakra. The rules are relatively simple. You probably know them even if they were not preached to you: don't steal, don't harass, don't kill, be kind. If you are Mortal, you have more freedoms. But if you are Talented, like Kipp, you're not allowed to be free."

"What do you mean?"

"Most of those with Talents are servants—not to say that some aren't soldiers—and they all work for the PCP, in some capacity. It's not a choice you get to make when you have Talents. Unless you are destined for something else. Most Telepaths are.

"The men and women chosen to be PCP soldiers, or guards, or servants, or whatever you want to call them ... are the true seers of everything. They are usually linked to at least one Telepath. They can be anywhere and everywhere, all at the same time. You might see one walking down the road in front of you, and not even know they work for the town's Telepath."

"Kipp hinted at that."

"They're considered the eyes and ears of Telepaths who have leadership positions. There are a lot of eyes and ears out there, and just as many Telepaths, most of which are under the rule of Hakra. They are loyal servants. That's how he becomes the overseer of so many things. He's got people in nearly every community blasting their telepathy, corrupting minds. It's twisted how he uses those of us with Talents."

How much of this I should believe?

Not wanting to argue with her, Irwin changed the subject. "What type of clothing do you think I should wear?"

"Well, I would like to get you some better shirts and pants—maybe a new belt, boots, and hat, and a jacket, or vest perhaps. We'll also need to get you a PCP uniform. I need you to look the part if the need arises."

"Why do I need a uniform?"

"Because of your smell; those Clan-Duins who are in service to the PCP and noblemen alike, will smell you coming. They will know something is off about you. And any Telepath within mind-reading vicinity will realize that they cannot read your mind. If they cannot read your mind, then they will want to know why. They'll want to interrogate you, or worse; if you do not look the part, Irwin, they'll pick you out and eat you up."

"What if I tell them I am a miner?"

"All the more reason you need to wear either rich-appearing clothing or a uniform. If any of them were to know exactly what it is you do, they would want you for their own. Your power." Her eyes dilated slightly as she explained. "What you do is very special, Irwin. If others knew about you ... as it is, I must forget everything I've seen you do. If a Telepath were to probe my mind, I can't let them see my thoughts about you. It's best you look the part as either a rich telepathic-type man, or PCP. You know, be inconspicuous."

"But if I look PCP, I will get the same amount of scrutiny."

"If you look PCP and are escorting a young lady such as myself, you're less likely to be approached." She winked at him. "It makes you look like you have a job, a mission. You've been entrusted to take me somewhere, deliver me to someone. And if you dress like a rich man, and are with me, then we are just a young couple traveling together. People will not question us. Maybe we just got married and are touring the countryside. Or maybe we are moving to a big city or going to visit family. I mean, have you seen all my baggage?"

She is overreacting. Clothing does not make the man. It seems Yace enjoys drama and pretending a little too much.

He looked ahead to the shadowy road, wanting to ignore her.

But she kept on. "We should also think about selling your Jennies and trading them for faster horses. I don't think we'll get war horses out of the deal. You must prove that you are PCP to get one of those beasts."

"I will not sell my Jennies."

"They are slow and stubborn ... really, really slow. I didn't know animals could walk that slow! Except for turtles, maybe. They will hold us back. They *are* holding us back!"

"I am not selling them." He glared at her. "Besides, since Kipp had his talk with them, they have been walking faster."

"Not fast enough."

"I really do not understand why you are in such a hurry?"

"My father's dying! Alright? I need to get to him as fast as I can. I thought I told you that." Spit flew from her mouth; anger wrinkled her forehead.

"How do you know he is dying?"

"Nonbry has been in communication with him. Many, many years ago, Nonbry knew my father. They traveled together when they were young and never lost touch. And then I came along. Nonbry didn't know I was related to him until recently. That was when I began hearing voices—other people's thoughts—and could not turn them off. Neither Nonbry nor Dana could help me. They're not like me. They are Telepaths and I am Coterie. When they figured that out, Nonbry called out to my father. And, well, long story short, we are heading to see him."

Irwin waited for more.

"I'm a little messed up in the head right now. Nonbry told me I need someone who is Coterie, family, to help me understand ... to help me unlock my potential, as he put it."

"Do you believe your father will be able to help you?"

She shrugged. "I must. My mother is presumed dead, and I don't know to what extent her powers were, so she can't help. If I am to have any peace, I need someone of comparable or greater power to help me. Neither Dana nor Nonbry can fathom my powers. They don't know what my true potential could be. But they say I will be strong. I can feel myself growing more powerful every day, but what am I to do? How can I control, stay in control of myself? It's so hard to ...." she trailed off and picked up her stride again.

Irwin watched her walk ahead of him. He did not press the issue, though he had more questions. He was thankful to have Blacky's help to pull Jenn Jenn and Nee Nee along to help him keep up with Yace.

By midmorning, they found the edge of the urban sprawl that encompassed the city of Jo Hara. It took them until mid-afternoon to make it to the other side of the large city. During their long walk through the bustling streets, Yace held close to Irwin, and so did Kipp. They ventured into the open markets to purchase more grain for his Jennies and some extra provisions. It was there that he spotted the kind of clothing Yace had talked about.

She came up behind him and scoffed at the soft tunic he was looking at. "Rich men don't wear things with patterns or whimsical sleeves like that."

"I was just looking at it." They shuffled down the aisle of the clothing market. "I have a few fancy pieces of clothing I can show you tonight. I do not need any new clothes, Yace. I also have boots I have not worn yet. They are nice and clean." He ran his fingers through his thick hair. "I have a well-conditioned canvas jacket that is the same color as the boots. Oh, and I also have a woolen vest that looks nice with my red button-up shirt."

Yace seemed preoccupied. "Sure, alright, whatever."

They perused a few more storefronts but found nothing of interest. The three of them continued on down one of the city streets, trying to find an Inn.

"Are you alright, Yace?" Irwin asked, noticing her twitch and fidget—those blue eyes of hers darted around.

She stopped and looked back at the way they had come. "I'm fine." She smacked her lips and on she went.

Irwin hung half a stride behind. Yace was swift and decisive. He could feel her listening to people's thoughts. She paused again, peering around as though someone was after her or something inhabiting her. Irwin also felt the call of metal. He had to ignore all those songs and the urge to release the precious ore from its positions. He could feel it moving all around him, at various speeds, or standing idle while sweetly singing at him. The rush of sounds and feelings unnerved him.

They were near the eastern edge of the city when they came upon a sleepy little Inn. Though they were still close to the stores, there was a park nearby and very few people were around. It appeared to be a quiet place, and there was not much metal or locals on the move.

As requested, Irwin purchased one large room to share with Yace. "We should appear as a couple traveling together. Or else people will question our relation-ship." Apparently, all this pretending did not bother Yace, but Irwin was wary of any ill intentions she might show toward him later that night.

He asked for a bath for himself to be drawn immediately. But Yace declined a bath.

"I still need to purchase a few things."

"Do you want me to come with you?"

"No, I'm fine. Stay here with Kipp and get things done. I'll be back soon." She left him to pay for it all. She did not stay around to help him with the animals or their baggage; instead, she set out by herself to find Kipp some PCP clothing.

There were two stalls at the Inn's stable for Blacky and the Jennies. The animals were fed, watered, and allowed idle time. Kipp was given a place to rest for the night, outside those stalls. Irwin noticed the tired canine lay down on a spread of hay meant for the donkeys to eat later. He watched his friend from the corner of his eye and felt the Clan-Duin perk up, watching him unpacking the animals. This would have been Kipp's job had he not lucked out and been given canine status. A smile drew upon the dog's wet mouth.

Irwin saw the expression for what it was, and he joked with Kipp. "You think this is funny?" The brown dog nodded, and Irwin laughed. "I hope she remedies this situation. I prefer to talk to you in your two-legged form." They were alone in the barn, except for a few other animals confined to their stalls and hay piles. "When you are up on two legs, I will buy you a meal. How about that? Anything other than fish or dried venison. Perhaps a whole chicken or a roasted goat's leg?"

Kipp barked in agreement, startling Irwin with the outburst. "Or maybe meat pie!" Kipp barked again. "How about an ale? You want one of those?"

The Clan-Duin barked twice. Irwin laughed at their peculiar conversation. And then Kipp sounded like he was heaving up a hairball, losing his mutation.

"And a saloon!" It was obvious Kipp was happy. He seemed glad to have a moment away from Yace's constant prying.

Yet, as if slapped across the face, Kipp gave Irwin a fearful look. "Dang me. Yace shouldn't have gone shopping by herself, Irwin. You need to go after her."

"Why?"

"She's used to the Gypsy, not the city of Jo Hara. It might get overwhelming out there for her."

"She told me she was fine."

"And you believed her?"

Irwin nodded. "She told me to stay here with you, that she will be back soon." He then began to think about Yace's reactions and her off-the-subject outbursts while walking through Jo Hara. He remembered how close to him she had been once they were in the heart of the city, especially in the markets. At one point she had touched him, but he had glared at her, and she backed off. Had she been altruistic and he ignorant? He realized she needed his help back then. Although she acted tough, Yace did need protection from the mental in-pouring of voices and information.

Kipp's eyes and ears were focused on something outside the barn. Immediately, he shapeshifted.

A young woman stepped inside carrying linens. She stared at Irwin as he turned around, knowing someone was there.

Kipp remained intent upon her with his puppy-dog eyes and smile.

She gleamed at the canine and then looked at Irwin. Appearing jovial, she asked, "Is that who you were talking to?"

"Yes."

"The bath you requested is ready any time you are, Sir," she said. She must have noticed he was still unpacking the animals. "Oh, I can get my brothers to come and help you if you wish. They're doing nothing but playing cards."

Irwin said, "Do not worry about this, I am almost done. Most of it can stay here." He pointed toward the bags with his eyes. "Only those need to be taken to the room, and I can do that."

"Are you sure? My brothers are incredibly lazy and are doing nothing. Please, let me offer our services." She smiled at Irwin and leaned into him. "And if there's anything else you need," she winked, "I am at your service. My name is Coralin." Her brown hair and eyes matched, as did her face full of freckles. She was no older than fourteen and appeared used to getting friendly with male customers.

Irwin heard Kipp whining. He glanced over his shoulder at his canine comrade, realizing that the dog wanted her attention also. "This is my dog, Kipp, and I am Irwin."

The Clan-Duin barked. Not knowing if he had said something wrong, Irwin corrected himself. "I mean, I am Kipp, and he is Irwin. I am sorry. I am tired." He said and looked back at Kipp.

I hope I am saying the right thing.

Coralin was blushing as she tried to help correct him. "Lady Yace called you Irwin Samuel."

Trying to brush off his insecure moment, Irwin said, "Yes, I will take your brother's help. And thank you for letting me know about the bath. I will be right in." He looked over at Kipp again.

"Alright!" she said, "I will let them know. See you inside, Mister Irwin." Coralin called back and then waved, "Bye-bye puppy Kipp."

Kipp waited only a moment after she left the barn before transforming back into his two-legged self. He slapped Irwin on his shoulder. "Dang me. She's something to be watched out for. Reminds me of Yace. Don't get too close to that young thing, Irwin, unless you want her to sink her teeth into you."

"She is not Clan-Duin, is she?"

"No. She's Mortal."

Irwin wondered what Kipp knew, that he did not.

"And she likes you."

The Clan-Duin helped Irwin get everything ready to be hauled upstairs. Then he mutated back into his canine form and waited for Coralin's brothers.

23

CORALIN

After Irwin was done with his hot bath, he found his room and the comfortable bed. His bags were artfully arranged along the wall next to the door. He did not bother retrieving any clean clothing. The only thing he wanted now was to sleep on that bed. He curled up in the blanket and fell into a deep slumber.

Sometime later, Yace came into the room and plugged up his nose. "You were snoring."

He sat up, not fully awake, and she threw a uniform and a pair of fancy pants onto the bed. He noticed that the uniform matched Kipp's new attire. She had bought three sets of dark indigo pants, very basic, with black stitching. All pairs of PCP pants and tunics matched and appeared to be form-fitting. The fancy pants had red stitching along the cuffs and seams. She insisted he try them on to see how they fit.

He obeyed, and they were a little large for him.

"That looks good, sort of," Yace said. "You'll grow into them, hopefully."

"Hopefully." He agreed and took off the new pants. "How are you doing, Yace? Are you still hearing thoughts everywhere?"

She ignored him. "Hey, wait, leave those on Irwin! They look good on you."

"What do you mean? I do not have to wear this now, do I?" He folded them and placed them on the edge of the bed.

"Well, no, you don't. I was just hoping you would. They look good on you."

He did not enjoy feeling Yace gazing lustfully at his body. He retrieved the red blouse and a well-worn pair of hemp pants and began to dress.

"Oh, no! Please don't wear that."

He didn't know what was causing Yace's hysterics this time, but he wanted the honest truth. "Is it the pants? Because I think those other pants, as large as they are, would look better with this top."

"Yeah, they would, you're right. Put them back on," she said, still watching him change. "Alright, if you do that, then you need to wear those things you wore a few days back."

"Which things?"

"Those calf chap thingies, and your boots. They match nicely and would go well with my belt; it's the same color. You shouldn't need your new boots if we shine up your old ones." She reached for his boots, retrieved a rag from a small pouch, and began cleaning the boots.

It took her no time to spit-shine the brown leather boots while he was fishing his calf-chaps from his packs. They doctored his clothing by hiding the bottom hem of his pants inside the calf-chaps. The top of his pants ballooned out from the calf-chaps, making his legs go from slender to fat, then tapering up at his waist.

"Tuck in the red blouse." She pulled out a large brown leather belt. They agreed that would tie Irwin's outfit together. It also made Yace laugh aloud.

"What's the matter? Should I not wear the belt?"

"No, the belt makes it look great. I just never thought ... I mean, where did you ... where did you get that lady's blouse?" She could not hold back her hilarity. "It's so bright! But those pants and ... well, it is you, Irwin. That is definitely your look."

He looked down at himself. He was trying to understand. "What do you mean?"

"It fits you. Kipp could never pull off something like this. He's too ... furry."

He bowed at Yace's. "Well, thank you."

"Good, now go take these to Kipp, and tell him to meet us at the bakery. He'll know where it is."

"Bakery?"

"He'll smell it."

"Oh, right!" Irwin took the bundle of soldier's clothing and hurried out of the room. Descending the stairs from their third-floor shared bedroom, he was certain he was seen only by Coralin as he exited the building. She had been feeding Kipp leftover pieces of uncooked chicken, mostly giblets and pieces of fat and skin. The Clan-Duin was taking the food and doing tricks for each bite, his tail wagging.

Coralin had changed clothing. Her soft blue dress fit her body too well, pushing her chest up towards her neck. Her breasts heaved every time she opened her mouth. "Oh, Mister Irwin, Sir, your dog, Kipp, is it? He's quite a trickster."

"I need to go see the animals, make sure they are good for the night," Irwin said and stumbled around Coralin, pressing the package of clothing behind him, then up his shirt. He saw Kipp glancing up the young girl's dress as she held it up by the hem and stepped back, making room for Irwin to descend the steps.

"I made sure my brothers took all your belongings up to your room, and I organized them a bit by size and weight." Her bright brown eyes and keen smile meant something, but Irwin wasn't quite sure what.

"Can I come to the barn with you?" She said, and without an answer moved to join him. "All your animals appeared well-watered and well-fed a while ago when I went to see them."

Whining insistently, Kipp was trying to keep Coralin's attention, trying to allow Irwin a moment of time to shuffle into the barn with the clothing.

She jumped back and began engaging the canine again. "Oh, that's right, huh Kipp? You want more treats?" She gazed up at Irwin. "Your dog is amazing."

It was plain that this Coralin wanted Irwin's attention, but Kipp was the only willing participant. "He can sit, and lay, and he rolled over and barked on command. He is full of tricks. He is very smart for a dog. You have taught him well, Mister Irwin, Sir."

"Yes, he is smart."

She coerced the animal by bending over and allowing her cleavage to spill forth, all the while clapping her hands and shouting, "Come Kipp, come!"

Kipp jumped up and darted around like a playful dog. He bounded ahead of them into the shadows of the barn; then he darted out, and back again. Coralin hooked Irwin's arm with her own and pulled him along. "How long have you and your female friend been together?"

Startled by the question, Irwin hesitated. "Yace? I have known her for a while."

They stepped inside the barn; it was dark. Coralin leaned in close, her breath warm on his neck. "How long is a while?" He tried not to freeze. "I don't mean to question your passions. I noticed you allowed her to go off by herself. She said you two were traveling together, not that you were a couple.

"Most men escort their women. But you just let her go." She continued to press into him. "Most of the people who stay here are old. And I am young. And my sister left with the last young man who came through here. And your woman friend doesn't seem really interested in you. I saw her bossing you around. Are she and you meant to be together, I mean, forever?"

He was abashed that this young woman was so bold.

"No man dresses this way without wanting some sort of attention. And I don't think your woman friend is anything other than a friend." Coralin then quieted her voice and added, "But I can be so much more for you. I'll let you boss me around. I'll do whatever you want me to do, Mister Irwin, Sir." She then laid a hard kiss on his cheek.

Kipp barked when Irwin pushed Coralin back.

"Am I not pretty? Is my dress ugly? Am I unworthy of your affection? Look at you, Mister Irwin, Sir. You are so handsome tonight." She licked her lips and pressed forward. "And it would be a shame if your female friend did not see that. I see you want attention. And I'm here ready to give it to you if she won't." She studied him longingly. "You would not wear such bright clothing if you were already courting or married to that woman."

Coralin didn't back down. "You wouldn't have to pay much to keep me. I don't eat a lot. I would clean your clothing and cook for you too. You could speak to me as you want. I will not berate you; I will not bully you, unlike your friend."

Kipp laughed by barking again, though this startled Coralin. She rushed to his side. "Oh no! Your dog … he's choking!"

"No. Kipp is not choking. He is laughing."

"Laughing? He laughs?"

"He is a funny dog."

"I guess so." She might have been only fourteen, but clearly, Coralin wanted to be older, was trying to act older. Again, she tried to kiss him.

And again, he pushed her away.

She looked down at her hands. "Tell me I'm ugly and I will leave you be. But I'm willing to do anything asked, and not give lip back, unless you like my lips." Her smile was desperate. "They enjoy pleasing men."

Irwin knew he had to diffuse this. "You are a little young for me."

"I'm nearly fifteen and am suitable as any other female. Do I not have large breasts? Do I not smell to your liking? I will meet all your needs and expectations."

"You are pretty. And your smell is very pleasant."

Coralin's smile rose slightly. "And my breasts?"

Irwin looked at her breasts. She was still growing, still developing, but obviously wanting male attention now. He could see that, as could Kipp who appeared to be hypnotized by the young woman trying to throw herself at Irwin.

Not knowing what to say or do, he could tell she was awaiting some answer from him. "They are breasts."

And then she fell to her knees and goaded his dog into her arms. Kipp came over and licked her face. She cried, "Your dog likes me more than you do."

Irwin recognized the jealousy in the Clan-Duin's eyes. "It sure looks that way."

"And you're okay with that?"

Irwin laid the folded clothing in the stall where Blacky was eating. He was not attracted to this young teenaged hussy. Her behavior made her look ugly, even if she was pretty. And how she used her body to get attention repulsed him. He wanted to leave, but he knew to be polite. "I guess so." He turned away from her, stepping over to the open barn door.

"Mister Irwin, how long do you plan on staying here at my family's Inn?" She followed him, leaving Kipp behind in the barn.

This young woman spooked Irwin. She was relentless. There was nothing he could say to keep her at bay. "I only paid for tonight."

Please let us leave tomorrow; please let us leave early tomorrow.

"Is it alright if I show your dog to my siblings? They would love to see his tricks, and he'll be fed well."

The young women clung close to his side. "Just as long as you don't scare him off, you can feed him and show him to your siblings, yes."

From his periphery, Irwin caught Kipp racing out of the barn, carrying the PCP clothing in his canine jaw—quick to scurry away from Coralin.

"He ate all the leftover gizzard pieces I brought him earlier," she said, eyes wild. She followed Irwin back into the Inn, keeping close to him still. "He really likes those."

"I am sure he does," he said, no longer caring to be part of this exchange. "Have fun with Kipp."

He found the stairs and saw Coralin run into the kitchen. Irwin raced up the stairs, three at a time, and found their shared bedroom. Yace had just pulled a dress over her head and shoulders and was trying to pull the braided strings together, trying to close the back. "You're just in time! Can I have some help?"

He stood still, just beyond the closed door. "Why am I dressed like this, Yace? Because if it is to get the attention of women, I am not so sure I want to."

"We're going to a Saloon, Irwin." Her head was held high in defiance. "Kipp needs it. I need it. You need it! It will be good for everyone. Now please help me."

Irwin was wary of going to any Saloon. Just the thought of it triggered memories of the fiasco with his father. "No. I am not comfortable with that idea." But he stepped forth to aid Yace in getting dressed.

"We're going to go so Kipp can relax. He's been so uptight since his family broke apart, and I've wanted to take him to a Saloon ever since the whole debacle occurred. He needs to see some pretty women dancing and drink some liquor until he's too drunk to remember."

Irwin closed his eyes.

Okay, I will do this for Kipp.

"Oh! Well then, in that case, I guess I will come along. And you will be there, so we can sit together if Kipp goes off to have some fun with a lady."

There was a mischievous sparkle in Yace's blue eyes. "Don't worry, Irwin, we will have fun too!"

"Is that why you are dressed like that?"

"Yes, to have fun."

He studied her. "Saloons usually are packed. Are you not worried about the voices?"

"Oh, that's what alcohol is for. It dulls the senses." Yace winked and tapped her forehead. Then she pulled out her pouch with combs, brushes, glass bottles of perfumes, and tins of makeup. She pulled out a round mirror fixed to an ornately gilded piece of metal. There were mirrors on both sides; one side made Yace's face twice as large.

Irwin had never seen such a mirror that could distort one's face. He made faces in the mirror while Yace looked at herself on the normal side. He watched his silvery eyes bubble out and then opened his mouth to see his teeth. He examined his nose, and then his eyes again, before Yace realized what he was doing.

She made a face at him and then turned the mirror over to use the other side.

Irwin was having too much fun playing with his reflection to notice what Yace had done.

When she put the mirror down on the small table, Irwin saw that she had put charcoal around her eyes and rouge on her eyelids, cheeks, and lips. She looked made up, like women in Saloons.

"Why do you look like that?"

"I am out to have as much fun as I can."

"But you look like one of the Saloon Ladies."

"I'm not going out like this to find a man, if that's what you are thinking. Don't worry Irwin. Tomorrow we're getting an early start, so we need to have as much fun as we can tonight. There are no cities like Jo Hara until we reach Onj Raha. The best Saloons for those with Talents are always in the larger towns and cities. I happen to know that there are a few saloons here that accept people like us." She picked up the mirror and glanced at herself one more time. "Now, it would be best if we left all your metal here," she said. "Put it wherever you can, you know, like in your bags, or coat, or the floor. I don't care. Just make it so that no one can steal it."

"I do not get why I should leave it all."

"The smell, mostly. I heard Kipp's thoughts earlier. He knows that your death-ly scent diminishes when you're not holding metal inside your flesh."

"I must leave all my metal behind?"

"No. Bring a pouch of coins." Yace said. "Kipp thought you would be a liability if we go somewhere where there are other Clan-Duins, like a saloon. We don't want your smell to call undue attention."

Unlike your makeup.

"I do not have to go."

"No, you don't have to come with us. But I thought I'd at least offer. Kipp really likes the saloon scene. And it's been so long since we've been in one. What he really wants to do is try his hand at a game of cards with people he doesn't know. He's been coached by one of the best card players in the Gypsy, Olei." She brushed back her hair. "Olei can play cards! He can sense inflections in heart beats and smell the first drop of fear. And he is really good at seeing people tense up at the slightest change in cards.

"We've got some good card players in our bunch. Our Erthin man, Fish, counts cards. He tried to teach me once. I kind of got it, but card playing is not as much fun for me. I'd rather flirt and watch. Besides, I can listen in on player's thoughts, so where is the fun?"

She scowled as she moved toward the window. "You didn't tell Kipp to meet us at the Bakery."

"I did not have time," he said, "Coralin interrupted. How do you know?"

"Kipp is outside," she said, looking out the window. She approached Irwin and their stack of packs at his feet. She pulled out Kipp's bag and found his boots. "He wants these."

"Should I take them to him?"

"Only if you want to be cornered by Coralin again," said Yace. "She's just outside the door, trying to decide if she should knock or not."

I am so glad I did not ask Coralin to wash my clothing!

"No thanks. I think I will stay here."

Yace returned to the window, opened it, and tossed down one boot at a time. Then she returned to her beautifying ritual. From another small pouch, she pulled out an ornate box carved with waves of elaborate designs. She pulled the lid off, revealing several pairs of earrings all mixed together. She found the pair that matched her dress and stuffed them through her earlobes. Then she turned to Irwin and adjusted a few stray strands of hair around his ears.

"You look handsome tonight. I ask that you open all the doors and take my hand once we are down the stairs. Oh, and try not to engage Coralin more than necessary. And please, only bring a pouch of coins. No other metal."

I do not need to be nitpicked.

"How many coins do you think we need?"

"Oh, not much more than five or six each for drinks and supper; although Kipp might need more." She took up a floral hand-knit pouch and pulled out a vial of liquid and another of powder.

Irwin made and tossed down thirty coins onto the bed. Each was stamped with the Hakran emblem. This one trick he had perfected.

Picking up one of the coins, she looked it over and said, "Watching you do your magic will never get old."

He stepped back and placed his hand on the wall next to the door. He pushed out silvery metal from his flesh, coating the entire wall in a shiny mirror-like finish. Then he fished out his vest, pulled it on, and removed a small coin purse from an inside pocket. He placed his coins inside the pouch.

"Wow." Yace looked at the silvery wall, her mouth agape.

"When we leave, I will lock the door," he said.

"But it doesn't lock."

Irwin gave her a mischievous look.

"Oh, I get it!"

24

<u>Telepathic Talk</u>

Irwin opened the door for Yace. He would have done so even if she hadn't suggested it. And there was Coralin, leaning against the wall. She gleamed the moment the door opened, but she dropped the smile when she saw Yace. Irwin saw this over Yace's shoulder. When he came out of the room, her smile reappeared. As he closed the door, he placed his hand on it, pulling the metal on the other side of the wall across and doorway from inside. Their bedroom was sealed. No one could enter without him.

As he turned to follow Yace, Coralin opened her mouth, ready to say something. He wanted to get as far away from the young woman as he could. Closing his eyes, hoping she did not speak, Irwin heard her lips shut. She did not move.

He was one step behind Yace as they descended the stairs. And like a gentleman, he walked at her side to the front door, and then opened it for her. She stepped outside into the night. Irwin shut the door and took up her arm in his.

"I did not expect you to be so ..." *Handsome!*

Irwin tensed, hearing her voice echo in his head.

"I will never harm you, Irwin. I will never violate your mind again. It's just ... when we're this close, it's just easier than talking aloud."

That is what you believe.

"I hope your father can help you." He could hear her thoughts.

"Same here." Yace leaned into Irwin and thought, *I know it is hard to understand me.* "For now, though, you are my savior." She kissed his cheek and then placed her head on his shoulder.

He fought with himself to keep separate from her, but still by her side.

Being this close is so uncomfortable for me.

He tried not to grit his teeth. "How did you do it without me? Shopping for clothing?"

"There weren't that many people busy buying. Most people shop in the morning. It's always easier if I'm around one or two other people in small shops. In a larger store filled with a lot more people, I have problems focusing. Markets are the worst." She continued to lean into Irwin. "It was good that we went there together. But if all the sounds get me fretting, I try to keep focused by thinking about what it is I'm trying to do. Sometimes I repeat my purchasing list over and over, or look for words on signs, and not at the faces that surround me."

Again, Irwin heard her thoughts.

If I see their faces, I cannot stop hearing their thoughts.

He tried to ignore her personal thoughts. "I do the same, but sometimes I just count. It is good to know you have ways to subdue the thoughts of others."

She shrugged. "It works sometimes. But having you here at my side really helps." She put her head on his shoulder again.

Trying to brush off her affection, Irwin asked, "Where are we going to meet Kipp?"

"I told him to meet us at the bakery when I dropped him his boots. Earlier while I was shopping, I saw a narrow alley between there and the—"

"I am behind you now, Ma'am." Kipp spoke from three strides behind.

"Good to see." Yace brought her head up off Irwin's shoulder and glanced behind them.

Irwin jumped at hearing Kipp's voice. He had not detected the Clan-Duin's approach. And there was no one else along that particular bend in the street to notice either. The Clan-Duin had just appeared from a dead-end alley between the residences.

Kipp followed behind at the distance required for a man in uniform to be with his benefactors. At the next intersection, Yace slowed their pace and Irwin glanced over his shoulder to see where Kipp was. The uniformed Clan-Duin held his eyes to the ground.

Why is he acting that way?

Try to ignore Kipp for now. Yace's thought traveled around Irwin's mind. *This is what they are supposed to do. People like Kipp aren't allowed to be out wandering the streets, except with their benefactor, or with brigades at this time of night.*

Why? Why is it this way? Why cannot Kipp just walk around like you do, like I can? Why must we play this charade?

Irwin, there are three types of people on Urthis. Those who have nothing—no power or talent, no wealth, no land, nothing to call their own, but the children they bear. And even then, if they are workers on a plantation, their children are not really theirs. Those people are usually Mortals, but Clan-Duins and Erthins are susceptible to the same fate. That's not to say that others, Mortals that is, can't live lives in cities and townships. They can be a productive member of society.

She paused for a moment.

But really, it's the smarter people, those who believe they can have something to call their own, who know they can be something. They're the ones who ruin everything.

Usually, it comes from positivity taught by parents and social circles. Having money also helps. Living in a larger city can be a component of success, too. But most of those types of people have jobs working for one another, making things for each other. They've been taught trades, like you; knowledge is usually handed down. They can be or carpenters, or blacksmiths, tailors …. These people believe they have the power to change society.

She chuckled. *Telepaths are the ones who have power.*

Irwin looked toward the sky.

Of course!

They live in society without being questioned, unlike a Clan-Duin, Erthin, or Mortal. The thing about Telepaths is that they usually look Mortal, like me, pale skin …. And they're usually better dressed. They tend to own lots of land and will have a ménage of people working for them. They feed on everything and everyone, manipulating things for themselves. And I should know, I do it and I don't mean to. But it's the nature of the telepathic beast. She glanced over her shoulder toward Kipp. *I hate not being able to hear his thoughts.*

Irwin asked, *Is this how you two walk every time you venture into a town or village?*

Actually, this is the first time we have done this walk without supervision. Yace's body shook, as if she had just realized she was without a chaperon. *We've been taught how to act and what to say, but this is our first time all alone. We know what to do when approached. So, I am not too worried. It's just that, with you at my side not allowing me to hear Kipp … it's a little too quiet.*

Irwin chuckled.

I cannot imagine that Kipp thinks all that much about anything. He always looks like a stone.

Yace replied, *Oh, he does! And he's much more impulsive than you. For sure!*

Is he more impulsive than you?

Yace did not act like she had heard him, but a smile lifted her mouth at the corners.

Irwin studied the young woman who clung to his arm.

So, you are implying that not only are Plantations death traps for those with Talents, but towns and cities, and even villages, are all managed by Telepaths? And they are all under the rule of Hakra?

Yeah. They are.

I think you are overreacting.

No. I am not overreacting. It's all true.

He studied her from the corners of his eyes.

How do you know it is truth?

Nonbry and Dana and Tamera and all Gypsy have stories. They've told me what they know. I don't just jabber whatever I please. I know what's going on out there. Urthis is a very scary place.

Indeed.

I know there are some plantations made up of a group of mean, mentally sick Telepaths who suckle every little piece of energy. They will beat and starve their servants to keep them meek and make them serve. Those people do not learn to question. They're not allowed to have a voice, or a thought, for themselves. They also don't live long.

A mayor of a town or city will encourage you to work harder as he passes you by in the street. He will hold you accountable and expect you to work. And he will make you wrong, in front of family and friends if you don't. He'll tax the money you make, taking it for himself without regard for you or your family. That mayor, that Telepath, has no other job than to make sure everyone is working. And what are they all working for? To serve Hakra. In return, you get to believe that you actually own a home, and that you are working a job you love. Wait, what was your question again?

Are you implying that there are Telepaths everywhere?

Yeah. They are!

And that they are all working for Hakra?

In some capacity, yes. Or their personal gain.

He still was not ready to accept Yace's explanations.

Are there really that many Telepaths?

Oh yeah, they are. And they live everywhere! Most of them are in it for Hakra. They believe that he'll give them everlasting power. Most are too blinded by greed.

But not even Hakra has everlasting power. And then, like I said, there are some mentally twisted ones who do things for their own amusement. Then there are the few, like Nonbry and Dana, and myself, who are kind and nurturing and want to help—like my father.

How is all this possible? Telepaths are everywhere.

Just then, a passing thought fluttered forth; *Mayor Yurpton had blue eyes.*

That's a telepathic trait, one of the biggest, besides the blonde or blonde-white hair, like mine.

How does the Gypsy do it? How do you all stay safe? If there are Telepaths out there trying to manipulate you, trying to take you for their very own, make you work for them ... how do you stay protected?

Having a powerful Telepath like Nonbry helps. But in reality we can't. We just keep going and never look back.

Sometimes you need to look back.

Yeah, you're right. Sometimes we must face the truth. The truth is Telepaths like to control. It's a sad sight. I mean, there are people like Kipp. They have amazing power, amazing abilities, and can do well for themselves if they try. But they are also easily corrupted—mentally, that is. And because of how they look, they have swagger over the Mortal man, which is why Telepaths use them. That's why there is such racism against those who look different. Mortals instinctually know to fear those who have power. And if the Telepaths say, 'Hey, these Clan-Duin's are the people to fear', then Mortals fear them. Even though it's those Telepaths you should really be worried about.

Says the Telepath.

He chuckled out loud.

Yace held tighter to his arm. *Fear is the one emotion the powerful use to keep the powerless oppressed. And those of us with Talents, we are fearful and fearless. That's the reason we all are sought after, in one way or another. A Telepath is scarier than an Erthin, and an Erthin is scarier than a Clan-Duin. But now a Telepath with an Erthin and Clan-Duin, that is an oppressive look indeed. That's why they lay claim to people with Talent more so than Mortals. 'If you are not claimed or owned, you will be', that's the mindset of Telepaths. And if it happens to you, hopefully you'll be under the rule of one who does good for others. If not, then you become enslaved to people who see you as nothing more than a piece of money.* There was no pause in Yace's ranting. *Do you know how many Clan-Duins have been killed because they weren't claimed? Every day the number grows. And not much can be done unless they're rescued and taught a different way to live.*

That's not to say there are no safe places—like the mountains were for you. But down here on the flats there are places, whole towns, and villages, where people like Kipp are accepted. Those places are called sanctuaries. But I don't think there are any around here. Yace paused, perhaps trying to recall some place she might have known.

Although in bigger towns and cities there are Districts—places where Talented people live and work for one another. Sometimes it's one block of land in a town, near the edge usually. We are going to that area in Jo Hara now. She kept on rattling in her thoughtful conversation, filling Irwin's mind.

I can only imagine that Onj Raha has many city blocks dedicated to those with Talents where Kipp could walk around without worry. Well, for as long as he looks to be going somewhere, and not up to mischievousness. She glanced back at Kipp. *The thing is, even if you run free in one of those districts, you still must prove that you are property to someone. But especially if the PCP catches you doing no good. I'd like to think that those with Talents who are not claimed know better than to appear mischievous.*

I am guessing this is why my father kept us hidden.

Probably.

Well then, how do they know if you have been claimed?

Tattooing. Or a piercing. Tattoos can be simple in design, or complex, depending on how mean your owner is. Some are put in specific spots, like shoulders, arms, lips, forehead, and neck. All PCP have a symbol on their right forearm.

Are Mortals owned in the same way?

Yeah. Those who have lesser means or are just plain stupid and of the type who do as told. I've met many Mortals barren of tattoos. So, I would say less than half of them, whereas it's all of us.

How is one tattooed?

With a needle and ink, usually indigo, though I have seen green and red inks. Mean owners will brand you.

I am glad that I do not have a tattoo.

You are lucky in that respect. Being Gypsy, we try to avoid any meetings with the PCP.

Yace stopped with the mental chatter finally and pulled her arm away from Irwin. She rolled up her sleeve and exposed a small circular tattoo on her left shoulder.

Everyone in the Gypsy has the same tattoo, Tamera made them. This allows Nonbry to lay claim to all of us. She drew down her sleeve and pulled Irwin forward again. *When we're approached, and we have been multiple times over the years, Nonbry usually deals with issues that arise. We must be careful of what we say and how we act everywhere we go.*

Why is that?

The Gypsy harbor several PCP dissidents. They've lived with us for about two years now. I would like to think they'll stay on permanently, but who knows?

Is your family the only Gypsy caravan out there?

Oh, no. There are other Gypsy camps doing exactly what we do. There are about half a dozen troupes who roam around and free those in need. There are so many Talented people, Irwin. And almost all of them are enslaved. You'll find them everywhere across Urthis.

Then there are bastard children. They are paler, usually mixed breed, half Mortal, half Talented; usually direct descendants of PCP soldiers.

Irwin tried to process it all.

Some PCP men enjoy taking advantage of powerless Mortal girls. They don't care that they are breeding. Or maybe it's part of Hakra's plan. She tightened her grip on Irwin's arm once more. *Those children don't even know they're children of soldiers. They don't know that they have extraordinary powers until it's too late, and they have already been put in service of PCP. Some are put in the gallows.*

A chill wind came up behind them and billowed Yace's skirt. Irwin felt it in his bones while she rattled on and on in this conversation of the minds.

It's the Gypsy mission to help all we can, for as long as we can. It's a challenging task to roam around and save those who need it. But it's necessary. Many of those we've saved we've educated and invited them to stay on and help us rescue more. But most don't stay. They see us as a catalyst to something better. And we are for some. We teach them how to stay alive in this less-than-friendly world.

Thankfully, there are many places of refuge for us, but only that's if we're willing to drive for years to find them. There are smaller towns all around Urthis filled with the Talented, but they are always tucked away. Nonbry talks about them, but we've visited only a handful in my eleven years of traveling. It's in those towns that most we've rescued stay—in those safe zones, those sanctuaries. But if someone chooses to stay with the Gypsy, then the Gypsy owns them. That's how we survive.

Irwin hoped they would reach this saloon before his head spun off from over stimulation.

We have to act, to put on a charade if we're approached by a PCP squad … keep ourselves from being enslaved or killed. If I act as the benefactor … and I am right now. I look like a Telepath, or a richly common woman. Then Kipp has a place to be. If he were to go out without me near, there might be a problem. He might get picked up by a PCP unit.

You sure talk a lot.

She droned on over him. *On the other hand, being Erthin is different. They can walk through the city at night so long as they are wearing appropriate clothes—PCP clothes.*

Our Gypsy mate, Fish, is a fire-water-air wielding Erthin. He comes and goes from camp as he pleases, setting a terrible example for the younger Gypsy. Since he is Erthin, and if he dresses up in his PCP garb, he probably wouldn't be approached by a squad of PCP, even if he looks to be up to no good. No one wants to accidentally cross a Fire Erthin! And though he does walk around in a PCP uniform, it's not valid. But he doesn't care. He doesn't care about much except alcohol and women and money. Just so you know, Fish is an annoying guy, but in the world of the Talented, that gets him merit.

He wondered, *What if Kipp was with me? I mean, I look Mortal. I even smell it right now. Could I be his benefactor?*

Yeah, I guess. Yace did not sound so sure. *I spoke to Nonbry this morning. He told me that Fish is here in Jo Hara, taking a reprieve from camp, as always. He's an asshole, and we're going to meet up with him now, by the way.*

They approached a lively sounding building, gleaming with lights and sounds of laughter and shrieking poured out the front door.

This is one of the more upscale Saloons in the two Talented districts here in Jo Hara.

She finally stopped the mental chatter and looked back at Kipp who had been following in silence.

"Here we are," she said, tapping her side, snapping her fingers.

Kipp played his part. "Good Ma'am." He was looking around, scouring the streets.

The saloon was filled with men and women. Irwin saw a woman leaning on the bar smoking; he saw several men and women flirting; two men in the corner were arm wrestling. The music was loud and lively; people were dancing, and the smell of food wafted throughout the place.

Irwin and Albert had entered the Hairy Yak; the door swung shut behind them. Irwin held back. A stout middle-aged woman behind the bar's long oak countertop watched the two mountain men. Her hair was braided and pinned around her head. Irwin nodded toward her and had then chased after Albert who was heading toward his favorite table.

They took seats on two wooden chairs that Albert had scraped noisily across the floor. He ordered the same meal and drink he did every time. Irwin kept an eye on him. Albert's behavior could change like a winter storm coming from the north at any time. The whiskey helped calm him, but not much.

An older woman shuffled toward the piano in the back of the room. Her fingers raced across the keys, and the melody soothed Irwin, soothed the ringing in his ears. He closed his eyes and there came a smack on the back of his head; he lurched forward in the chair. He had let his mind wander.

The woman who delivered their whiskey and introduced herself as Rosi brought them their hot meat pies; the ceramic plates clanked onto the table.

"Another drink, Sir?"

"Yes! And one for my son." Albert's eyes turned from gold to silver. "Make them both doubles. Irwin here will need as much courage as he can muster tonight!"

"Yes, Sir. Will that be all for now?"

Albert pulled out a small satchel of silver coins. He held it up, feeling its weight, then absorbed several ounces of silver through the material and into his flesh before handing the satchel to Rosi. "Tell your proprietor we will be staying the night. I assume this will be enough for meals, drinks, and women."

She peered inside the purse. "Yes, that should suffice, Sir."

"Tonight you will become a man!" Albert stared at him, eyes changing again from silver to gold.

"Become a man? I do not understand. I thought I was a man."

"You are a boy, nothing more. A boy and a smart ass." Albert's eyes narrowed. "Maybe tonight you will learn something. To be a man," his father snarled, "you must learn to fuk a woman."

Irwin closed his eyes and received another slap to the back of his head.

Albert's eyes swirled with silver and gold, occluding his irises. Irwin was aware of the man's power and his habit of lashing out at him—same as he would to one of the donkeys. He could feel his father ready to explode. It happened whenever they were here in the city filled with all kinds of metals that both of them voluntarily, and sometimes involuntarily, absorbed into their bodies. Irwin was aware of this power, but he had learned early on to keep it to himself.

Rosi appeared with two more cups of whiskey. Albert yanked one from her and cast the whiskey down his throat. With a hard hand, he slammed the ceramic cup onto the table. He took the other double shot and threw that down his gullet too; his flaming eyes never left Irwin's. "Bring us another set of doubles."

Irwin watched Rosi scurry away, empty cups in hand. He squirmed under his father's glare.

"A woman like that is too meek for you. I promise you, my boy, you will learn something from this night I am paying for."

Irwin watched the woman he remembered as Saryh walk past.

"Good choice! Do you like her? Of course you do. You will have Saryh tonight."

"Yes, I like Saryh. She is nice."

"Nice has nothing to do with it."

He poked at the meat pies. They were the perfect temperature to eat. Albert grinned, exposing his yellowing teeth, when Rosi appeared with more shots of whiskey. The grizzly man was in a mood to drink, and fast, meanwhile Irwin sipped on his. Their dinner was turning into a drinking contest for which he wanted no part. But again, another round of whiskey, and again ....

"Your Grandfather Jebadia wanted this night to happen while he was alive." Albert was already slurring his words. "He wanted you to learn how to procreate another generation. I knew you were too young before he died, but now ... now you are ready to learn how to be with a woman." He slapped Irwin's shoulder. "Drink it!"

Irwin had not wanted to anger his father who was drunk, but his shoulder stung. With a quick hand, he flung a mouthful of whiskey down his own throat. *Ugh!*

"Swallow boy!" Albert shouted. "Another round for us!" He stared at Irwin. "Tonight we will make you into a man." He slapped Irwin's shoulder again. "By the end of this night, you will know what it means to be a *real* man."

"I thought all the hard work in the mines made me a man."

Albert had leaned so close to Irwin's face he almost gagged on the odor coming from his father's mouth. "Knowing how to create children makes you a man. You can work your ass off for eternity and not know what work is until you have a child. We need another generation for the mines. Hopefully, your prick will not disappoint."

"You gonna be alright?" Yace asked, bringing him back to the moment. He nodded at her, and she pulled him along and into the hectic business.

Irwin sensed that nearly all the patrons here were Talented in one way or another. He noticed many shades of black and red hair, reddish-brown, dark brown and olive skin tones; gray, amber, and hazel-colored eyes. There were Erthins here and twice as many Clan-Duins. He saw men sitting closest to the door notice Yace as they entered. Her platinum blonde hair hung straight down her plum-colored dress, and her deep V neckline showed off her pulled-together cleavage. Yace was not as well-endowed, so she played herself up with makeup and fancy clothing.

She held onto Irwin when they called to her from their tables.

Her voice floated around his head once more. *Don't forget to pay Kipp.*

He felt for his coin pouch.

"Kipp." Irwin called to the Clan-Duin, but apparently so just had their fellow Gypsy, Fish. Kipp stepped over to Irwin who shook out ten coins for the Clan-Duin to play with.

Kipp rushed to seek out Fish at one of the many card tables.

Yace pulled Irwin to a small table with two seats near the front of the room. They had a prime place to sit and watch the dancers. Yace scooted her chair close to his.

They were serviced right away. A young Clan-Duin woman sauntered over, wearing a short skirt and see-through blouse. She sat on Irwin's lap and tried to cuddle him.

He stiffened.

"A carafe of wine for us to share," Yace said, appearing not to notice Irwin's discomfort. "And two house-plates, please."

"Yes, Milady, and thanks to you." The Clan-Duin waitress ogled Irwin and sauntered away to the kitchen.

"See Irwin, all you have to do is just relax, and the women will be all over you." Yace smiled at him and kept her hand on his. "You are so handsome in those clothes."

"Though I appreciate your kindness, Yace, I am not so sure I am ready for this." He looked mournfully at the dancing women kicking their legs up, showing their privates—spinning and spinning.

25

<u>FRIENDS</u>

Yace's hand felt warm on his. "I know what happened to you. I can assure you it will not happen again. Your father is a cruel, cruel man who deserves to be punished for what he's done. But being in places like this will help you move beyond your past. Here ... tonight ... nothing sexual must happen. Only fun!" She leaned back as their waitress returned with a carafe of wine and two small glasses.

"That'll be two silvers." Irwin paid without hesitation. After their waitress left, he studied Yace. "You did not tell Kipp what happened to me, did you?"

"I thought you would. The two of you act like you are best of friends. Besides, it's not my place to tell Kipp your secrets." She glanced at Kipp who happened to be looking at her just then.

Irwin watched Yace smile at her longtime friend.

"By the way, I need to thank you, Irwin. Kipp's resolve would have wavered by now if you weren't here. He has told himself that the only reason he's coming along is not for me, it's for you."

I do not even know what that means, best of friends.

"Why would he think that?"

"He was ready to turn back those first few nights. Kipp really wants to rescue Flinn. He wants to take her and go off and live in the forest, just the two of them. But being around you kept him here."

Kipp acts like he is indifferent to me being here.

He raised an eyebrow. "I do not believe you."

"I'm not lying! If you hadn't shown up, I would be all alone by now. I might not have made it this far. I might have turned back." Taking the carafe, Yace filled their glasses. "I want to thank you for journeying with us." Her voice was quiet now. "I hope you don't grow to hate me as Kipp has." She raised her glass. "To a swift journey to Onj Raha." She tapped her glass against Irwin's, and then drank the entire glass of wine in a few gulps, then poured herself another and drank that one too.

"Wow! I think you should slow down."

"Irwin, I've got this." She poured herself another glass and chased it down.

By the time she pulled the third glass away from her lips, it was clear she was feeling the wine's effect. She closed her eyes and turned her head back and forth. "Irwin, this is how I am only when I am this way." She poured herself another glass of wine.

He intercepted the glass, pulled it from her hand. "I think you need to wait for some food." She swayed with the music. Her hand fell away, and her eyes glazed over.

There was a young piano player in the corner, his back turned to everyone. He did not look up to see the show going on around him.

Four scantily clad dancers wearing makeup, nails and skin painted, their hair piled high, were trying their best to be seductive, beautiful, and enchanting. Irwin was paying attention to the other men. Watching how they were all acting toward their servers who maneuvered between bodies and arms, and around tables. The men grabbed and pulled, touched and fondled every chance they could.

Soon, their smiling Clan-Duin server stepped up to their table with a full tray of meat pies. She set two plates on their table and requested four more coins. Irwin paid her.

"She is pretty, huh, Irwin!" Yace was tipsy. "Don't you think? The next time she comes over here, I'm putting a move on her."

Irwin did not understand what Yace was implying. Her head still bopped around to the music. Then she began emulating a few of the women's gyrating motions; she stood and mounted their table. Several of the surrounding men began hooting at Yace, encouraging her.

Irwin tried to get her attention. "Yace, your food is ready."

"What? Oh yeah, I'm starving!" She sat back down and peered at the steamy meal. Without so much as a pause, she started shoveling the hot food into her mouth.

He tried to ignore all those men still watching Yace. While she was dressed to get attention, for now she appeared content to be eating her meat pie, barely stopping to breathe. She finished and belched loudly. The men sitting behind them cheered her on. Irwin stopped in mid-bite to watch the fevered pitch that Yace kept, to watch Kipp over at the card tables laying down his hand, a smug grin on his brown face as he collected his bounty. Once Yace's plate and glass were empty, she was back on her feet dancing to the music. The song ended.

The men hooted for Yace, even after the dancers bowed and stepped off the stage, making room for the next set of dancers. Yace stood there watching, waiting, and then clapping loudly when their server stepped out on stage. The piano was alive again, and five new dancers all began shaking their torsos in unison. Yace mimicked their movements.

She danced closer to the stage; then onto it. The dancers encouraged Yace's liveliness. Amid cheering for her to take off her clothes, she pulled up her skirt and showed off her pale white legs.

Though Yace acted intoxicated, she did manage to show restraint when it came to keeping her clothing on, but she flashed the crowd a view of her breasts a few times. The encouragement did not go unnoticed, and the dancers began to mimic Yace's style of dancing. They all swooped around Yace, pretending to kiss her. She seemed to blossom from the attention, and then followed the dancers off the stage, back behind the curtains.

His meat pie half eaten, he never would have guessed that Yace would be so bold, though he knew she was wild. He sat there, waiting, but did not know exactly what for. Yace was gone, as was the wine and their server. He did not know what he wanted more, Yace at his side, or some alcohol to numb his mind.

One of the men who had been sitting behind Yace took her seat next to Irwin. His breath smelled of alcohol, and his clothing smelled of fish. Irwin tried not to breathe in, as the older man asked, "Where did you find such a thing? Most women from 'round here aren't so much fun! What's her name?" He was nearly twice Yace's age and looked like what Irwin had once heard called a lech.

It was hard for Irwin to hear the older man, and he tried to ignore him, but then realized he was insulting the old man by not responding.

"What was that?" Irwin asked loudly, attempting to play stupid. "I blew out my ear in a mining accident. I cannot hear too well."

As if she knew Irwin needed to be rescued, Yace reappeared. She slipped past the edge of the curtains and darted across the stage, straight toward him. He saw her wave at their waitress who quickly retrieved them another carafe of wine. "I am so sorry, Irwin. I got all caught up. That was so much fun. The ladies and I are going to do something a little later." Their waitress came over and leaned forward extra low. She planted a kiss on Yace's cheek.

Yace turned toward the crowd of gawking men. "That was just a peek at what's coming, boys." She tossed her hair.

Irwin stared at Yace. Why was she sending out sexual messages to all the men in the room?

Is she trying to use her powers on all these drunken sots? She cannot control anyone other than Kipp, can she? Does she know what she is doing to all these gritty men, and what they might do to her?

He leaned in toward her. "How much longer are we staying?"

She ignored him and poured herself another glass of wine. Then she refilled his. "You're not drinking enough." Then she downed hers.

Irwin asked with increasing concern, "Will you be sober enough to walk tomorrow?"

"This is short-lived, my friend. Nothing I do tonight will affect my tomorrow; much." Yace hiccupped.

She kept on moving in her seat to the piano music. She looked around, appearing eager for their waitress's return. Those blue eyes sought out Kipp who was still sitting with Fish and the other card playing patrons. Then she leaned in close to Irwin.

"I thought I'd see Kipp trying to get a woman on his lap."

Irwin shrugged. "Maybe he is not that interested."

"Oh, wait, there he goes, catching a feel."

Kipp was grabbing the buttocks of a short and stout Erthin woman who had extra of everything, including laughter. "He likes Clan-Duins, but sometimes flirtatious redheads catch his eye."

Irwin peered at his Clan-Duin friend, then regarded his glass of wine. He would never have walked in here voluntarily.

I am here for my friends.

Then he took Yace's advice; drank down the glass of wine and filled it again.

"Good job," she said.

Irwin watched Yace scan the room and all the men in it. "He's handsome." Her gaze stopped on a violet-eyed, roughly cut man leaning against the wooden bar. He too was surveying the room and caught Yace's attention.

The man was unshaven. He wore a deep-purple buttoned shirt tucked into dark suede pants. Irwin also thought he was the handsomest man in the saloon. The barmaid caught the man's attention, and he turned his lustful eyes to her.

Once more the dancers emerged, dressed as if going to a ball. Their costumes flared out as they twirled around, then stopped. The women all harmonized themselves, began singing, holding still, if for only a moment, then the dancing commenced. This was the main show, the one reason all these men were still here—more than the alcohol, food, card playing, or body grabbing.

Irwin wondered how far these women would take their shenanigans. All the men began clapping, shouting, and hollering; everyone except Irwin.

He tried not to feel more uncomfortable than he already did. He felt sorry for these women who had to flaunt their bodies in order to have food, a roof, and clothing. They had to humiliate themselves every night, and allow themselves to be grabbed and touched, just so they could live. How could these women do this? He wondered how many of these women would be robbed of their lives.

As Saryh had.

Yace put her hand on his. "Are you alright, Irwin? You're looking extra pale right now."

He shook his head, felt nauseated, felt the wine trying to come up. He jumped to his feet and managed to maneuver around the hollering men. Irwin pushed past many people, hand on his mouth; ran toward the doorway.

The front porch was empty.

Irwin barely made it down the last step before the wine he consumed spewed through his fingers. Everything he had consumed that evening came up and out.

The meat pie tasted great going down, but not so much coming back up. He found a place to sit and lean against the saloon's façade. Irwin waited for a time before he stood back up. He stumbled toward a nearby watering trough across the road.

Away from the lights and sounds of the saloon, he washed off his hands and face and sat on the edge of the trough. His body shook; memories of Saryh flooded his thoughts.

She was so kind. Saryh did not deserve the death given to her.

He wondered how many of the women in that saloon he had just left would be raped, sodomized, or beaten that night. Or killed. He tried to erase those thoughts.

He held still in the shadows of a closed shop, listening only to his breath and his heartbeat. There were no lights on him; no prying eyes would see him there wondering where and why this life had taken him here.

He had said he would do this for his new traveling companions, but now he regretted his promise. All he wanted to do was curl up into a ball and cry.

Irwin was slow to stand, legs shaking. The road was empty; it was late in the evening, and they were all in there watching the dancers. He washed his hands in the trough one more time but was not ready to go back to the saloon. The cool crisp air felt good.

He ambled around a block of stone and mortar buildings. There was a foulness of dead livestock lingering in the air near a refinery and slaughterhouse one street away from the butcher's market. Just beyond was a leather store with dozens of well-tanned pieces of animal hides hung on display in the front windows. He recognized the horse, cow, and bear hides, intermixed with larger moose and caribou skins. Then he noticed a shoe store with tall leather boots on display in the window; they were lined with wool. Next to the boots were leather slippers, perfect for lounging around the homestead.

He passed by a wax shop filled with colorful candles and trinkets made of tin. The sound the tin made was a higher-pitched ring and slightly sour to Irwin's ears. He ignored that, and all the other pieces he felt. Right now, he was more overwhelmed by his thoughts and his emotional state than the reverberations of metal.

His stomach felt better, and after a while of looking into the storefronts, he was ready for more food, though wary about any more wine. He had never tasted anything as bold as what had been served in that saloon.

I did like it, but next time only one glass.

That wine had been as strong as the whiskey his father had raised him on. He wanted his mind to stop spinning, to feel clearer than he was. Irwin dawdled along the block, still examining storefront windows. Jo Hara was an amazing city, and much like Kobiton in many ways. But Jo Hara was probably four times larger than Kobiton.

His attention wandered here and there—not a good thing to do here, in this place. Though Yace had brought them to the side of town where she said they would be more welcome, Irwin didn't know this was the bad side of town. He meandered down a wooden walkway. A few stragglers out on the road were already keenly aware of his presence. His back to the roadway, he heard the two sets of boot steps only a second before the men were upon him, before he felt their metal.

Knives drawn, the larger of the two men was upon Irwin before he knew what was happening. The knife slid through his red blouse and into his flesh far too easily.

He swung around to look at his assailant, and the man further twisted the antler hilt of his blade, cutting Irwin's shirt open. Irwin did not react like a man who was being knifed, and he noticed that confusion in his attacker.

The man growled. "Give me your money!" That thief then yanked the empty hilt from Irwin's flesh and took several more jabs before realizing he had no blade. "What the ...?"

The second man, the lookout, turned to see what was happening.

Now Irwin could see both thieves clearly. Both were plainly in shock, both studying the barren antler hilt.

Irwin reformed the knife's blade. "Is this what you are looking for?"

The Erthin's hand began glowing, and he summoned a fireball onto his hand. He threw that fiery ball at Irwin, clearly meaning to set him aflame.

Irwin put his arm up to shield his face, and the flame hit his hand and died out immediately. He had grounded out the fireball. Angered that his ball of fire was extinguished the Erthin grabbed Irwin's forearm.

At the same time, the Clan-Duin mugger took the blade from Irwin's hand. He shoved the knife into Irwin's eye. Again, the metal turned fluid and floated past his eyeball and back into his flesh.

There was nothing these two would-be thieves could do to take Irwin's money, short of asking politely for it. His unflappability and his abilities horrified these would-be assailants. There was plainly nothing they could do to this man that would cause him pain or end his life—not with a knife or with fire.

The two assailants rushed away, scattering between two buildings.

Irwin stared at his hands.

Father did the same thing.

He had been tested before by thieves who had been easy to terrorize. He now realized he did not have much to fear from Fire Erthins.

Yace is right. There is something grounding about me.

His confidence surged.

I wonder what else my Metalist power can do?! But first I need to return to Yace. And I should rid my skin of this metal. I do not want to irritate anyone at the saloon.

He turned the metal blade into more coins. They glistened like silver but were, in fact, made up of all the different alloys of that blade.

He went back to the saloon. His feet fell hard upon the ground as he walked with newfound confidence. As he took those first two steps up to the saloon's front doors, Irwin felt as if his feet could smash through those wooden stairs and meet the ground. The piano playing had stopped, but the chattering was still teeming. About half the patrons had left the barroom, but the waitresses continued to maneuver through the crowd that was left—still trying to avoid the random hands grabbing at their bottoms and their breasts. He knew that many of them would sleep with some of these men tonight for more money. By morning, they would be ready to clean up and do it all again. This was their life, their existence. It saddened his soul to know this.

Yace was dancing with their waitress on a tabletop at the other end of the saloon. They were kissing and groping each other. The men who surrounded their table visibly boiled with emotions that Irwin did not understand.

He headed toward Yace, but Kipp intercepted. "I was about ready to lose and come find you. Where'd you go?"

"I lost my supper. I had to clean up."

"Dang, that bites! Those meat pies were amazing. Way better than the giblets that Coralin fed me. I hate giblets. You'll have to get another pie before we leave."

"Maybe," Irwin said, and regretted his words. He was ready to go back to the Inn and to bed right now. Even with this new sense of confidence, he was ready for this outing to be over.

Kipp read him, "You look like you wanna leave."

They both watched Yace, and the waitress tumbled off the table.

"Yes, I do. But is Yace ready?"

A man shouted, "Kipp-man, get back here! It's your turn!"

Irwin did not understand the game of cards, and he was not interested in learning. He managed to push past a few of the burly incoherent men to get to Yace. She was on the ground, still making out with the server. The two were enjoying themselves, feeling each other's breasts, caressing one another's skin.

Yace laughed at Irwin peering down at her. "Wanna join in Irwin?" She must have noticed something in his expression. "Something happen?" Immediately she appeared sober, even though he had seen that their table now held three empty wine carafes. He offered his hand, and she used it to pull herself up off the floor. "What happened to you? Where did you go?"

The surrounding men were still begging her to carry on with the waitress. They were cooing and shouting, "More!" Yace ignored the men and pulled Irwin close.

With the contact of her hand upon his arm, Yace had the ability to extract those recent memories, but did not. Irwin was aware she did not want to violate him again. She pulled him out onto the porch. No one was there. "Irwin, are you alright? Tell me what happened. Why is your blouse ripped?"

"I got sick. Puked up all I ate and drank."

"This is a clean rip. But I see no blood. What happened!"

Nothing got past Yace. Even when she was reeking of wine and her eyes noticeably bloodshot, she was still keen.

"Thieves thought they could stab me and take my money."

"What did you do to them?"

"I scared them."

Her eyes suddenly scoured the quiet roadway. "With your powers?"

"Kind of."

"How many were there?"

Irwin knew she wanted to know how he got away with his life. "Two." He added, "One tried to stab me multiple times. I manifested his knife in my hand. But that was after he realized it was no longer attached to his hilt. And then the Erthin standing guard tried to light me on fire."

"Irwin!"

"Do not worry, I am alright. And they are long gone."

"Don't worry?" She pulled herself and Irwin further away from the main doors. "Erthin fire can eat you from the inside out! Erthins shouldn't be antagonized."

"No, I do not think you understand, Yace. The fire went out as soon as it made contact with my skin." He pointed at his unmarked forearm. "That Erthin thief whimpered like a scared Billy goat, and then they both ran off."

"Irwin, this isn't good." She peered into the saloon, trying to catch Kipp's attention, but he must have been absorbed in his game. "We can't stay here." She left Irwin on the porch to fetch Kipp.

He watched her approach Kipp from behind, bend down, and whisper in his ear.

Yace reappeared as quickly as she had run off. "We'll have to go back another way."

"Another way? Why?"

"You are probably being watched right now, Irwin." She wrapped her arm around his. "Anyone with rare Talents is considered dangerous. And if they were owned thieves, their benefactor will know about you directly."

26

<u>SHOWING OFF</u>

"**S**uddenly I wish you were a Clan-Duin or Erthin—not a magical miner."

They waited for Kipp to collect his cash. He stepped out onto the covered porch, counting the coins he had won.

"Ha!" Kipp said, "Broke even!" He handed the money to Irwin. "Thanks. That was one fun evening."

Irwin helped Yace descend the three steps onto the graveled roadway. She was still visibly buzzed from all the alcohol. But the steps were the only time she seemed to need assistance, even though she had consumed at least four carafes of wine. Once they were squarely on flat ground, she let go of him and took a half step lead.

As they moved away from the light of the saloon's porch, Kipp must have caught sight of Irwin's ripped clothing. "Yace said you'd been in a scuffle ... wish I could've been there."

Being on the Talented side of Jo Hara kept them on their toes. When they walked through hours earlier, there were no worries. But now, Irwin knew Yace was keenly aware of what could happen. He, too, knew to be cautious. The streets were peaceful, though there could be eyes watching from above.

Yace grabbed Irwin. "Do you have any metal absorbed?"

"No," he said, "I did not want to upset anyone at the saloon. I made it into coins."

"Can I have the metal?" She put her hand out. He summoned the metal from his pocket and gave it to her in one large ball. Her eyes darted around, hearing the thoughts of those who were watching. She peered over her shoulder at Kipp who was using his Clan-Duin senses too, listening and watching. A few of the saloon's patrons were following. Yace pulled harder on his arm.

She grumbled at the metal Irwin had given her. "The least you could have done was make it into a dagger or something of use, not a rock."

With a wave of his hand, Irwin shifted the metal, sculpting it into a dagger with a handle. Yace stayed close, looking at her hand, and glancing over her shoulder again.

"Thank you, Irwin." To Kipp, she said, "Follow accordingly!"

The Clan-Duin paused to study the men following them. He remained three steps behind them.

What horrors might be lurking around these corners? He had a notion his newfound friends knew.

Kipp sniffed the air at the next intersection. Their pace quickened; Yace apparently knew where they were going.

This was not the way they had come. Yace darted down an alley, and the three of them slunk through dark shadows between buildings for several blocks.

These two seemed to innately know the harm that would befall upon them if they did not keep themselves hidden.

It is hard to believe that there are people worse than Albert in this world.

But he was coming to realize that there were worse monsters out there; until now, unfathomable to him. He was beginning to understand that his mining world had been safe and simple compared with the reality of living on Urthis.

What was my reasoning for leaving the mountains?

They crossed several avenues, keeping to the alleys.

Kipp slunk toward the next crossing street. Irwin watched him study both directions before motioning them to exit the narrow alley.

Yace pushed Irwin forward, glanced at her Clan-Duin, spurring him to take position once more. Even in the dead of night, she clearly wanted their relationship to look legitimate. Kipp had to pretend to be their servant at all times, and Yace was always to be known as the benefactor. Irwin was just along for the ride.

Back out onto the primary road through Jo Hara, Yace took up Irwin's arm once more. Kipp stayed three strides behind. Now they found themselves five blocks away from the Inn. Yace had taken a side route through a residential district that wound up in the park. Once they were safely inside the Inn, Kipp headed for the barn. Yace and Irwin moved stealthily through the front room. A fire smoldered in the hearth. They carefully ascended the stairs to the third floor, to their shared bedroom.

And there, sitting on the top step, was Coralin, her eyes puffy and red. Her lower lip trembled. "I'm so sorry, Mister Irwin, Sir. Your dog ran away.

"I don't know what happened. I brought out the giblets and more fat and skin. I mean, Mother was cooking up two chickens, and there were lots of extras. I told him I would be back with more treats. But he didn't come when I called. I had my sisters and brothers look everywhere for him, even in the park." She began to sob. "I am so sorry, Mister Irwin, Sir. I did not mean to lose your dog."

"It is alright, Coralin. Kipp probably heard another dog's howl and sought them out. He is a dog, you know. That is what they do."

Yace moved past Coralin and Irwin and tried to open their bedroom door. Apparently, she forgot that Irwin 'locked' it. She glared at him. "Irwin, are you coming to bed?"

"Yes." Then to Coralin, "I would not worry about Kipp. He will be out there waiting for us at sunup."

A weak smile grew on Coralin's face. "I sure do hope so, Mister Irwin, Sir. I would hate for your dog to have run off."

Irwin saw Yace rolling her eyes from beyond where Coralin stood. He moved to pass the young woman. "Good night, Coralin."

Her smile sparkled as did her eyes and her voice, "Good night, Mister Irwin, Sir."

Irwin placed a hand on the wooden door and worked his magic.

"She's got it bad for you, Mister Irwin, Sir," Yace snickered.

She lit the lamp as Irwin closed the door, then went and opened the window. "Alright, Irwin, from the beginning, how did you get knifed?"

Irwin sat on the bed and began peeling off his calf-chaps and boots.

Yace bounced on the bed, waiting for a reply.

"Well, after losing my meal, I went for a walk. I was looking at the storefronts, and that was when they approached me. One of them said 'give me your money'."

"What did he look like? Was he Talented?"

"He appeared to be Clan-Duin. His skin was paler than Kipp's, but he was larger than Kipp and had the same dark hair and brown eyes. I would say he was my father's age. And he was not wearing a uniform, nor was the other man. That Clan-Duin then put his knife into my back."

"Did you feel the blade coming?"

"Of course I did. He only caught me slightly off guard. He stabbed me many times, but he mostly bruised me with the antler hilt." Irwin chuckled and removed his vest and unbuttoned his torn blouse. "I thought it was funny how the thief stared at me. It was like he was waiting for me to do something."

"Oh, I don't know, maybe for you to scream in pain?"

"It was not until he pulled the hilt away and noticed the metal was gone that he realized he was not hurting me. And then his watchman, the Erthin, tried to light me on fire."

"What do you mean, he tried?"

"I am still trying to understand exactly what happened. It reminded me of the blowout with my father when that Erthin soldier threw flames at him as we were on our way out of Kobiton."

My father was also unscathed. In fact, he heckled that Erthin into firing more at him.

"I find it suspicious that you say Erthin fire can ignite a person from within. How do they do that?"

"Oh, they can! It's like they just think it, and it happens. I don't know the process, but I know that Fire Erthins can make fires any which place they please ... if properly trained. Most PCP Erthins are trained, but not all Fire Erthins know the trick to incinerate from within. Most of the time, they must touch you to ignite you. If he works for some rich noble person, it's possible he might know a few tricks more than igniting a ball in his hand or making a fire in a firepit. But it doesn't sound like it."

"He might have known what he was doing."

"What did it feel like? When he tried to ignite you?"

"It tingled as it went through my body. It tickled really ... went down my arm, to my chest, through my body, then out my feet."

"Sounds like you dissipated the fire effect ... grounded it out."

"Yes, exactly. It was like what I did with Kipp that first night we met." He paused to reflect. "Both you and Dana have told me I am a grounding person. Maybe that is another aspect of how my Metalistic power works. And I never knew."

But my father knew. And he never told me.

"It was funny to watch them be so startled. I mean, they looked at me the same way I have looked at my father. They were scared."

"I think they realized something bad would happen to them if they messed with you anymore."

"That is possible. But I was not being aggressive."

"So, they tried to stab you and light you on fire."

"Oh, and then the Clan-Duin stabbed me in the eye! That was after the fire went out on my arm."

"You didn't tell me that before!?"

He took off the red blouse, saying, "Is it relevant? They wanted to kill me and take my money." Then he added, "What else could I do?"

"Oh, I don't know, defend yourself maybe. But you were stabbed in the eye!" She peered into both his eyes. "How is it possible that you were stabbed? I don't see a mark."

"Of course you do not; I absorbed the metal."

"How is it possible to absorb metal into your eye?" Holding the dagger he had made in her hand, Yace brought up the knife and pretended to stick it in his eye.

The blade's edge wavered a few millimeters between his iris and the blade turned fluid, melting around his eye. All the metal was absorbed into his socket and surrounding flesh.

"That's so gross!"

"It does hurt, you know."

"It does? Oh, I'm sorry Irwin, I wouldn't have done it had I known."

"I am joking. I do not feel a thing unless you jab me with an antler hilt."

"Can I see your wound?"

"It is not there. I have already healed."

"How is that possible?! Only Erthin healers can do that."

"My skin heals almost instantly when I have metal in me. If I do not, it takes a bit longer, but not more than a day." Irwin watched her rosy lips part, but she did not speak. "Broken bones usually heal within one to two days, depending on how badly they are broken."

"That's called instant regeneration. I've heard of regular Erthins being like that. But true Erthin Healers are exactly like that. They regenerate almost instantly. You cannot kill a true Healer Erthin, unless you cut off their head. You'll never see bruising and they can heal their own bones within a day, if that. And if their skin is cut, it fuses back together as its being cut. It's amazing to watch."

Irwin watched her study him.

"How long have you been like this?"

"My whole life."

"Your whole .... Have you ever been sick?"

"No, not that I remember."

"What happens when a blade is stabbed into you? It doesn't even touch you, does it? You absorb it too quick for that to happen."

He nodded and pulled off his wool stockings and threw them across the room onto their baggage.

He was learning how to change the subject with her. "When are we leaving tomorrow? I must buy a few things, like red thread. I should probably get myself a new shirt too … if you want me to dress richly."

She shook her head, her long hair whipping from side to side. "You cannot leave this room. You're now too much of a liability to be seen in Jo Hara, Irwin. We can't let you walk out and about like we did tonight. You've been made a mark. Guaranteed, the local Telepaths know about you. Even if we both go with you—" She talked as if Kipp was there with them. "—we'll need to be next to you the whole time. We'll have to protect you. No, we cannot do that. I'll have Kipp go retrieve the supplies. No, dang it, I'll have to do it."

Irwin was amused at the spectacle of her thinking out loud, staring off, but annoyed too.

"That means I need to wake up before dawn."

He said nothing.

"I wanted to visit the markets once more and get some fresh produce. Maybe a loaf of bread, or sweet rolls, but now …."

"I do not know why you are so worried, Yace. I can handle myself."

Her blue eyes stared right through him. "You still don't get it, do you? There are people who will try to take you away. They will use you."

"It sounds like you are trying to scare me. I do not scare easily, Yace." Irwin tried to put her at ease. "Trust me, if you cannot hear my thoughts, then no other Telepath will either. I know I am not easily swayed by words. I am highly skeptical about everything. And I usually think things through, almost too much sometimes."

"How will you defend yourself?"

"I think you know that if I had to defend myself, I could. But I do not want to be brutal. I much prefer to use my words and walk away."

"The problem is, Irwin, you were seen. We don't know if those two thieves were servants or soldiers. At this point, it doesn't even matter. They will talk none-the-less. All the Telepaths in Jo Hara will know your face soon enough."

"But we will be leaving tomorrow, so why does it matter?"

"It matters." She was pacing, grumbling to herself. "The sooner I wake up and get to the markets, the better.

"I will buy you a new shirt and repair your old one. And when we find our place to camp tomorrow evening, I'll wash your clothing too. I'm offering to do this, Irwin; really, I don't mind."

"Why?"

"Because I know you want to wash your clothing, but you just didn't want Coralin to touch it."

He frowned at Yace.

"I didn't read your mind. I just heard you thinking it while we were close tonight." She winked at him.

It had ruminated in his mind a few times during the night. He recalled watching Yace attempting to clean her clothing and the dishes during prior evenings. Everything she did was done half-assed. "But will you wash them well, or just give them a rinse?"

"I'll clean them thoroughly. I'll use soap and a brush." The tension between them eased up a bit. "Once I get what we need, we'll leave. It'll still be morning. You'll stay here and sleep. I don't even want you to leave this room for breakfast."

He was not sure he liked that idea.

"You need to stay hidden. I can't assure you that the PCP will not bother you. I mean, I think we did good at covering our trail back there, but who knows?

"But for now, we need to work on a few things. I think we should hone your senses before you should show your face in public again." She cocked one eyebrow. "I'd like to see what else you can do with this metal."

"What do you intend for me to do?"

"Can I have that dagger back?" She put her hand out. "I want to see how far your abilities extend."

He had to smile.

Her mouth also twisted with amusement.

"Take this from me."

The blade lay flat in her palm.

He extended his fingers to grab it, but Yace slapped his hand away. "No, not physically, but metaphysically."

"Metaphysically?"

She nodded.

"But I was never allowed to play with metal apart from extracting it."

"Is your father here now?"

"No, but—"

"Then don't let him stop you."

I was always told no.

He felt himself shake.

Breathe. It is alright. I cannot be beaten now. Albert is not here. Breathe. Let us see what I can do.

He stared at the blade glistening in her hand and said, "Metaphysically."

Breathe.

He closed his eyes; exhaled. At once, the blade turned liquid and flew into Irwin's hand and was absorbed.

Yace squealed with delight. "Yes! I knew you could." Her smile broadened. "Give me the metal again," she laid out her hand flat.

He reproduced the blade again and put it in her hand.

Finding a spot farthest across the room from him, Yace asked him to try again. As soon as he put his hand up, all things metal in their room flew into his hand, including the knife. The metal pans and pots from the packs were drawn across the floor toward Irwin. He let go of his power.

"Oops!" Yace giggled, "I hope we didn't disturb anyone." She was eyeing the mess of baggage.

Irwin looked at his hands, recognizing that the power he held was vaster than he had ever imagined. He then understood the extent of her warnings. "We probably should not do this around people." He replaced their baggage upright against the wall.

"Yeah, you might be right about that. We'll have to keep trying to see how far away the metal can be before you cannot retrieve it."

"I am a magnet for metal. I can hear it singing everywhere I go. In that saloon, I could have told you how much silver and gold and copper pieces there were collectively, amongst all those people, by the pound. I could have told you who had the biggest dagger. I felt all the gold teeth, and rings, and ...."

He did not want to admit to Yace what she should probably know about him, about his metallic knowledge. He wanted Yace to understand how he felt when being close to all types of metal. It was akin to her being around people with active thoughts. With eyes closed, and the truth serum of alcohol still floating around his head, he said, "I cannot go anywhere near an active forge. The sound of the metal being hit, hearing it being cooked and cooled ... I want to save it." He could see

Yace attempting to grasp the extent of his words. "When you ask me if a woman is beautiful or not, I see nothing but the metal if she has any. And if she has none, I see nothing." He hesitated, knowing how that must sound.

"No, it is not that I do not see her. I do see her. Her eyes and her hair, her outer beauty, but it is not what I see. It is what I feel. The metal makes me smile. It is hard to explain."

"I think I understand. Kipp is the same way. He loves looking at all the women, but only true Clan-Duin women, voluptuous and honey-skinned women turn him on the most. Everyone else is just a blonde or a redhead. He couldn't care less."

Irwin nodded, not knowing if that was the best analogy. "I guess it is the same." He placed his hand on hers so she could hear his thoughts.

I am glad to have met you, Yace. Thank you for letting me be me, and at the same time, trying to keep me safe.

She reached to pull Irwin in for a kiss.

He pulled away.

"I'm sorry, Irwin. I wanted to kiss you because I love you. I mean, I love you as a sister would a brother, well more than that, dang it, I just do not want you to hate me. But I do love you. And I appreciate you, too."

Irwin dropped his head, ashamed that he assumed too much. "Thank you."

Yace stood, turned around. "Can I get some help out of this dress?" She had pulled off her outer dress but had an under outfit he had not seen before. She wanted help to unbutton the numerous buttons that held her corset together.

He fumbled as he undid each button. He was not used to this type of clothing. "How did you get yourself into this?"

"Very carefully; I shimmied myself in mostly. Being skinny helps. Women do bizarre things to make themselves presentable for men."

He sighed. "I wear clothes so I am not naked. I do not really care what they look like. And I do not care what other people think, unless they are trying to get something from me because of how I act or look."

Yace placed her hand on his bare chest. "You did look handsome in that blouse. I'll mend it for you."

"I can mend my own clothing, Yace. Beyond what Kipp believes a man and woman should do, I know we can do the same things, like cooking and cleaning. I do not need someone to help with that. My father taught me to be self-sufficient. And up until, what, six days ago, I relied on myself for everything."

Yace poked him with her finger.

Now what?

"And for how long had you been reliant on just yourself? You had help here and there along your journey. And when you lived with your father, you had his help too."

"Well, yes, and no. With Albert, I had to do as told. I helped my father live. He taught me to be self-sufficient."

"With him, you weren't given much of a choice. Your circumstances were beyond anything I could've ever imagined. You were never given a choice, so I understand why choosing now can be hard on you. You did what you could to avoid being punished or humiliated, and you still do."

Has she seen my memories again?

"What I am getting at, Yace, is though I appreciate your help, it is not needed."

The dress slipped off her shoulders but clung to her body. "I didn't mean to offend you, Irwin. You just have this 'all-by-myself' mentality. Now you have friends you can count on. Kipp and I are here for you." Her voice softened. "Thank you for unbuttoning me." She set the corset aside and retrieved her nightgown.

Irwin held up the corset to see how it worked. "I cannot imagine wearing something like this."

She giggled. "It's the only thing that gives me cleavage." Irwin moved around the bed and sat to examine the rip in his shirt while Yace changed from one undergarment into another. He kept his eyes to himself.

"So, which side of the bed do you want?"

"I will sleep on the ground."

"Wrong. You are sleeping up here with me, and not in any other way than just sleeping. I prefer to sleep on my left side, so I'd like that side of the bed, if it's alright with you."

There is that coy smile again.

Stifling a yawn, he shrugged. He knew that no matter where he slept, his slumber would be sound. He rolled across the bed, allowing Yace to have her side. She slipped under the covers. Irwin pulled out his blanket roll and slept on top of the bedcovers. His back against Yace's. Soon, they were both snoring.

27

<u>Social Cues</u>

He woke in an empty room, famished. Although she had told him not to, Irwin needed food. He dressed in the clothes he wore the day before and descended the stairs into an empty dining room. He sat down and waited for one of the young children to come through the dining area and take his order.

He asked for potatoes and chunked chicken. He drank three mugs of mint tea with his breakfast, and with a full stomach, returned to the room. Tired, he lay down, hoping to catch a nap before Yace returned.

But too soon, there she was in the doorway, ready to go.

"Hey, Irwin, I thought you'd be packed and waiting for me? Are you just now waking up? You're not hungover, are you?"

"What? No?" He stood, alert and ready to leave Jo Hara.

She does not look tired.

"Hungover? What does that mean?"

"Still feeling the alcohol!"

"Maybe."

She tugged at their bags and started ordering him around. "We need to get everything packed. Let's get going!"

Irwin put his dirtied laundry into a separate sack and then stuffed that into a larger saddle bag. "Where is Kipp?"

"I believe he's in the barn. Coralin was wooing him when I left this morning. She was so happy he returned. That is not to say that Kipp wasn't having fun with her too, licking her face and breasts. That's what they were doing when I left." She stopped, eyeing him carefully. "Huh, but neither was in the barn when I returned."

You could easily locate Kipp.

"Where do you think Kipp went?"

"He's a dog."

That's what he had told Coralin.

"Dogs do what they want. They come and go as they please. There's nothing I can do to stop him short of feeding and sleeping with him every night. He's got a one-track mind, as you've seen. He's out feeding himself, most likely."

"She would not steal him, would she?"

"Ha! I'd be more worried about Coralin stealing you, or Kipp stealing Coralin." She was still grabbing and struggling with her bags.

"The stairs are too narrow for all that."

She put one of the smaller bags back on the floor.

"Let me help, please." He grabbed the largest bag. "I will come back for the rest." With his own bags slung across his shoulder, Irwin opened the door. Yace took the lead.

It took two trips to bring all their baggage out to the barnyard.

Yace retrieved the donkeys and Blacky, tying them to a hitch post at the end of the barn. She then snapped at him, "You need to get them ready."

What is she miffed about now?

Irwin ignored her but did as ordered, gathered wooden pannier frames and their camping supply packs. He needed to move fast. Yace was impatient. He watched from the corner of his eye as she attached the saddle to Blacky, and that took no time even though he was a giant beast. After Blacky was cinched up, she tied her bags along his sides, not across the seat, as she had in days past.

"I need to tie your pillow bags on Blacky," he said.

"No, the Jennies need to carry my stuff. I'll be riding today."

"Well, then should I attach my Jennies to—"

"Yes, Blacky!"

"Why are you being so pushy?"

"I want to move fast today. We've had our rest."

"How fast is fast?"

"You'll be running." She said, double checking the cinch. "Give me their lines. I'll tie them."

Irwin was not finished making sure his bags would not fall. "Give me a moment, please." He adjusted, secured, retied, and cinched tight several bags before giving Yace the lead ropes.

She tied his Jennies to the back of her saddle and mounted Blacky. The lumbering horse began to move. Both Jenn Jenn and Nee Nee were pulled along, their heads held high.

Irwin could keep up, but he had to smack the donkeys to get them to follow without fighting against their tie-downs.

Yace glanced over her shoulder. "Now we're going to jog."

"For how long?"

"Until we're out of the city."

Kipp appeared and began loping along Irwin's side, who was trying to keep up with his Jennies who were slowing down Blacky. They did not want to go fast, nor did Irwin, but that's what Yace wanted. He pulled out the willow stick he had made into a whip many days before and tapped the Jennies to give them a bit of incentive.

Yace glared at Kipp, "Fix them, will you!" She ordered the canine who then barked at the donkeys. After a few loud barks, the Jennies moved faster, leaving some slack in their lead lines. Now it was Irwin who had to keep up.

He was not by nature a runner. If he had to, he could, but not for long distances. Running, unless escaping a cave-in, was uncalled for in his line of work. They proceeded quickly through the east side of Jo Hara.

Yace's pace did not slow, even after they came to the fence-lined pastures on the far side of the city. Rock walls broke up the contoured land and lined the roadway for half a day, where a multitude of herds, sheep and goats mainly flocked. They passed plantations where people were working on the ground and on horseback. The sun was out, but occasional clouds blocked its warmth throughout that day.

Irwin and Kipp stopped at a watering hole where two aqueducts met, forming a pool. The Clan-Duin lapped at the water and Irwin drank with his hands. They exchanged glances, but neither spoke. There were random workers throughout the acres of cultivated land, and they gawked at the travelers as they passed by. Others were tending to the fields, appearing to be unaware of them.

They pressed on well into the afternoon, jogging to keep up with Yace. Clouds grew thicker than they had been. The sun hid behind towering treetops, as did the occasional opening of blue sky. The roadway was well cared for, smoothed by daily wagon usage. They passed produce-filled wagons driving toward Jo Hara. Soon the sky grew dim.

By the time they reached the next plantation, it was dark. Kipp smelled Yace pass by a well-lit building, but her scent did not linger. He urged Irwin to stay on the roadway, away from the plantation lights. Meanwhile, the Clan-Duin loped off to investigate scents. The two met up further down the road, well beyond the lights, beyond any more sightings of people.

They had not passed Yace. Would they find her, or would they have to walk all night to catch up? They were too tired to keep going after they found another aqueduct to drink from. But they could hear Yace cursing at her tent only a few hundred feet beyond.

It was dark. Clouds were thick and threatened rain. A few drops fell, large and cold. Kipp led Irwin into Yace's camp. There was no fire. The horse and donkeys were still attached to one another, tied to a sapling tree.

Irwin walked past the animals to pick up kindling for a fire.

He left Kipp to deal with Yace who was arguing with her canvas tent. He saw Kipp mutate into his nude, two-legged form.

With a calm voice, Kipp said, "Maybe you should have waited for us."

Then he heard Yace. "This is important to me, Kipp! I want to see my father before he dies. He's supposed to help me. He's supposed to make me better. Nonbry, nor Dana, can help me, you know this! No one can, except for a family member." Her anger sounded like it had turned into tears, but he knew she would keep those tears from forming. "I asked you to come only because I knew you could keep up!"

Irwin walked past them with a small bundle of mossy sticks and twigs. He was going to start the fire but stopped to explain himself. "I am sorry Yace, I know I am slow. This is not Kipp's fault. This is mine."

"It's both your faults. Kipp should have been nipping at your heels the whole time! In the next town, we're buying you a real animal to ride! Sell those girls, trade them, I don't care. But you are no longer a miner, Irwin. You do not need those donkeys."

Irwin hated arguing. "Do not blame the donkeys for me being slow, Yace. They kept up with Blacky just fine. This is my fault. I have never been fast at anything. And I am not a runner."

"That's for sure."

Irwin knew there was nothing anyone could say that would settle her temper. "I will try harder tomorrow."

He left her, placed the kindling at the fire ring, and retrieved his fire-making satchel. He then went to work stoking their campfire to life. Just a bit of lantern oil on dried pieces of horse manure, and the fire was soon ablaze. There was enough warmth to dry out the kindling and moss stacked atop the fire. Though he had finally been successful at something, Irwin kept his eyes down, avoiding Yace's scrutiny.

She is acting like my father, ready to burst for no apparent reason. I wonder why? Should I ask? No.

He crept over to his packs and retrieved the kettle and a flask.

Kipp had been speedy in setting up her tent. "There you go Yace." He stepped back, proudly taking in the finely erected tent. Then the Clan-Duin headed over toward the pannier bags.

Yace called after him, "If you're going to get some food, bring the flasks too."

She sat down by the fire; her usual perky attitude gone.

Kipp returned with the food and water. He passed the flasks to Yace and Irwin and then took a seat to hand out Irwin's dried foods.

Yace grumbled and went toward the edge of the campsite. She returned with more than enough plums for herself, but she did not offer a piece of fruit to either man as she took her seat by the fire. They sat in silence as they ate the dried foods; Yace ate her plums.

When done, Yace tossed all her bags into her tent. Bitterly quiet, she took her small lantern, lit it, and retreated to her own space.

Irwin and Kipp sat next to the fire, and the rain began to fall. Slow at first, the wet sky soon deluged the campsite. Kipp kept his Clan-Duin form and found a place to sleep under a low-lying branch, away from the dying fire. Irwin glanced around before heading to Yace's tent. He did not want to put his tent together in the rain; it was late.

He opened the tent flap; the lantern was beginning to fade. Yace lay skewed across a layer of plush pillows. She had blankets thrown across the pillows and had curled up deep inside a thick covering. He tried to be quiet, but Yace heard him open the tent's portal.

"What is it?"

Irwin was wet from the rain. "Can I sleep in here tonight?"

With a grunt, she rolled over. He couldn't tell if she said yes or no, but then Yace clearly said, "Good night."

He didn't think she would kick him out, especially now that it was raining. Irwin removed each wet boot, each piece of wet clothing. Then he took up one of the many unused blankets. He curled up with his back against hers for warmth.

Kipp woke Irwin by putting his hand on his arm. Irwin was startled and moved out of the tent, his damp bundle of clothing in hand. He knew to give Yace her time and space in the morning.

"I'm amazed you slept with her," Kipp said. "She was cranky last night." The Clan-Duin had on a pair of pants, but he was bare chested. The campfire crackled, and Kipp turned toward it. He was already boiling water for a porridge breakfast.

"Why does she get so cranky in the evenings?"

"She was probably picking up on my thoughts last night," Kipp said. "I know she has a deep fear of plantation houses. There are good people out there, kind folk, who do put people up for the night. The Gypsy have stopped at places like that. I bet if we had stopped at that plantation house back there, we'd be put up. Instead, she's daring to push our journey faster, and make us sleep out on the side of the road in the freezing rain. She's bound to get sick!"

"I am alright with sleeping at these campsites," Irwin said, "Though this one is not as nicely kept as the others."

"That's something the Gypsy do. Nonbry calls it paying it forward. When you have twenty able-bodies, and half of them are bored, we tend to find things to do."

"Do all Gypsy do that?"

"No. I think we're the only ones. We've come across campsites that were completely broken: trees, tethers, boulders covering the firepit."

"That is rude."

"Yeah, well, all these campsites were made for and by the PCP. Not many travelers are as kind as the Gypsy."

"I thought these spots were made for pilgrimages."

"All of this is for Hakra."

He saw a twinge of jadedness in Kipp's eyes. "It was a nice gesture for other hikers, like me—firepits covered with branches and preset kindling piles, and stacks of pre-cut wood. Very thoughtful, indeed." Irwin remembered what he really wanted to talk to Kipp about. He sat down next to the Clan-Duin. "I am curious; how is it that Yace drank four carafes of wine, but she didn't seem drunk by the time we were back at the Inn?"

Kipp snorted; snot flew out of his nose. "Oh, yeah, you'll never want to try to out drink Yace. She can get drunk, and then level off and sober up while you get shitfaced and pass out."

"Why is that?"

"She's told me it's because she's Coterie. I think it's just her. She's not like most of those who are telepathic, which is why she needs to see her father before he dies.

"She's serious about you getting a horse, though. I could see her eye twitching in that way that lets me know not to press an issue. You'll get that look from time to time too; I imagine." Kipp sighed. "Ah looks ... that Coralin, she was so happy to have found me." He elbowed Irwin. "She threw herself upon me." He licked his lips.

"I do not understand why she was like that. But now that I think about it, the few Inns I have stayed at most of their older daughters acted that same way ... although Coralin was more forward than any other."

"They probably were hoping you'd save them from a life of servitude." Kipp sniggered, "I bet women dream of being saved by someone like you."

"What do you mean?"

"They're not dreaming of me saving them."

The tent flap moved, and Yace stepped out. Dressed in her nightgown, she strode across the muddied ground over to the fire. "What are you two doing out here? Talking about fornicating with women?"

Kipp glared at her while she stepped around them and their humble fire in search of a water flask. "Pull out the dried fish. I want something good to eat before we leave." It was Irwin who complied.

Yace was quick to dress and tossed her bags out of the tent. She hauled the cumbersome baggage toward the donkeys.

Kipp had taken nothing from his own luggage, so he had nothing to put away, and neither did Irwin. They watched her grunt and rant while tying her belongings to Jenn Jenn. "Are you going to stand there and gawk or help Kipp? Irwin?"

Irwin handed over the satchel of dried fish meat that they had eaten while waiting for Yace. She seemed more than angry, possibly hungry too. Now that she was breathing down their necks, they knew not to stand around. He helped Kipp dismantle the tent.

Yace sat back and ate her share of dried fish and plums while they packed up. The rain had let up during the nighttime, but now, as they began their day, it started to drizzle. And with the clouds as low-lying as they were, the fog pushed down occluding treetops. It was not going to be a warm day.

Yace mounted Blacky with Kipp's help. Irwin tied on his Jennies. She urged Blacky forward. Her words trailed off as her horse sprang into a fast trot. "Keep up this time."

The Jennies knew to follow the fast pace the lead horse was setting. They had no choice. They would be drug along if they did not.

28

<u>THE PCP</u>

It was still raining when they found Yace at that night's campsite; she had taken shelter under the trees. It was obvious that she had not been waiting long. They were quick to set up camp. Everyone wanted to get warm and dry.

She seemed more amicable on this night and shared her fruits with Irwin and Kipp. She asked Irwin to sleep next to her again—even offered Kipp a spot inside her tent, but he turned it down. The Clan-Duin would sleep outside, ears alert.

Yace's attitude lightened. If they did what she expected them to do, without being asked, backtalk, argue, or point out something they shouldn't have, she was happy. With the pace she set, they arrived every two days in towns and villages that were usually, under normal conditions, a three-day walk. Now they never stopped to enjoy a night on a soft bed, but they did pause at local taverns for a fresh meal and drink. From just before sunup until the last bit of daylight, Yace led a hearty trek along what felt to Irwin like a never-ending journey. It was hard for him to adjust to the hard-set pace. But by the tenth day, he could keep up with a certain ease of body and mind.

He had always been a walker. Now that Yace had lit a fire underneath him, he accepted his role as a runner. His body was built for it—gangly long legs and a sleek torso.

It appeared that when he put more effort into helping Yace her drive to see her father seemed less urgent. She continued to push them but allowed reprieves.

The forested countryside went from steep U-shaped valleys to rolling foothills along the Kruluver Mountain Range. Thick evergreens gave way to deciduous trees and large open spaces and wildlife were ever-present.

As they descended in elevation, following the hillsides and ever churning river, the cool crisp air turned humid. The transition was gradual, but one night as they settled into camp, there was no reprieve from the ever-pressing humidity. It was then that Irwin realized he had finally found what he wanted: warmer weather.

But this new humid climate was disagreeable. He was used to cold, crisp nights. It was a peculiar feeling, being warm all the time. Still, he was happy to be in weather more suited for how he wanted to dress. He preferred his red silky shirt rolled up to his biceps or a sleeveless tunic, tucked into his soldier's pants. He felt liberated from the thick hemp clothing he had worn all his life. They packed the long jackets, hoods, and cloaks away.

As they continued their daily descent, they found clear-cut areas. There were many deforested hillsides where logging roads slithered away from the clear-cuts and down toward the river. Logging was the livelihood in every village they passed through. From there, the wood supplies were barged downstream to Onj Raha.

The river grew wider, and the forests grew thicker with many tree species that Irwin had never seen before. Then the river departed from the roadway that zigzagged down a steep grade for several days. They passed through a mining village and kept on going.

For two days, they had no direct water source. Irwin and Kipp had to hike into the forest in search of a chasm of a creek for watering the animals and themselves. Coal was being mined further upstream. They both smelled it in the water. A day later, that creek led them back to the massive river they had been following from the start.

All that day, there was a constant rumble in the distance. They were approaching an enormous waterfall. At an elbow-turn on the roadway, their next campsite came into view. And just beyond, above the treetops, they saw that they were camped at the base of a massive cliff. This place was large and well-graded, but the campsite lacked much of what they were used to, although there was a giant bounder firepit in the center. Massive fir trees barricaded the thunderous rush of water. From the camp, there was no way to see the depth of the falls until they hiked down a well-worn trail.

They did not unpack their animals before journeying with bathing supplies down the winding footpath. Everyone wanted to see the grand view of that mysterious rushing sound. Thankfully, it was a short hike. The trail had been carved between protruding rocks and boulders—steps meandering up and down into a punchbowl chasm, a tight fit even for a person.

The river had etched away at the hard, rocky landscape for thousands of years. Large boulders had been broken and parts left behind. They descended into a rocky jumble, leftover from years and years of water churning sediment downstream. Light gray rocks gave way to a great wall of plummeting water. They had heard its low rumbling for half of their day's journey. Now they stood before its power and stood back in awe. Hundreds of thousands of gallons of water spilled over the edge of the towering and wide cliff side every moment of every day. Expansive, the wall of water cascaded into the rising mist and made it difficult to make out the opposite side of the river.

The waterfall they approached was an offshoot from the major river, broken apart by a rocky ledge where a few trees tried to thrive. There was an overhang where the water sprayed down into a pool below—knee-deep and five times as long as the falls' drop.

Yace peeled off her layers of sweaty clothing. Their entire ride that day, she had been ruminating about the idea of a cool shower. Irwin and Kipp also hastily removed their clothing.

The young woman grasped a small satchel of toiletries strung around her wrist and went in first. "It's kind of warm." Yace looked back at them, disappointed, as she stepped into the pool. "I was hoping it would be deeper. We could climb over these boulders to those other falls." She pointed to the main part of the river and falls.

"You said you wanted a shower. There you go," Kipp said, "That, over there, will take you downstream … if you're lucky."

"But I want to get cool." She turned away.

Kipp stood back, watching Yace.

It appeared that Kipp saw more to women than Irwin. To him, the Clan-Duin was animalistic, even somewhat hedonistic. He noticed saliva pooling at the corner of Kipp's mouth and felt embarrassed to be standing next to this flesh-hungry man.

Irwin studied Yace with a sense of humility. With her clothing on, she appeared larger than she was. He saw the clothing as armor for Yace, keeping her safe, making her feel protected. Without her clothing, she appeared frail. Her petite and slender body did not have curves like Saryh's. And Yace's skin was so pale she almost disappeared in the glimmering light of the pool's reflection. Though Irwin had seen Yace naked a few times, he felt he was seeing another side to her now.

I need to keep her safe.

She walked over to the small waterfall where enough water poured forth for a decent shower. "Yeah! This water is cooler than that pool," she called back and stepped under the falls. Her hair collapsed around her, clinging to her slender body. When her hair was dry, it hung to her hips, but when wet, it covered her buttocks. Once all her hair was soaked, she soaped it and her body into a frothy lather.

He knew that Yace knew they were watching. She peered out from under her soapy hair and glared at Kipp. "Are you two going to watch me the whole time?"

Her words felt like a hard slap to Irwin. He looked away, but Kipp sustained his lustful gaze.

Irwin left Kipp's side and approached her.

"Can I get you to wash my back?" She asked.

Irwin stepped up to her with his scrub brush and bar of soap. She pulled her hair across her shoulder, and he helped her with a few stray strands. He tried to be thorough about washing Yace's back, but her body felt weak, and he held back his force. The closer he was to her naked body, the more he realized he was scared for her.

"You can scrub harder," she said. "It's been a few days, and I'd like to get the sweat off my backside."

"I do not want to hurt you."

"You won't hurt me. Scrub harder," she said, turning away. "You're looking good these days, Irwin. With all that running, you're becoming lean and fit. Like you needed that, but you are looking really good. I almost feel as if you grew taller, too," she said. She turned around, facing him, staring at him.

She moved closer, her body nearly pressing against his. "Let me scrub your back," she said, urging him to join her under the waterfall.

He turned away and put his arms against the slick, rocky waterfall wall.

"This is how we do things in the Gypsy camp. We help each other," she said, scrubbing Irwin's back harder than he had done hers. She was leaving marks, but Irwin kept quiet. He enjoyed the hard scrubbing; it felt good.

Once Yace was done washing his backside, she pulled out her bathing oils and finished her beautifying rituals.

Irwin prolonged his enjoyment of the cool water, washing the rest of himself with a square of soap.

Kipp appeared as soon as Yace left the waterfall. He moved close to Irwin, crowding him under the water. Irwin stepped back to give his friend room to shower. The Clan-Duin spoke so that only Irwin could hear. "I know I can be a dog sometimes, but dang me! Yace was really trying to get a rise out of you." He slapped Irwin's shoulder. "Maybe one of these nights you should try cuddling with her under the covers. Most likely, she won't turn you away."

Irwin sensed Kipp was testing him. He asked, "You would be alright with that?"

Kipp's eye twitched. "Of course!"

"Just so I am clear on what you are implying. You are saying that I can couple with Yace? The woman you covet?"

Kipp threw his hands up. "Hey, as long as she takes to bed someone I approve of, I'd be alright with that." His eyes faltered. He was bluffing and Irwin knew it. He knew the Clan-Duin would not be alright with anyone else taking Yace to bed.

Yace stood on the shore's edge, drying off with one of her undergarments.

Kipp stepped out of the shower, eyeing Irwin. "What I mean is, I trust you to keep Yace safe."

That was the only genuine statement Kipp had delivered just then.

"I have no intention of coupling with Yace. Wanting to mate with her is not why I travel with you two." He shrugged and gazed down the obscured line of waterfalls. "Warmer weather is what I long for, and it is what I have found. As for flatter land, those are not mountain peaks." He pointed at the beautiful sight. "All my expectations are fulfilled."

"You are still heading to Onj Raha with us, right?"

Irwin chuckled. "Yes. I still plan to follow you two, just as we have talked about, and there is no way I could leave you now, anyway. I am curious to meet Yace's father. Besides, I have also been entertaining the idea of going on an adventure with you after all is done, if that is alright. Like you had said, you do not have to go back to the Gypsy right away. That is, after Yace is safely delivered."

Kipp nodded. "We should do that! If she doesn't accept me, after all we've done together .... You and me, we should go on our own adventure. Go study the women and the sights of the eastern seaboard." Again, he slapped Irwin's shoulder. Kipp's eyes glowed golden—possibly excited by the prospect of exploring Urthis with his new friend. "Dang me, I am glad to hear that! I was hoping you wouldn't just end all this once we got to Onj Raha. Maybe in the next town we buy some playing cards. I'll teach you how to play; how to count cards. Maybe we can make some money along the way."

Irwin was not keen on the idea of counting cards. He did, however, like the idea of learning how to play card games using his wit and cunning. "Yes, we can do that."

"Can you scrub my back?"

Irwin helped clean Kipp's backside, but then left his friend at the cool shower. Yace was gone from the water's edge, naked and carrying her clothing.

Rather than hold out for a change of clothing, Irwin put his pants back on. They were only dirty by a day. He strolled back up the rocky pathway.

Ambling along the narrow trail between the trees, listening to the birds and rustling of leaves, he felt a pang that told him that they were not alone. There, in dark blue uniforms with blackened cufflinks and hard black boots, four PCP soldiers had come across their animals. Yace stood away from the trailhead, fear in her eyes, two Clan-Duin patrolmen standing at her side. Irwin saw her shaking and sobbing. The soldiers held long blades against her naked flesh. Two other Clan-Duin soldiers were going through the packs on Jenn Jenn. Blacky and the donkeys were partially asleep, tired from that days' journey, and they paid no attention to the four Clan-Duin Patrolmen, or their large warhorses tied to a tree by the roadside.

"Well, hello there, stranger." The lead Clan-Duin called to Irwin when he stepped into the open camp area. He stopped the ransacking and moved toward Irwin.

Yace turned to him.

"Irwin!" She clutched her clothing against her naked body, her blue eyes filled with terror. The men pushed their long knives against her skin. There was one blade at her throat, the other pressed at her abdomen. Had she been able to telepathically communicate with him, she would have shouted, *get these knives off me*! He saw that look in her eyes.

He suddenly wished they had worked more on his abilities after that first night. She was nearly fifty feet away. He knew he could not summon the metal from that far away.

I need to get closer.

He raised his hands, dropping his belongings on the ground, advancing slowly. The lead Clan-Duin soldier growled. "Stop where you are."

Irwin tried to summon the metal from where he now stood. Still, he could not. "What is it you are looking for, gentlemen?"

The larger of the two patrolmen rummaging through their belongings strode toward him. Irwin stood frozen to the ground. The soldier's stride and his size were immense. He looked up at the large-shouldered Clan-Duin man. The soldier sniffed the air around Irwin. "You smell. That wash did you no good."

Irwin kept his hands out and up. He dared to smell his armpits. "That is interesting. I used half a bar of soap."

Yace's voice shook. "Irwin?"

Irwin rued the idea of fighting. Even when his family members beat him, he had succumbed to their will. They used their powers against him. If he was forced to, he would; at best, his Metalistic ability needed training. He could mine, but he did not know how to defend himself properly, nor could he talk his way out of a conflict. All he could do was to take their blades. His eyes locked with Yace's right before the soldier threw a punch to the side of his head.

He went flying and landed on a layer of small rocks, closer to Yace.

"Irwin!"

He was not knocked out, but he could see spots floating in the air in front of him. No matter, he was now close enough to liquefy the metal daggers piercing Yace's flesh. In one millisecond, he extracted the metal from the oblivious men who were laughing at him. He had found his center.

He stood, wrought the stolen metal, and flushed it across his skin. Now they were alert that Irwin was Talented, and that they had lost their blades. They relaxed their stance long enough for Yace to try and free herself. She spun sideways, but a Clan-Duin soldier grabbed her arm. The second soldier forced her to drop her clothing while he grabbed her other arm.

Had Irwin been disoriented too long? Yace shouted for help again, and a patrolman lunged toward him, broadsword outstretched, keen on destroying him. The sword, the patrolman, and Irwin crashed to the ground. Again, Irwin absorbed the metal saber just as the back of his head met a hard, jagged rock, this time knocking him out while the real fight began.

29

<u>Kipp to the Rescue</u>

Yace cried for help and suddenly Kipp was there, racing into the campground from behind the soldiers. On four legs, he dove straight for the soldier closest to her, knocking him off Yace's arm. That maneuver gave her enough time to free herself from the other soldier's grasp, but they struggled against one another.

Across camp, a larger, older soldier was ransacking their belongings. He wasn't bothered by the fighting and kept on piling their rations onto the ground. A wild cackle parted his lips when he found the large cache of silver rocks Irwin had stashed deep within his packs.

In that moment, the Jennies must have realized the commotion happening around them. They immediately became agitated when seeing their caretakers under attack. Some sort of animalistic communication happened between Jenn Jenn and Nee Nee, and Blacky too. And suddenly the animals pulled themselves out of the loose tie down Kipp had made. Although they were still tied together, the horse and donkeys became free and gave the ransacking Clan-Duin trouble. They took off, and he had to race after them.

Meanwhile, Yace made desperate use of her telekinesis skills and levitated herself and the Clan-Duin, who wouldn't let go, up and into the air. He panicked. That was the opportunity she needed to pull away. Yace landed on the ground, yet her hold on the soldier remained firm. He floated in the air from her telekinesis. Angrily, she then smashed his body against the hard, rocky ground, extinguishing his life. Wasting no time, she levitated that deceased soldier over the trees, and threw them toward the falls.

The soldier who stood over Irwin's unconscious body was dumbfounded by his own lack of a blade. He became Yace's next target. Somehow, she managed to telekinetically grab that soldier by the throat and collapsed his entire neck as he stood there. She watched him struggle for his life. But soon she levitated him too and tossed him toward the falls. Now her attention turned to Irwin—still unconscious.

Kipp had been taught how to fight by master fighters, *Shayot*, and the most loyal of guardsmen under Hakra himself. Alio and his brother and sister, Olei and Leola, along with Koloto, had been saved by the Gypsy a few years back; in turn, they offered to train anyone who wanted to know how to fight in every imaginable manner. The young Gypsy Clan-Duin used this knowledge to toss around the guard who had held Yace in a death grip. He found pride in throwing kicks and punches to that PCP soldier, clearly young and naïve about his Clan-Duin powers. It was obvious that this guardsman had little knowledge of hand-to-hand, or canine-against-canine combat. Kipp was sure this must have been his first outing since being enlisted to serve the PCP. As Kipp morphed from one body into another, the soldier was no match for him. Kipp played with him as a canine would with a ground rodent before finally landing a deadly blow, killing the adolescent PCP soldier. Standing over the dead man, who was now bleeding out on the dirt ground, Kipp smiled victoriously.

All around them dust had risen. Blacky and the donkeys were maneuvering this way and that, racing around the large barren campground, trying to get away from the soldier running after them. They narrowly missed plowing right across Irwin and Yace twice as they kick up rocks and dirt in the middle of the melee.

Watching the frantic moment, Yace joined the chase, though all she wanted was the soldier. She caught the Clan-Duin who was still running after the horse and donkeys. With her telekinesis, she grabbed him as he raced by. She was ready to end his life too, but Kipp intervened. Leaping through the air, he grabbed the soldier by the shoulder, threw him down, and went for the throat, snapping that man's neck with his hard and jagged teeth, and left him to bleed out.

As Kipp walked away, he morphed back into his two-legged body and wiped the blood from his face. "Dang me! I'm gonna need to take another shower."

"Not now, Kipp! We're leaving."

"Why? You think there'll be more?" Kipp said, "That's the first brigade we've seen since leaving Jo Hara. I don't think there'll be another one for a while."

"I don't care. I don't want to stay here."

"What about Irwin?"

Yace replied, "He's unresponsive, but he's not dead."

"We shouldn't move him."

"But we must leave. I don't trust that there won't be more soldiers."

"Were any of them telepathic?"

"No, I don't think they were. At least none of them said anything telepathically. But they knew not to hold my skin ... except with their blades."

Kipp stood above Irwin, studying him. "There might be a larger town down river. Remember, we passed that small village about a day ago?"

Yace also gazed at their unconscious friend. "Okay, fine, I guess we stay. I'll make him a poultice. Retrieve their clothing; then take their bodies to the river to dispose of them."

"That sounds like a lot of work. Why strip them?"

"Their clothing!"

"Have you looked in their baggage? They'd have cleaner clothing in there, probably."

Kipp went to one of the soldier's horses and rummaged through the saddlebags. Yace walked over to Blacky and the donkeys. They had finally stopped racing and were now parked near the soldier's horses.

Kipp loudly commented. "I was right!"

"You are?"

"Yeah. They're not from anywhere around here. Their bags are decently packed with clothing and rations. I say we take them, and anything else they have that we need. And we'll take two of their horses. Sell the others in the next town."

"Why would we do that? Think about it, Kipp. Why would anyone sell PCP horses?"

He stared at her before replying. "They wouldn't."

"Exactly! We'll let them go. They can fend for themselves. Who knows, maybe the Gypsy will find them and take them in. With two more, they could have their own patrol. They could be an acting escort or go pillage."

Kipp chuckled, "Your mind sometimes."

She took out of her bags their medicine sack and returned to Irwin to address his injuries. But there were no apparent contusions, only a bit of blood on the rocks below his head. She used smelling salt, even plugged his nose to wake him, but he remained still for some time. In the meantime, Kipp set up camp, and did all the chores—sorting baggage, feeding the animals, and looking around on the ground for anything the soldiers may have dropped in the scuffle.

Kipp then caught a meal near the river's edge and found rosemary and wild chives on his way back to camp. He tried his hand at making dinner, using what he had found and from Irwin's sack of herbs. Meanwhile, Yace watched over Irwin as he slept.

Irwin remained unconscious until suppertime. When his eyes fluttered open, Yace was the first thing he saw.

A smile spread across her flat lips instantly. "You're awake! I tried everything I knew: poultice on your head, salts to wake you. We thought you were dead, but you were breathing so .... I'm sure you were hit really hard by a rock." He blinked several times. "You know who I am, don't you?"

He wiped his face and the sleep from his eyes. "You are Yace, and he is Kipp." He groaned. "Beyond that, I ... I remember nothing."

"You were knocked out by a brute of a Clan-Duin."

Kipp said, "We need to teach you how to fight, Irwin! Yace said all you did was take their metal, which was a good start. But maybe next time, put up your fists. Maybe encase *them* in metal, throw a few punches. You know, engage the enemy."

Irwin felt the back of his head where he had hit the ground. Had he been anyone else, he would have died from the head trauma. He looked around at their camp. "You two are alright?"

Yace said, "We didn't get as hurt as you did."

"She killed two. I killed two. And we already disposed of their bodies. We're gonna take two of their horses, too. We were lucky. Those Patrolmen were trying to ransack us. They would've killed us.

"They rove in fours," Kipp added, "usually on half-moon patrols ... unless there is a major city nearby. But Yace, you said that Onj Raha is still half a moon away, right?"

Yace nodded.

"Most likely, that'll be the only pack we'll see between here and there."

"I hope you're right," she said, "or we'll be knee deep in PCP by morning."

Irwin put his hands up. "At least you two are alright. And we still have all our belongings, correct?"

Yace said, "Yeah."

He smelled rosemary. "What's for supper?"

"Well, I started fixing the fish like you do, but I added too much water. So now it's soup." Kipp said, "Fish soup!"

"I still have some of that flat bread from the last village," said Yace. "It might be a little mangled after those guys ruffled up our packs, but probably still edible."

"Just crumble it into the soup." Kipp peered into the pot of simmering fish soup.

Irwin rubbed his head again and looked at Yace. "Is it usual that the PCP ransack animals left unattended?"

Kipp answered. "It happens all the time, especially if you are meek and fearful of the PCP. They're bullies. They take advantage of the weak, as any prey animal would." He pointed toward the mountains. "It happened to the Gypsy outside of Akarah."

"I don't think that counts, Kipp," Yace said. "The Gypsy saved Alio and Olei, Koloto and Leola that day. Had they not interfered with us, they wouldn't have seen the error of their ways. Sometimes it's good to come across PCP, but not all the time."

"Koloto? He traveled with you?" Irwin was stunned. "Large, thick body? Could heft a moose across his shoulders?"

Kipp gasped, "Yeah! You've met him?"

"Irwin passed the summit, Kipp," Yace said. "He met Fay and her charming sisters ... stayed at their place for a night. Of course, he would meet Koloto."

"Ah, the women at the summit of the Kruluver Mountain range. I remember them well ... Fay, Eliza, and Cheryl."

"What do you remember about Koloto, Irwin?" Yace asked.

"Koloto? He was terrifying ... now I know why my smell agitated him. But his horses were like Blacky, large and intimidating. It was the second time I had ever seen any horse that big."

"Koloto has the biggest horses I've ever seen too," Kipp said, "Probably because he's the biggest Clan-Duin/Erthin hybrid you'll ever meet."

Irwin remembered looking at Koloto's beasts. "I was not sure what they were at first. All I saw was steam coming out of their noses. They did not look like horses."

Kipp said, "I remember his horses as playful. They would chase the chickens, and the goats too."

"We stayed at the summit for what, half a moon's time? It was obvious to everyone that Koloto wanted to be with Fay," Yace said. "They hit it right off. And soon thereafter, he told us Gypsy he was going to remain behind ... never saw him smile in the two years he was part of the Gypsy. But Fay made him smile."

Irwin said, "Koloto definitely looked Clan-Duin. I did not know he was Erthin too."

"He's a mixture of Clan-Duin, Erthin, and a little Mortal; but mostly Clan-Duin." Yace gazed at the setting sun, the twilight that Irwin loved so much.

"Was that your first fight, Irwin?" Kipped asked, probably not wanting to let go of that bone.

"Outside of family members beating me, yes, that was my first fight."

"Yeah, that's what I figured." Kipp picked up the pan of fish soup. "We should probably have a meal before combat class."

He filled and passed bowls of salmon soup to Irwin and to Yace. Irwin devoured his. But Yace critiqued Kipp's cooking while they ate. Then they fought over what Irwin should learn about fighting first.

This is tiresome.

"How about this ... let me show you what I can do first." He flushed metal across his skin, coating his hands, his arms, then his entire torso until his whole body, including his clothing, was encapsulated.

The two stared in awe; then Kipp asked, "Can you throw the metal from your skin? Like daggers?"

"Maybe orbit metal around you?" Yace added. "I've seen earth Erthins do it with rocks and dirt. I can levitate only a few objects at a time, but the more things I have, the harder it is to control. That's why I need to see my father."

Irwin tried everything they suggested. They made him push spikes across his flesh, making him appear monster-like. They asked him to summon cooking pots and turn them into spears and daggers.

That night, they pushed Irwin's limits, but he was gaining important knowledge about his abilities.

By the end of that first night of practice, Irwin could throw small thumb-sized daggers at nearby trees, pegging them precisely every time, but only from short distances. His ability to control the metal as it left him was not as easy as it was to pull it into his flesh. Once he was further from his target than twenty feet, his control diminished. But the distances were less cumbersome when it came to absorbing metal. After practicing with Yace, he could feel and summon metal objects into his outstretched hand from fifty feet away.

This is new.

Learning to utilize the talents given to him was the simple part. Learning how to be defensive was more difficult.

Kipp was trying to introduce every style of physical combat, working on all aspects of warfare with him. No one training session was the same. Luckily, he already had well-defined muscles in his arms from working the mines, and quick legs now from chasing Blacky and the donkeys.

A daily routine ensued.

Every morning before they took to the road, he and Kipp went over body-building techniques that had been taught to Kipp by Olei and Alio. And before bedtime, he worked on his Metalistic skills with Yace.

She encouraged Irwin and his Talents further than he ever thought possible.

30

<u>ONJ RAHA</u>

After watching how Kipp rode, Irwin tried to keep the same standing position while learning to be an equestrian. His butt hovered above the saddle but was still beaten up by it. He just didn't have the balance for such things. He bounced around, trying to keep control of himself and his horse. After a while, he made them go slower, despite Yace's objections. It was hard to keep the giant horse from taking large strides and bouncing around. These warhorses were built to cover a lot of ground in little time. Irwin's first riding lesson consisted of learning to slow his horse down, to keep his balance in the seat. The first day, he hurt from one end of his body to the other.

By the end of day two of riding lessons, although incredibly sore, staying astride, communicating, and keeping a good cadence now seemed easier. He learned to have better balance, seemingly overnight. The donkeys were also improving at keeping up with the horse. And when they stopped, the smaller animals would stand under the enormous beasts for shade. They would gallop along the side of Irwin's horse as it trotted at a wild pace.

At the next town, Yace used some of the money they had taken from the PCP and purchased them a good night's rest, well-laundered clothing, hot baths, and a couple of good meals. By the next morning, they were well-rested and ready to move on.

They held to their daily routine, except when stopping for a night in a town or village. Otherwise, they woke up, ate, and the men practiced sparring. Then they rode on. In the evenings they stopped before the day's light was gone to make camp, eat supper, practice Metalistic skills, and then sleep. They barely had time to recuperate from their ride or their rituals. There was no free time. And now, because they each had their own warhorse, Yace made the men dress the part of soldiers. She kept her focus on making their drive to Onj Raha unyielding and without further incident. She was making up for what she felt was lost time. Irwin knew this and did his best.

During that time, Yace had become more annoying. The closer they were to Onj Raha, the more she talked about her father. Everything she said was speculative, but it was all she talked about: What was his life like, his lifestyle, his money, his family? Did she have siblings and, if so, how many? She wondered aloud about his likes and his dislikes, often ruminating to no end.

Irwin figured the reason she rambled on like this was so she would not be disappointed when she did meet this old and dying father. But it was the way she talked about his imminent demise that made their race against time more tangible.

From the streets of Jo Hara to the first signs of rural Onj Raha, they had ridden for a moon's cycle: thirty-two days—a trek that would normally take fifty-five days. And in all that time, they passed only one other brigade of Clan-Duin PCP soldiers who did not stop the three travelers, probably because they looked the part.

Their last day on the eastbound road was at a slow trot. Tired eyes stared forward, studying the oncoming horizon. The people laboring in the fields were watching their approach. Outbuildings, mostly for food and livestock storage, popped up now and again throughout the cultivated landscape. There were many aqueducts running parallel and perpendicular to the road, furnishing all the crops with fresh river water.

To the east, in the distance, they closed in on the urban sprawl. Even further were large spires and towering buildings which marked the center of Onj Raha. Houses lined the lanes and spread out on grids just like the aqueducts. Stone and mortar and wood buildings were sporadic at first, but soon they clustered, forming dense neighborhoods.

Before long, the muddy gravel roadway gave way to cobbled roads. Now four and five-story buildings crowded the skyline. The further into the city they traveled, the more the building façades changed; it was as if they were going back in time watching the architecture change from stark to more ornate in design, structure, and flow.

Yace led. Irwin and Kipp kept their horses side by side behind her steed. When people heard the horses' mighty hoof steps hitting the cobbled roadway, they parted. Some dared to look up, while others looked away. No one ever made direct eye contact with Yace or her men. Nearly everyone, everywhere, it seemed to Irwin, feared PCP soldiers. Yet within a city of this size, there were many PCP and most they saw were on foot, not horseback.

The men kept a look-out for roaming brigades. They had passed several sets of walking soldiers, mostly Clan-Duin. And then they saw the first all-Erthin entourage on warhorses, three blocks away and closing in on them. He saw Yace's head moving around as she tried to navigate physically and mentally through the crowded street. He knew she was trying not to hear all the surrounding voices. Had she not seen the four soldiers trained upon them?

Irwin turned and saw that beyond those soldiers, they were the only ones on horseback for many blocks.

"Yace!" He shouted at her.

Kipp also tried to get her attention, "Yace! The livery. The livery!"

She looked around toward the open stable yard and spun her horse in that direction. She did not look down to see the people her horse nearly stepped upon. Nor did she look back at her companions as she rode into the open barnyard.

Chickens and pigmy goats scattered.

Yace dismounted first and greeted the stable manager. Irwin and Kipp stood near one another, looking on from afar. Her words were drowned out by the hum of city life. Soon young stable hands jumped from the hayloft, startling the chickens back out into the enclosed yard, and took the horses from them.

"He says there's an Inn around the corner ... says it's quiet with laundry service," she said upon returning to her friends.

Irwin watched Yace's face struggle with a range of emotion. She was having a challenging time, ignoring all the city people's meandering thoughts.

He put his hand on her arm. "You are tired." He had to remember the formalities. "My Lady." He then addressed his friend, "Kipp, please take care of the baggage on the donkeys. I will take Lady Yace to the Inn."

Yace smiled at him. She was clearly tired. "Thank you, Irwin." It was late in the afternoon, and everyone on the streets was headed in all different directions. He had to let go of Yace when they stepped into the street. And once he did, her stride became three times as quick as his own. He had to push through the thong of people to find her halfway up the steps to the Inn's front room. Irwin ran to get to the door before it closed.

He stood behind her, straightening his wrinkled uniform. An old woman at the front desk asked Yace to repeat herself several times. She glanced back at Irwin. He knew she wanted him to touch her again, needed to take the voices away, needed to remain calm.

The old woman finally got it right. "One night, three rooms, meals, and baths for the lady and her men. Would you like your clothing cleaned?"

Yace had already told the woman they had dirty laundry. She jumped when the door flung open, and in came Kipp, overloaded with their belongings. He used his boot to close the door.

Irwin tried to grab a few of the bags, but Kipp held tight to everything.

Yace spoke through gritted teeth, "Yes, linens too."

"Okay then." The old woman licked her pencil and entered the requests in a ledger. "That will be thirty silver pieces."

"Thirty silvers?!" Kipp said, "For only one night? That's a bit high, don't you think?"

Yace indicated to Irwin that she expected him to produce the silver.

He did not hesitate. He gave a large handful of coins to the woman. She examined and counted each piece before smiling at him. "It's rare to see a Mortal PCP." She studied them both. "He is a handsome one."

No one said a thing.

"I am Gladis, by the way. Gladis Humphries. Follow me, please."

Gladis moved slowly up the stairs, and they shadowed her with impatience and exhaustion.

Kipp was covered in sweat when they arrived at the top of the stairs. He dropped the baggage in the middle of the hallway. There were six rentable rooms, and Yace had bought out the top floor where there was a shared bathing room at the end of the hallway with a water closet and a small tub. Gladis showed them how to work the gravity-fed water. Then she showed them the rooms, opening one door at a time. Yace took the largest of the three, a suite with a bed big enough to sleep all three of them. Gladis also showed them the laundry chute and said that supper would be ready soon. "Many thanks for staying here." The gray-haired woman repeated this a few times and then went back down the stairs.

Kipp said, "Well done, Yace. We are finally in Onj Raha! Now, where does your old man live?"

"I'm supposed to contact Nonbry before we go anywhere. He knows approximately where my father is located." She was studying them both. "I need you two to organize the bags and put my stuff in my room."

Kipp grunted but did as instructed.

Irwin could see she was tense. He put his hand upon her shoulder, and she sighed. "Thank you for grounding me." She took several deep breaths.

"That is why I am here, correct?"

How are you doing, Irwin? I sense you are bothered by the amount of metal in the city.

I am coping. If I do not think about it, I am alright. What about you?

I'm a wreck.

You are afraid something bad is going to happen?

No, well yeah. I'm just glad we are finally here … and I'm scared. I hope my father is still alive! I don't know what I'll do if he isn't.

Kipp glared at the two of them huddled together and pushed past them. He flung Yace's bags onto the bed. "Anything else?"

"No." *He's jealous.*

Why would he be jealous?

Because he's afraid of you. He thinks you want me. We both know how much he covets me.

Afraid of me? That is just silly. Kipp has nothing to fear from me.

"Thank you, Irwin, for grounding me." She winked at him. "You two go eat. I'll be down soon. Once I've contacted Nonbry."

"Will you be alright doing that by yourself? I can stay here with you if you need."

"No, go and eat, Irwin." She pulled out the talisman from a small pouch.

Irwin heard a twinge of hesitancy in her voice, noticed her studying the small wooden necklace with a forlorn look. "You will be alright doing that alone?"

"I've done this alone before. Why should tonight be any different?"

He shrugged. "See you downstairs." He followed Kipp to the main floor. And as they reached the last steps, Kipp came bounding back up. "She requests our soiled linens now."

Back up they went to gather their clothing.

The stairway was long and spiraling, and by the time they reached the bottom step again, they were both out of breath. "We should race up that tomorrow morning a few times for our morning workout."

Irwin's leg muscles were already burning. "Maybe, if they were in a straight line."

"Yeah, but who likes easy?"

Gladis came out from the kitchen and looked almost as if she had forgotten them. "I am sorry." She corrected herself. "My name is Gladis Humphries. Let me know if there is anything I can get for you."

"Here are our dirtied linens."

"We are hungry, Gladis." Irwin said as Kipp handed off the bags.

"Supper will be finished soon." Gladis was short and thin, but the energy she exuded was thick and beaming. She took the first sack of laundry, Yace's belongings. "I have access to the chute, over here." She took them around a corner and opened a hatch. Dropping Yace's bundle into the chute, Gladis held the opening for them to do the same. "I'll get those cleaned after supper. Will the Lady be joining us?"

"Yes, after a while," Irwin said. "She is resting for now. Our ride was a hard one."

"Oh, alright. What brings you to Onj Raha?"

"We are escorting Miss Yellsen to meet her father. He lives here in Onj Raha. His health is failing him, and she wants to be with him before he passes."

"Is she close with her father?"

Kipp answered, "This is her first visit here, to Onj Raha."

Gladis nodded. "Death is a hard reality. I am so sorry for what she must be enduring. My husband, Carl, went with Death recently. It's been hard on me." She glanced around at the walls. "This place was much easier to run when he was here. Things are breaking now. And people are not stopping here anymore. But I am so happy to have three of you to serve. I hope you enjoy your stay." There was a spark of despair in the old woman's eyes.

"Tonight, I am making my husband's favorite meal. It's my favorite too ... a lot of food for one, but I feed the stable boys every few days.

"Had you not shown up, I would be eating lamb and potatoes all by myself. But I enjoy sharing. If you've been traveling for a long time, I would expect you to be famished for fresh-cooked food, not living off the land type of food. I have a leg of lamb with chutney, baked beets, and potatoes.

"I also have wine that Oliver, the livery owner, makes. And my sour bread will be done soon. I trade bread for wine frequently.

"My husband and I never had children. That's why we bought the Inn. We wanted to make a difference in people's lives, especially since we couldn't have children. Had I not been plagued with a barren belly; all my recipes would be handed down to our next generation." She motioned them to come inside the warm kitchen and renewed her chattering.

After sampling some of her food, Kipp said, "Your food is comparable to a cook we met along the way. Everything she made was magical."

Irwin knew he was comparing Gladis to Patrice.

"Yum, this is really, really good."

Irwin and Kipp set the large dining table with plates, cups, and serving utensils. They helped carry out bowls of potatoes, beats, chutney, a leg of lamb, and sourdough rolls.

They waited for Yace as they sat at the table and passed around the food. But she did not appear. So, they continued to listen to the old woman who only stopped talking long enough to chew and swallow.

"You like the meal?" she asked after finishing her first bite. "This was my husband's favorite."

"It's delicious." Kipp said.

Irwin was glad he was being kind to the old and lonely woman.

"Carl, my husband ... did I mention him ... went with Death recently? It's been hard on me ever since." Gladis looked around the dining room again. "This place was much easier to run when he was here. How things are breaking, now. And people. They just are not stopping by anymore. I'm so happy to have you two staying here. I enjoy sharing my meals. My husband and I never had children, which is why we bought this Inn. We wanted to make a difference in people's lives."

Irwin smiled and nodded while stuffing himself with the tasty meal. Both he and Kipp managed to eat half of the lamb's leg, along with all the extras Gladis had prepared. The men also enjoyed the wine Gladis had opened, leaving a drink for Yace who finally turned up only after they were finished eating. While Yace ate, they sat back, stuffed from their meal. Gladis kindly served Yace a plate of cooled lamb and chutney and filled her glass with wine before reminiscing once more.

31

A MEETING WITH DEATH

I t looked like Yace was enjoying the home-cooked meal and the wine. The old woman retold her stories again: about her husband, her lack of children, and how much she enjoyed cooking.

Irwin and Kipp left her to eat and listen while they went back upstairs to wash up and get ready for whatever might happen next. They bantered back and forth while the Clan-Duin washed up first, and Irwin organized his belongings and shaved. Once Kipp was done, Irwin entered the water closet, rinsing grime from his body.

Before he could finish drying, Yace appeared in the hallway, grabbing his arm as he stepped out of the bathing room. "I need you two ready to go."

"I just threw my soldier clothes down the chute."

Yace went into Kipp's room.

Irwin hustled past Kipp's room; he could hear him bowing to her demands. "Yup, yeah, ready to go!"

She stormed into Irwin's room without knocking. "Do you have any clean clothing?"

"Yes."

Here we go.

"Do you know where we are going?"

"Yeah, I know where we're going. What are you going to wear?"

"Trust me, Yace, I will not embarrass you."

She bit the inside of her cheeks. "You'd better not."

He wanted to touch her, ground out her angry energy. But the look she held gave him the chills. And she stepped back out of his reach with a defensive posture, glaring at him.

"Are you sure you want to do this?"

"What? Yes! Get dressed, now!"

He could hear her grumbling at Kipp again and then slamming the door to her own room.

Kipp stood at Irwin's doorway. "She's turned moody! I'm guessing she didn't finish that glass of wine."

Irwin put on his red blouse and the dark blue embroidered pants with red stitching. It all fit better now that his body had grown with muscle. He slipped his vest over the shirt—made sure to wear the rich attire Yace preferred. The calf-chaps were a little tight, but still fit over his boots. But he did not have a belt that matched.

He looked at Kipp, hoping for confirmation that he was well dressed. "Acceptable?"

"Decent, I guess. She's the one you must please, not me."

He clomped into Yace's room. She peered up at him. "Thank you. That looks better than anything else you've worn in days."

He wanted her approval as much as he wanted her peace of mind. "Are you going to be alright?"

"Yes. Of course! Stop asking stupid questions."

"Do not snarl at me like my father would."

She is nervous.

"Let's get going." Yace glared and swooshed past him to descend the stairs.

He and Kipp followed her down to the main room. Gladis was nowhere to be seen or heard, probably down in the basement doing their laundry. Yace led them down to the city streets, less crowded than earlier that day.

"Irwin." Yace waited at the end of the steps for him. Her eyes demanded he take her arm, help ground her out. Thank you.

I hope this goes well for her. I hope she gets what she wants from this. I will be sad for Yace if this does not go the way she hopes.

Can you please be quiet with your thoughts? Her angry voice cut through his random mental conversation.

Sorry.

They rounded the corner of the alleyway and stepped onto the main roadway. The last leg of their journey had begun. They traversed from the west side to the city center, and Irwin kept close to Yace's side. Kipp remained three strides behind. Arm in arm, Irwin was close enough to talk to Yace. But it was apparent she wanted them to keep silent. There were people, Mortals mostly, walking in small groups. There were also more PCP soldiers patrolling on both foot and horseback at this time of night. As long as they continued on as they were, they most likely would not be bothered.

After a while, Irwin asked, "Do you know where we are going?"

"I had to ask Gladis for directions. What Nonbry told me made no sense. Anyway—" Yace rolled her eyes. "—Holy Hakra, that woman can talk!

"Nonbry mentioned a black spired building ... said it's located in old town Onj Raha. Gladis says it's in the sultry district where the Talented live. She also said someone like me shouldn't go there. Then she proceeded to tell me that she might have met my father once, and—holy Hakra—she did not like him. She said the building with the dark towers is in the middle of the Talented District, not in the old part of town. Nonbry told me my father owns an herb shop at the base of the spires. Potions and Remedies. That's what we're looking for."

"Gladis met your father?"

"She thinks she did; her impression was that he is rude. She didn't like him ... said he's a surly old man who is spiteful. I'm not sure how much I trust an old woman like her. She seems a bit full of herself. And I thought I talked a lot."

"We were glad to leave the table when you arrived. Gladis must have repeated herself at least five times."

"Twice for me. Good thing I can eat fast."

She held the instructions Gladis sketched on a piece of ledger paper. The map was not detailed, but there were a few named shops as points of reference, and only two street names. She studied the uneven pencil markings when they stopped under a mounted lantern. Yace turned the paper around a few times, then pointed the way.

Irwin kept quiet. He walked along her side, even after she had dropped his arm. As they went further away from the Inn, there were fewer people in the streets. Now the only types of people they saw were those with darker skin or vibrant red hair, people with Talents.

They had found the sultry side of Onj Raha. Dark and olive skinned, scantily clad women whistled down from windows at the men who passed by their saloon. It was that time of night. Kipp motioned toward the nearby saloon and signaled Irwin to take in the dressed-up women.

But Irwin was eyeing the metal gates across the street from the rambunctious brothel. Like Yace, he had to keep his focus.

Walk forward. Follow Yace. Keep Calm. Breathe.

They were still looking for the black spired building that towered above the stone and mortar structures surrounding them.

Shadows moved behind closed curtains. They heard babies crying, children laughing, and adults loving and fighting. A dog barked in the distance, and the wind lifted scraps of litter. They followed Yace down another street, and then they saw the spires two blocks ahead.

"Gladis was wrong about the streets." Yace put the piece of paper between her breasts. "I can't fault her. She's old and doesn't like to leave her home." She picked up her pace and Irwin and Kipp followed.

They sped down the street and stopped in front of the dark building. Spires rose from each corner of the block-long structure. It looked like all the rest of the buildings they had passed except for the intricacies at its edges. There was the herb shop called Potions and Remedies that reeked of herbs, where bunches of sage hung from the interior rafters for drying. No light emanated from inside the store, but they could see a lantern shining from a back room.

Yace opened the unlocked door and walked inside.

"Are you sure about this Yace?" Kipp asked, following close.

They ventured through the shop, toward the light, like bugs to a flame. Yace stepped through the back doorway where they found a long stairwell that led to the residence above. There was nothing either man could say or do to stop her at this point. Yace remained in the lead, up the stairs to the second floor.

Now they stood before large, wooden double doors, closed tight. Yace did not falter. She knocked with all the fierceness she had used to lead them here.

After a long moment, an old Clan-Duin man answered. His light amber eyes surveyed all the faces before him but held still on hers the longest. "Good evening, my Lady." His dark bald head gleamed in the dim light. His brown face, bushy black and white eyebrows, and large ears were the only hairy parts on his head. He wore a drab gray servant's uniform, looked to be past his prime by thirty years.

The elderly man bowed his shiny head. Did he know who she was? The servant did not speak to Yace, but their eyes locked briefly. He motioned all of them into the long foyer. The ancient Clan-Duin studied Yace again. He bowed once more and held forth a sweeping motion with his left hand. "This way, please." He led them into a grand residence and up another flight of stairs.

They ascended four more flights and finally reached the top floor. It was warm and filled with stagnant air. The elderly servant's hand shook when proceeding to an enormous door and opened it. Immediately they were blasted by the odor of defecation, urination, and decomposing body stench.

The old Clan-Duin stood at the door. "He waits for you." The man addressed Yace. Once they passed through the threshold, the old servant left.

Kipp said, "Yace, I don't think he's alive." He could smell each odor and delineate it. "Yace?" Kipp turned to Irwin. "Why are we doing this again?"

Yace pulled her sleeve across her nose and mouth. She did not look back at Irwin or Kipp. They had stopped halfway into the dark bedroom and were taking in the deadened sight.

Kipp pinched his nose and closed his mouth, but he kept close to Yace.

Irwin did the same, two steps behind Kipp. The room was long and vaulted, surrounded by enormous dormer windows covered in dark curtains. It was all but barren except for drab paintings and an oversized bed piled with blankets. A lit tin lantern hung above the bedside, shedding a shard of light upon her father's withered body.

Yace approached the bed and stopped at her father's side. He was tucked below an array of blankets; his right hand protruded from beneath the layers. Yace took his hand. She held it for a long time, and at last he gripped her back.

The corpse's eyes shot open and stared at Yace. They were white—bone chilling. His short white hairs appeared to stand up on his head. Her father was as pale as Yace. He had appeared dead until that moment. He stared at his daughter and said nothing the other two could hear. They watched the exchange, startled.

Yace did not fight against her father. Her other hand sought out his under the covers. Grasping both her father's hands, she leaned in close. Their intense gaze did not cease.

Neither Irwin nor Kipp blinked or took a breath while watching the exchange between father and daughter.

Suddenly, Yace slumped forth, falling across her father's body. The old man's eyes slid sideways as if he were now really dead.

Kipp was first to her side. He picked up Yace, rolling her into his arms. "Irwin! Make sure he's dead."

Startled by the request, he complied, if only out of fear. Irwin took coins from his pocket and transformed them into a short knife. He began stabbing the deceased man. He had never killed a person before, only animals for food. But his fear helped him knife the cadaver.

Yace was vague about what it was we were coming here to do. I do not think she knew. But how she acted, she must have known something. How would she know? These last few days she has been burdened. Maybe she envisioned something. I wonder if Dana envisioned this. I do not want to think something bad has befallen Yace, but something is not right about any of this.

He walked away from the bloody bed, from the death scene.

Even after smelling the deathly room, she still went to what appeared to be a deceased body. She touched the outstretched hand. That is not like her. Slugs scare her!

He glanced around and examined the hoary bedroom, pilaster and paint chipping off the walls and ceiling—the floor discolored by the sun where the carpets were not laid.

She did not stop to question what she was seeing. Yet she always does. It is her nature to ask questions. What is going on here? Yace did not pause for thought, but she would have if this was anything else.

He shuddered, remembering how her touch had brought her father back to life.

The room seemed darker now. The lantern's light next to the bed dimmed, and he closed the door behind himself as he left the death room. "I am not prepared for any of this." He was the only person out there on the top floor. Kipp was halfway down the stairs, calling for the servant.

"Hey Clan-Duin! Hey servant! Come out wherever you are!" Kipp shouted. "I can smell you!" Kipp was sniffing, following the scent of the ancient Clan-Duin.

Irwin descended to the next floor down, below the one Kipp was clomping through. He opened doors to all the rooms, examining all the dusty places.

Kipp's voice echoed through the old house, "Dang it! Where are you, old man?"

All the rooms Irwin stepped into were empty. The last set of doors he opened led into a grand living room at one time. In that one room, all the cabinets, chairs, beds, and piles of crates were covered in dusty sheets. There sat the old Clan-Duin servant on one of the couches, a candle his only light, stoking a pipe with the flame.

"Kipp! He is in here!" Irwin called from the doorway. He stood guard at the entrance to the room, watching the old servant smoke the pipe. He waited for Kipp.

"What is your name, Sir?" He asked from the doorway.

Kipp's feet announced his rage. Together they approached the old, dark-skinned man.

With a low growl, Kipp said, "What did your benefactor do to Yace?" And grasped Yace tight against his chest.

Her father was dead, and now she was unconscious for no apparent reason. Kipp did not back down.

The old man coughed out smoke. "Paulur Cirmon." His aged amber eyes looked toward Kipp. "I do not know what my Master did to the Lady. He is near death, so he cannot do much. All I know is that he wanted to see her." He gummed his lip; his mouth had no teeth. "Care for a toke?"

"Why would she collapse?" Kipp demanded.

"I do not know why the Lady would collapse. But I can retrieve a healer if you wish."

"She does not need a healer." Kipp growled louder. "Tell me about your Master." Kipp tossed Yace around in his arms. "What type of person was he? Do you know exactly what his Talents are?"

"My Master is a good person. And yes, he is quite Talented. He's telepathic."

Irwin pointed to a sheet-covered bed. "We can put Yace over there."

"Oh, no!" Paulur Cirmon said, "That is moth ridden; I wouldn't. She can lie in my room ... put her on my bed."

"No, Yace isn't leaving my sight." Kipp was trying to keep control. His eyes insisted Irwin go and check the bed in question on the other side of the room.

Irwin lifted the covering sheet. Indeed, the mattress was full of holes and moth balls. He glanced at Kipp, confirming the situation with the bed.

"Where's your room, old man?" Kipp moved closer to the servant.

Paulur Cirmon led them away from the dusty room, down the hallway to a small chamber next to a lavatory. Kipp whispered to Yace as he walked. "Wake up Yace. Please, wake up."

The bedroom was small. There was no window, and only a small corner cabinet next to a cot. Kipp placed Yace on the cot. Paulur handed him a blanket. He tucked in Yace and stepped with care out of the room.

Paulur was under Irwin's supervision.

Kipp turned and stood at the door, watching Yace. He hissed, "Tell me everything you know about your Master ... or I'll kill you where you stand."

32

LORD MASTER DEPHEN ISHIK

The old man sniffed at Irwin. He took a partial step closer to Kipp and began to confess what he knew. "Dear Sirs, I'll tell you all I know. Master Ishik is an old man, much like me. And he's of the telepathic nature. He's also feeble and riddled with joint pain—doesn't move around much anymore.

"I have worked for Master Ishik for several years now. It wasn't until recently that he became bedridden. Now he uses his telepathy to summon myself or other servants for his daily needs."

Irwin said, "Master Ishik? I thought Yace referred to him as Dephen?"

"Dephen? His name is Master Ishik. I know no Dephen. All I know is that my Master has been dying for some time now. We've had healers come and give him life daily. For many days now, he has barely held on. I believe that it has been only his want to see his heir that has kept him alive." He peered up at Kipp, who towered over him. "The shop below, Potions and Remedies, that is his primary business. And the women who work it are also personal servants of Master Ishik. They've been with him for almost as long as I."

"How long is that?"

"Many years, I do not recall the number. Since being bedridden, I've been his primary caregiver. He has required much devotion. I told him I would remain to help him during these last days. And I will stay with him until he passes over. And, of course, if the Lady requests my servitude, I may consider staying on while she adjusts.

"Even though I'm old and ready for my time, it would be my pleasure to offer my assistance to the Lady. The women who work at the herb shop will also help the Lady. I know they wish to remain in their positions. They are most loyal to the business, and to our Master Ishik.

"I know that Master Ishik comes from wealth and has much influence in this community." He was moving from foot to foot, trying to gain distance from Irwin—it seemed. "He's done much for the people here and me.

"Before working with Master Ishik, I worked for a Mistress Pamona Omone of Orten city. Once her children left the manor, and her husband deceased, she had little use for me. I was her groundskeeper for twenty years. After she died, I moved here to Onj Raha to find a new master. I've been a loyal servant to all I have served. And will continue to do so for the Lady."

"All I'm hearing is all about you." Kipp said through gritted teeth. "How powerful of a Telepath was your Master Ishik?"

"I'm Clan-Duin, he's a Telepath! I cannot gage his power. But I will say this: he has such a presence, even after becoming bedridden. Master Ishik can still command."

Irwin peered into the bedroom at Yace. He regarded this Paulur Cirmon again who was watching him closely.

Paulur said, "She is beautiful. Looks just like her father ... his blue eyes and, no doubt, his same grand smile. I know that Master Ishik is very smart, even witty at times. He loved to lure in beautiful women—beauty comparable to the Lady."

Kipp snarled, "Are you saying he'd want to fornicate with his own daughter?"

Irwin understood what the older Clan-Duin man was insinuating. He could not see Yace being born to an unattractive woman, though he found it creepy that an old man might be lustful for such young women like Yace. Then it occurred to him to ask, "Was he particular about things, or quick to change moods?"

"Oh yes. Nothing could be out of place. He did not like his food to mingle on his plate. Yes, he was fussy about many things."

"Sounds like Yace." Irwin said.

"He's not much fun to be around if things are askew. Paintings, carpets, and such. At one point, before he became bedridden, Master believed the manor was out to get him. Made no sense to me. I think his mind had softened. And by the time he was bedbound, he had trouble speaking—aloud, that is. He became confused by the spoken word easily. He now only communicates through telepathy."

"Why is his bedroom on the top floor?" Irwin asked. "I would think it would be easier for everyone if his bed were on a lower floor?"

"That room keeps him the warmest. It also allows the sun in. If he wishes."

"Why was it so important for Yace to get here before he died?"

Paulur Cirmon was beginning to sweat. "Well, I guess he needs to know she is worthy of what he offers."

Kipp snarled, "Worthy? What does that mean?"

"Master Ishik confessed to me that he would bestow a great gift to his coming heir. The Lady will receive everything he owns. And he owns an empire here in Onj Raha. She will have his fortune and his businesses. He wanted to make sure she was worthy of such a task—inheriting an entire estate."

Irwin eyed Paulur. "How would he know if she was worthy?"

"I'm uncertain."

"Would he have held out for another heir if she was unworthy?" Irwin pressed.

"I'm unaware of any other heirs. She was the closest one willing and able to come."

"None of this explains why she collapsed!" Kipp heaved, clearly ready to attack the old man.

"Master Ishik has been holding on for her. These last few days were hard for all of us. He died many times, but we kept bringing him back. He's hoping to show her a better life, young man. A life she could be proud to live. She has lived as a Gypsy before coming here, correct?"

Both men nodded.

"Well now, she can live as she wishes. I know he wants to give her a place she can call home—a life worthy of living."

"That was not the reason she was given for this meeting," Irwin said. "She was told he could help her. That he would teach her to use her powers without hurting others. It was not until she left the Gypsy that we were told of his dying condition."

They eyed Paulur, waiting.

Paulur glanced toward his bedroom door. "Maybe the Lady is tired. You have come from a far distance. Your travels surely tired you too. It has been a long day for me, my friends." Paulur yawned, stretched out his arms, and pointed to the ceiling. "I must go and take care of the master's pots before I retire."

"No need for that. Your master is dead," Kipp said.

"What? No! That can't be! I'm sure he was alive when you arrived."

"Yeah, he was dead! But then was magically revived by her touch, if only to die again."

"That is most unfortunate."

"Yeah, for you, old man."

"I am sorry, but I don't know what you want me to say. Master Ishik is a good man who's been running away from Death, hoping to bestow his fortune upon his heir. The Lady must be fatigued or collapsed because of the situation. It all could be too much for her to take in."

"Is there another bedroom like this one?"

"Why yes, up one flight of stairs, right above this room." He exposed his toothless grin again.

"Irwin, escort Paulur to the room he just mentioned. We'll wait until Yace has slept off her tiredness. Make sure he can't leave. I'll stay here with her."

Irwin signaled for Paulur Cirmon to lead the way. The old man took a wide berth around him. Paulur tiptoed down the hallway and up the stairs. The time-worn wooden steps squeaked as they went. The room looked exactly like the one below, but not as comfortable. The cot appeared ready to rip apart, and there was no light. No window. No blanket. The room felt chilly. Paulur took a lantern from the hallway and glanced back at Irwin. He closed the door, leaving Irwin alone in the hallway.

Something about this does not feel right.

He wanted to keep his friends safe. Swiping his hand across the front of Paulur's door, he used some of his metal to lock the servant inside. There was no way Paulur could escape, not without Irwin knowing.

He returned to the floor below and found Kipp slumped across Yace. His Clan-Duin friend sat up. "She's still breathing." He wiped a tear from his cheek.

Irwin patted Kipp's shoulder, just as the Clan-Duin had done for him many times after a good joust. "Yace is strong. Do not worry, Kipp, she will be alright."

"Dang it! Why did this happen? I can't believe …. It smelled fowl in that room. I shouldn't have let her go in there."

"We both went with her, Kipp. It is not like she was alone."

Kipp stared at Yace. "For all we know, she was," he said, "She walked into that room; too determined in my mind. And then she reached for that dead man's hand." He shuddered. "She didn't squeal." He stared at Irwin with pleading eyes. "That's not like Yace. She's afraid of snakes and spiders and things that move in the forest at night." He cackled, as if he was beginning to lose his mind. "And how did Yace's touch bring that dead, withered old man back to life?"

Irwin shrugged. "I am trying to imagine how Yace felt. She was not acting herself since leaving Miss Humphriess' inn."

"Those are my thoughts exactly! She would've squirmed, or squealed, or moved away, but she didn't! She just took both of his hands and then she succumbed to who-knows-what?"

"It could be fatigue, like Paulur suggested."

"I don't know what to do. I wish she'd wake up."

Kipp strode out of the room and then poked his head back in. "I'll be right back. There's no chairs. Watch her closely. Don't let her leave."

"I do not think she will just stand up and walk out of here without us seeing her." Irwin stood inside the doorway. He watched Yace inhaling and exhaling. She appeared to be in a deep slumber. He was too scared to get close; he did not want to disturb her. From where he stood, he could see no marks upon her hands from the old man's grasp. She looked as lovely as she usually did when she slept. Nothing about her was different.

Kipp returned with a chair for each of them. He placed his chair in the doorway and turned toward the bed. He put Irwin's chair against the wall in the hall, facing the stairwell.

Then he asked, "Did Yace ever tell you why she wanted to come here?"

"She told me it was because her father could help her. That only someone from her family could help her understand her powers."

"Nonbry knew him."

"Yes, Yace and you have told me this story; they traveled together."

"From what I understand—not that I was paying attention, as Yace puts it, but I was—Nonbry helped this Ishik fellow out somehow. This was back before any of us were alive. I think he lived with the Gypsy for several years, touring the land, helping those in need. And then he left them for a more permanent residence. Nonbry and Ishik stayed connected, as Telepaths do, I suppose. I don't know exactly how they realized that Yace was this Ishik fellow's child. Maybe because she looks like him, as the servant suggested."

"His name is Paulur."

"Once her telepathic powers developed and her telekinesis grew stronger, well, there was no one in the Gypsy camp who could help her. I mean, none of them knows anything about telekinesis in the first place. And levitating wagons, horses, even other Gypsy in her sleep was scary. She was told to practice. But Yace being Yace, she didn't know what she was doing. She hurt people. Accidentally, of course. And that's when the concern began to arise. Everyone was talking about it in camp.

"Then one day Nonbry suggested she needed to find her father. He hadn't said anything up until then that he knew her father. But he was the one who filled her mind full of thoughts that she should try to find her biological parents ... that they could help her." Kipp went on. "You want to know what I believe. I believe Nonbry was trying to get rid of Yace. I think he saw her as a threat. How he looked at her. And sometimes he reeked of jealousy. I don't know how he could ... how he would reject her one moment, but then try to teach her the next. I think Nonbry always held spite toward her.

"The sad thing is, Yace has always looked up to him. She's always wanted his approval, his acceptance, but she'll never get it."

Sounds like me and my father.

"That is sad."

"Yeah, I know! What's worse is even Dana seemed fearful of Yace these last few moons before we left. Not all the time, but there were times—usually in the morning—she did. Especially right before Yace made the decision to leave the Gypsy and travel here to Onj Raha. To me, this all seems too coincidental ... and spooky. I'm not sure I should have volunteered, but what can I do now? Here we are, waiting for something to happen."

Kipp was acting like Yace—trying to fill the air because the silence was terrifying. "At this point I don't trust Telepaths at all ... but I trust Yace. I know Yace. I know her really well. All she's ever wanted was to be loved, accepted, and feel like she belonged ... that she mattered to someone." He looked lovingly down at his friend.

Just like me.

"How long has Yace known about her father?"

Kipp had to think for a moment. "I believe it was before we got to Kobiton. Or maybe it happened after we got to Kobiton. I don't remember exactly when she was told. But Nonbry came to Yace one day and sat her down in private—though it was not like the rest of us couldn't hear.

"He confessed that he, Dana, and Captain Hari had located her father. They're all Telepaths, so .... But you should have seen her, Irwin. She nearly exploded. I thought she was going to pee herself. She was so happy.

"She was so excited to find out her father was alive that she never questioned the impulse behind it. But I think Nonbry and Dana were trying to get rid of her—to send her away to make her someone else's problem."

"You really believe that?"

"Yeah. I mean come on; she was levitating carriages and animals. In her sleep! She was scaring all the Gypsy."

"I have never seen her have any problems with accidentally levitating things."

"I made her practice after she was asked to sleep away from camp. I didn't want to be levitated either. She's gotten much better. You should've seen her in that fight—snapping necks and throwing bodies hundreds of feet to the river."

They fell silent, and then Irwin said, "Yace always talks about being Coterie. Is her father Coterie, or is he just a Telepath?"

Kipp shrugged.

"Maybe something else happened beyond what we know."

"Yeah, like what?"

"Well, neither of us knows much about Coterie, except what Yace has told us. And I know very little about telepathy, other than what Yace has made me privy to. Maybe he is more powerful than anyone knows. Maybe he is teaching her about her powers. Maybe he is passing on his memories, everything about his businesses and his personal life so she can take over his empire. Maybe that is why he needed her to come here. Maybe that is why Nonbry sent her."

"That's a lot of maybes," Kipp said. "I know that Nonbry has been known to withhold information."

"You remember what Yace said about Coterie? She gloated at the fact that they can do it all. We already know she has the telekinetic power ... had it long before Nonbry rescued her.

"A while back, she told me what being a true Telepath entails. There must be many aspects of being Coterie too. They are telepathic. She has said that over and over. And Telepaths come in all different types. There are the visions and dreams of which Dana knows all about. And then there are the voices." Irwin knew the feeling. "I mean other people's thoughts in your head. We both know that one. She does not mean to hear the thoughts, it just happens. She told me that one aspect of telepathy allows a Telepath to control impulses and thoughts of other people.

"And then there is full-on mental manipulation. I know you know this one, Kipp, where you do not recall anything you said or did."

Kipp made a face.

"But the one that really sounds creepy is the ability to look through other people's eyes and see what they see. How can that be possible?"

Kipp did not react.

"She confessed she had tried it with you a few times. Although she did not like the images she saw through your eyes, it worked."

"It's her fault for watching."

"Yace also told me that Coterie can shapeshift. It is similar to how you do it, but she cannot change into anything four legged. And since she is female, I think she can only change into other female bodies. I know she does not know how to do it, but she honors how you do it. She told me that is a rare Talent for Coterie. I remember her wondering if she would ever be able to change like you do." He looked at his friend, felt his worry, his regret. "Do you not recall her ranting and raving about that these last few days?"

"Dang me! No. I must have been ignoring her. And we know she doesn't have control over most of it. Dang me!" Kipp's eyes fell upon Yace lying there on the narrow cot. "Wake up Yace.

"Whatever happens after this, she's gonna be more powerful than anyone. And all that money and property she just inherited will not help her control her gifts. Most likely it'll do the opposite. It'll go straight to her head. I mean, she already thinks she's powerful. Dang me, Irwin. I wish we weren't here. What I wouldn't do for one more night out on the road."

"She will be alright," Irwin said, "Like Paulur insinuated, she just needs to sleep it off."

Silence set in between the two men. Kipp's eyes never left Yace. Irwin leaned back in his seat, playing with two metal balls he formed, like Yace had shown him many days prior, twirling them around one another. The metal balls spiraled in and out and across his fingers. He tried to not move his hand as he was playing with his Metalistic power.

After a while, Kipp had fallen asleep. And soon, so did Irwin. They slept lightly, waking from time to time to kick the other awake.

33

FOLLOWING TELEPATHIC TRAILS

He awoke to Kipp punching his arm.

"Yace is gone!"

A tapping sound came from the room above.

Kipp raced up the stairs and toward the bedroom door where Paulur Cirmon was knocking from inside. He pulled on the door handle. "You really locked it!"

"Of course I did. We did not want him to get away." Three strides behind, Irwin wove his hand through the air and the metal beamed into his flesh.

Kipp swung open the door and yanked Paulur out of the room. "Where is she?" He spat on the old man. "Where is she!?" He shook him. The old Clan-Duin gasped as though he couldn't breathe.

"Kipp! Kipp, let him go."

The young Clan-Duin let Paulur down, but he continued to grip the old man's arms. "Where is she?"

"The Lady Yace?"

Kipp growled deep, drew his hand back into a fist.

"I don't ... I don't know, Sir .... Please ... please do not kill me." Paulur cowered under the powerful grasp.

"I smell her! She came here! She was here not long ago." Kipp dropped his grasp upon Paulur and turned to follow the illusive odor. "I smell her! Yace!" He tore up the stairs, two steps at a time. "YACE!"

Paulur moved toward the stairs too, trying to skirt around Irwin, but he grabbed the man's shirtsleeve. "Please!" Paulur turned and fell backwards against the hardwood floor. "Please, do not hurt me." The old Clan-Duin cowered again. "I fear you more."

"I will not harm you unless provoked." He put out his hand.

"Thank you." The old man grabbed Irwin's outstretched hand. As he found his feet, something peculiar happened. Paulur blinked several times, then he looked around groggily. He sniffed at Irwin and balked, "Let go of me!" He then jerked away from Irwin's hold.

"Are you alright, Paulur?"

The grizzly man stepped back; his face wrought with fear. "Who are you? What can I help you with?" He took a step away from Irwin and found the wall behind him. That seemed to spook him too.

"What do you mean, 'what can I help you with'? You and I are waiting for my friend to find Yace."

"The Lady ... Lady Yace? She's here? She's young, correct, and is blonde with blue eyes?"

Irwin nodded.

"Huzzah! Lord Dephen's daughter is finally here. They must be so happy!"

"Lord Dephen?"

What happened to Master Ishik?

Kipp flew down the steps, landing loudly. "Yace!" Ignoring the two standing there, he persisted down the next flight.

"Yes, she arrived. We have been here for a while. How could you not remember?"

"You have Sir? Has she met her father?"

"Yes, but you did not refer to her father before as Lord Dephen. You said you had never heard of anyone with that name."

"What did I call my Lord?"

"Master Ishik."

"Master Ishik? I do not know a Master Ishik. I serve Lord Dephen. Is it possible you're in the wrong manor?"

"No, you let us in last night. You took us up to Master Ishik's dreary room where the Lady Yace met her father. And then, after everything happened, we talked to you."

Paulur was apparently frozen with fear.

Kipp's shouts for Yace echoed through the house.

"I don't recall any of that." Paulur licked his lips nervously. "I do not remember what happened last night."

Silver swirled around Irwin's eyes. His metal flushed across the rest of his flesh. His shiny silvery eyes stared at Paulur. The old Clan-Duin soiled himself. Irwin meant to intimidate, and he did not let up. He stepped forward, noticed the urine pooling upon the floor. "Tell me everything about Lord Dephen."

Paulur gummed his lips and his hazel eyes darted. He looked ready to run.

Irwin would not let him go. "If you move, you are as good as dead. Now tell me about your Master."

"Wha-what do you want to know?"

"Everything."

"My Lord ... My Lord Dephen. I have known him for many years. He's a good man. Ah, he came to Onj Raha to live out the last of his days. That's what he confessed to me. I, a, I know he comes from wealth, though he never disclosed much about his upbringing, his past. He has always represented himself as a humanitarian and has used his wealth to help those who have need." He paused. "I know he was a pirate for many years. Said he's sailed all the oceans." Paulur bit his lip. "And he was a Gypsy. He told me he toured both land and sea for many years, trying to save those like us. That's why he's lived so long. It's why I serve him.

"Lord Dephen hired me as his personal assistant when he first moved here several years ago. Even though I was old then, he saw my value. I have no children, no wife, no responsibility to anyone but myself. He's allowed me to handle all his personal matters over the years. It's been an honor to serve him. I've helped him hire and fire many people. Even the ladies who run Potions and Remedies, I hired. He believes in people but expects much from them.

"And he's always been good at managing businesses. He knows what to do to get the job done and does not compromise. He expects profits and gives promotions when deserving. For many years this manor was teaming with life. We minimized staff a while ago. Now only myself and the two women who run Potions and Remedies remain.

"Until recently, he owned this entire building—the entire block of shops and residences. When he moved to Onj Raha, he bought this place from another wealthy Telepath who was moving out of town. Potions and Remedies has always been his front business. The other businesses and tenants rent their spaces from him. Not long ago, My Lord sold it all to a rich man who lives across the river. But he gave the herb shop to the women who've worked here since the beginning. They've served him as long as I have. Once My Lord goes with Death, this entire space will be theirs too."

"Lord Dephen sold this place, the whole building?"

"Yes."

"Why?"

"Because of Death. He knew his heir wouldn't be able to take on such responsibility ... wouldn't be able to follow in his footsteps. He believes his heir should have a choice about how to deal with their inheritance. The responsibility of owning and renting should not be taken lightly, especially for a Gypsy such as the Lady Yace."

"Just a little while ago, you said that Lady Yace would be inheriting it all, his businesses and residences."

"I did?"

"Yes."

"Well, she inherits all his worldly possessions. They are downstairs in a large gathering room, all stacked together. She can take what she wants; everything else will go to auction. And, if the Lady wishes, she will get all the monies from that auction."

"How much money will she inherit?" Irwin could feel substantial amounts of gold on the floor below. Paulur also had a small satchel of gold on his person tucked under his clothing.

There is approximately eighty pounds of gold in this house.

"There's some money left from the sale of his estates, though most of it went to the tenants. There are a few chests he received from the purchase of this building that are hers. I know that he didn't want his heir burdened by his possessions, or his lifestyle."

"Did he have anyone else close to him besides you? Maybe other family members lived close by? A brother or sister?"

"No. He never spoke of family. And none of his heirs live close—that I know of. There's never been a Lady of the house, although he has had many ladies over the years." Paulur chuckled. "I do know that Lord Dephen has many sons and daughters born to brothel wenches and wandering maidens. He has many heirs, but none live locally. He also has many business acquaintances and friends, but no brothers or sisters or parents that I know of."

"What was the reason Lord Dephen gave you for summoning his daughter?"

"Lord Dephen beckoned her because he wanted her to carry on his legacy."

"What legacy is that?"

"I assume it is his charity work. But I do not know what all he wanted to discuss with her." They stood in silence, staring at each other, and then the old servant said, "He was aged, but able-bodied, when he called for her. He had ideas of what he wanted to teach her .... But after being poisoned, there was an urgency for her arrival."

"Poisoned? When did that happen?"

"It has been over a moon's cycle since, maybe forty days. At one time, he wanted any of his heirs to come to him. He sent out the message to all who knew him to help find any of his remaining children. But after the attempted assassination, he knew he had little time. I know he felt rushed by Death.

"He's been holding on, putting Death at bay for so long. I know he hoped to see his daughter before he dies." Paulur, still shaking, smiled wearily at Irwin. "I am glad she arrived, and before Death, a cruel spirit."

The servant was assessing Irwin's metal façade. "I will admit that Lord Dephen is a womanizer. He bedded many women in his life and was proud of that. I am sure that is why he was poisoned. He told me many stories of the women he has taken to bed over the years. Being the man he is, I would have thought he would pass his possessions to a son, but he chose the Lady Yace."

None of this makes any sense.

"How was he poisoned?"

"It was on purpose! An evil plot by a whore of a servant, and thankfully she is no longer alive. The PCP made an example of her. They hang assassins, and though she is gone, my Lord Dephen has lived on despite it. We've used Erthin healers every day to keep him alive."

Kipp was still shouting for Yace.

Paulur said, "There are not many places for anyone to hide in this manor! If he cannot find Lady Yace, she must be gone from this place."

Irwin's silvery eyes studied the elderly man.

I do not know what stories to believe.

The servant knew more than he was letting on. "What is your hunch? Where do you think Lady Yace would have gone?"

The old Clan-Duin shook his head and shrugged.

Kipp could be heard bounding back up the stairs. "Where is she?" He stormed over to Paulur.

"He says he does not know anything of Yace's whereabouts."

"I think he does." Kipp was shaking, growling.

"I know nothing of the Lady Yace. What of My Lord Dephen? Maybe she's with him. Did you check his room?"

"She's not here, she's not there." Kipp spat and glared at Irwin. "What's with your silvery glow?"

"It seems that Paulur Cirmon's memories have changed." He glared at the old man. "And, by the way, as we have said, Lord Dephen is dead."

"What? Did she touch him before Death did?"

"Yes, she touched him." The silver in Irwin's eyes churned. "Why does that matter if she touched him?"

Paulur's eyes darted from one man to the other. "His request was to see her before he died. He wanted to see her, touch her, and know that she was his, that she was worthy."

Kipp spat, and said, "Oh, he saw her! But your Master was already dead before she touched him."

"He couldn't be dead," Paulur said. "Lord Dephen's been running away from Death, just for her. We had healers with him last morning. They assured me that he would be powered until the coming day."

Kipp said, "Oh no, he was dead, but then came alive for her!"

"Good, I'm glad that he saw her. That's what he wanted."

Kipp turned to Irwin. "I don't have time for this. Her scent trails down through the store and outside. We need to follow."

"Now?"

"Yeah, now! And you lead, but without the whole metal thing." He turned to Paulur. "Lock him in again."

"May I please have a water flask?" Paulur pleaded as Irwin grabbed for his arm and led him back into the bedroom.

"I am sorry. I do not have a flask. But I have a feeling we will be back." Irwin closed the door. With a wave of his hand, he locked the door up tight.

Kipp was already heading down the stairs. "Hurry up! Her scent will fade the more people walk through it."

They sprinted through the closed Potions and Remedies shop. Outside, the sun was barely up, but people were already on the move. "Lead," Kipp said, and pushed Irwin ahead.

He strode on and heeded Kipp's directions. "Right turn," and then, "Ahead." Once they came to the main thoroughfare, the roadway widened.

This is the way back to Gladis Humphries' Inn.

Irwin knew where to go from here and picked up his pace. He could hear Kipp behind him. They had to look the role, even though Irwin smelled of Death. Any

Clan-Duin brigade they passed would catch his metallic stench. But they moved across the city without incident.

The stable yard was open for business. Oliver was selling one of his hens to a customer as Irwin approached. The wide stable doorway was the perfect beacon for him to locate the Inn. Most of the buildings in this section of Onj Raha looked alike. He crossed the paths of wagons, carriages, and pedestrians, straight for the narrow alley and up to the Inn.

Kipp jumped ahead of Irwin and ran up the stairs. "I smell her! She went upstairs. I'll go up there. You look down here. Her scent isn't as fresh in that direction, but maybe Gladis knows something."

Irwin felt as if he were following Clan-Duin impulses and not true facts. Yet he had no time to talk to Kipp about what he had noticed with Paulur's change in demeanor or change in his story. He headed into the kitchen where he was overcome by the smell of baking bread. Gladis was humming a song, pulling a loaf of bread out of the oven.

"Oh, my! I'm glad to see you've finally arrived. I've made some more of my sour bread. Yace said you men raved about my food on your walk last night."

That conversation only happened between Kipp and Irwin while they were readying for their night. No one else had been present to overhear. "Is Yace here?"

"Ah, yes, the Lady is here. She said she was going to pack. We ate a wonderful breakfast. She talked nonstop about her interesting evening with her father. I fed her well and gave her all your cleaned clothing. She should be upstairs."

"How did she look?"

"Oh, exhausted. But she was hungry and full of conversation. I offered to put you all up for another night. She said you two might want to stay, but she is leaving."

34

<u>LIES, EVERYWHERE LIES</u>

Kipp burst into the kitchen. "Yace isn't here."

"Really?"

How convenient.

"Gladis was just telling me about the conversation she had with Yace at breakfast." Irwin subdued the urge to grab her and squeeze information from the old chatterbox.

The old woman eagerly agreed. "Oh, yes. She happily confessed that she would be moving in with her father immediately. I'm so glad to hear that she was able to see him before Death steals him away. She said he was alive and well and overjoyed to meet her; seemed elated to have been reunited with him."

"None of that happened." Kipp's hands formed fists.

Now the older woman turned bitter. "Lady Yace also told me that you two were under contract through the PCP. And now that you have delivered her to her father, you are free to return to the Hall." There was something about how Gladis talked, and her eyes, which spooked Irwin.

He muttered, "Contracted through the PCP?"

Kipp moved closer. "She's not moving in with her father!"

"That isn't what she told me. She said her meeting with him went quite well. And she would be moving in and taking over his businesses and his burdens. What an honor for her. And yet, it must be sad that she has come to see his end."

I am not so sure how much of this is true. It is time to provoke.

"That is a lie! He sold his businesses and his manor long before we got here."

Gladis's eyes turned gray, menacing, and then she clicked her tongue. "I had asked where you two were. She told me you both stole off to a saloon." Wiping her hands on her dirty apron, she added, "I know you are both men and have needs, but places like those should be avoided in Onj Raha. Only ragamuffins and hooligans run in those types of establishments. In fact, that whole industry should be banished. You shouldn't associate with those Hakra-awful people."

"That never happened!" Kipp muttered just loud enough for Irwin to hear.

I cannot believe what this woman is saying.

"It sounds like Yace was lying to you," Irwin said. "There is no way she would move in with her father. He is dead. But beyond that, he sold his residence and businesses. What she told you makes no sense unless she outright lied to you."

"Dear Hakra," Gladis blustered, "Does she know her father is dead?"

Kipp barked, "Of course she knows; she was there!"

Gladis struggled for breath, took a step back.

Irwin extended his hand to help steady the elderly woman. "Gladis, are you alright?"

The haze in Gladis's eyes fell away at the touch of Irwin's hand. "What's happening?"

"What do you mean 'what is happening'?"

She tried to loosen his grip on her arm. "I mean, what happened? Why are you holding me? Where am I? Oh, my! I don't remember anything." She pulled away, staring at her calloused fingers, and then grasping them to her bosom. A tear trickled down her cheek and she closed her eyes.

He asked Kipp, "What did Yace take?"

"Her packs. Everything!"

What is going on?

Irwin rubbed his hands across the top of his head. "Gladis, do you remember anything else Yace said or did?"

"Your lady friend, Yace, she's not with you?"

Kipp leaned in. "What's going on here, Irwin?"

"I do not know."

I have a few ideas.

"Gladis, you just admitted to us that Yace returned here this morning." He glanced over at Kipp. "You two had breakfast. And she spoke to you in detail about her father. She told you that she is going to move in with him." She shook her head, looked around as though hoping someone else might save her from this questioning.

Irwin turned to Kipp again. "I need you to go to the Livery. Please go and see if Yace's horse is still here."

Kipp nodded and sprinted from the kitchen and out through the front door. Gladis was studying four loaves of freshly baked bread cooling on the countertop. "I don't remember baking these; don't remember kneading the dough." She brushed her hands over the messy counter, flour dusting her apron and dress sleeves. "But it looks like I made several loaves."

She began opening cupboards, jugs, and totes, as though looking for something she had lost. "I believe there is food missing."

Irwin examined the ransacked crates of fruits and nuts. It looked like someone had taken food items and left bags, jars, and boxes exposed. Yace was someone who left things that were not hers out of place. "I had a bag of apples. I remember buying them. I was saving those apples to make a pie for the stable boys. They come over for evening meals every third night. I usually make a pie for them." She was examining the half-empty bag of apples. "Things have been much harder around here without Carl."

He gave his hand to Gladis. She dried her eyes on her sleeve, now flour spotted her face. He felt sorry for the older woman. "What was Carl like?"

"Oh, I think Carl would have liked you. You are soft and kind like he was. He loved to listen. And he always asked the right questions." Her smile brightened. "Though he was not much of a talker, he cared about everything. He paid attention to details that often fall by the wayside now.

"There was this one time when we were young and foolish. We dared to sneak into the theater to watch a play. It was called Emboldened Regrets. I had already seen the play with some friends, but Carl wanted to see it. It's a play about two lovers, where one finds death before the other.

"Carl and I got caught trying to find some seats. We didn't have tickets, but there were empty seats up high. I managed to talk the usher into giving us those seats.

"Carl was amazed by me back then. We were young. He said I could talk a bull into marrying me if I tried hard enough. And, you know, he was probably right." She wiped tears away.

"I am impressed that your memory is still with you, even though you cannot recall your conversation with Yace, or even remember her being here this morning. You remembered everything until I touched your hand. You said you two talked in depth. You fed her and gave her our cleaned clothing. But once I touched you, all those memories went away."

What is going on? This looks like telepathy. There is no other way to explain it.

"Dementia," she said, "It happens to us old people. Usually right before Death takes us. I can't even remember what I ate for breakfast." She glanced around the kitchen as if looking for the answer.

"I am sorry Gladis. You are a sweet woman. You do not deserve any of this."

She peered up at him. "Do you know if your lady friend has powers?"

Irwin had a growing sense for the signs of telepathic exploitation, and he was beginning to see a pattern. He said nothing.

"I was kind enough to put you all up, even with a Clan-Duin traveling with you. But at this point, he's the least of my worries." Gladis glanced at her old hands again. "She seemed like such a nice young woman. She didn't look Talented, but now I'm not sure what I saw. Are you Talented, young man?"

"I wish." Kipp and Yace had been stern about what Irwin should divulge. He scanned the kitchen, feeling all the metal items. "My Talents are cooking good meals and cleaning things. I am also well-versed with using metal utensils, keeping them sharpened, trimming horse hooves, and things of that nature."

Gladis's eyes sparkled. "Are you a blacksmith?"

"Yes, I can do blacksmith work," Irwin said, "Although, I do not have a forge. Where I am from, I would use the local forge to make things."

"Oh! That is a respectable job to have," Gladis said. "Do you carry tools with you?"

"Yes, in my packs."

Kipp appeared in the doorway. He was out of breath. "She took," he struggled for breath. "She took two of the horses. The livery owner said she was going back to her father's. She also told him that someone would be back for the other animals. She left without paying, so he won't release our animals until he's paid."

Irwin's heart felt heavy. "She is not coming back."

"Why do you say that?"

"Because of what I have been seeing, as opposed to what you have smelled."

"What are you saying?"

Irwin glanced at Gladis, hinting to keep quiet.

"We should probably pack up and pay for the animals," he said. He motioned for Kipp to follow him upstairs.

Once they were on the top floor Irwin said, "Yace cannot move into that grim manor; it is not hers, nor is the business or that building."

"You said that before." Kipp's furry eyebrows narrowed. "How do you know that's true?"

"This is all a telepathic spell," Irwin said. "I see it now. I mean, I saw it before, but now I really see it. I am sure something happened to Yace when she touched her father. Those haunting white eyes—something beyond what we saw happened."

"What makes you say that?"

"Paulur! When I touched him, he changed? He confessed things he had not mentioned before; his Master was called Lord Dephen and not Master Ishik. He also told me that his Master-Lord had sold all his large possessions—the building, his business and residence—and that was after telling me his Master would bestow everything he had to Yace. And then, get this, he said his Master gave most of that money away."

"And you believe him?"

"He also told me that his Master had been poisoned. That happened over a moon ago by a female servant. That is why only Paulur and the two ladies in Potions and Remedies work for him. Everyone else was laid-off. And the servant who tried to assassinate, she was killed. I believe that is why Yace had such a sense of urgency to get here. All Yace knew was that he was dying, not that he had been poisoned. That is where the urgency came from. That was why her father was 'holding on' and in need of Erthin healers. That was why he betrothed her with his legacy."

"Wait, what?"

"While you were running around searching for Yace this morning, I confronted Paulur. We had a scuffle, and I touched him and grounded out the spell Yace had placed on him."

"Is that why you were all silver?"

"Yes."

"That's why he soiled himself?"

"Yes. But that does not matter. There was something different in how he talked, his mannerisms. He was more truthful too. That was when I realized she had placed a spell on him. It's possible that she was speaking through him before I ground out the telepathy. Do you see?

"And now the same thing happened here with Gladis. Her story and memories changed after I touched her. You saw it! The tone in her voice, how she spoke. I know you saw it. It was exactly how Paulur changed—even how the words were spoken. You were there; you heard the difference in her stories."

"She's old."

"I talked to her more while you were at the livery. It is not dementia, Kipp. Gladis is not *that* old." He took a different tactic. "She is about as old as my grandfather Jebadia when he died. And he died from over-use of his powers, not from old age. My elder, Edwin, died from old age. He was near a hundred years old when Death took him. Gladis is not that old."

Kipp scoffed, "Remember the stair incident yesterday?"

"What is hard for me to understand is why does it appear that Yace is going to great lengths to manipulate this situation?" He looked out the window, searching for an answer. "This reminds me of that first night we met when she took your mind to keep you from divulging information. But what I am seeing here is ... is more powerful.

"Yace confessed why she could control you. She said it was because of the bond you share." He was hinting at the times Kipp and Yace had coupled, a long time ago. "But she is not bonded to Paulur, or Gladis, or even Oliver, so how can she affect them the way she is? Why is this happening? What is the motivation behind this? If Yace wanted to leave us, all she must do is say so. She knows we are not bound to her." He cleared his throat, allowing time for Kipp to take in what he was saying. "This is not like Yace. She has no reason to concoct something like this. None of those people care about her. But we do. This is all for us."

"Why? Why is that?"

"That is what I keep asking myself. Do you think Yace would have left us back there at her father's manor?" He did not wait for Kipp's response. "No, she would have woken us up! If she had inherited the manor and businesses and all that responsibility ... moving her in, that would be something we all would have done together. You know that! Like everything else up to this point, we have worked together."

"But she did leave," Kipp said, "like she said she would. Maybe she's lying to make it easier for us. She owes us nothing. We both volunteered for this. She told me in the beginning that once I was done, I could do whatever I want. Maybe she is trying to make the break easier."

"First off, that was so long ago she said those words. Secondly, where would she go? If she was leaving, and her father's manor is sold, where is she going to go? Back to the Gypsy? Thirdly, do you think she would have left us without saying goodbye? If she were going back to the Gypsy, or her father's manor, or wherever, do you not think she would say parting words?"

"Goodbye is permanent. It's like saying have a good life, see you never."

"Yace is not that cruel. She would not just leave us."

"How sure are you, Irwin? She can do whatever she wants."

Silence enveloped them and Kipp paced around the room.

Irwin moved past the doorway, stood in the hallway listening to Kipp.

None of this makes sense.

"I do not think Yace would have left us like this," he said, leaning into the doorway. "I believe something sinister has happened. It was during that moment of contact with her father. I do not know telepathy, but you do. You have seen more of its effects than I have. But what I am seeing, what is going on around us, makes no sense other than telepathic manipulation."

"I've had more telepathy done onto me than I have witnessed," Kipp said from the confines of his room. He moved toward the door, toward Irwin. "All I know is what I saw. She touched the hand of a dead man and brought him back to life. That's not a power Yace has. That's only something an Erthin Healer can do. It could've been something a healer implanted. I don't know."

"Something else is happening here, Kipp. Coterie-esque, maybe," Irwin said, "I mean, can you explain Paulur and Gladis's behavior, or Oliver's memories of her?"

"She can tell them what she wants. It's her life. It's her lie to make up if she wishes. If this is how she wants to depart from us, I can be mad, but—"

"You actually think she would *want* to lie? I do not think you understand, Kipp. This is not a lie we are hearing. This is a telepathic spell."

"I wouldn't trust much of what that old Clan-Duin said. He fears us. Fear has a way of making people say things that aren't true to get out of a situation.

"We should pack up and be gone from here." It was unusual to see Kipp so certain.

I know what I saw. Kipp is acting on instinct. Maybe this is what he is supposed to do. I do not want to argue. I just want to figure out what is going on.

He moved down the hallway, stopping at Yace's room. It was as clean as it had been the night prior. A pile of gold was stacked on the nightstand. He heard the golden call—its hum hypnotizing, as was the feel of it beckoning him into her room. The wooden talisman sat on top of the golden bounty. The song was his weakness, but it also woke him.

"Kipp, come here, please."

"Why?"

"I found something."

The floorboards squeaked. "What did you find?"

"A trap."

"Where did she get all this gold?"

"Her father."

"Why would she set a trap?"

"She knew I would be summoned to the gold. And she knows that if I touch that talisman it will no longer work."

Kipp grabbed the talisman and stuffed it into a pouch that hung from his woven belt. "You might be right. Something else *is* going on here. I hate to think that we have to contact Nonbry."

I know I am right.

"Do you think Nonbry knows what is going on?"

"He's a Telepath. I don't know what he knows. And I'm not sure I want to. Let's go back to her father's manor. Maybe we can find out something before we need to contact Nonbry. Maybe talk to that old servant some more. Maybe she's just there unpacking, trying to forget us."

"And if she is not there?"

"Then ... then we'll find an Oracle and get answers from Nonbry," Kipp said. "You should dress in a uniform, so we look the role."

"I think it would be better if I wore this."

"Yace isn't here. You need to be in uniform."

I do not think this is a good idea. But I should not question Kipp. He has been trained for these situations. Kipp knows what to do. He has been trained.

His clean clothing had been folded neatly and laid out on his bed. He changed as fast as he could and stuffed the rest into his bag. He grabbed the rest of his belongings and hoisted them across his shoulder. By the time he emerged from his room, no one was around. The silence felt eerie, ominous. He nearly fell into Kipp's backside at the bottom of the spiral staircase.

Gladis was standing there with two packages. "I have little to offer, but you two have been kind and helpful." She smiled at Irwin. "If I could give you more,

I would." She handed the wrapped bread loafs to Kipp. "I hope you find Lady Yace. And if I see her again, I'll surely tell her you're looking for her."

Kipp handed Irwin the loaves of bread.

Irwin gave Gladis five gold pieces. "Thank you for your hospitality, Gladis. Goodbye."

Huh. It is just like saying 'see you never'.

Yace had taken off with Blacky and one of the other warhorses, leaving them the horse named Bodi to share.

She did this on purpose. This is a ruse. There is something sinister going on. I just need to see the entire picture.

The animals were tacked up and ready. Oliver stood next to the saddled horse and the packed donkeys. The large pale-skinned Mortal man petted Bodi, and he watched them approach. Kipp reached for the horse's reins, but Oliver waited for payment before relinquishing the animals.

Irwin stepped forward. "I am sorry we did not pay for their board sooner." He shook Oliver's hand. "But I thank you for taking diligent care of our animals." Irwin passed him five gold pieces. Although Oliver appeared dazed by Irwin's friendliness, he said nothing, and Irwin felt his fear and confusion. The man took the gold.

They packed their belongings onto the donkeys and secured them onto their mount. Irwin whispered to Kipp. "Did you see that exchange?"

Kipp did not respond. His attention was on the animals, and probably his own internal dialogue.

"You're sitting on the back of the saddle."

"We are both riding?" Irwin continued to go along with Kipp's suggestions.

The Clan-Duin's dark facial expression was stoic. They mounted the warhorse, and Oliver opened the bulky gate, allowing them passage. The donkeys clopped along behind.

Irwin sat astride Kipp's blanket roll, only marginally comfortable. He grasped onto the back of the saddle's seat and Kipp guided the warhorse at a fast pace down the busy avenue. Neither spoke, keeping their eyes open for soldiers on horseback and on foot.

Kipp seemed to know the quickest way to Lord Dephen's manor. He navigated down the cobbled streets and straight to the dark spires. Stopping the horse at a tie-rack, they both dismounted.

Irwin secured the animals and Kipp resumed his hunt for Yace. Back inside the herb shop, the two women were helping a customer. Kipp strode on through the shop, toward the back room and the stairs, but was intercepted by a middle-aged redheaded Erthin.

"Can I help you?"

"We are here to see Master Ishik."

The Clan-Duin woman handed a parcel to her customer and turned back to Kipp. "I believe you are lost. There is no Master Ishik at this place of business. And no one lives in the residence above."

Irwin knew Kipp could smell Yace, and he was growling at the women. The Clan-Duin pushed his way past. "I need to go upstairs," said Kipp.

The Erthin woman asked, "Why? It's vacant."

Irwin took a calmer tone. "We have come to see Lord Dephen."

The women stepped back and gave Irwin a wide berth. They passed without more provocation. Irwin felt them watching as he stepped beyond the doorway. Kipp hustled up the steps. The door to the manor was unlocked, and they went in. The Clan-Duin sniffed the air and ascended the next flight of stairs. Irwin was several steps behind and tried to keep up.

Kipp's nose led him up to the top floor. His foot falls echoed as they entered all the rooms and then backtracked down the stairs. The Clan-Duin was chasing the scent of Yace toward Paulur Cirmon's room.

The door had been ripped off its hinges and lay upon the floor; the scent of blood was thick in the air. The bloodied body of Paulur Cirmon lay on his bed. The old man's wooden pipe was broken, and its pieces were on the floor, just past his dangling hand. There were no apparent wounds that either of them could see, only blood seeping out the elder Clan-Duins eyes, nose, and ears.

Irwin said, "How is this possible? I set the metal into the frame of the door. Only someone with Talents like mine could have done that."

"I smell Yace everywhere," Kipp said, "Dang it. Now we have to contact Non-bry."

"We sure do."

35

<u>NONBRY</u>

They apologized to the women of Potions and Remedies, then asked them to recommend a reputable Oracle. Irwin bought salts, herbs, and spices. He gave them money, hoping for any information they might divulge. The gold Yace had left behind in her room came in handy. But even with the extra coins and Kipp's flirtations, they learned very little.

Neither woman had any recollection of their proprietor, Lord Dephen, nor Master Ishik. This, of course, made no sense. The women claimed to be the sole owners of Potions and Remedies. "No one has lived in that abandoned residence for years," they were told. And neither had seen anyone come or go all morning. He wanted to touch the women, to see if they too had telepathic spells covering their eyes but refrained.

What is happening here? Telepathy. It must be telepathy. There is no other explanation. But why? This is not like Yace. Why is she doing this? She is not doing this. This is something else, someone else. What are we to do? Nonbry will know. Will he?

They excused themselves, leaving the herb store for a place called the Oracle's Den, just around the corner from the black-spired building. They waited there to be served for the rest of the morning. A distraught mother and daughter had taken up a lot of time with the resident Oracle. Soon the plump Oracle waved goodbye to those two and turned her attention to Irwin and Kipp.

They were eating one of Gladis's loaves, trying to soothe their hunger. By the time they were greeted, Kipp was ready to leave. He looked ready to find Yace's scent on his own. The emotionally driven Clan-Duin's eyes were livid with anger. Meanwhile, Irwin sat back, watching people pass by out the window. He knew not to be too emotionally attached. But he was compiling a list of questions for Nonbry.

Kipp stood to engage the fat female Oracle, a crossbreed. She had a bit of Erthin, Clan-Duin, Telepath, and Mortal blood running through her. Her skin paler than most people of Talent, yet it held a hint of Erthin olive-green. Her eyes were mostly hazel with a small ring of blue around the iris. Thick, auburn-brown hair, bushy eyebrows, and broad nose suggested Clan-Duin traits.

She took Kipp's hand and placed the other hand on his cheek. "I am so sorry for your loss. It is never easy when a parent dies. I am Mistress Guveir."

"I'm looking for someone," Kipp said.

Irwin felt his friend's ambivalence to the woman's suggestions of sympathy.

"Please, come into my room." Mistress Guveir motioned to Kipp, then turned to Irwin. "You will stay here."

"He stays with me." Kipp took charge.

"He is a succubus of energy," she said.

"I can make him use that energy on you if you don't help us."

Clearly Mistress Guveir did not like Kipp's bullying. She folded her arms across her thick chest. "The cosmos says I cannot help you today."

Irwin pulled a gold piece from his pocket and held it out. "We need your help. Neither of us wants any provocation. We are having a bad day and just need some help."

She was slow to take the money. Her eyes shifted from one man to the other. Then she relented. "Follow me." She led them into her small, well-suited fortune room. Sheets of painted fabrics were drawn from the ceiling to the floor. She shut the curtains and motioned for them to sit. Two small benches faced one another, a short circular table between. She sat across from them.

Mistress Guveir put her hands out, motioning for Kipp to reciprocate. He pulled out the talisman instead. "This is from our benefactor. We use it to contact him. His name is Nonbry."

She stared at the talisman.

"You are a Telepath, aren't you?"

She took the talisman, turning in around in her hands. "Telepathy by proxy takes time." She continued to study the wooden talisman. It was simple in design, with only a few circular grooves, and was soft to the touch. She caressed it with eyes closed. Her body shifted as she attempted to make contact.

After what felt like a long time, her eyes shot open, white now instead of hazel. "What is the meaning of this?" Her voice no longer sounded like her own. Instead, it was thick and gruff, like Nonbry's. "I asked to be disturbed at night only. I am trying to drive! Why do you call for me at this time?"

"Sorry, Sir," Kipp said.

The Oracle looked around the room. Was Nonbry seeing through her eyes? He grumbled through this woman with the white eyes. "Where is Yace?"

"I don't know where Yace is, Sir. That's why we've contacted you. It seems that she has left us." Kipp fidgeted, crossing and uncrossing his legs.

The Oracle blinked, and the white eyes disappeared. She appeared ready to speak, then blinked; her eyes turned white again. "I'm driving! I don't have time for this."

"We believe something bad has happened to her."

The lips of the Oracle twisted with anger. "Did she meet up with her father?"

"Yeah, Sir."

"Then she's no longer your responsibility."

Kipp glanced at Irwin and said, "We … we all saw her father. He, ah, he appeared to be dead when we arrived. That is until she touched him and brought him back to life." There was no reaction on the face of the Oracle. "Something happened between them. They grasped hands and locked eyes and stared at each other. It was creepy. And then Yace fell forward, into a deep sleep of some sort." They waited for Nonbry to have a reaction. "And then during the night, she woke and left his manor without waking us."

The white eyes blinked. "Why should I care she left you? Once delivered to her father, she's no longer your responsibility."

Irwin stared at the Oracle while Nonbry spoke through her. He wanted to ask a question that had been on his mind since Yace's moot slumber. "Is it possible for a dying Telepath to overtake a living one?"

Nonbry gasped—the first sign of emotion other than anger from the old man. The Oracle grumbled, "When did you last see her?"

"Last night, we watched her sleep. But then dozed off." Kipp stammered, "Like I said, Sir, she left us sometime in the night, while we were asleep."

The eyes shifted color again, unnerving Irwin. "Why does that keep happening?"

Mistress Guveir's eyes had changed again to white. Nonbry grumbled at Irwin. "I'm driving! Doing telepathy by proxy takes mental energy. And I do not trust my oxen to follow this section of road." His voice rose. "Your mission was to take her to her father's manor. Anything beyond that—"

Kipp would not let it go. "But sir, she left us without waking us. Without saying goodbye! That's not like Yace. And I've been following her scent everywhere. She's leading us on a run-around. And she's lying to everyone. It's the same lie too. Why would she lie to people we'll never see again?"

The old man, through the fat woman, looked as if he was half listening, half paying attention to driving his oxen.

"She backtracked to the Inn where we rented rooms and took all her stuff and two horses. Then she went back to her father's manor." Kipp paused, looking at Irwin for help. "She went back to murder her father's caregiver, Sir. This is unlike anything she's ever done. As of right now, we don't know where she is, or why this is happening."

Irwin took over. "Paulur, Lord Dephen's servant, is the one Yace murdered. When we confronted the servant last night, after Yace had collapsed, he referred to Yace's father as Master Ishik. This morning, he and I had a scuffle and when my hand touched his, his story changed. His mannerisms, his facial expressions, many things about him changed." Irwin made it a point to remind Nonbry, "Both Yace and Dana said I am a grounding post. I have witnessed this power several times now. I have been grounding out telepathic spells all morning long. After I grounded off the spell on Paulur, he referred to Yace's father as Lord Dephen. You told Yace her father's name is Dephen. So, who is this Master Ishik?"

Nonbry was silent, but the Oracle, or Nonbry, was obviously analyzing and scrutinizing everything he said.

"Nonbry, Sir, I have been witnessing instances like that all morning. Another example is Gladis, the woman who rented rooms to us last night. She was speaking to both of us about Yace, going on about her morning meal with her. And then when I touched her arm to help steady her, she forgot her story. She could not recall one thing that happened before the moment of our contact.

"And then there was Oliver, the Livery owner. Kipp said he told the same story as Gladis. I shook his hand upon paying him. He blinked and grimaced and then appeared agitated, as if he knew something magical had happened. I believe I felt the spell melt away upon contact again that time.

"And then the ladies at Potions and Remedies kept their distance from me. They watched me like predators' mind prey. Even after I paid them for information, what they told us amounted to nothing ... another bunch of lies created by Yace." He paused, hoping that Nonbry wanted to ask a question. "But by the time we spoke to them, it was a different lie. They said they did not know anyone we mentioned, including Paulur Cirmon. Yet he told me he hired them. What is going on here? Do you know?"

Nonbry asked, still seemingly indifferent, "What story is she leaving in her wake?"

"That her father is alive. That she inherited everything: his house, businesses, and his love. But none of that is true."

"How do you know?"

Kipp chimed in. "That thing with Gladis could have been dementia. She's old!"

Irwin shook his head. "Really? We are going to argue this again?" He addressed Nonbry. "Paulur disclosed the most about this Lord Dephen, Master Ishik, person. And I believe that is probably why he lost his life.

"During our first conversation, Paulur talked about Yace inheriting the manor and all of Master Ishik's businesses. But after I touched him, he had said all of Lord Dephen's possessions were sold. He said that Lord Dephen did not want his heir burdened by his lifestyle. Perhaps that makes more sense than her inheriting everything and being expected to know what to do with it all. He also implied that Lord Dephen wanted to bestow his legacy upon Yace. And yet he was not sure what that meant. He speculated that it was charity work." Irwin clenched his teeth. He did not want to sound demanding, but he wanted answers. "Nonbry, can you explain what is going on? Who is this man? Is he Master Ishik or is he Lord Dephen? Is this Coterie magic? Or is Yace just trying to get rid of us in the rudest way possible?"

A calculated look came over the Oracle's face. Irwin guessed that Nonbry was withholding, analyzing the moment. He continued to press. "Kipp says that Yace has left her scent everywhere. And at the same time, she is leaving a trail of those she has lied to. This is all for us. No one else would care. If she really wants to leave us behind, why would she go to such great lengths of deception?"

Nonbry said, "Lord Master Dephen Ishik." After a long pause, he added, "You're on your own."

"Wait," Irwin said, "We need to know what to do!"

Mistress Guveir's eyes ebbed back to their hazel color. "Is it over yet?" She placed the talisman on the table.

"No, no, it's not," barked Kipp.

Her hands clasped the wooden item again, and she closed her eyes. They sat in silence for a long time. After a while, she opened her eyes and said, "I am sorry, but I cannot reach Nonbry." She passed the talisman to Kipp.

He took it and leaned forward, his head between his hands, his elbows on the table.

Irwin watched Mistress Guveir study Kipp, plainly a wary and frustrated Clan-Duin.

"I might be able to help, even if your benefactor cannot." She spoke in a motherly tone.

Kipp rose from his seat, pushed past Irwin, and left the room.

Irwin wanted to follow, but he turned to Mistress Guveir. "Have you ever heard of a man called Lord Master Dephen Ishik?"

Her eyes narrowed. "Ishik? The name is Lord Master Dephen Ishik? He must be family to Emperor Somer Ishik, of Daos Territory. Are you familiar with the Ishik Empire?"

He shook his head. "Enlighten me."

"The Ishik Empire condones people like us, people of Talent. We're not allowed to cross his lands. If we're seen, we're killed. And beyond disregarding people like us, Emperor Ishik is a dangerous man. He uses the people of Daos for his own purposes. They are all Mortal, and they only live to serve him. Some of us Telepaths believe he uses their eyes to seek out those who have Talents. Talented people are born everywhere, but in Daos, they're not allowed to live. The Ishik name and Empire are very powerful. They've been in control of Daos people for several millennia. And they have also control over the oceans of Bounen and Osouf. They pay pirates to keep unwanted guests at bay."

She leaned close to Irwin. "The Ishik family are powerful Coterie—the last of the true Coterie. Though how true could you be when your family lineage is based on incest? Defects happen from incest, mental and physical. Either they don't see it that way, or they don't care. But they heavily promote cronyism—the best way to ensure pure lineage and ultimate power. It's sickening, really. Those of Ishik descent are not to be trusted ... just like you."

Irwin glowered at the woman.

Kipp called from the waiting room. "Let's get going, Irwin."

"One last question," Irwin said, "Can a spirit, a telepathic spirit from a dying or dead body take over a living person's body?"

"That is powerful magic you speak of. I have heard of it, but never seen it." Mistress Guveir smiled, as if addressing a different person. "You ask good questions, succubus. If you need my help again, please feel free to stop by."

"Thank you." Irwin tossed her another gold coin and left.

Kipp was already outside, climbing onto their shared horse. He offered Irwin a hand up onto the woolen bedroll secured behind the seat. Irwin steadied himself, grasping the back of the saddle. They meandered into the crowded streets again. Neither said a word.

What have we gotten ourselves into?

36

<u>ISHIK EMPIRE</u>

Kipp finally said, "Nonbry did that on purpose. He wants me to find Yace on my own."

"That is possible."

Something else is going on here. Something Nonbry wants us to figure out. This must be Coterie magic.

"I was supposed to be at her side the whole time. I'm supposed to be her guard, her servant ... her friend. How could I've let this happen?" Kipp's head hung low.

"You did not let this happen."

This feels planned out. How could being poisoned be part of any plan? Shit. I did not mention that to Nonbry. I should have. Details, there are too many details.

Kipp leaned back into Irwin's chest. "Hey, what did you ask? The Telepath, what did you ask her?"

"I asked if she had ever heard the name Lord Master Dephen Ishik."

"What did she say?"

"She said the name Ishik is linked to the Daos Territory. That they are cruel rulers and have been for millennia. And that the Ishik family—"

"Ishik?! I knew that name sounded familiar. I think I remember a lesson with Dana. And Daos ... Daos." Kipp fondled the reins. "Dang me, I should've paid more attention. But that explains how Yace's got Coterie blood."

"They are very powerful," Irwin continued, "but they promote incest and cronyism, and prohibit people with Talents from living on their land."

"Oh, yeah," Kipp interrupted again, "I remember Dana saying something about Daos being the only territory on all Urthis that doesn't allow people with Talents to exist. We're killed the moment we're seen."

"Yes, according to Mistress Guveir, that is true. Only Mortals are allowed to live. Probably because they are easy to manipulate. If Yace is truly of Ishik blood, it would explain all the telepathic spells we have witnessed today."

Kipp gripped the reins tight. "Telepathic spells. Ishik name."

Four Clan-Duins crossed the street in front of them. They were all on foot and did not look up at the horse and riders. Irwin held still against Kipp, watching the pack move on down the street.

He whispered in Kipp's ear, "Why would an empire of Coterie abhor those with Talents when they themselves are Talented?"

"Because we can't be trusted."

They fell quiet, and the city droned on around them. Kipp led their mount along Onj Raha's only road in.

"What do we do now?" Irwin felt lost.

"I don't know."

"You do not know? I thought you and Yace were trained for this."

"I was never trained for a situation like this. Only if we're confronted, do I know what to do."

"We are not leaving Onj Raha, are we?"

"No."

"Where are you taking us?"

"I think we're being followed. I'm trying to make it look like we're leaving."

Irwin grabbed Kipp's midsection to hold as he turned around to see if they were being followed. He saw no one in pursuit. Yet as he let go his grasp, Kipp pulled his hand back. Irwin leaned in. "What is it?"

"Someone is trying to tap my mind."

"Why would they probe you?"

"Because we don't look the part. We'll keep riding. Maybe they'll lose interest."

"I need you to forget everything you have seen me do with my powers." Irwin whispered, recalling a conversation with Yace. She had remarked that every day she tried to forget what she knew about him and his powers.

After a few kilometers, the cobbled road gave way to dusty well-ground gravel. The looming buildings shrank in size. Now there was no shade on the street, except for storefront awnings. It was the heat of the day. They were hungry and thirsty, as were the animals. Kipp stopped at a water-trough, told Irwin to dismount and tie up Bodi. After the horse and donkeys drank their fill, they found two small taverns. Entering the first one, they realized it did not accept people of Talent and crossed the road to the other.

Irwin looked down the road and saw no sign of soldiers on horseback. He followed his friend into the tavern.

The other tavern served Mortals only. This one was visibly for the Talented, dark-skinned workers and patrons watched them enter. A reprieve from the afternoon sun felt good, but it was still humid. Sweat trickled down Irwin's back as they ordered a meal and some ale. They sat in a booth next to one of the front windows. They glanced across the road to their hitched-up animals, and both directions on the roadway.

"I don't know what we're gonna do," Kipp said. "We need to think like Yace."

"Yace is not thinking like Yace." Irwin's brow wrinkled.

I thought Kipp would know what to do, but he does not. I need to come up with a plan.

Kipp was staring out the window. "She made it seem like her father would be warm and welcoming, that we would have a place to stay. But here we are, trying to figure out what went wrong."

The Clan-Duin peered down toward the city's center. "Dang me, we are being followed." He grabbed his mug and took a large gulp. "We should've kept going."

Two of four PCP dismounted out front.

Kipp snorted, "Erthin Soldiers. Dang it, what are we gonna to do, leave town? We can't. We can't leave without Yace."

"Calm down, Kipp."

"We need to leave here. Now."

"If we act antsy, the people in this bar may take action against us," Irwin said. "We have done nothing wrong. We are just here to eat and drink, correct?"

They watched the first soldier enter and exit the tavern across the road. Another peered into the window where they sat. Kipp locked eyes with the sun-kissed Erthin/Clan-Duin, a well-kept soldier with a shifty appearance.

"I don't want to be here."

"What do you think will happen to us?"

Kipp kept his eyes on the PCP soldier who walked in and over to talk to the barkeep. Kipp looked from the bar to the soldiers out in the street who were now moving toward the tavern. "If we are approached, let me talk."

Ha, let you talk. We will see how that goes.

Irwin took a sip of his pint of warm ale and made a sour face. It was not his drink of choice, but it was all they served here. He set the mug down and studied Kipp. The Clan-Duin was plainly trying to contain his emotions. He took a slug from his pint.

There were booming footfalls as the other three PCP soldiers entered the building. They all looked alike in their indigo garb and black boots. Each soldier had a saber attached to their hip. Their red hair was pulled back or cut short, their faces clean-cut. They strode over to the bar, to their fellow officer, and ordered drinks. They leaned forward, talking to the barkeep. Two of the soldiers observed the quiet tavern.

There was another brigade of Clan-Duin soldiers sitting in a booth close to the bar. They nodded at their PCP counterparts.

One of the bulky Erthin soldiers approached Irwin and Kipp's table.

He sat down next to Kipp and gave Irwin the once-over. The soldier drank his beer and then helped himself to Kipp's mug. They were outnumbered and outmatched. And though they were both hungry, and had paid for their meals and ale, Kipp signaled for them to leave. The PCP soldier held Kipp's cup for a while, his hazel eyes on Irwin—a greedy smile etched on his face as he drank the ale.

Slamming the mug against the tabletop, the Erthin pointed at Irwin and said, "You don't belong."

Irwin nodded. "We will go then."

At once, the soldier's hand was around Kipp's throat. Irwin held his breath. The soldier was trying to strangle Kipp, but his grasp was too light to do any physical harm. "What are you? You look Mortal, yet you wear a uniform and sit in this tavern. What's your Talent?"

Irwin had one hand under the table. He looked at Kipp, who shook his head as best he could, urging Irwin not to do anything stupid. Irwin raised his hand above the table, and his fingers came together on the tabletop. "I am Erthin. A very weak Erthin. I have been told I might be a healer. But I can heal only myself, no one else."

The soldier kept his hand on Kipp's throat. Irwin kicked off his boot and shoved his sweaty foot up Kipp's pant leg to touch his skin. The Erthin glared at Kipp; then his eyes shifted to Irwin. "I don't believe you."

Irwin watched his friend struggle to swallow. He leaned forward and smiled at the Erthin. "Try your power on me. I guarantee I will live through it," he said, and gave his friend a look. He hoped he could ground out this Erthin's power as he had before.

The soldier touched Irwin's forearm, and he felt a spark; a force of energy flowed through him, down and out his feet. It felt as if the Erthin's flesh was trying to merge with his. He hoped his opponent did not feel what he was doing. This Erthin was not one who could harness fire. He was an Earth Erthin. He could only move earthly materials such as soil, trees, and rocks. Irwin felt the trace minerals that rushed through this man's blood, making him capable of holding power over everything that had organic mass.

In that moment of contact, Irwin also felt the magnetic pull of this man's blood; the iron content was thick. He now understood why Earth Erthins were the way they were. He felt many other metals living within this Erthin man, giving him the ability to summon only earthly materials.

To the Earth Erthin, Irwin was a magnet. Their arms attempted to fuse together. He suckled the Erthin's power into his flesh. He could stop his magnetized power but did not. The Erthin tried to move his hand away, but their skin was straining to meld together.

Irwin turned off his magnetic power.

Staring at the Erthin, he saw his grasp on Kipp loosen. The sleek-haired man gasped. "That was unlike anything I have ever felt. It was as though my arm could move through yours." He looked at his companions, dumbfounded by what he had stumbled across. "He's an Erthin. Says he's a healer, and something else. Some sort of crossbreed!"

Kipp stared at Irwin who held his emotions intact. He did not believe the Erthin could have sensed his true power. He had done nothing other than magnetize his skin. Although in the future, he now knew not to be too revealing of himself.

The men across the room looked on suspiciously. The Erthin man's breath stank. "We've been looking to add a healer to our gang. Though five is an odd number; we could do formal escorts with riders and a carriage. You could be the driver. Think about my offer." The Erthin was drunk.

"Only if you stop taunting my friend. He has done nothing to you."

"Are you positive you can't heal others?" The Erthin soldier asked, glancing toward his companions.

"Yes. I have never been able to heal others." He peered at Kipp and shifted his glare to the Erthin. "If I can, I do not know how. I do not have any formal training, that is ... I am merely a son of a soldier. We came from Kobiton. We were commissioned to deliver a woman to her father here in Onj Raha. It was a long and tiresome journey, but we accomplished it today. Our plan is to fill up with rations, and head back home."

The soldier's attention did not waver from Irwin, who stared back defiantly. He knew that if this Erthin was also telepathic, he could not penetrate Irwin's mind. But he had not heard any telepathic inklings when they had made contact—and his eyes were hazel, not blue.

The soldier was gruff when he said, "All soldiers must check in. Leaving without doing so isn't allowed. If your fathers were soldiers, they would've told you this." The Erthin continued to study Irwin, and then glanced back to his friends. "Now, if you two have markings, you need to show them now and 'fess your lies. If not, we're escorting you back to the Hall where you'll be interviewed."

"The Hall?"

"Yes, the Hall. It's a halfway house for soldiers who are in search of jobs or relocation. Don't worry, they'll feed you, clothe you, and give you a bed. All you must do is to be ready for an assigned job."

"But we are needed back in Kobiton."

"And if there is a brigade heading that way, you can go with them. Unfortunately, soldiers aren't allowed to roam free on this side of the mountains ... not without an assignment or benefactor."

Their food arrived.

The Erthin stood up when the server delivered the grub. He followed her back to the bar. Irwin and Kipp were left alone to eat the meat pies.

Kipp smashed his meal into pieces. "We never should've stopped. Me and my stupid stomach, and you, you've gone mad! What do you think you're doing?"

"They left us alone."

"For the moment," Kipp glanced at the soldiers. "They're gonna escort us to the 'Hall'. Alio has told me all about the Halls, and why we should avoid them." He shoveled in a mouthful. "That's where they'll lock us up."

He could barely understand Kipp, complaining away with a mouthful of meat pie. "I have decided to think like Yace."

"This isn't what Yace would do." Kipp swallowed the food. "She'd be looking to get us out of this situation; she'd dress up for something brash."

Irwin held his tongue, and emotions still.

Had I not changed clothing, this might not have happened. Maybe I take the lead. Kipp does not know what he is doing, but neither do I! I can fake it though. I have been doing that my whole life. Why stop now?

A different Erthin stomped toward them. He had an unfamiliar drawl. "'Ow's ya meal?"

Irwin stared, attempting to understand this Erthin's jargon.

"Ya 'ave 'er 'oblem wit me speeches?"

"No, Sir," Irwin said, "but I have never heard a tongue twang like that."

"'E from Porford."

He leaned toward the Erthin, drew his voice low. "Is it possible we could be overlooked? We just want to return to Kobiton. That is where we are from. We promise to go without incident."

"Sorree we 'ant let ya do 'at."

It took him a second to fully understand what the Erthin had said. "I don't understand why."

"'Cus ya no rumroun 'er."

Irwin returned to his meal, took a few bites and a drink off his ale. He felt Kipp eyeing him. The Clan-Duin was trying to eat all he could before anything else happened.

The Erthin at their table signaled for his comrades. Kipp dropped his fork. He glared at Irwin who now understood he had spoken too much too soon.

Immediately the Erthins soldiers, these PCP, grabbed them by the arms and dragged them outside. Hard hands held them, pushed them, leaving marks. Then they were frisked. Any coins or knives were taken.

They were pushed out into the blistering sun. Irwin was made to ride, and Kipp was forced to run alongside the soldiers and tied to a rope.

The trip back to the city center was quick. People parted from the clamoring of horse hooves.

Not knowing what would come next, Irwin knew one thing for certain: he was committed to their mission to find Yace, no matter what.

Whatever happens next will be nothing compared to my father's tyranny. At least I found what I was looking for; warmer weather, flatter ground, and a friend.

We will get past this Kipp. I promise. We will get away from these thugs. And we will find Yace.

To continue the journey, please click HERE, or visit www.kdlumsden .com! If you enjoyed Secrets of Urthis, please leave a review.

THE UNUSUAL CREATURES MENTIONED

ANCIENT DWELLERS

<u>APPEARANCE</u>: Unknown

<u>UNIQUE TRAITS</u>: Deities who created the universes. They wanted life to happen; to experience love, hate, melancholy, triumph, and sorrow. Everything exists because of them.

CLAN-DUIN

<u>APPEARANCE</u>: brown skinned, black hair, hairy bodies, eye colors can be gray/ green/ brown/ amber

<u>UNIQUE TRAITS</u>: shapeshifters, can be feline, canine, raptor, bear, ape, and/or marine mammals. Are very loyal companions, prefer to live in packs, but can be loners. Linear thinkers, they can be stubborn and foolhardy.

COTERIE

<u>APPEARANCE</u>: pale-skinned, white to blonde hair, white to blue eyes, but can take on darker appearances if bred with other creatures, such as Clan-Duins or Erthins.

<u>UNIQUE TRAITS</u>: Blended children of the Guru, infused with Mortal DNA. Their abilities are similar to Guru, but can be limited by Mortal blood. They are considered bastard children of the Guru and are impure. Often arrogant and egocentric, they live anywhere/anytime.

ELEMENTALIST

<u>APPEARANCE</u>: grey to olive-skin color, auburn-orange to red hair, green-hazel eyes

<u>UNIQUE TRAITS</u>: can harness every element known to exist. They can create elements from within themselves, or through interaction with organic and

inorganic life. They are known to have the ability to live out in space without oxygen or nutrients, they can oxygen exist inside their lungs without taking a breath. It is said they were the first beings created by the Ancient Dwellers, that they were necessary for creating the known universes.

ERTHIN

<u>APPEARANCE</u>: grey to olive-skin color, auburn-orange red hair, green-hazel eyes

<u>UNIQUE TRAITS</u>: hybrid Elementalist and Mortal. They can harness the five most powerful natural elements: Air, water, fire, earth, and spirit. They can be pure-bred and have all abilities, or part-breed and have abilities specific to person (ie. the ability to harness only one element).

GURU

<u>APPEARANCE</u>: white skinned, white-ashen hair, white-blue eyes.

<u>UNIQUE TRAITS</u>: Direct descendants of Ancient Dwellers. They have can use any type of power (teleporting, telepathy, shapeshifting). Considered living gods, they hide in plain sight and across all the universes. They can live every-where/anywhere/anytime.

GYPSY

An enclave of like-minded people, usually Talented, who tour Urthis rescuing other Talented people. They often take the rescued to sanctuary cities.

HAKRA (Urthis's God)

<u>APPEARANCE</u>: black-skinned, blue-eyes, hairless.

<u>UNIQUE TRAITS</u>: considered a living god who resides in Akarah City, capitol of Urthis. Has lain the groundwork for Telepaths to shape Urthis into an interstellar hub; keeps the general population subdue through religion. Every few years produces a Tome for the people to follow, hypnotizes the masses through telepathic ideology; zealot followers are devout enough to turn in their brother or neighbor if they believe they are Talented. Every few years his followers take pilgrimages to Akarah to stand in Hakra's presence with hopes to be bestowed a gift.

ISHIK EMPIRE

Current rulers of Doas Territory, the Ishik Empire have been in control for the last thousand years. Believed to be the last full-blooded Coterie family, they claim to be purebred; to couple with someone outside the family brings dishonor. They tout their land to be free of Talented people, yet employ Talented people to work at the palace. They maltreat their subjects, taking boys away from their families at 9-10, to work iron mines, daughters are married off by 8-9, families live in small dome-huts, and when compared to the rest of Urthis, Doas Territory is at least one hundred years behind in technological advancements.

METALIST

<u>APPEARANCE</u>: ashen skin color, gray hair, silvery-gray eyes

<u>UNIQUE TRAITS</u>: can harness all types of metal including, but not limited to; gold, silver, aluminum, nickel, iron, zinc, mercury, cadmium, cobalt, chromium, platinum, lead, etc. They can hold up to eight pounds of any given substance within their own flesh, flushed it under the skin to specific places. Their ability to manipulate metal starts with extraction, turning the metal into its liquid form, and integrating it back into its hard form, and can form anything imaginable with any amount of metal. They are known to give off a deathly scent when holding metal within. Direct descendants to Elementalist.

MORTAL

<u>APPEARANCE</u>: always pale-skinned, brown-eyed, hair light brown to dark-brown/black

<u>UNIQUE TRAITS</u>: Bipeds with no superhuman powers. One of the five eldest beings created by the Ancient Dwellers. They have been exported from their home world, brought to foreign worlds to repopulate but often exploited as cheap labor.

PLANETAIRY CONSTIBLE PATROL (PCP)

Comprised only of people with Talents. Telepaths are given powerful positions (Admiral, Captain, Colonel, Corporal, Sargent), Erthins can hold powerful positions (Lieutenant, Sargent), Clan-Duins are considered working soldiers or minions, but can be demoted and placed in a "court-yard sitter" position. Also called "Population Control Patrol". They usually patrol in groups of four and are seen riding large "warhorses".

SANCTUARY CITY

Not necessarily a city, but a place where people with Talents are safe from the PCP and Hakran ideology. Most don't allow Mortals to reside. Most require those looking for permanent residency to prove they are a positive influence, that they will help protect others with Talents, regardless of abilities, and not cause issue within the community. There are rules within each community to adhere, and if someone breaks that main rule they can be banished from one, or all sanctuary cities. (*Note: All Sanctuary cities are interconnected by Telepaths.)

TALENT, PEOPLE OF (aka TALENTED)

Any being who possess supernatural powers.

TELECAPRITIAN

<u>APPEARANCE</u>: pale skinned, white to blue eyed, white to blonde hair

<u>UNIQUE TRAITS</u>: can use telekinesis and telepathy, can shapeshift appearance but only into same gender roles. One of the five eldest beings created by the Ancient Dwellers.

TELEPATH

<u>APPEARANCE</u>: pale skinned, white to blue eyed, white to blonde hair

<u>UNIQUE TRAITS</u>: hybrid of TeleCapritian & Mortal, they cannot yield telekinesis. There are many types of telepaths; dreaming (they see visions future or past based), some can hear thoughts, some can manipulate beings though 'telepathic' brain waves, others can only do this through physical touch.

TELEKINESIS

The ability to move objects at a distance by mental power or other nonphysical means.

URTHIS

Fourth planet from the sun in the Oska'al solar system and one of the many places in the known universe that hosts supernatural and natural powered creatures. It is the planet on which Samuel Irwin Miner lives.

VOLATILE

A derogatory word used against people of Talent. (see: Talent, people of)

<u>Also By</u>

<u>The Metalist's Journey</u>
(Prequel) Flight of Yellow Falcons (2025)
The Metalist's Journey Prologue
Secrets of Urthis
Elements of Power
Sleeper Assassin
Land of Cannibals
(+2 more at least!)

If you liked this book please leave a review!

Want more information about Irwin and the world of Urthis?
Join KD Lumsden's newsletter at https://www.kdlumsden.com/

About KD Lumsden

A lifetime reader and writer of fantasy, Secrets of Urthis is KD Lumsden's debut novel. She creates fantastic worlds while drawing up architectural designs, and dreams up unforgettable characters while maintaining an equestrian farm. Supported by her loving husband and imaginative son, they enjoy nature hikes and playing at the beach when the Pacific Northwest weather permits.

eBook Blurb

In a world where metal sings with raw power, Irwin Miner's gift marks him as either savior or destroyer.

For nineteen years, he survived his father's brutality in the isolated mines of Urthis. Now his rare ability to manipulate metal has become both a blessing and a curse. Each surge of his growing powers draws him deeper into a realm of ancient mysteries and deadly secrets.

When Irwin meets the captivating telepath Yace and her fierce shapeshifting companion Kipp, he dares to dream of belonging. But their fragile bond shatters as Yace vanishes after a devastating encounter with her past. Hunted by the tyrannical Ishik Empire and haunted by shadows that shouldn't exist, Irwin must master his abilities before they consume him.

Every ally could be an enemy. Every choice could lead to destruction. And somewhere in the darkness, Yace's screams echo in his mind, driving him toward a confrontation that will shake the foundations of Urthis itself.

With its unique magic system and unforgettable characters, "Secrets of Urthis" weaves a spellbinding tale of betrayal, redemption, and the price of power. Perfect for fans of Brandon Sanderson's intricate world building and Sarah J. Maas's emotional depth.

Discover why readers can't put down this stunning fantasy debut. Let the magic of metal sweep you away on an unforgettable adventure.